THE PRICE OF FREEDOM

SOURCEBOOK

AUTHORS: Brian Campbell, Heather Curatola, Harry Heckel, Kenneth A. Hite, Ross A. Isaacs, Steve Long, Christian Moore, Nicky Rea, Aaron Rosenberg, John Snead, Ray Winninger

DEVELOPMENT: Kenneth Hite, Ross A. Isaacs, Christian Moore

EDITING: Janice Sellers

STAR TREK: THE NEXT GENERATION® LINE DEVELOPER: Ross A. Isaacs

GRAPHIC DESIGN: Anthony N. Vayos

ART DIRECTION: Christian Moore, Anthony Vayos

ORIGINAL ART: Bryan Gibson

PRODUCT DEVELOPMENT, PARAMOUNT: Paul Ruditis

PROOFREADING AND FACT CHECKING: Bill Maxwell

ADDITIONAL CONTRIBUTIONS: Matthew Colville, Ryan Moore, Jay Longino

SPECIAL THANKS: To Alessandra Isaacs, for making a trek across the country that seemed longer than a trek across the Federation; to Barry and Carol Moore, for everything; to Paul Ruditis, for answering the phone ten times a day; to Chip Carter, for letting us live in his world; to Ben Plavin and Allison James, for their endless patience; to Jeff Hannes, for his warp speed design work; and to the visionary sapients who conceived of the United Federation of Planets.

Last Unicorn Games
9520 Jefferson Blvd., Suite C
Culver City, CA 90232
WWW.LASTUNICORNGAMES.COM

Printed in Canada
First Printing—February 1999

TABLE OF CONTENTS

Introduction

Political union. Cultural melting–pot. Think tank. Peacekeeper. The United Federation of Planets stands as a testament to the collective vision of its member worlds. United by the precepts set forth by the Articles of Federation, its members have become the foremost guardians of freedom in the galaxy.

In the two centuries since its founding, the Federation has come to assume an almost mythical stature among both its member worlds and its starfaring neighbors. Starfleet vessels and officers, UFP ambassadors and diplomatic missions, Federation scientists and researchers—all have played pivotal roles in galactic history, and in many cases their exploits and actions have taken on the mantle of legend. The legacy of the UFP is one of vigilance, of hope, and ultimately of universal acceptance and freedom.

Remaining true to this legacy, the modern UFP stands for something larger than the sum of its many parts. Its very existence represents an association born of unparalleled cooperation and optimism, and its continued prosperity and growth serve to remind the entire galactic community that freedom and sovereignty are not mutually exclusive.

Since its inception, the Federation has enjoyed a colorful and storied history, and at times the fact and the myth collide. This book is not intended to be the "one true repository" of all things UFP; rather, consider it a collection of viewpoints and perspectives. It does not contain an exhaustive history or timeline of Federation events. Instead, it presents UFP history as a series of linked incidents and high points, often drawing on personal accounts in order to place events in the proper historical context. This method gives the Narrator a certain degree of freedom when deciding which events are appropriate for his own *Star Trek: The Next Generation* game series.

HOW TO USE THIS BOOK

This book gives players and Narrators alike an overview of this grand interstellar experiment. Curious about the origins of the UFP? You'll find the story within these pages. Want to know more about the politics of the member worlds? Look no further. Along with its companion volumes, *Planets of the UFP: A Guide to Federation Worlds* and *Planetary Adventures, Vol. I: Adventures in Federation Space*, this book gives players the most comprehensive picture yet available of this noble and far-flung alliance.

Within the pages of this book, players and Narrators alike will find the information they need to flesh out characters and events set within the Federation. Players can use the Overlays included herein to play characters other than Starfleet officers, yet still stay within the bounds of the Federation. Narrators will find this book useful for understanding how the Federation operates, opening up new possibilities for their series.

Included in *The Price of Freedom* are a number of alternate campaign ideas, from the Federation's Merchant Marine to a series set on a distant colony. Narrators can use the information provided to create supporting cast members, such as Federation bureaucrats, Starfleet diplomats, and members of the Federation Press and Information Bureau. Finally, this book collects and presents the history and organization of the Federation, its member worlds, its branches, and its Starfleet.

Chapter One discusses Federation history and chronicles the major events and conflicts that have shaped the UFP throughout its relatively brief existence. It also analyzes the motivating factors and circumstances that led the founding members to enter into this untested alliance. From the dark days of each of the five original members to the historic signing of the Federation Constitution and beyond, this chapter gives players and Narrators a sense of the forces that shaped what would become the strongest alliance for peace and justice in the Galaxy.

Chapter Two discusses the organization and administration of the UFP. To administer such a large amount of territory and keep the Federation's goals in focus requires a great deal of coordination. This chapter includes sections on the main branches within the Federation and their attendant duties, as well as important figures within the UFP. It details organizations like the Federation Press and Information Bureau, the Federation Internal Security Force and the Federation Diplomatic Corps.

Chapter Three details the rights and responsibilities of Federation members, as well as the process for joining this august body. With it, Narrators can set up episodes and series involving the admittance of a new planet, and players can take an active roll in bringing a new world into the Federation fold. Also discussed is the Federation's relationship with its many colonies, and both Narrators and players are provided with the tools to play a series centered on a colony, from initial exploration to establishing their own Federation colony.

Chapter Four details the Federation's relationship with other starfaring powers and species. From the Ferengi to the Tholians, this chapter provides more information on the UFP's history with these intergalactic powers, the structure of those relations, and how those groups relate to the UFP.

Chapter Five introduces a new group within the Federation—the Merchant Marines. Responsible for hauling everything from medical supplies to industrial replicators across the galaxy, the Merchant Marines are the grease that keeps the wheels of Federation commerce moving. Take on the role of a Merchant Marine crew, hauling supplies to outlying colonies (and perhaps have a few adventures along the way), or rescue a Federation freighter from imminent danger. This new group provides a new perspective to adventures in Federation space.

Chapter Six provides readers with a glimpse of perhaps the most famous UFP institution—Starfleet. How is this vast organization structured? How does Starfleet Command keep track of the fleet's myriad ships and missions? This chapter answers these questions and many others as you take a tour of Starfleet and its various branches. Within these pages, you'll find new Overlays—play a Starfleet cultural attaché, an investigator for the Judge Advocate General's

office, or one of Starfleet's intrepid marines. Narrators will find advice for running many different types of series.

Chapter Seven provides information and templates for close to a dozen new starships, like the *Steamrunner*-, the *Norway*-, and the much-requested *Akira*-class ships. Included in this chapter are expanded ship classifications, like the fast frigate and the heavy cruiser, and the many types of fleet operations.

Chapter Eight gives players and Narrators alike a host of new Federation technology to add to their games. Fly over an alien landscape with your flight vest, observe a new civilization from the safety of your holobase, or fend off a pack of enraged le-matya with a network of portable force field generators.

Finally, the Appendix provides information and game statistics for the crew of one of Starfleet's most famous ships—the *U.S.S. Enterprise NCC 1701-D*.

> STAR TREK: INSURRECTION: THIS BOOK CONTAINS INFORMATION FROM THE NEW STAR TREK FILM, *INSURRECTION*. INCLUDED HEREIN IS INFORMATION ON THE SON'A, MYSTERIOUS ALIENS RECENTLY ALLIED WITH THE FEDERATION, NEW WEAPONS LIKE THE ISOMAGNETIC DISINTEGRATOR, AND THE *U.S.S. ENTERPRISE-E*. FOR THE CONVENIENCE OF THE FANS, THIS INFORMATION CAN BE FOUND IN THE *HISTORY*, *DIPLOMATIC RELATIONS*, *TECHNOLOGY*, AND *STARSHIPS* CHAPTERS.

History

The roots of the Federation intertwine deeply throughout the histories of the five founding members. Alpha Centauri, Andoria, Tellar, Vulcan, and Earth all survived dark pasts when their civilizations teetered on the edge of annihilation. All five races overcame these threats to their existence, each race finding its own way to defeat its particular demons. The lessons of these times brought each race to an understanding of unity and helped forge the Federation into an institution that protects the fundamental rights of all beings and works to promote peace throughout the galaxy.

ALPHA CENTAURI IV

During Earth's nineteenth century, the Centaurans faced the threat of extinction. Many city-states experimented with biological agents following a worldwide nuclear weapons ban. Either by design or accident, a genetically engineered retrovirus was released on the northern continent of Alpha Centauri IV. This retrovirus quickly mutated into several deadly strains and spread to the four corners of the globe. Millions sickened and died. The different city-states declared war on the virus and on each other. World leaders desperately searched for an antidote or a vaccine. When that search failed, governments looked for scapegoats.

The Centaurans refer to this time of death and disease as the Plague Years. It lasted over a decade. Strains continued to mutate, exacting a terrible toll in lives. Well over a billion Centaurans died before the plague ran its course. The different governments of Alpha Centauri IV eventually ceased fighting—armies died faster than they could be trained—and began pooling their resources to combat the virus. The best scientists and doctors on Alpha Centauri IV gathered in an Emergency Medical Council to coordinate their efforts in fighting the plagues. Finally, in the Earth year 1871 this international team developed an effective antiviral agent and vaccine.

The Centaurans stopped the plagues, but they did not forget the lessons the Plague Years had taught. The Emergency Medical Council became a full-fledged world government only five years after the end of the Plague War, as every surviving Centauran city voted to make Dr. Kulei Asephas, the discoverer of the vaccine, its leader. Despite Dr. Asephas' objections, she became global president by acclamation.

Her government outlawed biological weapons and laid the foundations for a lasting time of world peace. This time of horror made the Centaurans realize how easily conflict could result in the destruction of all life on their planet. They learned to put aside their differences and work for the common good of all.

ANDORIA

The Andorians had a history similar to that of the Vulcans (see below). With their passionate and violent natures, the Andorian clans fought one war after the next, massacring their enemies. Some clans fought vendettas and wars against enemies on the other side of the world, and carried on blood-feuds for centuries. Seven centuries ago, during the Age of Lament, the Andorian civilization fell into complete anarchy. World trade collapsed, the economies of the Andorian families crashed, and in the ensuing starvation every Andorian blamed every other for the disaster. Infighting tore the clans apart as relatives even took up arms against each other. Archaeologists estimate that over a quarter of the population of Andoria killed each other at the height of the Age of Lament (roughly 1600-1670 Earth time).

Lor'Vela, an influential clan leader, sought to end the bloodshed. She instituted ritual dueling as a means to settle conflicts in her clan. All members of the clan swore an oath to abide by the results of these duels and not to seek revenge for those killed with honor. The process worked, and Lor'Vela's clan grew strong. Word spread across Andoria. A council of clan leaders gathered and agreed to unite and adopt ritual combat to settle differences between the clans. Lor'Vela burned the histories of Andoria to prevent old feuds from surviving in the minds of the new generation; the Andorian calendar begins with this act (the year 1692 on Earth). The institution of ritual combat saved Andorian civilization, and Andorians hold their rituals sacred to this day.

TELLAR

Tellarite histories tell of the Voice Wars, which wracked their culture in Earth's early twentieth century. The Tellarite fascination with engineering and mechanism spilled over into political science and anthropology around the same time as Tellar's industrial and scientific revolutions hit. Each Tellarite nation sponsored theories of perfectly engineered social and economic systems, none of them compatible with each other. For about a century, these theorists tried to enforce their idealized systems on the Tellarite people, with indifferent results.

According to Tellarite social science, resistance to scientific economics and politics resulted from "pre-scientific" languages. Since language obviously has an immense effect on thought patterns, Tellarite engi-

neers derived scientific languages to create properly malleable cultures. The new science of linguistics became the battleground as Tellarite nations made war upon each other to impose various scientifically developed languages upon their enemies' recalcitrant populations.

These Voice Wars spread across the continents of Tellar: Many smaller dialects and tribal languages were totally extinguished in the name of the newly engineered tongues and of scientifically perfected societies. The Voice Wars militarized Tellarite society to an unprecedented degree. Every single Tellarite was drafted and assigned a place in the vast machinery of a Tellarite national economy. The remaining Tellarite nations teetered on the verge of the Final Voice War when the mathematician Cherok began a program of public speeches and civil disobedience.

Cherok used chaos theory to demonstrate that scientific economics and politics were, in fact, impossible illusions, and that "dissent and diversity create harmony and peace." Cherok's movement promised a way out of the dead end of the Voice Wars; hundreds of thousands (and eventually, millions) of Tellarites refused to speak any of the new "scientific" languages, answering only "Ukora" ("No" in the most primitive Tellarite language) to any question put to them. Soldiers left the front lines, armaments workers went on strike, students refused to attend classes, and the carefully engineered war machines of the Tellarite governments crumbled. The Ukora Segment, as Cherok had predicted, provided the nucleus for a new society based on debate, diversity and personal pride. Ironically, it also served as the center of an almost accidental Tellarite world government after only four generations, as Tellarites refused to let national allegiances get in the way of free speech, free debate, and free exchange of information.

VULCAN

The Vulcans guard their past zealously, and they do not allow outsiders to see their records. Vulcan scholars say only that the early history of Vulcan was violent and destructive, colored scarlet and crimson with uncontrollable emotion. The few records to survive this Age of Wrath exist only as fragmentary legends of angry gods and endlessly raging battles. Without hard data, wild speculations rule the day.

Some theorists claim that these wars destroyed Vulcan's ecosystem, turning it from lush jungle to harsh desert. Others look to the Romulans for insight into prehistoric Vulcan, and claim that ruins across the spiral arm date from a primitive interstellar Vulcan tyranny. The wildest theories hold that one of the asteroid belts in the Vulcan system is the remains of the true Vulcan home planet, physically destroyed in a final war.

After centuries of intense fighting, the brilliant mentalist Surak developed a vital philosophy of logic, which could control the strong Vulcan emotions. Surak's teachings, which elevated peace as the precondition for rational thought ("The calm mind is the mind that truly knows") took hold across Vulcan and brought

about the Time of Awakening. Surak's personal sacrifices for peace convinced the few holdouts to end their wars and concentrate on building a future. Historians and xenologists believe that the Romulans may have broken from the Vulcans at this time rather than accept Surak's doctrines.

The Time of Awakening brought a flowering of Vulcan civilization. Building on Surak's philosophy, the logician Selok developed the Theorems of Governance, which reconciled the famous traditional Vulcan culture with Surak's logic to provide a basis for a unified planetary government. Unity, peace and logic advanced Vulcan science even faster than Vulcan warfare had. At the time of the founding of the Federation, the Vulcans were the most advanced of the five original member planets in theoretical science, although Vulcan cultural conservatism kept most of the innovations from disrupting the time-tested, logical Vulcan ways.

EARTH

The nations of Earth fluctuated between disastrous world wars and ever-more-widespread world governments for three centuries. The "Seven Years" and Napoleonic Wars (1754-1815) led to the Concert of Europe, World War I (1914-1918) led to the League of Nations, and World War II (1931-1945) led to the United Nations. Tiring of the ineffectual UN, a group of fanatical human scientists created a genetically altered master race in an attempt to forcibly impose world peace. The most infamous of these "supermen," Khan Noonian Singh, seized power in Asia in 1992 and used brilliant diplomatic and military strategy to conquer much of the developing world.

As he amassed an empire controlling almost a quarter of the Earth, Khan played politics, manipulating the world powers into appeasement strategies, while he demanded the reverence and worship of citizens in his empire. Forty other nations fell under the domination of Khan's fellow "supermen," but the United Nations coordinated efforts to stop the genetically altered conquerors. Cooperation between the unconquered countries of Earth, combined with infighting among Khan and the other "supermen," led to a slow, but inevitable defeat of the "supermen."

Khan and his followers fled into exile using a *DY-100* sleeper ship, the *U.S.S. Botany Bay*.

The Eugenics Wars were the turning point. Khan's war had so seriously damaged the world economy and ecology that no nation felt secure enough to support the New United Nations. Even the relatively rich and free United States suffered, both from domestic unrest and from economic decline. Colonel Green, an ambitious American soldier, attempted to launch a coup to restore American greatness after losing the 2052 Presidential election. Green favored exterminating the unfit and excess population, and historians credit Green or his followers with launching the volley of nuclear and biological weapons that started World War III in 2053.

Although the European nations originally stood as one against Green, after suffering devastating attacks several of the allies turned against each other. Bombs tore apart many European capitals. Destruction of trade routes left millions starving. Some accounts tell of cannibalism in heavily populated cities. Nationalist groups slaughtered minorities en masse in these areas. Revolution caught fire throughout Europe as some fought desperately to bring back a united Europe.

For obvious reasons, few records survive from these dark days. The war was over almost before it began, since nations simply collapsed into near-complete anarchy. Portions of the United States, East Asia and Europe survived, but the nuclear winter and ecological devastation hit even these relatively lucky regions hard. Famines, plagues, and riots killed billions. Civilization was knocked back to seventeenth-century levels in even the most prosperous regions, and almost to the Stone Age everywhere else. Only isolated groups of scientists and experimenters survived the chaos of the middle 21st century.

One such was Zefram Cochrane, who became the first human to break the light barrier with his ship, the *Phoenix*, in 2063. His flight alone might have restored hope across the globe, but when a Vulcan scout ship detected the *Phoenix's* warp signature, that first contact with Cochrane ushered in a new era on Earth. First the Vulcans and then the Centaurans worked to save humanity from its wreckage. Although the road to unity was difficult, no government would willingly

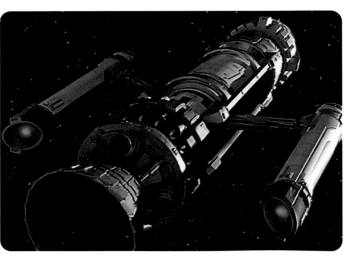

risk both its newfound interstellar allies and the future of the planet for another war.

In 2113, the European Hegemony and the restored United States of America merged as the United Earth Republic. The popular enthusiasm for unity swayed the South American Union and the Eastern Coalition, who joined by 2130 rather than be overthrown by their own people. Australia, the final holdout, joined United Earth in 2150.

A SHARED DESTINATION

Although each of the five founding members overcame its conflicts in its own manner, they all gained an appreciation of the same ideals and concepts. Each world had fallen to the edge of self-destruction and pulled itself back from the brink. These ideals would see their ultimate expression in the founding of the UFP. However, before the five worlds could join in the Federation, they had to venture into space alone.

ALPHA CENTAURI IV

Of all the five founders, the Centaurans had the least experience with spaceflight. The first Centauran astronauts landed on Alpha Centauri V only a hundred years before the Centaurans encountered Earth's starships. The Centaurans founded a colony and developed their famous terraforming technology to tame the hostile environment. Although they possessed vessels capable of traveling across their solar system, warp drives had eluded the Centaurans. When Earth made contact with Alpha Centauri, Centaurans considered it one of the greatest moments in their history.

Warp drives received from Earth sparked an explosion of Centauran exploration. The Centaurans established colonies on distant planets and charted unknown regions of space. Centauran innovations in starship design made vessels far more "liveable," and Starfleet has long recognized these significant contributions.

ANDORIA

The Andorians developed spaceflight around the Earth year 1800. Competing clans sent their own ships to the far reaches of their solar system, seeking honor and glory. During this initial period of rapid expansion, the Andorians established colonies throughout their system. The citizens of Andoria celebrated the conquest of their solar system and started looking toward the stars.

Andorian scientists worked to develop more powerful engines, but had little knowledge of warp theory. Using impulse drives, Andoria sent sleeper ships on colonization missions to nearby stars. These vast ships contained hundreds of frozen Andorians and repositories of data about Andorian civilization. Most sleeper ships malfunctioned and disappeared in the depths of space. A few succeeded and colonized new solar systems. Andoria sent robotic supply ships on multiyear journeys to support these colonies.

Andorian experiments with warp drives showed less success. Vessels exploded or vanished into subspace, never to be seen or heard from again. The *New Andoria* was a combined effort from leaders of each clan to construct a warp-drive vehicle. Once it was constructed, initial tests of the warp drive indicated success. However, when the *New Andoria* attempted its first interstellar flight, its unstable engines detonated, ripping a wormhole in the fabric of space-time at the edge of the Andorian system. This rift destroyed everything that it touched and Andorian explorers discovered that the laws of physics altered near it. As an unfortunate side effect, powerful ion storms were generated throughout the Andorian system, making all spaceflight more hazardous than ever.

The Andorians gave up on making their way to the stars for over a century and a half, losing contact with all of the Andorian colonies. Political movements on Andoria concentrated on domestic matters. At four different times, the Council of Clans narrowly rejected proposals to dismantle Andorian spaceports.

The spaceports and launch sites helped save Andoria. Global climate changes triggered by the ion storms brought a new ice age, which threatened to make Andoria almost uninhabitable. Andorian scientists designed a satellite weather control system, preventing this climatic catastrophe. Andorian spaceflight technology served them well and reminded the people of the time before the *New Andoria* disaster.

The unstable wormhole eventually collapsed, and the ion storms burned out. Although many Andorians were skeptical, spaceflight resumed and ships set out to discover the fate of Andoria's colony worlds. When contact was reestablished, the Andorians discovered that only one of their four colonies had survived. Geologic activity had destroyed the colony on Thalassa, while settlers on Quardis had died from supply shortages. Trilith VII's colony had simply vanished, leaving no trace (even modern UFP teams have not determined the fate of this lost colony). Only the Cimera III colony remained. The Andorians rebuilt their colonies on Quardis and Thalassa, but decided to leave Trilith VII uninhabited.

Finally, experiments in warp drive began again, despite major protests. Many scientists died in ritual

duels in order to restart the research. The launch of the new vessel, the *Lor'vela*, went perfectly—the data from over a century of studying the wormhole helped the Andorians to stabilize the *Lor'vela's* engines. Although now possessed of a functioning warp-drive design, Andoria lacked natural dilithium, a key element in stabilizing the engine cores. Due to the short supply of this resource, Andoria built one-shot warp-capable starships used primarily to improve transit to and from the colonies, rather than explore the galaxy.

When the *U.S.S. Challenger* entered Andorian space in 2144, warning shots were exchanged before the two sides hailed each other. Humans and Andorians found much in common (the name of the Earth vessel made an excellent first impression on Andoria's dueling culture). Contact with Earth quickly led to contact with both Vulcan and Alpha Centauri. The Andorians received dilithium through trade with their new allies, and began upgrading their fleet and exploring new worlds.

During the Earth-Romulan War, the Andorians constructed a fleet of ships with the intention of entering the struggle at Earth's first request. When the Federation was formed, the Andorian ships were converted to merchant vessels because they couldn't match the technology level of the Daedalus project. Since that time, Andoria has been a center of Federation interstellar trade.

TELLAR

The Tellarites have a long history of spaceflight, dating back several centuries. The first Tellarite astronaut was Ranx, a bold explorer/scientist who designed his own rocket ship in 1867. Ranx pushed the limits of his designs and perished in a landing on Tellar II, although he became the first Tellarite to enter the atmosphere of another planet in the process. He inspired generations of Tellarites to seek the stars.

Within twenty-five years of Ranx's death, the Tellarites had conquered their solar system. Colonies were started on the first, fourth, and fifth planets of their system and on three of the moons of Boragus, the sixth planet, a gas giant rivaling Jupiter in Earth's solar system. Tellarite engineers spent the next fifty years improving these outposts so they would survive

any disaster. Many of the engineers on Tellar's space colonies played major roles in the Ukora Segment, and the prestige of space contributed to Ukoran success in ending the Voice Wars.

As the colonies grew, so did the costs of launching ships from Tellar and landing vessels from the colonies. Talla, the head of Tellar's Engineering Council, proposed the construction of a gigantic space elevator, extending from the surface of Tellar into orbit. Her plans were ambitious but sound, and she challenged her fellow Tellarites to build this monument of the ages. The Tellarite Agora approved Talla's proposal and construction began.

The Tellarite Space Elevator was one of the most ambitious projects undertaken by any race. Tellarite engineers spent over thirty years constructing it, despite cost overruns, damage suffered from upper atmospheric winds, and occasional political uncertainty. When finally completed, however, it functioned exactly as Talla had planned, down to the decimal place. The Tellarites made the first day of its operation a global holiday.

With easy access to space laboratories ensured, Tellarite scientists developed basic warp drive almost a century before Earth possessed the technology. The Tellarites went to different star systems and swiftly grasped the dangers of interstellar travel. The Tellarite government had strong concerns regarding encounters with alien lifeforms. Like the Vulcans, the Tellarites began a policy of observation.

In 2105, the Centauran exploration vessel Shayna Kavic arrived in the Tellar system. Tellarite leaders were distrustful of the Centauran message of peace, but upon meeting the crew relations improved. The story on Tellar is that when the Centauran delegation first saw the Space Elevator they reacted with appropriate awe and wonder. The Tellarite leaders were so proud to have their works admired that they rapidly agreed to an alliance.

VULCAN

The Vulcans achieved spaceflight in their distant past. Although Vulcans rarely speak of them, many ancient Vulcan myths tell of visitors from beyond the stars, wars in the skies, and Vulcan heroes questing on

long odysseys through the heavens. The Romulans are believed to have exiled themselves from Vulcan over two thousand years ago, supporting the theory that Vulcans had interstellar travel even in the distant past.

Exploration of the stars leads to knowledge. Gaining knowledge is logical. After the Vulcans adopted the philosophy of logic, they began a more systematic exploration of space. They quickly discovered that most neighboring civilizations were less advanced than themselves. Although the Vulcans could have exploited these races and built an empire, they no longer desired war or conquest. The Vulcans were satisfied to observe. Several legends of unidentified flying objects among neighboring cultures, including Earth, are now attributed to Vulcan scout ships.

A millennium after the rift that separated them, the Vulcans and Romulans again encountered each other, leading to a sporadic war. The Romulans no longer possessed the technology to carry the war to Vulcan, and the Vulcan devotion to pacifism meant that the Vulcans never followed up on their strategic advantage. After a century, the Romulan threat receded and Vulcan forgot her foes. After this war, however, Vulcan scout craft carefully observed any new culture before making contact. Vulcan explorations, never plentiful, nearly ceased entirely for seven hundred years.

The unexpected detection of a warp-drive signature from the battered planet Earth lured a curious Vulcan scout into contacting humanity. Realizing the great potential of humanity, Vulcan advisors came to Earth and helped bring it about. As human explorers traveled to distant stars, Vulcan kept a firm alliance with Earth. After Earth faced down the Romulans, the Vulcan government felt creating a unified interstellar government of Earth, Andoria, Alpha Centauri, Tellar, and itself conformed with its philosophy of "Infinite Diversity in Infinite Combinations."

EARTH

Humans have dreamed about the wonders of space since their eyes first gazed up into the heavens. They built temples aligned to celestial movements and saw ancient gods in the patterns of the stars. For four centuries, humans have had the power of spaceflight, and their connection to the stars lifted them out of the dark nightmare of World War III.

In 1957, *Sputnik* became the first man-made satellite, and human exploration of space began. Yuri Gagarin, a Russian cosmonaut, was the first man in space. A race between Earth's two superpowers, the Soviet Union and the United States of America, pushed scientists, technicians, and astronauts to challenge the skies. The space race ended in 1969, when *Apollo 11* astronauts Neil Armstrong and Buzz Aldrin reached Earth's moon. Seven years later, two robotic *Viking* spacecraft landed on Mars in a search for extraterrestrial life. Both sites would become home to millions of humans by the 24th century.

In 1977, Earth's first reusable spacecraft, the prototype space shuttle *Enterprise*, completed its first suborbital flight. The shuttle *Columbia* achieved orbital flight in 1981. Several successful space shuttle

missions followed until 1986, when the space shuttle *Challenger* exploded, killing all seven astronauts on board. This tragedy crippled American spaceflight, although the Russian space station *Mir* launched in that same year lasted for decades.

The Eugenics Wars started a new space race as the genetically altered conquerors pushed the envelope of spaceflight technology. Khan Noonian Singh was successful in constructing a *DY-100* sleeper ship, the *Botany Bay*, which he and his compatriots used to flee Earth when they were overthrown in 1996. The new space race survived the Eugenics Wars. Unmanned spacecraft, including *Voyager 6* and the *Nomad* space probe, and manned missions, such as Shaun Geoffrey Christopher's pioneering flight to Saturn, continued sporadically until World War III.

When World War III began, spaceflight was all but forgotten. As the devastation and loss of life mounted, many lost hope that humanity could preserve its own civilization, much less reach for the stars. Zefram Cochrane's first contact with the Vulcans turned this defeatism into renewed hope. All nations worked together to launch new warp ships. The *Valiant* was only one of the early ships that vanished during this dangerous, mysterious period. The Cochrane, however, discovered another civilization on Alpha Centauri IV. When the Centaurans and Vulcans inspired Earth's nations to unite, the United Earth Republic established a United Earth Space Probe Agency to continue interstellar exploration.

UESPA ships encountered the Andorians and followed the Centaurans to Tellar, and their resourceful crews made fast alliances with these newly discovered races. Earth founded colonies and expanded its influence across space; many human groups dissatisfied with the United Earth left to found their own, more isolated, colonies as well. When Earth encountered the Romulans in 2156, she commanded the respect of her allies and had the most powerful fleet of any Federation founding member. The dangers faced by Earth forces made the people of Earth realize how important their interstellar allies were to the human destiny, and, before the war ended, politicians were carefully considering the merits of a galactic government.

THE ROMULAN-EARTH WARS

In 2156, the Earth starship *U.S.S. Endeavor* encountered an unknown spacecraft in orbit around Cheron IV. According to the *Endeavor's* log, the unknown vessel dropped several nuclear bombs on the planet's surface, then moved to approach. The Earth starship hailed the unknown ship, but received only a barrage of nuclear missiles. The *Endeavor* suffered serious damage from the initial onslaught. The unknown vessel then identified itself as a warship of the Romulan Star Empire and demanded the immediate surrender of the *Endeavor*. The captain of the *Endeavor* returned fire and used the ship's warp engines to retreat.

When the *Endeavor* arrived at the colony of Gamma Hydra IV, she had lost over 90% of her crew due to the failure of life support. The story of the attack spread throughout Earth's colonies. The leaders of the United Earth Republic sent several warships to the Cheron system and into the surrounding sectors. United Earth forces fought in their first interstellar conflict. Vessels armed with atomic weapons dueled in space, mostly in empty systems between the Romulan and Earth borders. No two combatants ever came face to face in the four years of the war. Both Earth and the Romulans suffered terrible losses in the initial stages.

As the campaign progressed, Earth proved to possess decisive advantages. The Romulans lacked Earth's reliable warp drives, instead using a precursor of the quantum singularity drive to power warp flight. These primative quantum singularity drives could only produce enough power to propel a Romulan ship one-way before the singularity collapsed. Once at their destination, they could only use impulse power, effectively stranding their vessels without warp drives. This meant that Earth starships could tactically outmaneuver the Romulans.

THE CHERON ENIGMA

As a final note on the Earth-Romulan War, scholars still remain uncertain of the reasons that the Romulans were in the Cheron system and why they bombed the planet's surface before engaging the *Endeavor*. The prevailing theory is that the Romulans had discovered alien artifacts or had built a special weapons facility that they feared would fall into Earth's hands. However, investigators have found no evidence of either at the bombing site, leading speculators to suggest that the bombing was a distraction, but for what no one knows. Many Federation experts believe that the Cheron system still holds a secret.

In addition, Earth's allies provided valuable support. Alpha Centauri donated medical supplies and food to help Earth in her war effort. The Vulcans gave insightful tactical advice on Romulan tendencies. The newly encountered Tellarites allowed humans to rent their spacedocks for starship construction. Toward the final stages of the war, the Andorians upgraded their fleet in hopes of giving Earth military support.

The war came to a conclusion in the same system where it had begun. In the Battle of Cheron, Earth forces decisively defeated the Romulans. A small detachment of Earth ships lured the Romulan fleet into a trap. When the Romulan commander decided that he had surprised the humans, he launched an all-out attack. Earth's reserves warped in on all sides of the Romulans, catching them completely unaware. No Romulan vessels survived the battle.

After the Romulans had suffered this humiliating defeat, both sides negotiated a peace over subspace radio. Like the war, the peace was conducted by remote control. The Romulans agreed to the Treaty of Cheron in 2160, which ended hostilities and established the Romulan Neutral Zone. Both sides agreed that violation of the Neutral Zone would be considered an act of war. At the end of the Romulan war neither side had yet seen its opponents.

The Earth-Romulan War's lasting impact was to remind Earth and her allies of the dangers that space could hold. Earth added defensive protocols to her exploration guidelines. The allied planets held numerous meetings and conferences to work out defensive measures in case of another encounter with hostile aliens. Every race was uncomfortably aware that although it was no longer in danger of destroying itself, it was still in danger of destruction by others.

TERRAN CONVENTIONS OF 2160

Even before the Treaty of Cheron, officials from Earth had met with Vulcan and Centauran ambassadors on the planetoid Babel to discuss increased trade and mutual defense alliances. After a successful round of agreements, the three powers invited representatives from Andoria and Tellar to join in the talks. The economic and military conference on Babel produced numerous agreements. During a late-night celebration of the accords (which some historians credit with introducing Andorian ale to the rest of the galaxy) the lead ambassadors—T'Shenn of Vulcan, Jasmyne Ray of Alpha Centauri, Mark Wells of Earth, Tarnoc of Tellar, and Sheras of Andoria—came to the mutual conclusion that the creation of a unified government and economy would benefit all five worlds.

Rather than merely reacting to future disasters, a new federation could head dangers off early and build a zone of peace and prosperity across the quadrant. Afterward, each ambassador returned home with news of the success and a recommendation for drafting Articles of Federation, tying all five worlds together in a single union. Federation historians still don't know which of the ambassadors first suggested the creation of the new interstellar government. Some suspect that T'Shenn was operating under a secret Vulcan agenda, and a few have gone so far as to suggest that the confusion over which ambassador first proposed the Federation was intentional. In any event, the citizens of all five founding worlds can make a valid claim that their people proposed the UFP.

Initial reaction to the ambassadors' messages was mixed. On Andoria, Sheras had to win a duel with his chief political opponent Rexar for the Council of Clans to consider the proposal. The Vulcans held numerous meetings where every aspect of increased contact with outsiders was analyzed in a search for a logical course of action. Jasmyne Ray of Alpha Centauri was hailed as a hero on her return, and within the year was elected President of Alpha Centauri. The Tellarites distrusted the concept and held a long series of global debates. Some say that the Tellarites finally were won over because they enjoyed arguing about the Federation so much. On Earth, reactions varied. Many people claimed that Wells was trying to sell out his own planet and that he had stepped beyond his authority as ambassador. A media report circulated that he had been seduced by Jasmyne Ray of Alpha Centauri into betraying Earth. Another story held that the Vulcans had mind-controlled the representatives from the other worlds.

However, with the Romulan War still going on, the logic behind the proposed Federation was clear to all. The veterans of the Earth-Romulan War came out in favor of the concept, as did the populations of the colonial planets. Once enough interest was generated, the majority threw their support behind the concept of the Articles of Federation. Despite the controversy, Earth was the first planet to vote for convening a convention, and so the talks came to be known as the Terran Conventions.

The three Terran Conventions began almost immediately after the Treaty of Cheron, on the joint human-Centauran colony of Epsilon Eridani. The Hall of Freedoms where their meetings were held stands today as one of the greatest symbols of liberty and interspecies cooperation in the galaxy. It is maintained by the five founding races as a shrine to the ideals which the Federation embodies. Large delegations from each of the five worlds came to draft Articles of Federation. Elaborate ritual and ceremony attended every moment of the convention. The peoples of the five worlds were confident that this meeting would result in the creation of a new interstellar government. Instead, the First Terran Convention of 2160 would demonstrate how much work needed to be done before the Articles of Federation could be drafted.

Protesters from all five worlds also arrived on Epsilon Eridani, loudly demonstrating against the convention. Delegates from different colony worlds, such as Mars, Cochrane, Alpha Eridani, and Epsilon Eridani itself, demanded to have a voice in any new interstellar government. Some politicians tried to use the event as a forum for the interests of their constituents or to boost their political careers. This chaos was exacerbated by the very process of five different civilizations coming to common ground at all.

The five species reviewed and examined each others' societies, histories, and values. They determined what the central social and political tenets of each society were. It was in making these determinations that some of the most acrimonious debates broke out among the delegates; many individuals have difficulty accepting a bluntly objective view of their society from an outsider. However, the perspective of truly neutral and alien viewpoints eventually helped create a newly mature self-awareness in each society (even that of the Vulcans). Then they compared their findings on each civilization to distill the "points of accord" between them. For example, it was determined that all five races' legal systems possessed some form of "protection against self-incrimination" which prevented the government from forcing someone to testify against himself (for example, by being compelled to give testimony, or being tortured for information).

In such a manner, the delegates came to basic agreement on political values and on the shape of the government, but could get no further. All agreed that the Federation should have a governing council, but they could not agree on representation. The plan proposed by Gnax of Tellar suggested basing representatives on population, while Dregas of Andoria firmly pushed for equal representation for each member world. Maria Gonzales of Earth voiced her concerns regarding the sovereign rights of each member planet, and those concerns resonated with beings on all five worlds. Centauran economists designed an interstellar economic system, based on the creation of a credit, but no one could agree on how to weight the economic strength of each world. The issue of representation and management of colonies led to endless hours of argument.

T'Shenn of Vulcan finally led her delegation out of the convention hall after suggesting that a new convention be held after two months, this time behind closed doors and without so much fanfare. After the Vulcans departed, the First Terran Convention of 2160 quickly ended. Before the remaining delegates left, however, all of the representatives resolved to reconvene as soon as possible.

Although contemporaries viewed the First Convention as a failure, later historians have come to regard it as a master stroke. The delegates arrived at major decisions such as the interlinked "economy of surplus" and the Federation Council's overarching authority, and holding the first convention publicly allowed dissenters to have their say immediately while convincing everyone that less publicity would lead to more progress. These two factors allowed further negotiations to advance in a spirit of compromise and unity. No planet wanted to be responsible for letting the negotiations fall apart, and the hard business of creating an interstellar Federation that was both free and strong could be done without fifty billion onlookers distracting the delegates.

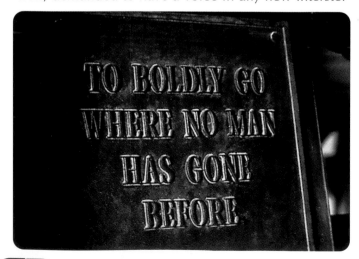

TO BOLDLY GO WHERE NO MAN HAS GONE BEFORE

The Second Terran Convention began ten weeks after the first convention ended. Sheras, Mark Wells, and Tarnoc were the most notable delegates absent from the first convention who attended the second. The meetings held behind closed doors raised even more issues than the first convention.

The delegations from Tellar and Earth wanted a supreme leader to administer the daily affairs of the Federation, but the Centaurans objected that an individual leader would be subject to corruption no matter how many checks were placed on him. Sovereignty issues were raised again even without Maria Gonzalez's voice. The Andorians wanted assurances that member worlds could keep their own military forces in addition to the proposed joint interstellar fleet. The first major accomplishment that came out of the convention was an agreement on the purpose of the UFP and the protection of the fundamental rights of all citizens.

T'Shenn of Vulcan left immediately after this agreement, citing personal reasons. Her departure raised alarms throughout the convention hall, much to the surprise of the Vulcans. Suvok of Vulcan took the lead of the Vulcan delegation, only to be greeted on his first day with a proposal drafted by the Centaurans, Andorians, and Tellarites which would establish Vulcan as the capital of the UFP. Only the humans seemed reluctant to embrace the idea of Vulcan as the capital of the UFP. When Suvok immediately rejected the proposal, several of the Andorians walked out of the hall. The Centaurans tried to convince Suvok to accept the offer. When he refused again, Achelos of Tellar demanded to know why T'Shenn had left and why the Vulcans were angry with the other representatives.

Only an appeal from President Ray of Alpha Centauri saved the convention. She spoke eloquently of the history of all five worlds, and how each of their peoples had overcome adversity and horror to reach the stars. She quietly challenged the delegates to complete the task before them and build a foundation for future generations. "On all our planets, we have found unity and peace only after terrible destruction. For once in our mutual history, let us strike the first blow for unity intelligently, as something we chose to do rather than something that history forced upon us.

As my Terran cousins are fond of saying, let us lock our barn doors now before the horses are stolen again." Suvok of Vulcan then suggested that Earth be made capital of the United Federation of Planets due to its location and its symbolic value to the human colonies, and to ease the concerns of Earth's delegation regarding sovereignty. The proposal passed easily, and the representatives began to hammer out other problems. Ambassador Tarnoc rose to the occasion, working compromises between delegations and using every ounce of his Tellarite debating skills to silence objections that threatened the convention. From this point on, the future of the Federation seemed assured.

Requirements for membership in the UFP were drafted and the Dregas plan for planetary representation won out over the Gnax plan for popular representation after Vulcan delegates raised the issue of hive races voting as a bloc. Despite the trials and tribulations, the Second Terran Convention was a success. All but the final drafts of the Articles of Federation were complete. The delegates returned to their homeworlds to present the documents to their governments, and set the date for a final Terran Convention at the end of 2160.

The Third Terran Convention of 2160 was everything that the dreamers had hoped the first convention would be. The delegates ironed out the few final difficulties, and all agreed to the Articles of Federation. Most of the voting and debating was simply a formality. The completed Articles of Federation protected the rights of self-determination for each world, and they contained the plans for a representative government which could make decisions for all members.

The Articles of Federation established an economic structure as well as a government, and, most importantly, they protected the rights of every Federation citizen. They were a testament to peace and to the vision of all five founding worlds. Once the Third Terran Convention of 2160 ended, the only step left for incorporation was ratification of the Articles of Federation by the member planets.

RATIFICATION

Tellar was the first world to ratify the Articles of Federation. Tarnoc led the campaign for passage, emphasizing the important place in history the Tellarites would earn as the first world to join the Federation. Tarnoc's political savvy, coupled with the people's desire to have defensive alliances with their neighbors, led to near unanimous passage in the Tellarite councils. When news of the ratification spread, celebrations broke out across the Tellar system.

Vulcan followed suit. The Vulcan High Council carefully analyzed the Articles of Federation, and in the final analysis deemed ratification logical. Although most Vulcans agreed with the decision to ratify, a minority voiced concerns over the potential erosion of Vulcan philosophy and identity by outside influences.

The Centaurans also quickly ratified the Articles. As on Tellar, ratification was cause for celebration. Copies of the Articles were placed on public display and officials began preparations for the planetwide holiday that would accompany the incorporation of the UFP.

Ratification was more of a struggle on Andoria. Different clans saw the political debate as a chance to gain power and humiliate their enemies. Blood filled the council chambers as different factions dueled for supremacy. Finally, Tharan, Dregas, and other supporters of federation triumphed and the Council of Clans ratified the document.

Earth was the last of the five founding members to ratify the Articles of the Federation. A few foreign observers commented that the slow ratification was part of the human penchant for the dramatic. The truth was that many citizens of Earth were concerned that their homeworld would lose its identity once it became capital of the UFP. Becoming a member of the Federation meant great changes and enormous responsibility. Many groups left Earth in a final wave of isolationist colonization rather than join the Federation. When the time came for the final vote, however, the United Earth Parliament ratified each article almost unanimously.

The final step in the process was a "framing" conference and signing ceremony in Paris and San Francisco on Earth. Unlike the Terran Conferences, this meeting was a smooth and festive occasion. Delegations from five worlds signed the Articles of Federation on February 22, 2161 in the San Francisco Opera House, officially ratifying them as the Constitution of the United Federation of Planets. The anniversary is still celebrated as Federation Day throughout the UFP. The Federation Council unanimously elected Earth's Mark Wells its first President, and the United Federation of Planets was born.

An Age of Exploration

The founding members of the UFP realized that their destiny lay among the stars. The first mission of the newly formed Starfleet was to explore space, to make first contact with new races, to find planets suitable for new colonies, and to spread the ideals of the Federation to the ends of the galaxy. The *U.S.S. Daedalus*, flagship of the new *Daedalus*-class starships, was the first ship to incorporate the technology of all five founding member worlds. Gnarr of Tellar designed the basic spaceframe of the *Daedalus* class, originating the primary/secondary hull with warp nacelles structure still used by Starfleet today. Manned by Starfleet crews containing a mix of elite personnel from each planet's navy, these vessels greatly expanded the boundaries of known space.

Many of the early *Daedalus*-class ships were lost on these first missions, such as the *U.S.S. Archon* in 2167 and the *U.S.S. Horizon* in 2168. First contact protocols weren't firmly established by the Federation, the new technologies required extensive shakedown testing, and even the Prime Directive didn't exist during this time. The natural evolution of several civilizations was tainted by first contact with the Federation.

No one can be certain that the legacy of the *Daedalus* class is complete. Rumors abounded of contact with powerful beings capable of destroying planets. Early scouts reported ghost ships, along with barbaric civilizations and strange space-time anomalies. Starfleet historians believe that the warp drives of some *Daedalus* ships malfunctioned, and that their crews live on today, trapped in subspace.

Although there were many failures during this time of initial exploration, on the whole the *Daedalus* class enjoyed immense success. In its first burst of exploration, Starfleet discovered dozens of new worlds and new civilizations. Many of them shared the ideals of the UFP and petitioned for membership. Within the first decade, the founding members were outnumbered on the Federation Council. Each new member world contributed its technology and culture toward strengthening the Federation. By the end of the 22nd century, almost fifty worlds belonged to the UFP. Membership would continue to grow over the next century, until the modern figure of over 150 members was reached.

Challenges to the Federation

In the first half of the 23rd century, the Federation confronted two of the greatest challenges it would ever face: an expansionistic new rival and a secession crisis. Both crises called for new responses from Starfleet. After the inhabitants of Qo'noS slaughtered a Federation diplomatic-xenological team and seized its ship (the *U.S.S. Ranger*), they reverse-engineered Federation technology to catapult the Klingon Empire into dominance over dozens of sectors on the Federation's rimward border. The Federation and the Klingons fought a series of running battles from 2223 to 2242, when Admiral Farsha of Cimera decisively halted Klingon expansionism at the Battle of Donatu V. The complete failure of standard Starfleet procedure in the Qo'noS contact led to the adoption of the Prime Directive.

The issue of the admission of Axanar nearly provoked the secession of Andoria, Vulcan, and many

other systems from the Federation. In 2253, the Axanarians attempted to win membership in the UFP by conquering several worlds on the Federation border and offering them to the Federation. Andorian Admiral Farsha, by now the Secretary of Defense, demanded that Starfleet move immediately against Axanarian aggression. President T'Pavis of Vulcan supported Farsha, although Earth, Tellar, and Alpha Centauri advised leaving Axanar alone. Earth and Tellar were still concerned about the Klingon threat, and Centauran Ambassador Eulis simply desired peace. Only after T'Pavis threatened the secession of Vulcan did Earth and Tellar change sides and vote for war with Axanar. Captain Garth of Izar, commanding a squadron of the brand-new *Constitution*-class starships, brilliantly decimated the much larger Axanarian fleet, and equally brilliantly negotiated a lasting peace in the sector.

The next ninety years were a time of incredible exploration by ships like Gan Laikan's *U.S.S. Asimov* and Robert April and Christopher Pike's *U.S.S. Enterprise*. Aside from a pinprick raid by the Romulans in 2266, brushes with the Gorns in 2267 and the Tholians in 2268, and similar brief skirmishes such as those with the Breen in the 2280's, they were also a time of relative peace and vastly increasing prosperity and technological progress. The Organian Peace Treaty of 2267 laid the groundwork for the Khitomer Accords of 2293, ushering in a new era of cooperation between the Federation and the Klingons. New races, most notably the Betazoids in 2294 and the Bolians in 2320, joined the UFP.

The 24th century has seen a return to the crises of the early 23rd. Starfleet has fought at least three major actions: the Cardassian Wars between 2347 and 2370, a war with the Tholians between 2353 and 2360, and a nearly fatal Borg incursion in 2367. The UFP has also had to deal with a Romulan-Klingon border war from 2344 to 2352, a Klingon civil war in 2367-68, and an outbreak of smuggling and piracy that resulted in first contact with the Ferengi in 2364.

Finally, tension with the Romulans has risen to new heights with incidents throughout the 2360's. The new *Galaxy*-class starships hold the line, however, and the dream of the Federation remains pure and strong even after more than two centuries. Through it

all, Starfleet and the UFP weathered these threats by holding dear to its guiding principles of peace, honesty and virtue. Yet the Federation would face new challenges in the years to come, putting its capabilities and resolve to perhaps the greatest test of all.

A TEST OF PRINCIPLES

This clarity of purpose and strength of ideals faced no greater test than the last three years. Once again, in 2373, the Borg would arrive to attack the Earth, taking the battle to Earth's past. During the heat of battle with a Starfleet armada, the Borg launched a sphere capable of creating a temporal vortex. By traveling back in time, the Borg hoped to prevent Zefram Cochrane's first warp flight, which resulted in first contact with the Vulcans. Thus preventing the alliance of worlds that would become the United Federation of Planets would have fundamentally erased all resistance to the Borg in the 24th century. As it had so many times before, the crew of the *U.S.S. Enterprise*, equipped with a new *Sovereign*-class vessel, saved the day. But a new menace, from an unexpected quarter, did more to threaten the existence of the Federation—and the entire Alpha Quadrant—than any previous adversary.

The discovery of a stable wormhole in the Denorios Belt in the Bajoran system was heralded as an opportunity to explore the distant Gamma Quadrant, and foster good will with whatever new civilizations were encountered. Quickly, rumors of the Dominion, a mysterious empire of ruthless shapechangers on the other side of the Bajoran wormhole, began to surface. By 2370, Dominion soldiers attacked and destroyed the *U.S.S. Odyssey*, to punctuate demands that the Federation cease all traffic through the wormhole. Exploration continued, but the situation deteriorated. The civilian-led government on Cardassia fell to a military uprising, leading to the rise of the Central Command, and an eventual alliance with the Dominion. The Klingons, suspicious of Dominion involvement, attacked the Cardassian Union, and withdrew from their alliance with the Federation in 2371 after the UFP failed to support the move. Events culminated in a Dominion declaration of war on the Federation in 2374, as enemy ships

Disobeying orders and flaunting the will of the Federation Council, Captain Picard and his crew successfully fought for the Ba'ku's rights, and exposed the plot to steal their homeworld from them. Their dedication to the Federation's ideals served as a clarion call to others: no matter the circumstances, no matter the danger, one cannot win by compromising their principles.

attacked both colonies and member worlds. The Romulans remained behind their borders, content to remain uninvolved rather than react to this threat to the entire quadrant.

Yet the Federation, hemmed in by the Cardassians, Romulans and Klingons, failed to give up, and eagerly cultivated all the allies it could. It reached out to the Het, the isolationist Gorn and the Tholians, with little success. When a new species calling themselves the Son'a contacted the Federation with offers of alliance, the Council jumped at the overture. In return for their alligiance, the Son'a asked only one thing: to mine metaphasic particles surrounding a remote planet in Federation space.

The Son'a suffered from DNA breakdown after years of genetic therapy designed to extend their lives. In order to survive, the Son'a required treatments of metaphasic particles, found only in the rings of a remote planet in a region of space known as the 'Briar Patch.' To save the Son'a from extinction required the collection of these particles, resulting in the destruction of the planet's surface.

The Son'a offered not only to share the benefits of this life-extending energy—thus nearly doubling lifespans throughout the UFP—but to join in the fight against the Federation's enemies. That the planet's inhabitants—the Ba'ku—would have to be relocated seemed a small price to pay. Blinded by fear of the Dominion and the opportunity a new ally presented, the Federation Council joined in a conspiracy to effectively steal the planet from its inhabitants. The Ba'ku, numbering a mere 600 inhabitants, were not indigenous to the planet; members of the Council could console themselves that this was no violation of the Prime Directive.

If the Son'a reputation for keeping indentured servants was not troubling enough, rumors of Son'a production of the narcotic ketracel-white and the suspected use of nucleonic subspace weapons (outlawed by the Second Khitomer Accords) should have been. The deal with the Son'a could not conclude happily for the Federation. In the end, no Cardassian, Borg or Dominion attack could have damaged the Federation as much as this compromise of ideals.

It was only through the dedication of the crew of the *U.S.S. Enterprise-E* that disaster was averted.

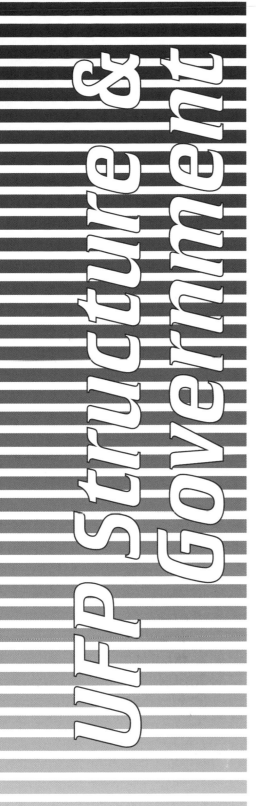

The United Federation of Planets—known universally simply as "the Federation"—is an institution formed in the year 2161 by five diverse species for the purposes of mutual defense, trade, diplomacy, and scientific and cultural exchanges. Based upon the principles set forth in the Federation Constitution, it embodies a government dedicated to freedom, fairness, civil rights, mutual respect among member species, and the rule of law. Although its own laws prevent it from interfering in local political situations or with the normal development of any society, whenever possible the Federation and its member states stand as bastions for the protection of individual rights and responsibilities that are, sadly, denied to many citizens of other governments.

The Federation does not exist to preserve cynically its own interests and power. The members of the Federation and the Federation's constitutional principles prevent it from becoming so self-serving an institution. Rather, the Federation has a proactive mission, a duty to promote and advance galactic civilization and to ensure basic individual freedoms for all sentient beings. It is a measure of the Federation's quality and moral strength that it is often successful in this mission without having to invoke its potent military arm, Starfleet. Starfleet, of course, stands ready at all times to preserve the Federation's mission and to extend the sphere of peace and freedom wherever possible.

The Federation Constitution

The bedrock upon which the Federation rests is the Constitution of the United Federation of Planets (often known simply as the Federation Constitution). The Federation Constitution serves two related functions. First, it establishes the framework of the government of the Federation. It sets forth how basic governmental units such as the Federation President, Federation Council, and Federation Supreme Court are to be established and maintained, what their respective powers are, and likewise what responsibilities and duties they have.

Second, and of equal or greater importance, is the Federation Constitution's role as a guarantor of individual rights and privileges. The very existence of the Federation government and its powers and functions is predicated, first and foremost, upon concepts of individual liberties. Governmental institutions and powers are derived from the citizens of the Federation, and cannot intrude upon or abrogate their fundamental individual rights, so it is important for the most important of those rights to be specified by the same document which establishes the government itself.

As such, scholars throughout the galaxy consider the Federation Constitution one of the greatest statements of individual rights and liberties ever made. It is often mentioned in the same breath as the Declaration of Independence of the former United States of America on Earth, the Fundamental Declarations of the Martian Colonies, the Statutes of

Alpha III, and the Vulcan Theorems of Governance. Many newer members of the Federation have simply adopted the Federation Constitution wholesale as the constitution of their own planetary governments. These constitutional principles and laws have guided the Federation for over 200 years with relatively few changes or additions. This longevity is testimony not only to the vision of the founders of the Federation, but to the dedication of several generations' worth of citizens to sustaining that vision.

Amazingly, the Federation Constitution is not the work of one species, but rather is the culmination of ideas and processes which arose almost simultaneously on five separate planets—Alpha Centauri IV, Andoria, Tellar, Vulcan, and Earth. On each of these planets historical events led the inhabitants to two principles. First, they concluded that the various disastrous events of their recent past, from the Andorian Age of Lament to the human Third World War, could not be allowed to repeat themselves. All of these species could see that they must not again allow their civilizations to descend into such darkness.

Second, they realized that, in order to prevent such evils from arising again, and to achieve the longevity and prosperity they desired, they had to look outward, beyond the narrow confines of their home planets or sectors, to establish a new galactic order. This new order would preserve that which was good in their societies by supporting and, when necessary, defending it.

THE DRAFTING OF THE CONSTITUTION

It was with these goals in mind that representatives from each of the five civilizations came to Epsilon Eridani in early 2160 for the first of three Terran Conventions. The stated purpose of the Conventions was "to define the goals and objectives of a grand alliance of our five peoples, that further effort may be devoted to establishing such an alliance." The Conventions exceeded even those high hopes, although, as the preceding chapter indicates, the road was not always easy.

The process began with setting forth broad philosophical and policy statements. They describe the "common ground" upon which the Federation was soon to be formed. During the course of the Terran Conventions, the delegations reconciled the differing versions of and perspectives upon each point of accord so that a unified alliance government based on agreed-upon principles could be established. During this process, each race was required to discard, or compromise, some details of long-cherished practices to ensure that unanimous agreement could be reached on each point.

Each race also had to agree to sacrifice a portion of its sovereignty so that the "allied government" would have the teeth to make effective policy. All chafed at this, but it is to the founders' credit that they were able to see past their selfish interests to the greater, and ultimately more "profitable," ideal of a common

interstellar community working to create an enlightened galaxy. Tellarite mathematical models and the rigorous example of the Vulcan Theorems of Governance were very helpful in demonstrating the "win-win" and "non-zero sum" nature of a Federation where all members gain great rewards by giving something up.

The final agreements became the basis of individual Articles, which expanded on the five species' common ground and set up structures to implement them. The ultimate product of the Terran Conventions thus became the "Articles of Federation." Upon ratification by the member worlds, the Articles of Federation became the Constitution of the United Federation of Planets. This landmark step made the year 2161 truly one of the great years of galactic history.

For the first time on record, formerly independent planets voluntarily joined without immediate threat and without suffering a debilitating war to enforce such unity. True, the Earth-Romulan War had demonstrated that interstellar space was not without its dangers, but fundamentally the Federation was an act of optimistic, intelligent planning rather than one of exhausted desperation, as the United Nations on Earth had proven to be. Even today some historians marvel that it happened at all.

THE ARTICLES OF FEDERATION

WHEN THE DELEGATES LEFT THE THIRD TERRAN CONVENTION OF 2160, THEY HELD DOCUMENTS THAT WOULD BECOME THE CONSTITUTION OF THE FEDERATION. ALTHOUGH SLIGHT CHANGES WOULD BE MADE DURING THE FINAL FRAMING, THE BASIC INTENTIONS OF THE ARTICLES REMAINED INTACT. THESE PROVIDED THE BASIS FOR THE OVERALL PHILOSOPHY OF THE UFP. THEY ARE SUMMARIZED HERE.

ARTICLES ONE AND TWO: CHARTER

THE FIRST ARTICLES OF FEDERATION LAY OUT THE CHARTER OF THE UFP. THEY STATE THE DEDICATION OF THE FEDERATION TO ITS MEMBERSHIP, AND EXPLAIN ITS GOALS AND OBJECTIVES AS FREEDOM, PEACE, PROSPERITY, AND THE EXPANSION OF KNOWLEDGE.

ARTICLE THREE: THE GUARANTEES OF LIBERTY

ABOVE ALL, THE FEDERATION IS DEDICATED TO PROTECTING THE FUNDAMENTAL RIGHTS OF ALL SENTIENT LIFEFORMS. THIS ARTICLE REAFFIRMS THE BASIC LIBERTIES OF ALL SENTIENT BEINGS AND EMPHASIZES THAT THOSE LIBERTIES ARE INNATE, NOT GRANTED BY ANY POWER. SPECIFIC LIBERTIES COMPRISE THE MEAT OF THIS ARTICLE, WHICH IS PRIMARILY A LITANY OF GUARANTEES. FOR EXAMPLE, THE SEVENTH GUARANTEE PRESERVES THE RIGHTS OF SENTIENTS AGAINST SELF-INCRIMINATION.

ARTICLE FOUR: SOVEREIGNTY

THE ARTICLE OF SOVEREIGNTY INSURES THE RIGHT OF EACH WORLD TO GOVERN ITSELF, SUBJECT TO PROTECTING THE FUNDAMENTAL RIGHTS OF INDIVIDUALS. THIS ARTICLE WAS ESSENTIAL FOR THE CREATION OF THE UFP. BY MAINTAINING THE INDEPENDENCE OF EACH MEMBER WORLD, THE FEDERATION PLACES EMPHASIS ON COOPERATION AND OPEN DEBATE. THE UFP WILL NEVER INVOLVE ITSELF IN DOMESTIC PRACTICES UNLESS INVITED BY A MEMBER WORLD OR TO PROTECT THE INTERESTS OF INTERSTELLAR PEACE AND CIVIL RIGHTS OF FEDERATION CITIZENS. UFP SCHOLARS SEE THE DIVERSITY OF GOVERNMENT AND CULTURE AMONG MEMBER WORLDS AS ONE OF THE STRENGTHS OF THE FEDERATION.

ARTICLE FIVE: DISPUTE ARBITRATION

THE ARTICLES RECOGNIZE THAT DISPUTES MAY ARISE BETWEEN FEDERATION MEMBER WORLDS. A FEDERATION MEMBER MAY BRING SUCH DISPUTES BEFORE THE FEDERATION COUNCIL. IF THE RECOMMENDATIONS OF THE FEDERATION COUNCIL ARE NOT AGREEABLE, BOTH PARTIES MAY SEEK ARBITRATION IN THE FEDERATION JUDICIARY. APPEALS MAY GO AS HIGH AS THE FEDERATION SUPREME COURT, WHICH HOLDS THE ULTIMATE JUDICIARY AUTHORITY.

Articles Six through Fifteen: Federation Council

These Articles establish the powers and duties of the Federation Council, terms of service, and other practical details. Article Thirteen establishes the seat of the Council on Earth, for example.

Articles Sixteen through Nineteen: Federation President and Secretariat

These Articles establish the powers and duties of the Federation President, and set out the general framework for the Federation Secretariat. These Articles, and the previous Articles dealing with the Federation Council, reiterate the principle of sovereignty established in Article Four. Among the responsibilities of the Secretariat addressed here is the maintenance of the Federation credit as a solid medium of exchange.

Article Twenty: Starfleet

Although this Article is technically part of the duties and powers of the Presidency, it deserves special mention. Starfleet is so important to the security, stability, and continued existence of the Federation that its powers and limitations are carefully spelled out in some detail.

Articles Twenty-one through Twenty-three: Federation Judiciary

Much as the previous fifteen Articles establish the operating framework of the Federation Council and President, these Articles map out the structure and jurisdiction of the Federation Judiciary.

Articles Twenty-four and Twenty-five: Membership

Since the UFP is meant to be open to all sentient species in time, these Articles lay out the general requirements for becoming a new member of the Federation. Article Twenty-five also establishes that all five founding members must ratify the Federation Constitution before it can take effect, which happened in 2161.

Article Twenty-six: Colonies

This Article discusses the special nature of Federation colonies and reiterates that individual planetary colonies may govern themselves in any way without Federation interference. Of course, if a colony world wishes to be admitted to the Federation independently, it must abide by the requirements in the previous two Articles.

Article Twenty-seven: Amendments

This Article discusses the procedure for amending the Federation Constitution. It explicitly forbids the amendment or alteration of Article Three.

However, as has been observed in countless history files, there were forces at work that helped convert a common desire into an actual institution. The first and foremost of these was a shared perception that a common government was, simply, needed. Today the Federation consists of over 150 member worlds spread out across more than 8,000 light years of space. Even in the days of its founders, their five worlds were separated by huge gulfs of open, and usually unexplored, space. Exploring and administering that much territory, with its attendant planets, moons, and other astronomical objects, is enough to strain the resources of even the most prosperous government. By uniting in the Federation, the founders were able to work together, establishing common policies and economies of scale that made it feasible to govern such an enormous area of space without having to resort to totalitarianism or military rule.

Similarly, defending their respective territories was becoming increasingly difficult. Given their commitments to their peoples' welfare, the five governments could only afford to devote a certain percentage of their resources to defense—a percentage far lower than what was needed to defend themselves effectively. The result was a constant security weakness for even the strongest spacefaring species, a vulnerability to attack from "whatever's out there" that scared each of them to the core. None of them were as powerful as they needed to be to handle the challenges the universe was likely to throw at them. However, by uniting as a Federation, they could pool their military resources in such a way as to create a synergistic effect, giving them a Starfleet that is stronger than the sum of its parts.

Going hand in hand with defense is foreign policy, which includes not only diplomatic relations with other spacefaring "empires," but also exploration of space (after all, one cannot have a foreign policy without knowing where the foreigners are). The members of the nascent Federation knew that by presenting a common front and speaking with a common voice, they would have more power and influence "abroad" than they could ever hope to have separately.

Each race also counted on experiencing greater prosperity as the result of joining an alliance. Along with common political and military points, the Articles of Federation included common economic points and plans. Each race wished to maximize its profit, and thus prosperity, without sacrificing individual rights. Thus, their political union was accompanied by an economic union which has seen interspecies trade increase many thousandfold during the course of the past two centuries.

Lastly, and perhaps most importantly, each species held a common hope for the future that bound their hearts together where their minds sometimes did not wish to agree. After triumphing over their individual periods of darkness and downfall, they could not help but view their outward expansion with anything but optimism. Their initial forays toward federation were accompanied by a certain benign sense of "manifest destiny" for freedom for all sentient species. The Federation still possesses this optimism today.

The Federation has been, from the beginning, an association of species predicated on an ongoing, and beneficial diversity. The founding species included, among others, two species (Terrans and Andorians) known for their often violent passions and emotions, and one species that had overcome such impulses in favor of pure logic (Vulcans). Centaurans saw art as argument, where Tellarites see argument as an art. More divergent viewpoints are difficult to imagine,

but nevertheless each of these species was able to see beyond itself and acknowledge that a mixture of philosophies was a good thing—Infinite Diversity in Infinite Combination, as the Vulcans would say.

Accompanying this faith in diversity was a corresponding faith in the concept of universal freedom, for without freedom diversity cannot maximize its potential. This philosophy is the backbone of the united Federation, because it emphasizes the contribution of each individual, however different he may be, to the whole. A single member planet or system may not be very powerful on its own, but as part of the Federation, in which it is a significant participant, it is part of the greatest force for peace and justice that the galaxy has ever known.

Without an acceptance of diversity, tempered by a willingness to compromise for the common good, the members of the Federation simply could not function together effectively. They could form a trade union, perhaps, or a defense alliance, but they would never have created the Federation Council or Starfleet. Accepting, even embracing, differences leads to strength, both of arms and of purpose.

Perhaps the greatest expression of these values is the Federation's Prime Directive, also known as Starfleet General Order No. 1. The Prime Directive states that Starfleet (and, by extension, Federation) personnel and spacecraft shall not interfere in the normal development of a primitive (nonstarfaring) society or culture in any way. Federation personnel willingly sacrifice their equipment, their ships, or even themselves to uphold the Prime Directive, if necessary.

Typically the Prime Directive only applies to pre-warp species, since a race capable of achieving warp speeds can explore the galaxy and its civilizations on its own, thus "contaminating" itself regardless of the Federation's policy of noninterference. However, even in the case of early warp-era cultures, the Federation remains reluctant to become too involved. This means that the Federation can approach "first contact" and early relations with species deemed "ready" by the Contact Commission from a mutual perspective of trust. While some species are openly greedy for the Federation's technological secrets, most understand, and respect, the purposes behind the Prime Directive. Indeed, some actually mandate an even less intensive level of contact with the Federation than the Prime Directive would allow.

Despite the sanctity with which the Prime Directive is held (it is, for example, the only Starfleet regulation whose substance has ever been debated as an addition to the Federation Constitution), even Starfleet has to admit that its personnel have been known to break it occasionally. There are times when the Prime Directive mandates what are widely perceived as injustices—the continuation of genocide campaigns, inability to save people from natural or social disasters which are wreaking havoc on a civilization, the suffering or death of Federation personnel for trifling violations of local laws—and in those cases, members of Starfleet sometimes cannot resist interfering, no matter how reluctantly. Depending upon the severity of the violation, and its effect on the society, disciplinary action may or may

not follow. Clearly such disciplinary action has done little to deter other violations. Fortunately, Starfleet engenders sufficient responsibilities in its commanders that violations seldom happen lightly.

Federation Government

In the two centuries since the United Federation of Planets was founded, it has grown into an enormous governmental institution employing several billion sentients on its 150-plus worlds (not to mention countless space stations, outposts, colonies and ships). Within Federation space, and in the areas immediately surrounding Federation space, it is the dominant political and social entity, dwarfing the governments of most of its member planets. Its policies and activities influence billions on a daily basis, and establish trends in government, social policy, and leadership that have affected dozens of widely diverse species.

The basic structure of the Federation is mandated by the Federation Constitution. It provides for a system of government with three primary branches: the Federation President (the executive branch), the Federation Council (the legislative branch), and the Federation Courts (the judicial branch). There is also the Federation Secretariat—the bureaucratic and administrative arm of the government (or the "bean-counters," as Starfleet personnel sometimes disparagingly call Secretariat employees). The Secretariat is something of a hybrid. Although it is technically the "meat" of the executive branch, the departmental Secretaries are always members of the Federation Council, which subordinates it to the legislative branch as well. Because of this structural ambiguity, and because it is so large and often so independent, observers often regard it as a "fourth branch" of the Federation.

Although most graphic depictions of the Federation government place the President "above" the Federation Council, the main power within the Federation government resides in the Council, not the President. Most laws, proposals, initiatives, and policies originate with it. Only when it is deadlocked does the President step in to cast the deciding vote—

though that has given him considerable power from time to time. However, there are periods (particularly times of war, conflict, or crisis) in which the situation reverses itself: A particularly wise, beloved, or well connected President may wield much more influence than normal, and the Federation Council, in deference to him, may take a lesser role in government than it usually does.

One of the key aspects to the Federation government is that it remains just what it says it is—a federation. That means the members have agreed to join together, and to cede certain rights and powers to the "group government," but not to relinquish their sovereignty entirely. The Federation Constitution is very specific in describing which powers are granted to the Federation government and which remain the province of the member planets. In general, while member planets can ask for the Federation's help in certain matters, the Federation may not dictate to its members, or of its own accord interfere in their local affairs. However, this rule does have some exceptions. The primary one is this: If a member violates the agreement that it makes when it enters the Federation (by, for example, instituting a war of aggression, establishing a class or caste system, or otherwise grossly interfering in individual rights), the Federation may intervene. In effect, each member agrees to abide by certain standards of conduct when it joins the Federation, and if it does not, the Federation is empowered to make it "behave." Fortunately, this situation arises so rarely as to be almost academic; the Federation has only had to "discipline" members on a few occasions. Most scholars attribute this to the fact that the benefits of Federation membership far outweigh the burden of the rules that members have to obey. After all, any civilization mature enough to join the Federation will usually follow those rules anyway.

THE PRESIDENT OF THE FEDERATION

The Federation President is the chief executive of the Federation. The office of the President is a curious one. Although the chief executive in most governments enjoys significant power, the power of the Federation President is limited in many ways. First,

since the President starts out as a Councillor and is elected by the Federation Council (see below), he is often obligated to the Council, and in particular to those Councillors most influential in getting him elected. During most administrations, the Federation Council is able to use this leverage to maintain effective control of the government. Only when an especially charismatic person holds the office of President is the executive likely to wield more power than the Federation Council.

Second, most of the President's powers are controlled, either legally or practically, by the Federation Council. For example, although the President is technically Commander-in-Chief of Starfleet, Starfleet Command is based in San Francisco (where the Council is located), not in Paris. Thus, the Federation Council has the opportunity to wield influence over Starfleet which dilutes the President's control. The President also lacks veto powers, although since the President is selected by a majority of the Council, he seldom strongly disagrees with them in the first place.

The general weakness of the President is one of the potential flaws in the Federation system, and poses some problems in day-to-day administration. A strong executive is frequently necessary to keep a government on track and provide leadership. On the other hand, since the Federation President is always a Councillor selected by the Council, the two branches often share basic assumptions and sympathies. Perhaps as a result of this situation, the Federation government functions so well most of the time that any theoretical weakness is not as dangerous as it would be in most governments.

POWERS OF THE FEDERATION PRESIDENT

• *Commander-in-Chief, Starfleet (and other Federation military forces)*: On paper, the President is the ultimate commander of Starfleet; Starfleet Command reports directly to him. (Since Starfleet acts as the Federation's "law enforcement" arm when necessary, the President is also the Federation's "chief lawman.") Starfleet goes where he tells it to and does what he wants (within the law, of course). However, he cannot declare war (the Federation Council does that), and is forbidden by the Federation Constitution

from engaging Starfleet in battles or conflicts for more than 60 days without the Federation Council's permission.

During times of war or crisis, the President's orders in military matters are final. However, when the situation has calmed down, the Federation Council is entitled to review his actions for violations of interstellar or Federation law, and, if it finds any, to issue reprimands or begin impeachment proceedings.

•*Federation Security*: Related to the President's role as Commander-in-Chief is his responsibility for Federation security. The Security Council and Federation Intelligence Service report to him (though also to the Federation Council), and he may call the Security Council into session if he deems it necessary.

•*Diplomatic relations*: As a single person, and thus an easily identifiable figure, the President is better suited than the Federation Council for making diplomatic overtures to new species, quarreling members, and the like. Although the Contact Commission is not an executive branch per se, its members always bear messages from the President, not the Council, when making "first contact" with a race.

•*Foreign relations*: For the same reason, the President is in charge of all relations with foreign entities, such as the Klingon Empire, Cardassian Union, and Romulan Star Empire. The President usually carries out the wishes of the Federation Council in such relations, however: The Klingon Affairs Committee directs Klingon relations, for example. He maintains close contact with the ambassadors to those realms, and the Diplomatic Service (see below) is part of the executive branch.

•*Committee and agency appointments*: As a check on the power of the Federation Council, the President has the power to appoint the chairmen or heads of all Council committees and agencies.

•*Tiebreaking*: In the event of a tie vote in the Federation Council, the President casts the tiebreaking vote.

It is also worth noting that the office of President carries a great deal of prestige, if not power. The Councillor elected to be President is typically one who has received the universal acclaim of his fellows after a lifetime of public service and numerous accomplishments. He is usually considered wise and capable, and his advice is not lightly ignored.

EMPYREAN HOUSE

The President's headquarters, known as Empyrean House (or, more casually, as the Silver Tower), is an enormous skyscraper located in the city of Paris on Earth. Although the main body of the building is only 30 stories tall, one section of it rises into a 100-story-tall tower. Its nickname derives from its silver-gray color. The building has a central courtyard where workers often eat lunch and which occasionally hosts public ceremonies.

Offices and facilities open to the public occupy most of the lower portions of Empyrean House. These include public relations centers, presentation halls and auditoria, art exhibits displaying gifts to the presidency by various planets and individuals, and the offices of some public agencies.

The President's primary office, called the Red Room for its decor, is located on the 30th floor. Depending upon the President's personal preferences, his quarters and those of his family may be on the 30th floor, or further up in the tower. Most of the tower is occupied by secured offices devoted to Federation security, defense, economic planning, intrafederation and interstellar relations, and the like.

PRESIDENTIAL ELECTIONS

As mentioned above, the President is elected, but not by popular vote. Instead, he is elected to a six-year term by the Federation Council from among the members of the Council itself. Any member of the Council can make a nomination, and any member of the Council can be nominated for the position. In some years this has resulted in a field of as many as two dozen candidates.

Candidates are allowed to "campaign" during a six-month period only in certain defined ways, such as scheduled debates and speeches. However, there is no denying human (or Tellarite) nature, and no one in the Council is likely to hold it against a candidate who spends some time subtly "working the room," trying to build up support among the Councillors by making a few campaign promises.

The voting is done by secret ballot; the ballots are counted by computer. With each round of voting, the half of the candidates (rounded up) who receive the most votes stay in the running. For example, if there are twelve candidates, after the first vote the six with the most votes proceed to the next vote. After that vote, the three candidates with the most votes proceed; this field is eventually narrowed down to two, who then go through one last vote for the position. If at any time a candidate receives less than 10% of the votes, he is automatically omitted from further voting. Eventually, the candidate who receives a majority of the votes wins.

The existing president has a one-month "lame duck" period during which he prepares for the transfer of power. The inauguration ceremony includes an oath of office in which the President swears to uphold the Federation Constitution and "never to conduct [him]self in any way which would tend to denigrate the Presidency or betray the trust of the peoples of the Federation."

There is no limit to the number of terms a Councillor may serve as President of the Federation. However, no individual may hold the office of President for more than two consecutive terms.

PRESIDENT JARESH-INYO

THE CURRENT FEDERATION PRESIDENT IS JARESH-INYO, A GRAZERITE. HE IS TWO YEARS INTO HIS SECOND SIX-YEAR TERM. HE WAS ELECTED TO THE FEDERATION COUNCIL BY HIS PEOPLE OVER THIRTY YEARS AGO AND HAS SERVED CONTINUOUSLY EVER SINCE, WEATHERING EVERY CHALLENGE TO HIS POSITION BACK HOME. DURING HIS TENURE ON THE COUNCIL, HE HAS HELD MANY OF THE BODY'S MOST PRESTIGIOUS POSITIONS AND COMMITTEE APPOINTMENTS, INCLUDING SECURITY COUNCIL, ECONOMICS COUNCIL, AND THE KLINGON AFFAIRS COMMITTEE. HIS WISDOM, INSIGHT, AND DECISIVENESS ARE VALUED BY THE ENTIRE COUNCIL AND THE SECRETARIAT.

JARESH-INYO IS SOMETHING OF A PARADOX. ALTHOUGH NORMALLY QUIET, RESERVED, AND DIPLOMATIC, HE IS SAID TO BE SUBJECT TO BURSTS OF CAREFULLY CONTROLLED FURY IN PRIVATE—AN EXTREMELY UNUSUAL PERSONALITY TRAIT FOR SOMEONE OF HIS NORMALLY PEACEFUL AND NONCONFRONTATIONAL SPECIES. HOWEVER, HE ALWAYS MAKES AN EFFORT TO CONTROL HIS TEMPER WHEN IN PUBLIC, AND THIS GIVES HIM A COOL, LOGICAL OUTLOOK ON MOST PROBLEMS THAT SOME COUNCILORS CONSIDER ALMOST VULCAN-LIKE. THIS STREAK OF EXTREME RATIONALITY ALSO MAKES HIM A SKILLED NEGOTIATOR.

IN PERSON, JARESH-INYO IS USUALLY VOLUBLE AND FRIENDLY, WITH A SOMETIMES PUCKISH SENSE OF HUMOR. HE APPRECIATES FINE ART, ESPECIALLY PLAYS AND SYMPHONIC MUSIC. DESPITE HIS RELATIVELY ADVANCED AGE, HE IS YOUNG AT HEART, AND HIS OTHER HOBBIES INCLUDE A VARIETY OF PHYSICAL ACTIVITIES, SUCH AS HIKING.

JARESH-INYO'S ADMINISTRATION HAS BEEN MARKED PRIMARILY BY SECURITY CONCERNS. HIS FIRST TERM SAW THE BORG REPULSED AT GREAT COST TO THE FEDERATION. HIS ADMINISTRATION STILL REMAINS FOCUSED ON DEFENSE ISSUES. HE HAS EXPANDED THE CONSTRUCTION PROGRAMS AT THE UTOPIA PLANITIA FLEET YARDS IN AN EFFORT TO REPLACE SHIPS LOST IN BORG ATTACKS AND OTHER ACTIONS AS SOON AS POSSIBLE. DESPITE HIS PEOPLE'S TYPICALLY PLACID NATURE, JARESH-INYO TAKES HIS ROLE AS COMMANDER-IN-CHIEF SERIOUSLY, AND HAS BEGUN SPENDING AT LEAST TWO HOURS PER DAY STUDYING MILITARY TEXTS AND MEETING WITH STARFLEET OFFICERS TO CONDUCT WARGAMES AND STRATEGY SESSIONS. AS OFTEN HAPPENS IN TIMES OF CRISIS, THE FEDERATION COUNCIL IS CEDING TO THE PRESIDENT'S WISHES MORE FREQUENTLY THAN NORMAL, AND JARESH-INYO IS TAKING ADVANTAGE OF THE SITUATION TO BEEF UP FEDERATION SECURITY AS MUCH AS POSSIBLE.

THE DIPLOMATIC SERVICE

Most major agencies of the Federation are committees of the Federation Council. The Diplomatic Service is an exception: It is controlled directly by the President, who appoints the Chief Diplomat and oversees all Service activities. Because both groups share a "special relationship" with the President, the Service often sees itself as a civilian equivalent to Starfleet. Starfleet officers, especially harried captains who have to deal with self-important civilian diplomats, often have a different opinion. Since the Diplomatic Service is so well connected, however, a politically minded Starfleet officer usually keeps his opinions to himself. Starfleet has its own Diplomatic Corps, which operates primarily on the far frontier as an interim diplomatic agency until the Federation

Diplomatic Service can send representatives to the planet in question. Many members of the Diplomatic Corps serve as military attachés in Federation Diplomatic Service embassies and missions, advising civilian ambassadors on military affairs, pursuing liaison work with local militaries, and keeping eyes and ears open for useful military data.

The Service is led by the Chief Diplomat, who is responsible for all issues of diplomacy and protocol within the Federation. The Chief Diplomat is usually a member of the Federation Council (since virtually all planets send their best diplomats to serve as Ambassadors on the Council), but this is not necessarily the case. During an official negotiation, the Chief Diplomat's orders regarding the negotiation take precedence over even the President's, though it is rare indeed for the two to disagree so strongly that this becomes an issue. As with the heads of other large bureaus of the Secretariat, the Chief is assisted by a legion of Undersecretaries, Deputy Secretaries, and Assistant Secretaries. He also controls the Federation's ambassadorial and diplomatic personnel.

AMBASSADORS

TO DISTRACTED STARFLEET OFFICERS ASSIGNED TO ESCORT FEDERATION DIPLOMATS HITHER AND YON IN THE QUADRANT, IT SOMETIMES SEEMS LIKE EVERYONE IS AN AMBASSADOR. PART OF THE CONFUSION COMES FROM THE NUMBER OF TITLES ANY GIVEN DIPLOMAT MIGHT CLAIM AT ANY TIME, AND THE REST STEMS FROM THE FEDERATION'S NATURE AS A COLLECTION OF SOVEREIGN PLANETS. FOR EXAMPLE, THE HEAD OF THE VULCAN DELEGATION TO THE FEDERATION COUNCIL IS TERMED THE AMBASSADOR FROM VULCAN TO THE FEDERATION, OR COLLOQUIALLY, THE VULCAN AMBASSADOR. A VULCAN DIPLOMAT SENT FROM VULCAN TO NEGOTIATE WITH AN INDEPENDENT PLANET SUCH AS BAJOR IS THE VULCAN AMBASSADOR TO BAJOR, AND ALSO REFERRED TO AS "AMBASSADOR." THE FEDERATION AS A WHOLE MAY ALSO COMMISSION AMBASSADORS TO FOREIGN CULTURES SUCH AS THE JARADA. IN MOST FEDERATION DIPLOMATIC CIRCLES, THE AMBASSADOR TO THE FEDERATION IS THE MOST IMPORTANT AMBASSADOR FROM THE PLANET (SOMETIMES REFERRED TO AS THE CHIEF AMBASSADOR). THUS, VIRTUALLY ALL MEMBERS OF THE FEDERATION COUNCIL, EVEN TERRANS, HOLD AMBASSADORIAL RANK: MICHAELA MARSHALL IS TECHNICALLY THE AMBASSADOR FROM THE UNITED EARTH REPUBLIC TO THE FEDERATION, AND THEREFORE SUBORDINATE TO PRESIDENT CHANG-LEWIS OF EARTH, EVEN THOUGH SHE WIELDS FAR MORE POWER THAN HE DOES IN FEDERATION AFFAIRS. AMBASSADOR IS ALSO A RANK IN THE FEDERATION DIPLOMATIC SERVICE (AND IN THE DIPLOMATIC SERVICES OF MANY OTHER PLANETS) ROUGHLY EQUIVALENT TO CAPTAIN'S RANK IN STARFLEET (SEE TABLE, P. 26). THUS, SAREK ROSE THROUGH THE RANKS OF THE VULCAN DIPLOMATIC SERVICE TO THE RANK OF AMBASSADOR, BECAME VULCAN AMBASSADOR TO THE FEDERATION, AND CONCLUDED HIS CAREER AS A FEDERATION AMBASSADOR TO THE LEGARANS. FINALLY, JUST AS AN ENSIGN IN COMMAND OF A SHIP IS REFERRED TO AS THE SHIP'S "CAPTAIN" IN STARFLEET TERMINOLOGY, THE DIPLOMAT IN CHARGE OF ANY MISSION, NO MATTER HOW JUNIOR, IS REFERRED TO AS THE "AMBASSADOR."

Perhaps the most important branch of the Service is the Federation Contact Commission, which is responsible for making initial contact with new civilizations. The head of the Contact Commission, the Undersecretary for Contact, is often the best-known person in the Service.

As its name implies, the primary purpose of the Diplomatic Service is to conduct diplomacy on behalf of the Federation—everything from ending wars, to preventing wars from starting, to establishing and maintaining trade. The Service typically represents the Federation to alien species. Most of this work is done by the Federation's ambassadors to member nations and other governments, but sometimes more senior negotiators are needed for more complex situations.

The agents of the Diplomatic Service are also available to conduct negotiation, mediation, or arbitration between any Federation members, if all parties involved so request. The Service conducts many of its diplomatic missions with alien governments or potential member planets at its extensive facilities on the neutral planet of Parliament. The Service mostly uses the planetoid of Babel for intra-Federation negotiations.

CHIEF DIPLOMAT VEI DAMRA

CURRENTLY, THE CHIEF DIPLOMAT IS VEI DAMRA, A BETAZOID FROM THE BETAZOID COLONY WORLD OF TRENNES III. BETAZOIDS OFTEN SERVE AS DIPLOMATS, OF COURSE, BUT EVEN FOR HER RACE, CHIEF DIPLOMAT DAMRA HAS A PASSION FOR PEACE. SHE BELIEVES WITH ALL HER MIGHT THAT THE ONLY ROAD TO PROSPERITY AND GROWTH FOR THE CIVILIZATIONS OF THE GALAXY IS A PEACEFUL, INTERDEPENDENT EXISTENCE. SHE SEES HERSELF (AND BETAZED IN GENERAL) AS THE CHIEF PROPONENT AND EFFECTUATOR OF THAT INTERDEPENDENCE.

A CONFIRMED PACIFIST, CHIEF DIPLOMAT DAMRA HAS NEVER CARRIED A WEAPON, AND NEVER WILL, EVEN IF HER LIFE IS IN DANGER; NOR WILL SHE EVER USE VIOLENCE OF ANY SORT. IN FACT, SO DEVOTED IS SHE TO THE CAUSE OF PEACEFUL COEXISTENCE THAT SHE USUALLY INSISTS THAT STARFLEET OFFICERS ASSIGNED TO ESCORT HER TO NEGOTIATIONS GO UNARMED AS WELL — WHICH HAS NOT MADE HER VERY POPULAR WITH STARFLEET, ESPECIALLY THE SECURITY BRANCH.

DAMRA'S BOUNDLESS ENERGY — SHE'S INFAMOUS FOR HER DOZEN-PLUS-HOURS-LONG NEGOTIATING SESSIONS — ONLY INCREASES AS SHE AGES. SHE WORRIES THAT IF SHE ENTERS "THE PHASE" (THAT STAGE IN A BETAZOID FEMALE'S LIFE CYCLE WHEN HER SEX DRIVE QUADRUPLES) WHILE HOLDING THE CRUCIAL POSITION OF CHIEF DIPLOMAT, IT COULD DISTRACT HER FROM HER DUTIES. A FEW TIMES IN THE PAST, SHE HAS SECRETLY RESORTED TO HORMONE RETARDANTS TO KEEP ON AN EVEN KEEL. AS SHE GETS OLDER, THIS PROBLEM IS ONLY LIKELY TO WORSEN.

THE DIPLOMATIC SERIES

AN ENTIRE STAR TREK: THE NEXT GENERATION ROLE PLAYING GAME SERIES COULD FOCUS ON THE EFFORTS OF THE FEDERATION DIPLOMATIC SERVICE TO AVERT WAR, DEFEND FEDERATION INTERESTS, AND EXPAND PEACE THROUGHOUT THE GALAXY. ONLY STARFLEET OFFICERS BECOME INVOLVED IN MORE UNUSUAL AND POTENTIALLY DANGEROUS SITUATIONS THAN THE DIPLOMATIC SERVICE DOES. WHETHER SOME HARRIED NEGOTIATOR IS WORKING OUT HOSTAGE RELEASE CONDITIONS ON THE ORION FRINGE, TRYING TO ENCOURAGE ROMULAN DISSIDENTS WITHOUT GETTING EXPELLED FROM THE EMPIRE, OR CALMING DOWN A NEWLY ENCOUNTERED SPECIES DEAD-SET ON NUCLEAR VENGEANCE AGAINST ITS TRADITIONAL RIVAL, IT'S NEVER A DULL MOMENT FOR THE SERVICE.

DIPLOMATIC SERIES CAN ALSO INVOLVE STARFLEET OFFICERS, WHETHER FROM THE STARFLEET DIPLOMATIC CORPS (SEE P. 41 OF THE STAR TREK: THE NEXT GENERATION ROLEPLAYING GAME CORE BOOK) OR FROM SOME OTHER BRANCH OF STARFLEET ASSIGNED TO THE MISSION AS A MILITARY ATTACHÉ. MIXED STARFLEET-SERVICE TEAMS OFTEN SERVE AS NEGOTIATING TEAMS ON DANGEROUS FRONTIERS OR NEW WORLDS. A DIPLOMATIC SERIES CAN HAVE ELEMENTS OF AN ESPIONAGE SERIES (P. 32), ESPECIALLY FOR DIPLOMATS ASSIGNED TO THE TURBULENT CARDASSIAN EMBASSY OR TO THE ROMULAN FRONTIER.

FOR PLAYERS INTERESTED IN STORIES OF ALIEN CULTURES, GAMES OF INTRIGUE AND POLITICS, AND AN EMPHASIS ON PROBLEM-SOLVING OVER PHASER FIRE, THE DIPLOMATIC SERIES CAN BE A REWARDING OPPORTUNITY.

NEW OVERLAYS

THE NEW OVERLAYS HERE AND IN OTHER CHAPTERS ARE THE POINT EQUIVALENTS OF THE OVERLAYS FOR STARFLEET BRANCHES ON PP. 66-67 OF THE STAR TREK: THE NEXT GENERATION ROLE PLAYING GAME CORE BOOK. TO CREATE FULL CHARACTERS WITH THESE OVERLAYS, SELECT A RACIAL TEMPLATE FROM THE ONES ON PP. 64-65 OF THAT BOOK AND ADD THE GIVEN OVERLAY. THEN ADD 5 POINTS FOR EARLY LIFE HISTORY (AS ON P. 71 OF THE CORE BOOK), AND UP TO 7 POINTS OF ADVANTAGES, DISADVANTAGES, AND PERSONAL SKILLS. (TYPICAL ADVANTAGES AND DISADVANTAGES FOLLOW EACH NEW OVERLAY, ALTHOUGH, UNLIKE THE TYPICAL ADVANTAGES AND DISADVANTAGES IN RACIAL TEMPLATES, THEY AREN'T AUTOMATIC OR REQUIRED.) THIS CREATES A CHARACTER SUBSTANTIALLY LESS SKILLED THAN A STARFLEET CREW CHARACTER, WHICH IS REALISTIC: STARFLEET TRAINING IS THE FINEST IN THE GALAXY, AND STARFLEET PERSONNEL ARE TAKEN FROM THE CREAM OF THE CROP. NARRATORS MAY, HOWEVER, WISH TO ALLOW NON-STARFLEET CHARACTERS TO TAKE MORE DEVELOPMENT POINTS (25 OR SO) REPRESENTING "LIFE EXPERIENCE,"

PERSONAL HOBBIES, OR ADDITIONAL TRAINING TO BALANCE THE GAME FOR ALL PLAYER CHARACTERS.

FOR PLAYERS INTERESTED IN STORIES OF ALIEN CULTURES, GAMES OF INTRIGUE AND POLITICS, AND AN EMPHASIS ON PROBLEM-SOLVING OVER PHASER FIRE, THE DIPLOMATIC SERIES CAN BE A REWARDING OPPORTUNITY.

FEDERATION DIPLOMAT OVERLAY

FOR PLAYERS OR GM'S WHO WANT TO BRING A DIPLOMAT INTO THEIR GAME, EITHER AS PART OF THE CREW OR AS AN NPC, HERE IS A FEDERATION DIPLOMAT OVERLAY. "POSTED PLANET" REFERS TO THE WORLD WHERE THE DIPLOMAT IS POSTED. SINCE DIPLOMATIC TRAINING MAY INCLUDE SPECIAL SKILLS RELATED TO THE SPECIFIC POST (FOR EXAMPLE, SAILING, FOR AN AMBASSADOR POSTED TO A WATER WORLD), BE SURE TO "PERSONALIZE" THE OVERLAY BY ADDING A FEW APPROPRIATE ABILITIES

ADMINISTRATION (BUREAUCRATIC) 1 (2)
CULTURE (POSTED PLANET AND ONE OTHER SPECIALIZATION) 2 (3) AND (3)
DIPLOMACY (CHOOSE TWO SPECIALIZATIONS) 2 (3) AND (3)
HISTORY (POSTED PLANET AND ONE OTHER SPECIALIZATION) 2 (3) AND (3)
INTIMIDATION (BLUSTER) 1 (2)
LANGUAGES
    CHOOSE ONE 2
LAW (INTERSTELLAR LAW AND POSTED PLANET) 2 (3) AND (3)
PERSUASION (ANY SPECIALIZATION) 1 (2)
SOCIAL SCIENCES
    (POLITICAL SCIENCE AND ONE OTHER SPECIALIZATION) 1 (2) AND (2)
WORLD KNOWLEDGE
    (POSTED PLANET AND ONE OTHER SPECIALIZATION) 2 (3) AND (3)

TYPICAL ADVANTAGES/DISADVANTAGES: ALLY, CONTACT, DIPLOMATIC RANK, HEAD OF MISSION, LANGUAGE ABILITY, PATRON, SHREWD; ARGUMENTATIVE, ARROGANT, RIVAL

NEW DIPLOMATIC ADVANTAGES

DIPLOMATIC RANK

TREAT THIS ADVANTAGE AS THE PROMOTION ADVANTAGE (STAR TREK THE NEXT GENERATION ROLE PLAYING GAME, P. 104) FOR DIPLOMATIC CHARACTERS.

COST	RANK
0	SECOND LEGATE
1	LEGATE
2	VICE-ENVOY
3	ENVOY
4	ENVOY GENERAL
5	AMBASSADOR

HEAD OF MISSION

THE EQUIVALENT OF THE DEPARTMENT HEAD ADVANTAGE (STAR TREK: THE NEXT GENERATION ROLE PLAYING GAME, P. 104) FOR DIPLOMATIC CHARACTERS. HEADS OF MISSION COORDINATE THE ACTIVITIES OF BROAD ELEMENTS OF THE FEDERATION MISSION ON A GIVEN WORLD: MILITARY, CULTURAL, INTELLIGENCE, ETC. THE COST OF THIS ADVANTAGE DEPENDS ON THE SIZE OR PRESTIGE OF THE FEDERATION MISSION TO A GIVEN WORLD; TO BE THE AMBASSADOR-IN-CHARGE OF A MISSION COSTS TWO MORE THAN THE STATED COST. (FOR EXAMPLE, BEING HEAD OF MISSION (MILITARY AFFAIRS) ON BAJOR COSTS 2 POINTS; BEING MINISTER (AMBASSADOR-IN-CHARGE) TO BAJOR AND RUNNING THE WHOLE FEDERATION PRESENCE THERE COSTS 4.

1	RESIDENT (SMALL, INDEPENDENT WORLDS, E.G., ACAMAR III)
2	MINISTER (MEDIUM-SIZED CULTURES OR IMPORTANT WORLDS, E.G., BAJOR, KTARIA VII)
3	CONSUL (SMALL EMPIRES, OR SECONDARY WORLDS IN LARGER EMPIRES, E.G., THOLIAN ASSEMBLY, KHITOMER)
4	AMBASSADOR (MAJOR EMPIRES, E.G., KLINGON OR ROMULAN EMPIRES, CARDASSIAN UNION)

THE FEDERATION COUNCIL

The Federation Council is the legislative arm of the Federation government. It is a highly respected institution that, despite the existence of a President, is widely regarded as the primary governing body of the Federation. During most periods of Federation history, that opinion has been an accurate one; only during times of crisis or when there was a particularly well liked President has the Council's power been secondary to that of the executive branch.

The Council includes representatives from every member of the Federation. Each member may send up to five representatives (plus appropriate support staff) to the Council, but regardless of how many representatives are sent or the population or importance of any system, each system is only entitled to one vote in the Council. The highest-ranking representative of each member's delegation is referred to as its Ambassador to the Federation; the other members (regardless of rank) are Vice-Ambassadors. Members of the Council are routinely referred to as "Councillors," not by any of their formal titles.

The Federation Constitution does not specify how each member planet chooses its delegation, leaving that up to local law. Some delegations are elected by popular vote, but it is not unheard of for them to be appointed. Earth's delegation, for instance, is appointed by the elected government of the United Earth Republic. Some members use other methods, such as ritual combat or games of chance, to determine their delegations. Appointment or election to the Federation Council is regarded as one of the greatest honors in the Federation. In the Federation's history, only one person, T'Pau of Vulcan, has ever refused a seat on the Council.

Each member government may determine for itself the length of time its Ambassador and other delegates will serve. The majority of members appoint their Councillors for life. The only requirements of the Federation Constitution are that a delegate's minimum term must be at least one year, and there can be no gap of time between terms of service in which the member is unrepresented.

The Council meets year-round; all Councillors are expected to maintain a home on Earth so that they can live near Federation Hall. The Council's busiest times tend to be in Earth's spring and autumn seasons. Many Councillors travel all over the Federation on factfinding missions, as ambassadors or negotiators for their own planets or for the Federation as a whole, or (in the case of Councillors with Starfleet rank) in response to military emergencies. Thanks to subspace communications, Councillors can keep up on business and instruct their deputies on votes and similar issues.

FEDERATION HALL

Constructed in 2162 following the ratification of the Federation Constitution by the five founding species, Federation Hall is the home of the Federation Council. It is located in the city of San Francisco on Earth, in a former industrial area called Hunter's Point. Its construction included stone and other building materials from each of the five founding species, giving it a somewhat eclectic, but nevertheless impressive, appearance. In the subsequent centuries it has been added to extensively. The entire Federation Hall complex is now a massive, sprawling collection of office buildings and other facilities.

Most of the activity in Federation Hall centers around the Council Chamber, where the Federation Council meets each day. It is an enormous room, capable of seating all Councillors of all member delegations at once without seeming cramped. The Speaker of the Federation Council and the other Council officers sit up front on slightly raised platforms. The other Councillors face them in a semicircle formation, each seated at his own desk or group of desks; each desk is equipped with a computer and electronic voting equipment. The podium is located midfloor between the platform and the Councillors; it faces outward, away from the Speaker. All sessions not involving classified information are open to the public, who can watch from galleries on the second floor or on public information subspace channels across the galaxy.

THE SPEAKER OF THE FEDERATION COUNCIL

The leader of the Federation Council goes by the title of "Speaker of the Federation Council" (SFC for

short). He is elected from the main body of Councillors by a majority vote for a term not to exceed three years. At the end of that time he can be reelected; there is no limit to the number of terms, consecutive or otherwise, that a Councillor can serve as SFC. At any time during the Speaker's term, any Councillor can call for a vote of confidence in the Speaker; unless a majority of the Councillors express their confidence, the Speaker is removed from office and a new Speaker is elected immediately. This has only happened three times in the history of the Federation, and in each case the Councillor calling for the vote of confidence was subsequently elected Speaker.

The Speaker's powers are not broad, but they are important. First, he is responsible for scheduling all sessions of the Council, including all formal committee meetings and all votes. If he deems it necessary, he can put off a meeting or vote indefinitely, subject to a two-thirds majority vote by the Council to override that decision. This effectively gives him the power to "table" legislation in some cases. Second, he controls all debate on the issues before the full Council. He chooses who gets to speak, and in what order. Although Council regulations forbid him to deny any Councillor the opportunity to speak, they do give him the power to force a Councillor to stop speaking after an hour (a rule designed, successfully, to eliminate filibustering). Third, in the event of a tie vote, which is broken by the President, it is the Speaker's responsibility to notify the President that his vote is required. Again, the Speaker can put this off indefinitely if he so chooses, subject to the two-thirds override. History shows that it is rare for a Speaker to use his so-called "delay powers," and that in most instances where he

does use them, indignant Councillors will vote to override. This ensures that the legislative process flows (relatively) smoothly and quickly.

IMPORTANT FIGURES OF THE UFP

Speaker of the Federation Council and Vulcan Ambassador

The current SFC is T'Nal, a Vulcan (in fact, Vulcans are frequently chosen as Speaker; their logical minds make them gifted parliamentarians). She has served in the Council for decades, and has been Speaker for the past eight years. Strongly devoted to the ideals of the Federation, she wields her power with a cold, precise logic that keeps things running efficiently. Councilors who attempt to balk or delay her are often invited to her office for a "private discussion" which involves a game of three-dimensional chess (at which T'Nal is an expert) and a long series of subtle, barbed arguments designed to sway the Councilor to her point of view — a tactic which usually works.

Tellarite Ambassador to the Federation

Norx is the current Tellarite Ambassador. He is one of the more aged members of the Federation Council, a fact that the silver-haired politician plays on during debates. Previously, Norx was the head of the Utopia Planitia Shipyards. He proposed building a Dyson sphere around Tellar's sun, an incredible undertaking that has grasped the imagination of many Tellarite engineers. Although he has a reputation as a vocal cynic on the council, Norx commands the respect of his colleagues through his well researched arguments and practical viewpoint.

Terran Ambassador to the Federation

Michaela Marshall was born on Mars in 2325, a descendant of some of the original Mars colonists. At age 17 she entered Starfleet Academy and after graduation spent ten years as a Communications Specialist, eventually attaining the rank of Commander. In 2357 she resigned her Starfleet Commission to enter the Diplomatic Service. Fluent in the major Federation languages (Vulcan, Centauran, Tellar, Andorian), as well as Klingon, Romulan, and Cardassian, she spent twelve years in various diplomatic postings, specializing in crisis situations. In 2367 she was appointed lead negotiator for the Federation-Cardassian talks. After the signing of the Federation-Cardassian Treaty in 2370, Earth's world government appointed her to the post of Ambassador to the Federation. With the posting, she became the first colony-born citizen to be appointed Earth's Federation Council member. No doubt due to her early training, Marshall staunchly supports Starfleet and the Prime Directive.

Centauran Ambassador to the Federation

Kolos Pallera began his career as a sociologist specializing in the effects of interplanetary contact. He also studied archaeology, mythology, and the history of Centauran contact with other worlds. A prominent scholar and speaker, he was the primary contact in helping Prof. Richard Galen decode the Centauran part of the universal message. After his work with Prof. Galen, the Centauran Council appointed him Alpha Centauri's Ambassador to the Federation Council. His appointment generated some controversy, as he had had little diplomatic experience. However, some elements of the Centauran government felt Alpha Centauri did not play a large enough role in the Federation. They believed Pallera's background would bring credibility and assure a strong Centauran voice in the review and admission of candidates for Federation membership. This view ultimately prevailed, and Kolos Pallera began serving as ambassador in 2369.

Andorian Ambassador to the Federation

Danos Kosk has held the position of Andorian Ambassador for over two decades. A former Starfleet officer, Danos possesses unusual control of his emotions. He fell into politics after his Starfleet career ended and has shown considerable talent at it. Most regard him as a consummate politician. He seems focused on the long term, and has spent much of his time collecting favors from more senior ambassadors. Danos has a strong interest in Cardassian relations, probably due to the time he spent fighting along the Cardassian border. A few critics believe that he strongly sympathizes with the Maquis.

POWERS OF THE FEDERATION COUNCIL

The powers of the Federation Council are extremely broad (as they must be to govern such a vast territory with so diverse a population). The most important ones include:

• *Electing the President*: Every six years, the Council elects the Federation President from among its ranks by majority vote. Depending upon the political situation, this process may be of little consequence, or it may have vital repercussions for the Federation. See above for details on the election process.

• *Debating and passing legislation*: All Federation laws and regulations originate in the Council, usually in committee (any citizen may propose a law; the President does so frequently). After preparing the proposed law for formal consideration, the committee presents it to the entire Council, which debates it and, ultimately, votes on it. The President has no veto power allowing him to override the Council's decision to create (or not to create) a new law.

• *Presidential oversight*: The Federation Council is responsible for overseeing the actions of the President, and, if necessary, holding hearings on whether to reprimand or impeach him for legal or Constitutional violations, breaches of ethical standards, and the like. A conviction in impeachment proceedings requires a three-fourths majority vote. No Federation President has ever been impeached.

• *Agency oversight*: Most of the agencies, committees, councils, and advisory bodies which are part of the Federation are formed by, and answer to, the Federation Council (though the President appoints each body's leader). Since these agencies are responsible for much of the day-to-day functioning of the Federation and enforcement of its laws, this is perhaps the Council's most important power after lawmaking.

• *Resource allocation*: The Federation Council is responsible for passing the Federation's annual budget and making sure that all Federation activities are properly funded. The consideration of the budget typically takes place during the month of March during the Earth year, making that the busiest month in the Council's schedule. The Federation Council allocates resources—from manpower to materiel—based on priority and perceived need. The Council determines the total need for duranium throughout the Federation, for instance, and ensures the demand can be met by requesting duranium from those planets that produce it.

After passing the budget, the Council is responsible for ensuring that all agencies receive their allocated resources. The Economics Council is in charge of this process, and also considers requests for new or additional resources.

• *Factfinding*: Delegations of Councillors are frequently sent to other worlds to observe, investigate, and determine a proper course of action in times of crisis or disaster. General economic and security factfinding tours take place throughout the year.

The key to the smooth operation of the Federation is the provision, enshrined in the Constitution, that members who lose a Council debate are required to obey the ruling of the majority of the Council. In short, you can't refuse to play just because you can't have things your way. If, for example, Earth wants to undertake an exploratory expedition into the far reaches of Beta Quadrant, but the majority of the Council votes to explore parts of Alpha Quadrant instead, Earth cannot refuse to participate in, or deny funding for, the expedition to Alpha Quadrant—the Federation Constitution itself requires Earth to take part.

The Council's powers are, of course, limited solely to Federation territory and activities. All other powers are reserved to the member governments. The Federation Council can make it illegal to carry weapons when on a Federation ship or in Federation space, but it cannot, for example, mandate that it is illegal to carry weapons on Andoria or on Andorian colonies. That is the province of the Andorian government.

THE POLITICAL SERIES

THIS SERIES CENTERS ON INTRIGUE AND MANIPULATION WITHIN THE RANKS OF THE FEDERATION COUNCIL AND SECRETARIAT. PLAYERS INTERESTED IN THIS MILIEU MIGHT WISH TO RELAX SLIGHTLY THE GUIDELINES FOR "HANDLING STARFLEET CONSPIRACIES" ON P. 42 OF THE *STAR TREK: THE NEXT GENERATION ROLE PLAYING GAME* CORE BOOK. GAMERS DESIROUS OF GRAND STRATEGIZING, HIGH POLITICS, AND TACKLING THE BIGGEST QUESTIONS OF RUNNING A UTOPIA MIGHT SIMPLY WISH TO TAKE THE ROLES OF VARIOUS AMBASSADORS FROM MEMBER PLANETS WORKING TO KEEP THEIR SPECIES' INTERESTS AND IDEALS ALIVE IN THE HURLY-BURLY OF FEDERATION POLITICS. RUNNING A "FAR ABOVE DECKS" EPISODE, WHERE PLAYERS TAKE ON THE ROLES OF FEDERATION COUNCIL MEMBERS FOR A SHORT INSIGHT INTO THE FORCES THAT DRIVE THEIR STARFLEET CAREERS, COULD BE AN INTRIGUING BREAK FROM A CONVENTIONAL SPACEGOING SERIES.

MAJOR COMMITTEES AND AGENCIES OF THE FEDERATION COUNCIL

In many ways, the heart of the Federation Council is in its committees and agencies, since most of the

"dirty work" is done there. That's where proposed laws are drafted, initial decisions are made, and information is gathered and turned into a polished product for the Council's consumption.

Pursuant to the Federation Constitution, the Federation Council is responsible for establishing these organizations and appointing or electing members to them, but the President appoints the group's leader or chairman. This requires the agencies to report to both the legislature and the executive, establishing a check on both branches' powers.

THE SECURITY COUNCIL

Since one of the primary motivations behind the founding of the Federation was mutual defense against aggressors, it should come as no surprise that the Security Council is regarded as one of the most important, if not the most important, agencies of the Federation government. It was the first such committee organized by the Federation Council.

The leader of the Security Council is the Secretary of Defense, who is appointed by the President for an indefinite term. The Secretary of Defense is not always a retired Starfleet veteran, but almost all the Secretaries of Defense for the last century have held at least a captain's rank in Starfleet. A world or race must be a member for at least ten years before it is eligible to hold a seat on the Security Council.

The Security Council is not a sitting body. It meets only when the President or the Federation Council deem it necessary to call it into session. These days, with all the security issues facing the Federation, the Council meets frequently—typically on a weekly, and sometimes daily, basis. Meetings are held in San Francisco in a secure facility in Federation Hall.

The Security Council's duty is to analyze, discuss, and make contingency plans regarding issues of Federation defense. It acts as the President's and Federation Council's chief advisor on all military and security matters, from ship construction and acquisition, to galaxywide tactics, to weapon systems. As such, it works closely with Starfleet's Joint Chiefs. Although it has no direct responsibility for issuing orders to Starfleet or directing Starfleet activities in any way, its influence over those who do, and its knowledge of every aspect of Starfleet operations, make it a very important agency to Starfleet. Most Starfleet commanders make a point of getting to know the members of the Security Council and establishing cordial relations with them.

The Security Council typically divides itself into two- to four-man "working groups" to research various issues or problems for the whole Council. Some of the most important working groups are the Borg Working Group, Romulan Working Group, and Ship Construction Working Group. The working groups have access to an enormous staff of administrative and clerical assistants, researchers, and advisors who help them get their job done. Among other things, these assistants maintain the Federation Military Database, an enormous collection of information on all friendly and enemy militaries, ships, weapons systems, and military resources. The advisors specialize

in subjects ranging from as broad as the Cardassian military to as focused as Romulan D'deridex-class ship weapons systems.

SECRETARY OF DEFENSE MORSHA OF ANDORIA

The leadership of the Security Council is currently vested in Morsha of Andoria, a retired admiral with over forty years' experience in Starfleet. Secretary Morsha started her career in Starfleet as an ensign and worked her way up through the ranks slowly and steadily. Her flair for politics, combined with her intuitive understanding of large-scale space warfare strategy, made her a natural choice for the top post. The other main contender, Admiral Terence Leyton, became Chief of Starfleet Operations instead. Morsha is particularly popular with Starfleet, which always prefers "the civilian" to be a veteran. Secretary Morsha is particularly concerned about the threat of the Borg, and is studying the situation intensely. This emphasis on the Borg makes some in Starfleet (including Admiral Leyton) and on the Federation Council uneasy, as they feel she neglects threats from the Cardassians, Romulans, and other species.

THE ECONOMICS COUNCIL

The Federation's budget amounts to hundreds of trillions of credits. The responsibility for budgeting, allocating, and disbursing these funds rests primarily with the Federation Council's largest agency, the Economics Council.

The Economics Council consists of thirty sitting members: one from each of the founding species, and twenty-five others chosen at random from the member worlds and species for six-year terms. Unlike the Security Council, a Federation member can serve multiple terms on the Economics Council if it keeps getting randomly selected, regardless of whether other members have served a term yet or not. During the history of the Federation, all members have served on the Economics Council at least once (and some as many as twelve times). The leader of the Council is the Secretary of Commerce (usually referred to as the Commerce Secretary), who is appointed by the President.

The Economics Council is a "permanent committee" of the Federation Council. It meets every day to consider economic or financial matters facing the Federation. Meetings are held in the Gervese Building, which is part of the Federation Hall complex in San Francisco. The Commerce Secretary, aided by his Assistant Secretary, presides over the meetings. The duties of the Economics Council are broad and far-reaching. Although it assists the Council as a whole in drafting the Federation budget, and works closely with the Assessment Committee to determine the contributions member planets should make to Federation operations, its primary duty is the maintenance of the Federation credit. In an interstellar Federation with nearly free energy and replicators, almost no regulation of trade, and (most importantly) societies which no longer feel any need for resource competition, conventional 20th-century economics no longer apply. The balancing of postmonetary services, rarities, and foreign exchange in the mighty abstraction called the Federation credit is a herculean task. Without the Federation's well earned reputation for fiscal restraint and prosperity, and without the replicator and antimatter conversion, it would be impossible even for the Economics Council. All important allocations or actions must be approved by the full Federation Council, but it is rare for the Federation Council to question the wisdom of the Economics Council, and rightly so.

The Economics Council has dozens of subagencies, committees, and councils. Some of the most important include the Dispute Resolution Agency (arbitrates economic disputes), the Federation Disaster Relief Agency, and the Inter-Federation Trade Development Council. The Economics Council and its subagencies are assisted by numerous specialists, researchers, and administrators. Most of these employees technically work for the Secretariat, which is responsible for the Federation's bureaucracy, giving the Council and the Secretariat strong ties.

SECRETARY OF COMMERCE KOLRAK

Kolrak of Tellar is the current Secretary of Commerce, having been appointed to that post by President Jaresh-Inyo. He is a serious-minded little Tellarite, and unusually sober for one of his normally outgoing species. He often seems completely devoid of any sense of humor except for the occasional "economics joke" that no one else, even other economists, finds amusing. His Tellarite propensity for debate takes the form of lengthy mathematical and econometric discussions rather than emotional disputation. He doesn't get invited to many parties.

Secretary Kolrak takes his duties very seriously, and questions any expenditures which he feels could be smaller. Anyone who comes to him with a funding request had better have all his supporting data ready and in the correct form, because he'll find the least little error and use it as leverage to reduce or deny the requested allocation. "You can't unspend credits" is his cherished saying, which more ambitious Councillors have grown very tired of hearing. Other members of the Federation government sometimes refer to him as "the Executioner" behind his back because of his predilection for axing budget requests.

THE FEDERATION INTELLIGENCE SERVICE

No government can survive without information—information about economics, communications, and enemy activity. The Federation Intelligence Service (FIS) was founded to provide the Federation with that sort of data.

It is important to note what the FIS is not: an organization of assassins and saboteurs like the Romulan Tal Shiar. It is also not a military intelligence organization devoted to gathering information about the Federation's enemies' military capabilities or to carrying out foreign espionage against military targets on other planets; Starfleet has its own intelligence arm for that. (And Starfleet Intelligence has its own book coming soon.) Instead, the FIS is a domestic intelligence agency similar to the Interpol or the FBI of 20th-century Earth.

The FIS's primary responsibilities relate to collecting and analyzing information, and then disseminating that information to the appropriate agencies within the Federation, as necessary. The FIS gathers information in numerous ways. First, the agency actively monitors publicly available information channels—newsnets, newspapers, government reports and statistics, and library materials. It's amazing what you can find out if you know where to look, how to look, and how to assemble dissimilar sources of information into a coherent whole. For example, statistics on the Romulan economy can tell the Federation not only where the Romulans are hurting financially, but where they are using most of their money, how much (roughly) they are devoting to military projects, and where they might be suffering from shortages.

The FIS is also responsible for all counterintelligence operations within Federation territory. In short, they catch enemy spies. The Tal Shiar and other enemy intelligence organizations are constantly trying to infiltrate the Federation and uncover its secrets. Their primary targets are military—shipyards, starbases, and the like, where Starfleet Intelligence is on watch for them. However, there are plenty of other things they want to know about. The most important is scientific

and technological developments. If they know how far Federation science is advancing in such areas as warp travel and replicators, they can predict future military developments, for example. Lastly, enemy spies want to gather information about Federation leaders, in case it is necessary to launch assassination plots.

The FIS does not accept applications, but instead recruits from desired sectors of the population—Starfleet Academy graduates, citizens who have extensive familiarity with enemy cultures and languages, and researchers skilled at data analysis. Once identified, these potential recruits are approached covertly. If they accept an offer of employment, they are sent to the Federation Intelligence Academy, in a well kept secret location, for training.

FIS AGENT OVERLAY

THE TYPICAL FIS FIELD AGENT IS NOT ONLY HIGHLY SKILLED, BUT ALSO CLEVER, RESOURCEFUL, AND ABLE TO ADAPT TO A WIDE VARIETY OF SITUATIONS. SOME FIS AGENTS SPECIALIZE IN INTERPRETING STREAMS OF DATA AND BUILDING AN INTELLECTUAL PICTURE OF ENEMY OPERATIONS; OTHERS TAKE A MORE DRAMATIC "OUR MAN BASHIR" APPROACH INVOLVING DISGUISES, ARCANE WEAPONRY, AND FAST HOVERCARS. FOR PLAYERS WHO WISH TO PLAY AN FIS AGENT, HERE IS AN FIS AGENT OVERLAY:

COMPUTER (DATA ALTERATION) 1 (2)
DISGUISE (ANY SPECIALIZATION) 1 (2)
ENERGY WEAPON (PHASER) 1 (2)
ESPIONAGE (CHOOSE SPECIALIZATION) 2 (3)
FAST TALK 1 (2)
LANGUAGES
    FEDERATION STANDARD 1
LAW (FEDERATION LAW) 1 (2)
PERSONAL EQUIPMENT (CHOOSE ONE) 1 (2)
SEARCH 1
SECURITY (SECURITY SYSTEMS) 2 (3)
STEALTH (ANY SPECIALIZATION) 1 (2)
STREETWISE (ANY SPECIALIZATION) 1 (2)
UNARMED COMBAT (STARFLEET MARTIAL ARTS) 2 (3)
TYPICAL ADVANTAGES/DISADVANTAGES: ALERTNESS, CURIOUS, EXCELLENT SENSES, LANGUAGE ABILITY, POLITICAL RANK, TELEPATHIC RESISTANCE; FANATIC, IMPULSIVE, SWORN ENEMY

THE ESPIONAGE SERIES

ESPIONAGE SERIES TAKE THE ASSUMPTIONS OF THE DIPLOMATIC SERIES (P. 26) AND ADD THE PHASER FIRE BACK IN. ESPIONAGE SERIES CAN TAKE ON ANY NUMBER OF FLAVORS, OR BLEND THEM ALL. THE NARRATOR CAN SPIN TALES OF BETRAYAL IN HIGH PLACES AND FACELESS AGENTS MANEUVERING FOR LOCAL ADVANTAGE IN THE BEST LE CARRE TRADITION. HIGH-TECH ADVENTURES OF STARFLEET SABOTAGE BEHIND CARDASSIAN OR ROMULAN LINES OR CARRYING OUT COVERT STRIKES ON BREEN PIRATE BASES MIGHT EVOKE THE TECHNOTHRILLER TRADITION OF TOM CLANCY. OF COURSE, THE "OUR MAN BASHIR" SCHOOL OF FAST GRAVCARS, BEAUTIFUL ORION WOMEN, PHASERS HIDDEN IN STYLUSES, AND MAD EL-AURIAN GENIUSES OUT TO DESTROY THE GALAXY HAS ITS PLACE AS WELL.

ESPIONAGE EPISODES CAN TELL ANY OR ALL OF THESE STORIES, BRINGING FIS AGENTS, STARFLEET INTELLIGENCE OPERATIVES, AND SCIENCE COUNCIL COVERT ENGINEERS TOGETHER WITH KLINGON "ALLIED ASSETS" (WHO, UNDER THE TREATY OF ALGERON, CAN USE CLOAKING DEVICES), ROGUE CARDASSIANS, OR FERENGI ARMS DEALERS. ESPIONAGE SERIES DON'T EVEN NECESSARILY NEED TO STICK TO ESPIONAGE. PERHAPS A SMALL TEAM OF FIS AGENTS TRAVELS TO EVERY CORNER OF THE FEDERATION INVESTIGATING EVENTS AND OCCURRENCES THAT VIOLATE EVEN THE OPENMINDED FEDERATION'S CONCEPT OF NORMALITY—A GHOST SIGHTING COULD BE A THOLIAN INCURSION, AN ANAPHASIC LIFE-FORM OR A HUNGRY DEVIDIAN ... OR SOMETHING EVEN STRANGER. AFTER ALL, JACK THE RIPPER TURNED UP LIGHT YEARS AND CENTURIES FROM HOME AMONG THE STARS; WHO KNOWS WHAT OTHER DARK TRUTH IS OUT THERE?

DIRECTOR OF FEDERATION INTELLIGENCE

T'omas of Tiburon serves as the current Director of Federation Intelligence. He is relatively new to the FIS, with a background in scientific research in xenology. However, the study of alien cultures teaches many lessons that apply well to domestic intelligence. Director T'omas has even been able to streamline and improve FIS operations somewhat by introducing scientific concepts such as reproducibility, multiple attacks on problems, and "tiger teaming" to the agency. A proponent of aggressive intelligence operations, T'omas is pushing the Federation Council to expand the FIS's role and powers.

OTHER IMPORTANT AGENCIES AND COMMITTEES

FEDERATION COMMITTEE FOR COLONIAL RELATIONS

This committee is responsible for overseeing the operations of the Bureau of Colonization (see below), and for all issues relating to Federation colonies. The Committee reviews all applications for colonization, and hears complaints from colonists.

FEDERATION DEPARTMENT OF TEMPORAL INVESTIGATIONS

Because time travel and chronal distortions exist, creating a real possibility of temporal disasters, the Federation established this agency. It is responsible for monitoring all time travel and temporal distortions, and for assessing their effect on the time-stream and the flow of history. Due to the importance of this issue, the Department's Chief reports directly to the SFC.

INTERSTELLAR RELATIONS

A committee of the Federation Council responsible for issues relating to trade and diplomacy between the members of the Federation and, to a lesser extent, between the Federation and other governments.

KLINGON AFFAIRS

A committee of the Federation Council responsible for issues relating to the Klingon Empire and Klingons in the Federation. Its importance rises and falls in relation to the current status of relations between the Empire and the Federation. There is a similar Cardassian Affairs Committee.

SCIENCE & TECHNOLOGY COMMITTEE

This committee is responsible for overseeing the Federation Science Council (see below) and for legislation dealing with scientific and technological issues.

THE FEDERATION COURTS

The third branch of government established by the Federation Constitution is the judicial system—the Federation Courts. The Federation Courts are responsible for hearing cases under Federation law, and for ruling on the constitutionality of laws passed by the Federation Council or acts of the President. Federation Courts also resolve disputes between member planets. Under the Federation Constitution, members agree that they and their citizens shall be bound by the treaty interpretations of the Federation Courts, and that if necessary Starfleet may be ordered in to enforce a court's ruling (in fact, the same applies to all of the Courts' rulings).

Most laws are local matters; each planet has its own legal code, often derived from antiquity (much of United Earth's legal code dates back to the formation of English common law, for example, in the 13th century). Federation law is restricted to matters like interstellar aggression, piracy, and treason. However, many member planets have revised their laws to make them uniform with, or similar to, Federation laws in most respects, thus minimizing problems that could arise because of differences between the two bodies of law. Over three quarters of the members also have laws allowing Starfleet to pursue Federation felons into local space and to prosecute them federally for crimes committed locally which would be Federation crimes if committed within Federation space.

CIVIL LAW

There is no Federation civil law. Civil cases involve noncriminal wrongs done by one person to another. These include breaches of contract, fraud, personal injuries resulting from negligence or professional malpractice, commercial disputes, and unfair business practices. In the advanced, almost nonmonetary societies of the Federation, such complaints are handled by professional arbitrators agreeable to both sides. Many Tellarites and Betazoids become professional arbitrators, and the few Vulcans who enter this field never lack for clients. Some planets employ domestic arbitrators (such as Tellar), while others have fully functioning civil court systems (such as Earth), and still others resolve noncriminal disputes in other fashions, such as the Andorian dueling codes.

Starfleet, meanwhile, operates its own military courts for violations of Starfleet procedure and regulations. Unlike most 20th-century military courts, however, Starfleet personnel retain their civil rights as Federation citizens even in a court-martial and will occasionally even use civilian attorneys rather than Starfleet-appointed military lawyers. Between this and the similarities between Starfleet military law and Federation law in general, Starfleet courts-martial often seem like civilian courts in uniform.

Because it is the policy of the Federation to rely on the good faith and sound legal judgment of its judicial officials, rather than on detailed and overly technical legislation, Federation laws are usually broadly worded. One result of this is that it is left up to the judge to determine whether a particular act falls within the law. Indeed, in many cases, the judge (which includes starship commanders, who are empowered to preside over cases where Federation Court judges are not available) serves not only as the presiding authority, but also conducts the investigation, questions people, cross-examines witnesses, and otherwise involves himself directly with the case in ways more reminiscent of 19th-century British judges than of 20th-century American ones. This gives judges a great deal of power, but they exercise it equitably, and the citizens of the Federation are generally quite pleased with the fairness, wisdom, and honor of their judges. In the event that a party to a case (particularly someone accused of a crime) does not believe that the judge can render an impartial verdict, he has the right under the Federation Constitution to request a new judge, but he can only do this once.

As a result of this less formal system (or perhaps as a cause), there are few Federation lawyers. There are still millions of lawyers in each member society, but they practice their local law, which in many instances is still quite procedure-laden and complex. In the Federation Courts, where there are few formalities, the average person is much less likely to need a lawyer to assist him through the legal process. Indeed, there aren't even any formal requirements to practice before the Federation Courts—someone who is involved in a case is just as likely to seek the help of a trusted friend or relative as he is to hire an attorney. However, for those situations where attorneys are deemed worthwhile or necessary, they are certainly available. Persons accused of crimes in Federation Courts have the right under the Federation Constitution to be represented by an attorney, at the Federation's expense, if they so desire. They can also stand mute under the Seventh Guarantee, which protects Federation citizens against self-incrimination. Seventh Guarantee questions (and the growing number of sentient brain chemistries that it failed to interpret correctly) have caused Federation and Starfleet courts to abandon the truth-detection equipment used in trials during the 23rd century.

THE COURT SYSTEM

The first level of the Federation Courts is not really a Federation court at all—it is the local, planetary court systems of the Federation's members. Normally local court cases only become involved with the Federation Courts if local law grants the litigants a right to appeal

to the Federation Courts (which is very uncommon), or if the local courts do something which one party to the case claims violates the Federation Constitution.

However, there are situations in which Starfleet personnel violate local laws. The question then arises as to which has jurisdiction over them—local law or Federation law (be it civilian or military law). The general presumption is that Starfleet personnel are subject to local laws when on a planet, and thus can be tried in local courts for violations of those laws. However, under the Federation Constitution, a Starfleet commander can override local law and insist that the crewman in question be tried under Federation law (usually by the commander himself, under the Code of Military Justice). This issue usually arises in criminal cases where local law is so manifestly unfair in Federation eyes (such as the death penalty for flower-destruction on Rubicun III) that a commander could not, in good conscience, subject Starfleet personnel to it.

Since the Federation no longer has a death penalty law (originally Starfleet's General Order 7, forbidding contact with Talos IV), commanders sometimes intervene to prevent their crewmen from being subjected to capital punishment under local law, preferring to try them under the more merciful Federation regulations. Given the reputation of Starfleet for fairness and rapidity of trials, local authorities will sometimes voluntarily remand Starfleet personnel to their ship for trial, with a local figure serving as prosecutor in the hybrid Starfleet-local trial that results. On other occasions, Starfleet will insist that local authorities provide prosecutorial personnel, or even allow foreign prosecutors in a court-martial, if the alleged crime has serious interstellar ramifications.

HIGHER COURTS

Cases appealed to Federation jurisdiction (or of violation of Federation law) begin in Sector Courts, assuming that an indictment in the case is returned by a Federation Grand Jury, a body of citizens which has the power to investigate crimes and subpoena witnesses. Appeals from Sector Court, if accepted, go to Quadrant Court.

There are two Quadrant Courts, one covering Alpha Quadrant and one Beta Quadrant. While the term "Quadrant Court" makes it seem as though there were only one in each quadrant, and in fact on paper there is, there are hundreds of Quadrant Court courthouses throughout each quadrant—there are too many cases for a single courthouse to handle them all, and travel limitations would make it impractical to use just one court in any event. However, all courthouses of a Quadrant Court answer to a single Chief Judge.

In those rare cases where a legal error slips past the Quadrant Court also, a party may appeal to the highest court in the Federation: the Federation Supreme Court at The Hague on Earth. As the ultimate judicial and constitutional authority within the Federation, the Federation Supreme Court receives tens of thousands of appeals per year, but it only hears those in which it feels a genuine legal error has been committed, or where a legal issue has been presented which determination is important for the entire Federation (for example, a new legal question that has never before arisen).

The Federation Supreme Court has jurisdiction over several types of cases. The first is cases that have been appealed from the Quadrant Court—"appeal jurisdiction." This is how it gets most of its cases. Second, some cases can come to it directly without going through the lower courts—"original jurisdiction." One type of original jurisdiction case is a dispute between two Federation members, for example a disagreement over who owns a particular asteroid belt (and thus has mining rights). In cases where the informal actions of the Diplomatic Service cannot resolve the situation, the disputants can petition the Federation Supreme Court for a ruling. Under the Federation Constitution, both parties are bound to accept the Court's decision without question; if necessary, Starfleet can be called in to enforce the order (this has never happened, however). A related type of original jurisdiction case is treaty disputes.

The Federation Supreme Court is also empowered to render "advisory opinions:" opinions not in a legal case, but on a general question of law put to the Court by the President or the Federation Council (for example, "Would it be constitutional for the President to appoint someone with no military experience or training as a Starfleet Captain?"). However, advisory opinions are rarely requested, and the Court does not like to consider them.

Lastly, but most importantly, the Federation Supreme Court rules on the constitutionality of laws and government actions. If a citizen believes that a new law is unconstitutional, he can file suit in the Federation Courts and appeal it all the way to the Federation Supreme Court for a decision on the issue. Constitutional challenges are unusual, but when the Court grants a constitutionality petition it ends up overturning the law as unconstitutional about half the time.

The Federation Supreme Court is composed of 25 sitting justices, who are appointed by the President and confirmed by a majority vote of the Federation Council; the appointment is for life. Each of the five founding species has a seat "reserved" for it on the Supreme Court; the others can be filled by a member of any race (even another one of the five). The leader is the Chief Justice, who under the terms of the Federation Constitution must be a Vulcan. The other 24 are Associate Justices. The current Chief Justice of the Federation Supreme Court is Tusar, an aged Vulcan known for his judicial temperament and his seemingly encyclopedic knowledge of Federation law. He is grooming one of the two Vulcan Associate Justices presently sitting on the Court so that she may succeed him.

THE SECRETARIAT

When tourists ask why Federation Hall in San Francisco is so enormous, their tour guide describes all the facilities for them and explains that it's necessary to keep them all in one place. What the guide usually doesn't reveal is that about 80% of the entire building is occupied by personnel of a single "branch" of the government: the Secretariat.

The Secretariat is the Federation's bureaucracy—the people responsible for sending correspondence, taking notes, filing records, maintaining databases, and performing other services to keep the entire organization running as smoothly as possible. Technically a section of the executive branch, and certainly under the President's direct control (divisions of it also report to the Federation Council on many occasions), the Secretariat is usually conceived of as a sort of branch of its own. As with any bureaucracy, it has a certain amount of prestige and power, since it has an institutional familiarity with the ins and outs of the Federation that more temporary Presidents and Councillors may lack. The titular heads of the various departments, such as Defense, Commerce, Colonial Affairs, etc., often find themselves completely dependent on their Undersecretaries for information and results.

BUREAUCRAT OVERLAY

ALTHOUGH IT'S VERY UNLIKELY THAT ANYONE WILL WANT TO PLAY A FEDERATION BUREAUCRAT, THE OFFICIOUS AND INTERFERING OFFICIAL IS A STANDARD ELEMENT FOUND IN MANY *STAR TREK* EPISODES. THIS OVERLAY IS PRESENTED, THEN, TO HELP BUILD THESE NPC'S MORE FULLY. SHOULD YOUR GROUP DECIDE TO PLAY A SERIES CENTERING ON POLITICAL INTRIGUE (SEE P. 29), PLANETARY/COLONIAL ADMINISTRATION (P. 26), OR EVEN ESPIONAGE (P. 32), THIS OVERLAY MIGHT BE HANDY FOR PLAYER CHARACTERS AS WELL:

ADMINISTRATION (BUREAUCRATIC MANIPULATION) 2 (3)
COMPUTER (RESEARCH) 1 (2)
CULTURE (FEDERATION BUREAUCRACY) 2 (3)
FAST TALK 2
HISTORY (FEDERATION) 2 (3)
INTIMIDATION (BLUSTER) 1 (2)
LANGUAGE
    FEDERATION STANDARD 2
LAW (FEDERATION LAW) 2 (3)
PERSUASION (DEBATE) 1 (2)
A FEDERATION BUREAUCRAT WILL ALSO HAVE A SKILL OF 1 (2) IN THE AREA HE OVERSEES: A BUREAUCRAT IN THE DEFENSE DEPARTMENT MIGHT HAVE A SKILL IN STRATEGIC OPERATIONS, ONE IN THE BUREAU OF COLONIZATION MIGHT HAVE A SKILL IN PLANETARY SCIENCES, AND ONE IN THE SCIENCE COUNCIL MIGHT HAVE A SCIENCE SKILL.
TYPICAL ADVANTAGES/DISADVANTAGES: ALLY, CONTACT, FAVOR OWED, PATRON, POLITICAL RANK; ARGUMENTATIVE, ARROGANT, RIVAL

NEW POLITICAL ADVANTAGE

POLITICAL RANK

THIS IS THE FEDERATION BUREAUCRATIC-POLITICAL EQUIVALENT OF THE PROMOTION ADVANTAGE (*STAR TREK THE NEXT GENERATION ROLE PLAYING GAME*, P. 104) FOR CIVILIAN FEDERATION GOVERNMENT CHARACTERS. (DIPLOMATIC SERVICE MEMBERS HAVE THEIR OWN RANK STRUCTURE; SEE DIPLOMATIC RANK, P. 26.). STARFLEET OFFICERS RARELY TREAT HOLDERS OF POLITICAL RANKS WITH THE RESPECT THE HOLDER WOULD LIKE; DIPLOMATS ARE, WELL, DIPLOMATIC.

Cost	Secretariat Rank
0	THIRD UNDERSECRETARY
1	ASSISTANT SECOND UNDERSECRETARY
2	DEPUTY SECOND UNDERSECRETARY
3	SECOND UNDERSECRETARY
4	ASSISTANT SECRETARY
5	DEPUTY SECRETARY
6	UNDERSECRETARY

HEADS OF IMPORTANT DIVISIONS OF THE SECRETARIAT USUALLY HOLD THE RANK OF SECRETARY (SUCH AS THE SECRETARY OF COMMERCE) OR UNDERSECRETARY-WITH-PORTFOLIO (SUCH AS THE UNDERSECRETARY FOR CONTACT). BUREAU DIRECTORS RANK APPROXIMATELY EQUAL TO UNDERSECRETARIES, ALTHOUGH DIRECTORS OF SOME IMPORTANT OR PRESTIGIOUS BUREAUS (SUCH AS COLONIZATION OR THE FIS) MAY HAVE CABINET RANK AND BE CONSIDERED SECRETARIES IN THEIR OWN RIGHT. AS WITH ANY BUREAUCRACY, THE FEDERATION BUREAUCRACY PLAYS BY ITS OWN RULES, AND SELDOM LETS OUTSIDERS IN ON THE SCORE.

DIVISIONS OF THE SECRETARIAT

The Secretariat is best known for the countless bureaus, divisions, agencies, and services which comprise it. Some, such as the Administrative Assistants Division, are relatively bland and functional, but they are as important cogs of the Federation machinery as are the more "colorful" divisions. These include:

THE PRESS AND INFORMATION BUREAU

PIB, as it is commonly known, is the Federation's press agency. Although regarded primarily as "the official mouthpiece of the UFP," it is actually more than that. While it does provide a substantial amount of information about the Federation to independent news agencies, it is also a broadcaster in its own right. PIB's Federation Information Network (FIN) broadcasts news, documentaries, and other shows of interest to the entire Federation. Due to the freedom of speech and press guarantees in the Federation Constitution, PIB has few oversights or restrictions, and operates in a quasi independent fashion. The only major limitation on PIB is the same as that on Federation citizens—it cannot broadcast classified information without the permission of the appropriate government officials. On the rare occasions when this rule has been broken, PIB has proven relatively immune to punishment, since it has successfully argued before the Federation Supreme Court that most of the penalties the Federation has tried to impose on it are unconstitutional.

Larger Federation starships sometimes have one or more PIB officers assigned to them. These officers are usually more tightly controlled by their commanders than "free" reporters, but they have learned not to complain about it, for fear of being banished from newsworthy Starfleet ships entirely.

REPORTER OVERLAY

PIB EMPLOYS TENS OF THOUSANDS OF CORRESPONDENTS, INVESTIGATORS, AND REPORTERS IN ITS SEARCH FOR NEWSWORTHY INFORMATION. PERHAPS THE LIFE OF AN INTERSTELLAR MUCKRAKER APPEALS TO YOUR CHARACTER. IF SO, TRY THIS OVERLAY:
ARTISTIC EXPRESSION (WRITING OR VIDEO) 2 (3)
COMPUTER (RESEARCH) 2 (3)
CULTURE (FEDERATION) 1 (2)
FAST TALK 2
HISTORY (RECENT) 2 (3)
LANGUAGE (FEDERATION STANDARD) 1
PLANETSIDE SURVIVAL (URBAN) 1 (2)
SEARCH 1
STREETWISE (ANY SPECIALIZATION) 1 (2)
WORLD KNOWLEDGE (CHOOSE SPECIALIZATION) 2 (3)
ONE OF THE FOLLOWING AT 1 (2) AS AN AREA OF PROFESSIONAL INTEREST: DIPLOMACY, ANY TACTICS, ANY SCIENCE. THIS REPRESENTS "BOOK LEARNING" GATHERED FROM REPORTING ON THE SUBJECT. A PIB REPORTER WHO REPORTED ON NEW DEVELOPMENTS IN SPACE SCIENCES (ASTROPHYSICS) WOULD KNOW QUITE A BIT ABOUT THE CURRENT RESEARCH AND INFORMATION IN THE FIELD, BUT COULD NOT DERIVE A CONCLUSION ABOUT A NEUTRON STAR FROM SENSOR PROBE DATA, FOR EXAMPLE.
TYPICAL ADVANTAGES/DISADVANTAGES: ALERTNESS, CONTACT, CURIOUS, FAVOR OWED; ARGUMENTATIVE, IMPULSIVE

THE BUREAU OF COLONIZATION

The Bureau of Colonization is in charge of the Federation's relations with its colonies. Although the Bureau does have to answer to the Federation Committee for Colonial Relations, since it handles most of the day-to-day contacts and crises, it is widely perceived by the colonists as being "in charge" of them back home. Colony governors report to the Bureau, further reinforcing the illusion of power.

The Bureau's power is not entirely illusory. In most cases the Bureau does have to submit requests for additional resources or assistance to the Federation Committee. However, in dire emergencies, such as natural disasters or a rapidly spreading plague afflicting a colony, the Bureau has the power to contact Starfleet or other branches of the Federation government on its own for aid. In these cases, the Bureau works closely with Starfleet's Office of Colonial Affairs. While the Bureau serves as the liaison between colonies and the Federation government, the actual logistics behind establishing a colony—transporting material and people—fall to Starfleet's colonial office.

Closely related to the Bureau is the Federation Terraforming Commission, whose members are selected from the Bureau and the Federation Science Council. As its name implies, the Commission is responsible for evaluating requests to terraform worlds, analyzing the worlds themselves to determine how terraforming could or should proceed, and overseeing the actual terraforming process. Due to the resources involved and the vast ecological transformations that terraforming works, the Commission tends to view applications for terraforming conservatively. This causes resentment among some pro-colonization groups.

THE FEDERATION SCIENCE COUNCIL

It has sometimes been stated that the Federation is a government founded upon rationality and science. If so, then the Federation's chief agency responsible for scientific subjects, the Science Council, must be considered one of its most important divisions. Centered in Geneva on Earth, the Federation Science Council serves as the advisory committee on scientific and technological questions to the Federation Council and Secretariat. The Science Council also engages in long-term research on warp propulsion, basic physics and cosmology, and other topics. Science Council committees also pursue topics of interstellar scope such as the nature of sentience or the question of warp-drive stresses on the space-time continuum. The head of the Science Council, known as the Chief Science Advisor, is appointed by the President and approved by the Federation Council.

Much of the Science Council's research efforts is conducted by the many research stations and institutes which it maintains. Chief among these is the Daystrom Institute, an enormous research and teaching complex located in Montana on Earth. The Daystrom Institute is devoted to research in all fields of scientific endeavor, from purely social sciences such as archaeology and anthropology to the computers and robotics beloved of its namesake, Dr. Richard Daystrom. The Federation's most respected and accomplished scientists have all worked or trained here at some point during their careers. In addition to campuses and study facilities from Earth to Vulcan to Omicron Theta, the Institute now has jurisdiction over an entire "planetary annex", Galor IV.

The Darwin Genetic Research Station, located on Gagarin IV, is one of the Federation's chief facilities for biological research. It concentrates on genetics research and has made some remarkable strides in this field, but also works in other areas of biology. It is well known for its near-disastrous experiments with the human immune system in the 2350's and 2360's, but this notoriety is not entirely deserved; most of its projects have yielded valuable information and caused no danger to anyone.

Another important scientific facility is the Sagan Institute for Stellar Research. Based in a large space station in the Gamma Eridani star system, the Sagan Institute studies all manner of astronomical phenomena. Its researchers are often granted permission to travel aboard Starfleet starships to study important stellar occurrences or conduct research that cannot be performed at the Institute itself. Being granted a position at the Institute, which requires a three-quarters majority vote by the faculty, is considered a signal honor in the Federation scientific community. Institute scientists have well deserved reputations for being pacifists, which sometimes causes problems when they travel aboard Starfleet vessels.

SCIENTIST OVERLAY

THE PART OF A SCIENCE COUNCIL SCIENTIST COULD MAKE AN INTERESTING CONTRAST TO SCIENCE BRANCH PERSONNEL ON STARFLEET VESSELS. UNLIKE STARFLEET CREW, A CIVILIAN SCIENTIST CAN CONCENTRATE HIS ENTIRE BEING ON RESEARCH WITH NO OTHER REQUIREMENTS. ON THE OTHER HAND, WITHOUT THE DISCIPLINE OF STARFLEET, CIVILIAN SCIENTISTS CAN PROVE FRUSTRATING TO WORK WITH. THEY CAN MAKE EXCELLENT NPC'S OR PC'S. HERE IS A SCIENCE COUNCIL SCIENTIST OVERLAY FOR EITHER PURPOSE:

COMPUTER (CHOOSE SPECIALIZATION) 2 (3)

PERSONAL EQUIPMENT (TRICORDER AND SPECIFIC SCIENTIFIC EQUIPMENT) 2 (3) AND (3)

SCIENCE, ANY (CHOOSE TWO SPECIALIZATIONS) 2 (3) AND (4)

SCIENCE, ANY OTHER (CHOOSE SPECIALIZATION) 2 (3)

SHIPBOARD SYSTEMS (SCIENCE STATION OR SENSORS) 1 (2)

CULTURE (SCIENTIFIC) 1 (2)

HISTORY (CHOOSE SPECIALIZATION) 1 (2)

ENGINEERING, ANY (CHOOSE SPECIALIZATION) 1 (2)

PERSUASION (DEBATE) 1 (2)

PHYSICAL SCIENCES (MATHEMATICS) 2 (3)

TYPICAL ADVANTAGES/DISADVANTAGES: CURIOUS, INNOVATIVE, MATHEMATICAL ABILITY; ARROGANT, OBSESSIVE TENDENCIES, PACIFISM, POOR SIGHT

Member Worlds & Colonies

The United Federation of Planets boasts a membership of close to 150 planets. In addition, hundreds of other colonies serve as homes for Federation citizens. This diversity of cultures gives the Federation strength. Different ways of thinking have led to scientific advancements. The talents of individual species working together give the UFP an edge in conflicts with any single species.

The Constitution of the Federation recognizes the equal rights of all sentient lifeforms, but the UFP takes primary responsibility for its member species. No part of the Federation is closed to citizens. A child born on a new Federation member world may dream of becoming Federation President. No member species are excluded from leadership positions in the UFP. You could be sitting across from a human Federation diplomat or an Andorian—both represent the Federation.

Perhaps more than any other part of the UFP, Starfleet embodies the philosophy of diversity. Crew members from all member species eat, sleep, and work together in starship communities. They must rely on each other's skills and abilities. They learn to appreciate the cultural idiosyncracies of their fellow species and spread their knowledge across the galaxy. They become friends; in many cases, crew members come to see each other as family members. This is the ideal of which the founding member worlds dreamed when they began this new interstellar experiment.

The Federation remains open to new members. Dozens of worlds petition for membership in the UFP. Most fail to meet the high standards set by the Articles of Federation. Those that make the sacrifices necessary to reach out to the UFP, however, find support and aid throughout the entire process. Many Federation leaders believe that as long as new planets join, the UFP shall survive and flourish.

Membership

Five systems founded the UFP and formed the initial membership: Earth, Alpha Centauri, Andoria, Tellar, and Vulcan. The Federation Constitution established guidelines for the review and admission of new members, and with the chartering of the new Federation Starfleet, the search for like-minded systems and species began in earnest. In the first century of the Federation's existence, the membership rose to over fifty systems. As new civilizations joined, the UFP prospered. Today, the number of member worlds stands at 150, with new applications received every month.

The eventual aim of the Federation is to unite all sentient beings in a single interstellar body, dedicated to protecting the rights of every individual and maintaining peace throughout the galaxy. The UFP sees all life as interconnected and all species as members of a single galactic family. These are high ideals, indeed. Few Federation citizens believe such harmony is practically possible, especially right now, but millions of men and women in the UFP strive every day to make this dream a reality. After all, they point out, the Federation itself would have been seen as impossibly utopian only two centuries before its founding.

RIGHTS AND RESPONSIBILITIES

Although the ideals embodied in the Constitution of the Federation appeal to many lifeforms, planetary governments must justify membership in the UFP to their people. Some worlds want Starfleet as a protector and a peacekeeper. Other planets wish to improve their economic ties with Federation neighbors. A few governments feel that gaining a voice in galactic affairs validates becoming members of the UFP. But each world that seeks membership learns to appreciate all of the rights of memberships and to shoulder the responsibilities that come with those rights.

PRIVILEGES

All UFP members enjoy the following privileges and benefits:

REPRESENTATION AND VOTE ON UFP COUNCIL

Article 9 of the Federation Constitution grants each member world representation on the Federation Council. All member worlds and systems are represented equally, possessing a delegation of up to five members and one vote, regardless of size, population, length of membership, or any other factors. The Constitution guarantees this right, and prevents any action which would proscribe a planet's right to representation, short of expulsion from the Federation.

ECONOMIC SUPPORT

The UFP Economic Council and its branches provide financial support to member worlds. Planets must request funds before they are released. Some worlds request funds for economic improvements, such as establishing new trade routes or providing investment capital for development projects. Catastrophes may strike any Federation world, and disaster relief is another part of the UFP's economic support. When a member planet suffers an economic collapse, whether due to a crisis or poor financial management, the UFP may help bail it out of dire economic straits and suggest measures that will reduce the likelihood of further financial difficulties.

LEGAL SUPPORT

The Federation's judicial system is open to all citizens and member worlds. The UFP maintains regional and sector courts. In addition, an appellate process guaranteed by the UFP Constitution helps insure that Federation courts reach fair decisions. Appeals may go as far as the Federation Supreme Court. The court system also hears disputes between member worlds and provides support to members on issues of local law.

The jurisdiction of the UFP extends primarily to interstellar law and the protections afforded to individuals by the Federation Constitution. Member worlds have their own laws and judicial systems which retain their authority to resolve internal matters. Federation legal experts will serve only in advisory roles on matters concerning the domestic laws of a planet.

DIPLOMATIC SUPPORT

The reputation of the UFP's Diplomatic Service extends far beyond Federation borders. Member worlds can request diplomatic and cultural support from the UFP. The Federation Diplomatic Service serves to keep the different member worlds at peace with each other by helping to open lines of communication and settle disputes. Federation diplomats will aid planets in improving relations with nonmember worlds and even negotiate treaties and trade agreements on behalf of a planetary government. They provide arbitration services to resolve internal political disputes or conflicts with colonies. Although few members join because of this benefit, those that take advantage of the UFP's diplomatic support find it extremely useful.

MILITARY SUPPORT

Starfleet provides for the defense of member worlds. For some planets, particularly those on the borders of the Romulans, Klingons, or Cardassians, this is the foremost reason to join the UFP. The Borg attack on Federation space has caused other planets to petition the Federation for membership, in the hopes that Starfleet will protect them from assimilation. The Federation Council takes the defense of its member worlds very seriously. Members can rely on Starfleet to defend them against any aggressor.

RESPONSIBILITIES

While member worlds enjoy the benefits of belonging to the UFP, they also take on important responsibilities. First and foremost, each member world swears to uphold the Federation Constitution. They agree to promote peace in the galaxy and respect the rights of all Federation citizens.

MUTUAL SUPPORT

Because of its size and diversity, the Federation has almost unlimited resources. While the Tellarites provide large quantities of toranium, should the demand exceed Tellar's supplies the Federation can obtain more from a dozen other planets. Each member provides what it can to support the UFP and its many endeavors. Most planets see this as a matter of pride and give generously to keep the Federation strong. The UFP uses these resources to administer the government and its branches. In times of need, the Federation sometimes requests additional assistance, from enlisting all available ships to evacuate a planet to providing food shipments to a planet suffering drought.

PERSONNEL SUPPORT

The Federation cherishes the strength provided by the diversity of cultures and abilities. Although no official requirement for personnel support exists, the UFP expects each member world to provide individuals to serve in government organizations, particularly Starfleet. To date, this unofficial requirement has never been an issue with Federation members. Following the battle of Wolf 359, which saw massive losses of Starfleet personnel, the issue has received some attention. Few ambassadors see any cause for concern. Most planets are proud to send their best and brightest to serve in the UFP.

JOINING THE FEDERATION

When Starfleet discovers a new civilization, regulations demand an initial observation period before first contact can be made. If observations prove that a race is significantly advanced, initial contact teams are sent to meet with the leaders of the planet. Initial contact teams educate the newly discovered race as much as they study them. In a few cases, a newly discovered world will ask to join the United Federation of Planets.

REVIEW PERIOD

After the initial contact teams have completed their missions, and a planet wishes to join the UFP, the planet is placed under Probationary Review. There is no predetermined length of time for this review; Probationary Reviews have been completed in as little as a few months, while others have been ongoing for decades. During this process, Federation officials evaluate the planet on a variety of factors to determine suitability for membership.

The Federation Council assigns a Federation Cultural Attaché to oversee the review. The Federation Cultural Attaché is assigned a review team to aid in the process. Members of review teams include individuals drawn from the UFP Diplomatic Service and Contact Commission. If special circumstances exist, the team may also include officers from the Colonial Office, Starfleet, or even the Science Council.

The review team conducts periodic surveys and planetside interviews, preparing both the populace and the government for full-fledged membership. Areas where the world does not adhere to UFP ideals will be pointed out to the planet's leadership, along with suggestions to correct the problems. The Federation Cultural Attaché and his team must make certain that their review is accurate and the leadership is providing them with all relevant information.

At the same time, the Federation Cultural Attaché must educate the people of the world about the nature of the UFP. Many worlds have a distorted view of the Federation, whether as a deadly interstellar empire like the Romulans or as the ticket to a permanent free lunch at Terran expense. The review team has the task of laying the groundwork for inclusion in the Federation and making the transition as easy as possible. Federation Cultural Attachés often find preparing any world for the changes that come with membership to be the most challenging part of their duties.

The primary concern of the team is to evaluate the world's capacity for full UFP participation. Technological development is important. A world may possess all the other necessary traits to join the UFP, but if it has not developed advanced technology fully, it may not be recommended. Spaceflight must be possible, and warp-capable civilizations certainly meet the Federation's technological criteria.

The world must possess a single world government. Planets without a single government or political

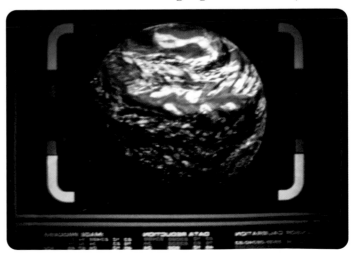

system are generally not considered. If the vast majority of the planet, ninety percent of the population or higher, possesses a single government, then the review team may continue to work with the world leaders until diplomacy can unite the planet's citizens.

Finally, the planet must protect the fundamental rights of its citizens. The interviews conducted by the review team are essential to making sure that the citizenry is not oppressed by a government. Even "private" discrimination, such as a caste system, will cause a planet to get a downcheck on Federation membership. Review teams see this work as the most sensitive part of their task.

After each review visit, the team makes a formal report to the Membership Committee of the Federation Council. Based on the team's findings, the Committee may recommend the world for membership. Based on this recommendation, the Federation Council will vote on accepting the world as a new member; the Committee's recommendations are not ironclad guarantees one way or the other, and many times membership for some new world becomes a touchy political issue in the Council. If the vote fails, the whole process repeats itself.

THE CONTACT COMMISSION SERIES

A STAR TREK: THE NEXT GENERATION ROLE PLAYING GAME series centering on the work of the CONTACT COMMISSION might be a specialized version of a diplomatic series concentrating on planet stories and exploration of new cultures. CONTACT COMMISSION teams include not only the CULTURAL ATTACHÉ, but also occasional Starfleet strategic experts and Science Council specialists performing technical evaluation. ANDORIANS might join the team because of the planet's warrior traditions; BETAZOIDS make excellent additions to any unit, like a CONTACT COMMISSION, devoted to reconaissance and reconciliation. An entire series might track one planet from first contact through covert surveillance and into the open contact, diplomatic negotiations, membership application, and probationary review period. To trace the development of an entire culture from an isolated, lonely planet to a full-fledged member of the FEDERATION could lead to some very rewarding roleplaying and interesting stories.

CONTACT COMMISSION series might concentrate on only one aspect of the process, of course. An entire series could be devoted to covert surveillance of a planet paralleling, and expanding on, RIKER'S adventures on MALCOR III in the episode "FIRST CONTACT." Let the players see how alien infiltration and conspiracy paranoia themes play from the side of the aliens!

Another CONTACT COMMISSION series could focus solely on the PROBATIONARY REVIEW period. Perhaps the characters helping to guide a new planet to Federation membership stumble on something more than the usual run of odd customs, misunderstandings, and comical UNIVERSAL TRANSLATOR glitches. Does the planet hold alien ruins, making it a potential target for robbers and hijackers from ORION to DESSICA II? Is the planetary government all that it appears to be, or are there shadowy species of energy beings working behind the scenes? Perhaps the world is unsure whether to join the FEDERATION or the ROMULAN EMPIRE and the characters find their paths blocked at every turn by a ROMULAN CONTACT COMMISSION team, which never hesitates to bribe, lie, or interfere to get a jump on its hated UFP rivals. Should the characters risk making the FERENGI into enemies by restricting the trade in nuclear weapons? Should the COMMISSION trust the new world; if not, how can it convince a new planet to trust the Federation?

EXCERPT FROM THE LOG OF CULTURAL ATTACHÉ ARTHUR KRIVAK

STARDATE 45739.1

0800 HOURS

It seems that each day brings new surprises. My team and I have been on MOLVOS IV for two weeks, yet I find myself unable to complete our report. Although I have served on review teams before, holding the position of CULTURAL ATTACHÉ puts things in a different perspective.

The MOLVONS certainly wish to join the UFP. The welcoming ceremonies lasted through the first week we arrived. I don't know if I can eat any more MOLVON delicacies after the THALOFIN BRAIN DELIGHT made me sick for two days. Still, the MOLVONS are friendly and enthusiastic. I'm just not sure they understand what it means to join the FEDERATION. The leadership speaks as if we offer them salvation, despite the advanced nature of their society. I think I've explained to ARCHON DALURION several times that becoming a member means that the MOLVONS are equal partners in our society.

Today, I'm going to tour a manufacturing facility and attend a major sporting event in the city of NYSTAR on the southern continent. I'm looking forward to the shuttle flight. If nothing else, MOLVON ergonomics could be a major contribution to the UFP. I love the seats on their vessels.

T'PAL has transmitted some new information on MOLVON weather-control technology. She indicates that it's not as effective as the MOLVONS stated, but I'll hardly hold a little exaggeration against them. At this point, I believe that they have met our technological requirements. They also definitely have a solid world government, but I'm still wondering about MOLVON rights. Hopefully, the rest of the team will have some interview information for me tonight, and I may learn a few things during my tour.

1400 HOURS

The shuttle flight was everything I expected. I wish the beds on this planet were as comfortable as the chairs, but MOLVONS don't believe in mattresses. I may sleep in my chair tonight.

The factory was impressive. Although the MOLVON officials seemed nervous about my visit, they had nothing to worry about. The workers I spoke with were very happy and their working conditions were excellent. They met all FEDERATION safety requirements and I found no evidence of rights violations. However, I was concerned about how little the average citizen knew about the UFP. One female thought that we were planning a complete takeover of the planet. If I recommend membership, I think we'll have a lot of work to do during integration.

I'm on my way to the NYSTAR GAMES, which are some of the most watched events on the planet. I'm hoping to gain a greater understanding of MOLVON culture and enjoy myself before I start poring through those interviews tomorrow. T'PAL will return to the capital tomorrow with her full assessment of MOLVON technology.

2200 HOURS

I'm not really sure how to begin this log. The NYSTAR GAMES were the most barbaric things I have ever seen. Apparently, MOLVON athletes are genetically augmented, pumped full of drugs, and then sent out to reenact mythical clashes between ancient gods. Not all the participants died, but there were heavy casualties during each event. The final ceremony was a struggle between different warriors armed with TRISKAS, a MOLVON bladed bola, for a shield with the crest of the UFP. The ARCHON just beamed proudly when the shield was revealed. I felt better after eating the THALOFIN BRAIN DELIGHT than when I witnessed that duel.

The manufacture ... breeding ... I'm not sure the appropriate word ... of these athletes and the type of competition they are put into raises serious questions about MOLVON regard for fundamental rights. I think I know what types of individuals the team will be interviewing next. I'm also not sure whether all of the homage paid to the ARCHON is just MOLVON culture or signs of a less open society than we previously expected.

Despite my shock, I think today reminded me of the good that the UFP can bring to the galaxy. Even if the MOLVONS are not accepted into the FEDERATION, I can help make this world a better place. Tomorrow will be another day. I'm going to see if I can make my bed slab a bit more comfortable.

END LOG

BECOMING A VOTING MEMBER

When a world has successfully completed its Probationary Review, members of the UFP Integration Commission join the Cultural Attaché to help the planet on its transition into full membership. During this time, the Federation officially gives the world status as an associate member of the UFP, which entitles the world to full Starfleet protection.

The economic transition is one of the key areas that the Integration Commission handles. Citizens of the new member world receive information on the interstellar economy and how their native currency, if any, converts to the credit. The Federation aids the associate member world in negotiating initial interstellar trade arrangements. Spaceports and docks are upgraded to UFP standards, so that merchants will not have difficulty arriving on the planet.

The associate member receives an influx of collected data from the Federation. If necessary, the UFP Integration Commission helps the planet establish an acceptable education system. This part of the transition to full membership is often the most difficult. Citizens must learn Federation law and culture, as well as adapt to new scientific information.

Politically, the world must adjust to Federation authority. Many associate members are surprised about the ease of this part of the transition. Since the Federation recognizes member sovereignty, little changes within a world's government. A representative delegation is sent to the Federation Council, but they do not vote until integration is complete.

Integration is a joint process between the Federation and the planetary government. When both the UFP and the world agree that the time has come for full membership, the planet gains voting rights in the Federation Council and becomes a UFP. The integration process can last for months or even years; on rare occasions, it may be as short as a few weeks. Each planet and culture adjusts at its own speed. The UFP Integration Commission always receives high marks from new members for the encouragement and respect they give associate members during this exciting and trying period.

Federation Colonies

The UFP maintains hundreds of colonies. Almost half of all Federation citizens live on Federation colonies. These settlements are found throughout Federation space, from the frontier to Mars, Earth's most famous colony. Life on these colonies can be harsh and difficult or filled with luxuries surpassing those on many core worlds. Starting with the drafting of the Articles of Federation, the status of colonies and their role in the UFP has occasioned numerous debates.

Colonies benefit the UFP in many ways. Colony worlds help relieve overcrowding on the core worlds of the Federation. They provide sources for recreation and rare raw materials. Colonies give the Federation a claim to large areas of space, allowing them to resupply Starfleet and prevent incursions from alien species. They allow religious and political groups to build their own societies without interference from

the Federation—and remove those groups' incentive to disrupt the Federation's peaceful society. Without colonies, the UFP could not survive.

COLONY DESIGNATIONS

Colonies may be categorized by their political ties. Many colonies belong to a specific homeworld, such as the Earth colonies of Mars and Cochrane. Humans founded these colonies before the UFP existed, and their governments are represented by Earth's delegation on the Federation Council. Several worlds with colonies, such as Earth, will often include citizens of their colonies on their delegation to the Federation Council. The affairs and concerns of these colonies are the affairs and concerns of Earth. The UFP sees the colonies of a specific homeworld as an extension of that planet's population and government.

The UFP also founds its own colonies. The Bureau of Colonization administers the affairs of these colonies. All species are encouraged to settle Federation colonies. Once a UFP colony is firmly established, the Federation Council will often invite the colony to appoint a Special Ambassador to the Federation Council. Special ambassadors may not vote, but they are allowed to speak at council meetings. Colonies established by the Federation, rather than by an individual world, are also called independent colonies, although this is something of a misnomer.

Neutral colonies, or unofficial colonies, are settlements of former Federation citizens that are not authorized by the UFP. In some cases, such as along the Cardassian border, the Federation has given up the rights to its colonies and has requested that citizens evacuate. In other cases, a group of colonists may decide to establish its own colony without the permission or assistance of Starfleet or the UFP. Although the settlers of these worlds are no longer Federation citizens, Starfleet monitors events on these planets. This is done to protect the UFP from interstellar incidents caused by colonists mistaken for Federation citizens, such as the Maquis, and for humanitarian reasons, with the hope that the colonists will seek to rejoin the UFP. Most unofficial colonies lie near the borders of the Federation. Neutral colonies are sometimes the sites of diplomatic meetings between the Federation and other interstellar governments.

The UFP has established joint colonies with the citizens of other governments, most notably Nimbus III, shared with the Klingons and Romulans since 2268. Unfortunately in the case of Nimbus III, all three powers agreed to abandon the joint venture in 2295: Nimbus III is a desolate sandball, and the Khitomer Accords made showy gestures of Federation-Klingon unity less meaningful than before. Administration of joint colonies has been strained. The UFP hopes that the establishment of joint colonies will improve relations between the Federation and her neighbors. The Bureau of Colonization and Diplomatic Service have made several proposals to the Security Council for presentation to the Federation Council, particularly in regard to more Klingon-Federation settlements.

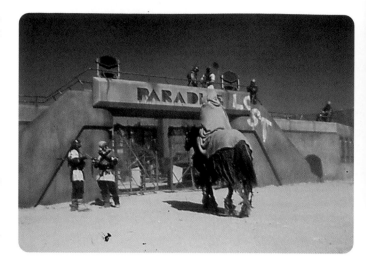

STARTING A COLONY

The Bureau of Colonization must approve the sites of all Federation colonies, and individual member worlds often seek Bureau of Colonization recommendations for their own plans. Colonies may only be established on explored worlds that have been visited by Starfleet's Survey Corps. Federation colonies usually require a colonization plan, which must contain an official purpose for establishing the colony and list a reasonable number of Federation citizens (ranging from 10 for scientific outposts to 3,500 for self-supporting farming colonies) who agree to join the colony. It must also include reasonable guidelines for the colony's development. If these conditions are met, Starfleet has no objection on military grounds, and the Diplomatic Service agrees that the colony won't upset the intergalactic peace, then Starfleet and the Bureau will assist the colonists in construction of an initial outpost.

The Bureau of Colonization will aid colonists in finding a suitable settlement site. Starfleet engineers may help in constructing appropriate shelter as well. The Bureau provides for vital necessities during the first five years of the colony's existence. The Bureau also helps refer would-be colonists to new colonies that might match their talents, interests, and biochemistries. Andorians, for interest, often settle on colder colonies, while the few Vulcan colonists tend to select hot, desert worlds. Many colonies rely on Starfleet heavily during their initial establishment. If the colony cannot provide for itself after five years, then Starfleet will review the colonization plan and recommend whether the colony should be maintained. Colonies that become self-sufficient in a shorter period of time are more likely to receive an invitation for a Special Ambassador and receive support from Starfleet for further projects.

TYPES OF COLONIES

Colonies are as diverse as the planets that contain them. However, basic types of colonies share many characteristics. Listed below are a few of types of colonies, along with a brief description of the life of a Federation citizen on one of these worlds.

DISSIDENT COLONIES

Colonial governments must report to the UFP, but colonies offer a great degree of political and religious freedom. Many dissident colonies are utopian experiments by citizens who are unsatisfied with their homeworld. Out among these colonies, the exception is the norm. Highly spiritual Tellarites may run a colony of poets and artists. Betazoids who take drugs to remove their telepathy might form another colony. Human experiments in genetic engineering are rumored to occur on some dissident colonies.

A Federation citizen living on a dissident colony may lead a very different life than does his counterpart on a core world. Most dissident colonies have some restriction on technology, especially communication devices. A few have governments which restrict individual rights to a far greater degree than most Federation worlds. Usually the site of a dissident colony has been chosen for its distance away from other worlds rather than natural resources, so colonists must often work very hard to survive. Most of the citizens of these worlds have roles to play within the political or religious structure which rules the colony.

Dissident colonies can be strange to Federation citizens, and most travelers should be careful to learn the specific laws of a planet before visiting. Although the founders of these colonies have different ideas, they are not necessarily hostile to the UFP. In fact, the ideals of the Federation which promote diversity are the very reason that these colonies can exist and contribute to the UFP, albeit not as member worlds.

ESTABLISHED COLONIES

Colonies like Mars, Cochrane, and Deneb II are firmly established worlds. They represent what many new colonies hope to become, integral parts of the UFP. Many of these older colony worlds are among the most important planets in the Federation. Established colonies are likely to be located in the center of the Federation, where the UFP's first explorations took place.

There is little difference between established colonies and Federation member worlds. A citizen of a colony lives the same lifestyle and has access to the same technology as a citizen on a member world. The only differences involve representation on the Federation Council. Although most worlds allow as much political participation for citizens of colonies as for citizens of member worlds, inevitably tensions arise. Some established colonies want to send their own delegations to the Federation Council and be recognized as full member worlds. However, some species without many planetary colonies fear this will unbalance the UFP in favor of more populous or widespread species, shutting them out of government. The issue of colonial representation is one that the UFP continues to debate.

FARMING COLONIES

Farming colonies supply the UFP with massive amounts of livestock and crops. Although farmers throughout the Federation gripe that replicators will end the need for them, the demand for real food remains great, especially on the frontier where energy can be precious. Since only the newest, rawest colonies actually depend on food shipments from other colonies, most farming colonies serve as experimental agricultural areas, such as Sherman's Planet, or grow luxury crops unavailable elsewhere, such as Ennan VI. Farming colonies often trade heavily with their neighbors. Many UFP citizens envision fields of grain and numbers of herd animals when they think of farming colonies, but these settlements also come in many other forms. Some consist of undersea domes where submarines harvest seaweeds and native krill. Other colonies specialize in particular delicacies, grown in inhospitable conditions. A few worlds are primarily vast vineyards.

Work is the order of the day on these colonies. Although most of these worlds have large amounts of automation, plenty exists to be done. Many colonists on these planets grow isolated from the UFP, since their work demands so much time and effort. Only those settlers who deal with free traders and Federation officials see many outsiders.

Until recently, farming colonies have not been very popular. A Centauran literary movement which romanticizes life caring for the livestock and harvesting the bounty of the soil has pushed many citizens to seek out these worlds. Unfortunately, the fortitude needed to handle the workload on these planets has proved lacking among these romantics and many soon return to the core worlds.

INDUSTRIAL COLONIES

Industrial colonies produce manufactured goods or process raw materials. Most of these colonies are located on the frontier or in intermediate areas closer to the core worlds. With replicators available all over the Federation, industrial colonies (like agricultural ones) usually specialize in one particular task that replicators cannot handle or that are best left on less-populated planets. Most of these colonies specialize in dangerous procedures, such as dilithium-cracking or working with toxic chemicals.

On industrial colonies, workers usually own part of the colony and profit not only from their work, but

also from the growth of the colony. Like many of the other profit-driven colonies, labor is a fact of life. Many industrial colonists spend their time inside factories, performing a variety of technical tasks. Most people don't enjoy life in an industrial colony and settlers may join the colony only to leave after a few months. If an industrial colony succeeds, those workers with seniority stand to receive the most benefit.

Accidents are a fact of life on these colonies, and Federation captains age a bit when they get a distress call from an industrial colony. Due to the dangerous nature of their work, any incident can turn into a colony-wide disaster. Although the Secretariat Health Department tries to enforce safety measures and emergency protocols on UFP colonies, many industrial colonies (especially planetary ones) fail to implement these procedures fully.

MINING COLONIES

Mining colonies are built on planets, moons, or asteroids which hold rare elements. Mining colonies may provide dilithium or rare crystals. Common metals and unique compounds are collected in mines. Many colonies provide a unique type of metal found only in a specific sector. The demand for high-quality metals and radioactives makes almost any mining colony worthwhile.

The people who live and work on mining colonies tend to be hardy and independent. They take meticulous care of their equipment, and when they aren't working make sure that they have a good time. Miners are known both for their well developed sense of humor and for clear thinking in a crisis. Most miners spend all of their time below ground and harsh lights may bother them.

Mining work is hazardous at best, even with 24th-century technology. Laser cutters, ion drills, and even environmental suits can kill with a malfunction. Unstable shafts and tunnels can cave in, trapping or killing miners. Tales abound of encounters with subterranean alien lifeforms, such as the Horta, which plagued the Janus VI pergium mining colony. When tragedy strikes, Starfleet often receives the call for assistance. Mining colonies reciprocate by treating visiting Starfleet personnel with extra hospitality.

PENAL COLONIES

As a last resort, prisoners may be exiled to a penal colony. These sites are off limits for most Federation citizens. All penal colonies fall under the jurisdiction of the UFP Bureau of Colonization's Penal Division.

Most penal colonies are high-security prisons or work sites. Colonial penitentiaries are established for the purpose of protecting Federation citizens from dangerous convicts. Even if a prisoner should escape, these colonies are so isolated that there is little chance he would find his way back to civilization. Work sites allow convicts to perform labor in return for shorter sentences. These penal colonies are similar to mining or industrial colonies, but contact with the outside is heavily restricted.

Starfleet barely monitors some penal colonies. Criminals condemned for life may be deposited on an M-class planet with basic supplies. After several years, Starfleet will send survey teams to check on the prisoners. On rare occasions, the communities established by these exiles have impressed the UFP enough for it to consider granting them full colonial status and commuting the crimes of the colonists.

Obviously, most penal colonists are criminals. However, support staff such as doctors, security guards, technicians, and bureaucrats also live on penal colonies. The rights of Federation citizens extend even to convicts, and Starfleet works to protect these worlds. Starfleet captains are also contacted to quell uprisings and riots on these colonies, missions that are never very popular with crews.

RESORT COLONIES

These sites cater to the recreational needs of Federation citizens. Usually, these are on terraformed worlds, designed to be a comfortable as possible for visitors. The actual administration of these colonies varies widely, crossing the spectrum of political systems.

Resort colonies come in many different varieties. Some have large zoos filled with interstellar menageries. Among these, a few offer safaris into specially designed "wilderness" regions. Spas are not uncommon, where citizens can have their health restored and work on physical development. Amusement colonies have thrill rides, holodeck shows, and performers from across the UFP.

More exotic resort colonies provide once-in-a-lifetime opportunities for Federation travelers. Aquatic sites may allow guests to swim with local wildlife or dive for ancient (or modern) treasure. Space station resorts usually provide tours of spectacular local phenomena. These orbital colonies often float near nebulae and several of them serve double duty as starbases.

Citizens of resort colonies tend to be entertainers, artists, technicians, and medical personnel. Although many of them spend their lives in a near-paradise, they all live with the knowledge that the success of the colony depends on its popularity. They work long hours and rarely take a day to rest, so that they can tend to the needs of others.

A few resort colonies reputedly cross the boundaries of Federation law, abusing staff or providing contraband to guests. This type of colony is rare, and those that exist lie on the edges of Federation space, especially in Orion-controlled systems. Rumors abound that a few such sites continue to be allowed by the UFP in order to support the activities of Federation Intelligence. The government firmly denies such claims.

SCIENCE COLONIES

One of the most important types of colonies, these are almost always founded under the auspices of the UFP. The colony administrator may be a member of

Starfleet or the Science Council. Each colony has a particular focus or special project. If a science colony is established for a particular long-term project, it may evolve into another type of colony once the research has been completed. Many times, residents develop ties to a colony world.

The personnel at science colonies are primarily researchers and support staff with little military equipment, leaving these communities vulnerable to raiders and space pirates. The staff spends the majority of its time working on experiments and maintaining equipment. Due to their importance, Starfleet keeps a careful watch over these sites, making a special point to visit them during space patrols. Sometimes the scientists on board a starship will share their findings with the science colony and vice versa, often leading to new insights into the nature of the galaxy.

The research done on science colonies produces benefits that far outweigh the costs of these undertakings. Many of the UFP's new technologies are based on work done on these distant colonies. Unusual phenomena can be studied for long periods of time from a science colony. Science colonies may develop rare medicinal compounds or conduct careful surveys of alien creatures in their native habitat. Not all science colonies manage to succeed in completing their primary missions, but the data from each one serves to expand the banks of the Federation's massive scientific library at Memory Alpha, and adds to the collective knowledge of the UFP.

STANDARD COLONIES

These colonies are established to help relieve overcrowding and to fill a need for challenges among Federation citizens. Standard colonies lack the unity of dissident settlements. They also don't have an immediate financial benefit or focus. Standard colonies spread their resources, trying to survive by any means possible. Many standard colonies don't survive. Accidents can destroy a sparsely supplied settlement. Other colonies lack leadership and dissolve after a few hard years. Some colonies are founded as a reaction to the crowding on Federation core worlds. A standard colony can be in any environment and have any type of political system. These colonies are extremely diverse and can be grouped only because they lack a specific function.

If these colonies survive, they are the most likely to develop into populous worlds. Because of the broad range of individuals and activities these settlements need to survive, they can grow easily into established communities. Those who manage the colony through its early years provide the leadership to attract new generations of pioneers.

The type of individual who lives in this colony is an independent, rugged survivor. People who make these outposts evolve into communities have faced tremendous challenges and beaten the odds. They respect Starfleet and the UFP, but they also feel that they have the best knowledge of how to run their world. These settlements often produce some of the Federation's most talented citizens.

The different types of colonies may cross and mix. Dissidents may build a mining colony. A resort colony could develop farming communities. Penal colonies may make convicts perform industrial work. Just as the members of the Federation are diverse, so are the communities they decide to create.

COLONY POLITICS

Federation colonies may have any type of political system as long as the rights of individuals are not violated. Some colonies have true democracies, where every citizen votes on each issue. Other settlements have monarchies, where a hereditary royal line holds power. Many colonies adopt historical or theoretical systems, such as the Delos colony, which bases its government on Plato's Republic. The Federation allows considerable leeway, only intervening to protect the rights of citizens.

Each colony has the right to self-determination for its form of government and plan of development. These communities may clash with the Bureau of Colonization or with Starfleet over issues of development. Usually these clashes involve recommendations for the protection of Federation citizens conflicting with the beliefs or practices of colonial leaders. The UFP cannot forcibly remove colonists from a planet, only refuse to recognize them as Federation citizens. Starfleet is usually willing to provide transport off a Federation colony for any group that claims the colonial government oppresses it, even if it can't intervene directly.

Starfleet or the Bureau of Colonization must provide colonists with adequate food and shelter, if the colony proves unable to meet these needs. A few hardy pioneers prefer starvation to receiving UFP aid. However, this does not release the Federation from the moral obligation to provide such assistance.

Colonial leaders must report to the UFP on the status of the colony, informing it of any recent developments. During initial stages of colonization, Starfleet carefully monitors any outside trade with the colony. A UFP-appointed colonial administrator may even serve to help organize the community. Both the Federation and the colony leaders carefully work to

keep relations amicable. When difficulties arise, members of the Diplomatic Service often have to resolve the conflict.

LEADERSHIP

Colonial administrators are initially responsible for Federation-founded colonies. These officials are sometimes members of Starfleet's Colonial Operations Division or representatives of the Federation Bureau of Colonization, but some specialized colonies may select their own administrators. The first duty of a colonial administrator is to make certain that the needs of the colonists are met. In addition, a colonial administrator is held accountable for the success of the colony.

These officials also serve as liaisons with the Federation. They must ensure that the colony follows all applicable Federation regulations. Colonial administrators are sometimes torn between their duties to the Federation and their duties to the colony. In a few reported cases, administrators have become petty dictators, using their influence with the Federation to threaten and cajole others into obeying their orders. Other times, administrators serve as puppets for strong-willed community leaders. Colonial administrators generally are found during the early years of a colony or on colonies that do not develop into strong communities, such as industrial or mining colonies.

Governors are colonial leaders, chosen either by the settlers or the colonial sponsors. Governor is the most popular title used by these leaders, but a variety of different terms are used. To some extent, colonial governors have the same authority as the head of a planet. They serve at the will of the colony or the sponsor. Individual governors have different degrees of power. Some are subject to considerable limitations imposed by colonial council. A governor may have nearly absolute power on his own colony.

Governors tend to have more influence in determining the course of colonial development than administrators. Most colonies feel a sense of loyalty and patriotism toward their elected leaders. The tastes of a governor may shape the culture of a colony for years after he leaves office. Some governors are venerated after their deaths and have monuments built to honor them.

Unlike the leaders of member worlds, colonial governors may be removed by order of the Federation Council. This is a rare event and only done when officials have reason to believe UFP laws are being violated. In colonies of member worlds, that world's government may also remove a colonial governor; this happens more often, usually because of domestic politics. On a few occasions, colonial governors have declared their settlements independent from the Federation. These declarations are usually acceptable, although Starfleet does send ships to the system to make sure that such declarations have the support of the colonists. Starfleet will evacuate all personnel who wish to remain Federation citizens.

COLONIAL ADMINISTRATOR/GOVERNOR OVERLAY

Although it is unlikely that a colonial administrator will have a starring role in a series, one can make an excellent "guest star" NPC. Of course, a colonial or diplomatic (p. 26) series might feature a colonial adminstrator as a player character. This Overlay represents a civilian administrator or governor from the colony, the parent world, or the Bureau of Colonization. Starfleet Colonial staff will generally use the Command or Operations Overlay.

Administration (Colonial Government) 3 (4)
Command (Colonial) 2 (3)
Culture (Colony Planet) 2 (3)
Language (Federation Standard) 1
Law (Federation Law) 2 (3)
    (Colony Planet Law) 2 (3)
Persuasion (any Specialization) 2 (3)
Planetside Survival (Specialization for colonial environment) 2 (3)
Security (Law Enforcement) 1 (2)
Social Sciences (any Specialization) 1 (2)
Vehicle Operation (any Specialization) 1 (2)
World Knowledge (Colony Planet) 2 (3)
Typical Advantages/Disadvantages: Contact, Patron, Political Rank (see p. 35); Arrogant, Dependent

THE COLONIAL SERIES

Another type of planetbound series is a colonial story arc set on one colony or in one colonial system. Tales of colonies can vary as widely as the types of colonies themselves. Individual *Star Trek: The Next Generation Role Playing Game* episodes might focus on a penal colony, for example, with stories of prison breaks (aiding or stopping), protecting a key witness against the Orion Syndicate from assassins, investigating prison conditions—or all three.

Other colonies also offer plenty of dramatic possibilities. Any colony can serve as the setting for frontier stories resembling adventures in the Old West. Are there dangerous savages or noble but doomed natives resisting the colonists, or both? Ferengi saloon keepers, Orion bar girls, Andorian phaserslingers, Vulcan monks, Bolian gamblers, human ranchers, Tellarite lawyers, Pakled prospectors, Breen rustlers hiding out in the ice caps, and any other character you can translate from your favorite Western can show up in a colonial series.

A darker series might center on a failed colony like Turkana IV. Here the series begins with a savage war of all against all resembling post-apocalyptic Earth and similar settings. Slowly, the characters learn to survive, then to trust each other, and perhaps to dream of building a new society worthy of Federation membership in the ruins of the old. This could be a truly rewarding campaign, and the Narrator who wants to avoid the "technology solves everything" approach of a starfaring series might be interested in the low-tech beginnings of such a storyline.

A colonial series might also be darker yet: a series of human struggle against some dark foe. After all, UFP colonies have seen aliens that humans would call vampires (M-113), ghosts (Caldos), deadly predators and parasites (Deneva), and devious murderers from Kodos the Executioner to, again, Jack the Ripper. In the far reaches of Federation space, not all the devils in the dark necessarily turn out to be friendly Hortas ....

Characters in a colonial series can range from colonists and administrators or governors to Starfleet garrisons to Science Council researchers or archaeologists.

The United Federation of Planets is not alone in space. Surrounded by other interstellar governments of varying intent, the Federation keeps close tabs on its neighbors. Each of these has their own cultures, histories, governments and priorities, often at odds with Federation ideals. Some, like the Borg and Romulans, are outright hostile to the Federation. Others, like the Tholians, remain enigmatic and aloof, or, like the Ferengi, take a neutral position. This chapter outlines the Federation's relationship with each of its star-faring neighbors, and, more importantly, their relationship to the UFP.

Borg Collective

BRIEF HISTORY OF RELATIONS

The Borg, native to Delta Quadrant, have been affecting Federation space at least since the 2290's, when they destroyed the El-Aurian civilization. However, the Federation first made contact with the Borg Collective not through its own efforts, but through the interference of Q. In 2365 Q propelled the *U.S.S. Enterprise* over seven thousand light years into Delta Quadrant onto the fringe of Borg space. Escaping only by virtue of a bargain with Q, the Enterprise warned Starfleet to expect a Borg incursion within the next decade.

That estimate proved to be wildly optimistic. In late 2366, Borg cubes obliterated the New Providence colony on Jouret IV, moving rapidly into Federation space after assimilating humans and other species there. A brief delaying action only succeeded in diverting the Borg directly for Earth after they temporarily assimilated Captain Picard of the *Enterprise-D*. At Wolf 359, the Borg decisively defeated an unprepared Starfleet, destroying 39 of 40 starships engaged. Only the last-minute reverse-engineering of Borg command architecture through Captain Picard's implants saved Earth. Since then, the vast majority of defense planning has focused on preparing for a second Borg invasion. The Borg threat was a major impetus in causing Starfleet to accept a draw in the Cardassian Wars. Last-minute concerns about theoretical genocide prevented the deployment in 2368 of the Trojan-horse invasive program through the isolated Borg "Hugh" (or Third-of-Five). The *Enterprise-D* repelled another rogue Borg invasion led by the android Lore in 2369, which demonstrated that more Borg ships than the Wolf 359 invasion force had reached Federation space.

Starfleet Command continues to consider the threat of the Borg a primarily military problem. Lt. Commander Shelby, one of the veterans of the Federation's first conflict with the Borg, has assembled a task force to further study the situation. The threat from the Collective remains constant. Any Federation vessel sighting a Borg ship is under standing orders to report the incident. Current fear of further attacks, however, has made this increasingly difficult. Characteristically, once rumors spread of a possible Borg sighting, many civilian vessels panic, misinterpreting sensor data as further confirmation of an imminent attack. Starfleet suspects some unscrupulous Ferengi and Orion traders of filing false reports to disrupt trade in some key sectors.

DIPLOMATIC RECOMMENDATIONS

Report of Commander Tal Malan, First Officer, U.S.S. Endeavor

As part of my duties as Starfleet Diplomatic Corps liaison, I have been asked to document my theories concerning a diplomatic solution to the Borg dilemma. I have expressed the opinion that we may eventually enter a dialogue of some kind with the Collective. My commanding officer, Captain Ar'iq, does not share this view. Despite this disagreement, however, the problem remains. The Borg are not simply a military threat. If we cannot overcome the Borg by military force, and we refuse to commit genocide against them, we must, by necessity, pursue other options.

At first, the idea of negotiating with the Borg—or establishing any form of diplomatic relations—certainly seems like a contradiction. The Borg do not negotiate; they conquer and assimilate. All discussion or negotiation concerning this conquest is irrelevant. It is impossible to maintain diplomatic relations with a culture that wants to assimilate you. Thus, formal relations with the Borg are nonexistent and decidedly hostile. The Borg have made their intentions clear, and the Federation has been unable to establish any fundamental dialogue. Nonetheless, I propose that this urge to acquire and assimilate new knowledge may prove to be a weakness of the Collective—one that can be exploited.

Let us briefly consider what we know so far. The Borg always negotiate from a position of strength, demonstrating an alarming single-mindedness in the pursuit of their goals. They will not stop to deal with a minor threat when a major conquest is at hand. This is understandable, as one who can negotiate from a position of strength has no need to negotiate. All distractions become irrelevant.

"Borg diplomacy," if I may use such a term, exhibits several unusual traits that build upon this arrogance and surety. Normally, in the practice of the diplomatic arts, one often wonders whether a representative can speak for his race with authority. If one strikes a bargain with a Romulan diplomat, for instance, there is little assurance that the politicians he deals with will agree. This complication is nonexistent with the Borg: The representative is the Collective. The Borg has no need to deceive or lie. Furthermore, their experience at dealing with a vast number of races has given them a remarkable insight into the many tactics of deception used by their enemies.

Yet, in recent months, we have been able to establish limited contact with isolated Borg. Captain Picard's latest discovery, a colony led by the "Sons of Soong," has led to a great deal of speculation. How do we know that this colony is the only one of its kind? I have no choice but to believe there may be further "families" or colonies of Borg possessing this, or similar, individuation. Further, if the Borg

goal is to evolve into the dominant life form in the galaxy, how can they dismiss the evolutionary possibilities "Hugh" presents? If such colonies or cooperatives of Borg exist, there may yet be hope for a diplomatic solution. It might even be possible to turn Borg against Borg, splitting the Collective.

Furthermore, I profess that other Borg may be made to undergo the same process experienced by Hugh, Third-of-Five. It is entirely possible that, through reeducation and conditioning, an individual Borg could be salvaged to provide us with further intelligence regarding this most remarkable life form—a "reverse Locutus," if you will. Information regarding the Borg is one of the most valuable assets we can have in our conflict with the Collective. The opportunity afforded by abandoned or stranded Borg should never be refused. The fact that the Collective immediately destroys its wounded, effectively preventing further examination, is confirmation of this.

While I am possessed of this uncharacteristically optimistic mood, perhaps I should advance another, more pessimistic, scenario. Suppose the Borg was forced to encounter a stronger civilization? They have, in the past, had no need to enlist allies, yet dare I say it? If the Federation and the Borg were ever threatened by another unfathomable and implacable enemy, we may find some common cause. Consider this: Faced with the first Borg attack, the Federation even managed to secure a brief opening with the Romulans. Stranger things have happened.

As we continue to theorize, the Borg continue to evolve. For now, so-called "Borg Space" remains quite distant from the safe boundaries of the Federation. Yet the expeditionary force that assaulted us is but the advance guard. As individuals, we must continue to theorize what may become of the Borg Collective. The alternative is abandoning all hope, surrendering to a force often described as the spread of a vast, unreasoning, and inhuman evil. As the incident of Third-of-Five attests, the strength of the individual may well be our greatest weapon against the Borg Collective.

CARDASSIANS

BRIEF HISTORY OF RELATIONS

Following first contact with the Cardassian Union in 2335, when the *U.S.S. Temple* exchanged shots with a Cardassian patrol ship, the Federation attempted to soothe the suspicions of this new neighbor. The Cardassians' possessiveness and their refusal to back down from conflict unless faced by an obviously superior force meant that tensions continued to flare. Occasional naval skirmishes only increased in the turbulent years following the Cardassian annexation of Bajor (2328), near the UFP-Cardassian border.

In 2347, the Cardassians attacked the Federation colony on Setlik III under the impression that it was a staging point for a Starfleet invasion of Cardassian space. The Setlik Massacre led to two decades of warfare between Cardassia and the UFP. Cardassian border attacks, and the Cardassian policy of looting any captured colonies, left virtually every citizen of the border sectors nursing a personal grudge against Cardassia.

At times, a lasting peace with the Cardassians must have seemed out of reach. The UFP Diplomatic Service continued negotiations with the Cardassians while Starfleet kept up a solid defense of Federation space. The truce of 2366 collapsed after the *U.S.S. Phoenix* launched a preemptive strike against Cardassian formations in Sector 21505. The next year, Captain Edward Jellico negotiated an armistice that held until the Federation-Cardassian Treaty of 2370 established peace in exchange for the neutralization of several border worlds in a Demilitarized Zone (DMZ). Cardassia gained dominion over some UFP worlds (and vice versa), but granted Bajoran independence.

Currently there is little constructive exchange or communication with the Cardassian Union, since they are unwilling to discuss military issues or trade technology and since they refuse any aid in other areas. The existence of both Federation and Cardassian colonies in the DMZ may lead to a better understanding between the two cultures in time. Until then, unfortunately, tensions remain high and many groups on both sides of the DMZ refuse to accept the verdict of the war. The Bajoran Wormhole remains a sticking point, as does the continuing presence of former Federation freedom fighters, the so-called Maquis, in Cardassian space.

CARDASSIAN MILITARY: THREAT ASSESSMENT

The Cardassians have a strong military, having spent the last several decades attacking, conquering, and stripping other worlds. Despite the current truce, they should be considered a major threat due simply to their firepower, their ruthlessness, and their highly disciplined structure. The Cardassians view every situation as a military exercise, and thus can be expected to seek every possible opportunity to gain territory or prestige. Their ships cover Cardassian space securely, patrolling against intrusion and dealing with any unauthorized entry with lethal force. They also travel to neutral areas and along the edges of contested areas, watching for opportunities. In particular, Cardassian *Galor*-class starships skirt the edges of the DMZ, constantly watching for the slightest excuse to enter that area or to demonstrate their power.

The Cardassians rarely back down from a battle, but they also do not commit themselves foolishly—rather, they wait until they are sure that there is at least a fair chance of success and also a reasonable level of potential reward. Once this is certain, however, they will commit their forces quickly and decisively, and are capable of coordinating dozens of ships in carefully arranged patterns and with multiple objectives.

It should also be noted that the Cardassians are not mere fighters—as any intelligent military must, they recognize the value of information, and realize that information obtained before battle and through noncombative means can often turn the tide of that battle when it does occur. They are known to have an extensive intelligence corps, and the typical Cardassian sense of dedication suggests that their agents are willing to wait for years or longer in the hope of obtaining useful information. The only two Cardassian ranks known are "Glinn," a medium-level rank roughly equivalent to Lieutenant or Lieutenant Commander, and "Gul," which is equivalent to Captain. All Cardassian vessels are commanded by Guls.

STRUCTURE OF RELATIONS

Relations with Cardassia are still strained, despite the treaty. The Federation is attempting to foster a less violent, more peaceful attitude on Cardassia, but such efforts have thus far met with failure, as the military mindset is deeply ingrained. The Federation Embassy on Cardassia Prime has top Starfleet Security specialists constantly working to foil Cardassian surveillance and spy efforts; Obsidian Order agents follow diplomats in the Cardassian Union everywhere. Only a few months after normalization of relations in 2367, one of the Federation ambassadors suffered an apparent mental breakdown and another diplomat disappeared

without a trace. The Cardassian Union professed surprise at these events and assisted in searching for the missing individual, but the body was never recovered. Relations have been slightly less dramatic, but no less tense, since then. Cardassian diplomats in the UFP are almost certainly all top Obsidian Order agents; a Cardassian cultural attaché on Earth was caught attempting to blackmail several Romulan emissaries, and took his own life before the FIS could fully investigate the matter. In addition to the inefficiencies this causes for Federation-Cardassian negotiations, it also implies that the Cardassian Union assumes that all Federation diplomatic personnel, military or civilian, are spies for Starfleet Intelligence.

One of the conditions of the Cardassian-Federation Treaty was that detainees had the right to representation from their own government in any proceedings. This is one of the services provided by the ambassadors of both sides, and requires large amounts of time and attention from Federation personnel.

MILITARY GOVERNMENT

Cardassia is ruled by a military government, overseen by the Cardassian Central Command, which in turn falls under the political control of the Detapa Council. Very little is known about this system, beyond the fact that it is rigidly controlled with detailed rules of conduct and clear duties and restrictions for each position. It is also known that the government keeps close tabs on every citizen. Reportedly, the Cardassian Bureau of Identification even requires that a molar be extracted from every Cardassian, to aid in verification later. Justice is meted out quickly and publicly, with all trials broadcast to the public—the verdict is always "guilty." Individuals are not valued strongly in the Cardassian system, as many are sacrificed to achieve objectives—it is only the overall goal that is important, and each person is only as useful as his position and strategic value.

Given the military structure, it is likely that political manuevering involves not only the usual level of deal-making and compromise but also subterfuge, strategic positioning, and even sabotage. A successful military record would be required to hold any high position, and each leader would attempt to position followers in key positions to control portions of the military, thus ensuring position and power, and preventing (or causing) an untimely military coup. This is all conjecture, however, as the Cardassians do not discuss their political matters with outsiders.

FERENGI

BRIEF HISTORY OF RELATIONS

Although their culture has apparently existed for several thousand years, the Ferengi were completely unknown for some time. The Ferengi may have been responsible for a number of ship disappearances in Alpha Quadrant, among them that of the *U.S.S. Stargazer* in 2355. The official UFP first contact with the Ferengi did not occur until 2364, at Delphi Ardu.

Upon learning of the Federation, this technologically advanced civilization immediately began trade negotiations, although they refused even to consider the notion of joining the Federation themselves. In many ways, this may have proved a wise decision for all concerned. As it stands now, the Ferengi are allowed free passage within Federation space and traverse it frequently, buying and selling goods of all types and to all types of people. They are shrewd businessmen and hold a business contract to be sacred, adhering to their own strict moral code. Because of this, and their familiarity with the Federation, they have sometimes been used as intermediaries between the Federation and some other civilization that does not wish for direct contact.

There are no Ferengi ambassadors, although at first there was no shortage of candidates—in fact, at one point there were at least three hundred Ferengi ambassadors on record, most of them engaged in personal negotiations with various other races or planetary governments. The Federation quickly issued a statement that, contrary to claims, there was to be no "ambassadorial discount" for the Ferengi in question, and began sending requests for routine paperwork to all of the "ambassadors." Since that time, not a single Ferengi has claimed the title or position. The closest thing to an actual ambassador is the Ferengi Trade Mission, which is a Ferengi diplomatic team. Their goal, however, is not to improve relations with other cultures, but merely to discover new ways of expanding Ferengi business interests.

Oddly enough, in a very short span of time the Ferengi have gone from being completely unknown (heard of only in rumors, and then only as thieves and scavengers) to being a major fixture in Federation life. Their ability to get almost any item or good has made them very important to many Federation businesses, and the fact that they are utterly unscrupulous in negotiating but completely loyal to a contract once signed has made them valuable business partners in many ventures. One can never trust a Ferengi not to overcharge you, but they can always be relied upon to deliver as promised. Be very, very careful with the wording of the contract, however—the Ferengi have an inspired ability to read meaning into vague language, and an innate knack for locating loopholes.

FERENGI NAVY: THREAT ASSESSMENT

The Ferengi do possess fairly impressive starships, labeled *Marauders* by Starfleet. However, unlike most cultures, they do not have an actual organized military. Instead, any Ferengi ship can apparently apply for the right to be in the "Navy," giving it the right to bear arms and to use those weapons to protect perceived Ferengi interests. It also receives a portion of any profits obtained during such actions, which are divided up according to rank. Interestingly, a similar practice once existed on Earth, when sailing ships known as "privateers" were given the right to stop, search, attack, confiscate, and, if necessary, destroy ships in the name of their country, and were authorized to keep any profits made.

This method of defense does not provide a solidly reliable military, nor is there any real way to create a cohesive force out of such individualistic and profit-oriented ships. It does, however, mean that there is always a ready supply of defenders, provided the price is right. In general, the Ferengi do not have to worry about fighting anyway—very few races are willing to attack them, knowing that the Ferengi are one of the best sources for weaponry and that it is not wise to attack one's own suppliers.

STRUCTURE OF RELATIONS

Most Ferengi do not seem overly fond of Ferenginar, their homeworld, perhaps because of its perpetually damp climate, but they do hold its offices in very high regard. Because of this, no non-Ferengi are allowed on the planet. Technically, others apparently are allowed on the planet, but only after the appropriate paperwork has been filled out, documented, filed, discussed, and approved, and (most importantly) after the necessary fees have been paid. Due to the length of time and the amount of money involved, and the ready accessibility of Ferengi off-world, no one has apparently ever considered it worth the added effort actually to set foot on Ferenginar.

The Federation's offers to send an ambassador to the Ferengi have been welcomed but have always received the same reply, namely, "How much will you pay the Ferengi Alliance for the privilege of sending us an ambassador?" The Federation has refused to pay another civilization for diplomatic relations, and therefore there is no officially designated representation to deal with the Ferengi or issues concerning them. Fortunately, there are no military issues beyond the occasional dispute over salvage rights, and the Ferengi have shown no desire to involve themselves in Federation politics beyond their usual desire to make a profit at every occasion. It is also exceedingly rare for a Ferengi to request the involvement of the Federation as a body, preferring instead to deal directly with individuals. The Federation has therefore allowed Federation members to handle their own interactions with the Ferengi Alliance, barring only such situations as deal with the Federation as a whole or with any aspect of its military.

GOVERNMENT

The Ferengi Alliance is headed by a single individual, the Grand Nagus. The Grand Nagus controls the Ferengi Commerce Authority, which handles business practices and the enforcement of trade laws, and is also in charge of assigning trade territories. Because the entire Ferengi Alliance is focused toward finance and profit, this power to determine who controls what location gives the Grand Nagus the ability to assure or destroy a Ferengi's future at a whim, which guarantees him complete obedience by all Ferengi. Political power is based entirely upon profit, and maneuvering is managed by amassing more money and by attempting to sabotage rivals' fortunes. Interfering with contracts, however, is strictly forbidden. In order to coax the Ferengi Alliance as a unit into taking part in any outside plan or action, it must be proven to them that taking part will be profitable for them, in specifically materialistic ways.

THE GORN

The Gorn are a race of bipedal reptilian humanoids approximately two meters tall, with impressive musculature which gives them great strength for both lifting and throwing. Observation suggests the Gorn benefit from both speed and great endurance. Their skin has a dull sheen to it and serves as armor, making them difficult to damage with blunt objects. Like many reptilians, Gorn have tails—thick, heavy appendages used to balance their muscular bodies. Though both hands and feet have claws, the hands have opposable thumbs, marking the Gorn as tool users.

The Gorn face is difficult for non-Gorn to read. Their heads are large, with the spinal ridge just visible above the browline. Their eyes appear bulbous and sport small pupils. The Gorn have binocular vision. Some observers report the existence of a nictitating membrane that protects the eye. The nose consists of large, flaring nostrils, while the mouth is wide and filled with sharp teeth, indicating that Gorn are primarily carnivores. Gorn sense of smell is highly evolved. One facet of their communication with one another seems to involve the release of certain odors indicating their frame of mind and readiness to mate.

The Federation first became aware of the Gorn in 2267 when the *U.S.S. Enterprise* under the command of Captain James T. Kirk arrived at the UFP colony on Cestus III. Kirk and his tactical staff transported down to the colony only to find it in smoking ruins, the colonists dead and an unknown force waiting in ambush. After a brief firefight, Kirk and his crew members retreated to the *Enterprise* and gave chase to an unfamiliar alien craft. Showing tremendous speed and maneuverability, the craft made several attempts to confuse the pursuit.

Stopped dead by a powerful race known as the Metrons, who resented both ships' intrusion into their space for a violent purpose, Kirk and the Gorn captain were placed on a distant planetoid to decide the issue by single combat. Each was told that the loser's ship and crew would be destroyed. During their interaction, Kirk discovered that the Gorn believed the colony placed on Cestus III was a deliberate violation of their space. When he eventually got the upper hand, Kirk refused to kill the Gorn over a misunderstanding. Pleased with his refusal to kill, the Metrons allowed both ships to leave their space. All Federation contact with the Gorn since that time has been colored by the Cestus III incident.

Aggressive and warlike, the Gorn evince cunning and ingenuity rather than mere brute strength. Willing to kill to protect what they consider to be their territory, the Gorn used great subtlety in setting a trap and might have slain Captain Kirk and his tactical officers had they not escaped via the transporters. The Gorn captain whom Kirk fought proved quite adaptable, setting traps and utilizing raw materials and the terrain itself to gain an advantage in battle. Federation analysts conclude that the Gorn receive training in primitive weaponry as well as more advanced armaments. Further, they exhibit knowledge of tactics and hand-to-hand fighting. Oddly, the Gorn captain offered Kirk a quick and painless death in return for Kirk's surrender, indicating that the Gorn are familiar with the concepts of both honor and mercy.

Although he used lures and traps, the Gorn captain betrayed a lack of imagination in his assessment of Captain Kirk's capabilities, apparently believing Kirk when the latter called out and said he was ready to "surrender." This may indicate that the reptilian race considers itself to be of superior intelligence and doesn't think other races capable of the same slyness the Gorn practice. Conversely, it may simply show that they are not able to judge human facial expressions and voice tones with any more accuracy than humans can judge the Gorn.

The Gorn have their own innovative technology. The ship which the Enterprise pursued showed an amazingly high rate of acceleration, pushing the Federation starship to its limits to maintain pursuit. Evasive actions occurred at high rates of speed, showing a level of maneuverability not then attainable by Federation craft. Shield capabilities and weapons appeared to be technologically commensurate with the engine design. Whether they continue to surpass

modern Federation craft remains undetermined.

Considering Gorn technological achievements, one question has plagued Federation analysts. If the Gorn possessed superior weaponry, why did they flee the *Enterprise*? Damage to their ship was minimal. Why did they not turn and fire, utilizing their greater maneuverability to best the Federation craft? Several theories have emerged to explain this curious phenomenon. Some argue that the Gorn are cowards, relying on tricks and surprise to overcome their foes. Others maintain that they fled from a craft whose technology they didn't understand, fearing other, more potent innovations. One academician has suggested that the Gorn are actually a servitor race for the Metrons and that when the Federation entered space claimed by those beings, they sent the Gorn to lure a starship into range so the Metrons might test them and judge our worthiness. Yet another proposal maintains that the Gorn may have impressive technology, but don't have much of it. What little they had was too precious to risk against a ship with the firepower of the *Enterprise*. Observation of the Gorn since the Treaty of Cestus III seems to indicate that all of these theories may have some merit (with the exception of the theory of Gorn as servants of the Metron, for which we have no evidence).

From what the UFP has learned in the intervening years, the Gorn are highly xenophobic. They just want to be left alone, and only attacked when the Federation unknowingly violated their space. The Federation has agreed not to intrude into Gorn territory—a mere handful of planets—or affairs. While the Gorn have no intention of crossing into Federation space, they hope to settle a number of worlds in their own sectors. A true Gorn empire could arise from such expansion.

Little is known about the Gorn form of government, although, based on observations by Federation diplomats and first-contact specialists, certain conclusions can be drawn. Our reports indicate that the Gorn are a matriarchal society, ruled by females who act as the thinkers, planners, artists, teachers, and philosophers. The ruling female is known as the Effri'a, which roughly translates to "Empress." She is attended by a council of matrons and a lesser council of important males. It is unknown whether these serve as the true government of the Gorn or merely act in an advisory capacity. Males do most of the exploration and trading, though those females who desire to travel often hold high positions aboard ship as well.

Observers have noted that male Gorn engage in ritual combat to win desired females for mating, a practice which prepares them for real combat when necessary. Though usually confined to ritual, it is not unknown for both male and female Gorn to engage in challenge fights to the death over slights and insults.

The noted Federation psychobiologist Kemmli of Rigel IV has developed a new theory concerning the Gorn attack on the Cestus III colony, based on Gorn mating behavior and olfactory communication. According to the theory, the Gorn had selected Cestus III as a suitable place for their rituals some years past, seeding the area with the appropriate pheromones so the plant life would carry a particular redolence necessary to their procreation. Arriving to prepare the site for use after waiting the requisite number of years for the plants to grow, the Gorn found humans there. Apparently the Gorn believed the humans deliberately ignored the Gorn's territorial markings. It never occurred to the Gorn that humans could not smell what was obvious to the Gorn. Interpreting the human presence as the intent to deprive them of their mating grounds, the Gorn attacked. To them, it was a clear case of protecting their race. Perhaps this theory, if proved, might shape our future relations with the Gorn. For now, they remain almost unknown, their territory off limits to Federation personnel and diplomatic duties handled through the Institute for Human-Gorn Relations on Cestus III.

KLINGONS

BRIEF HISTORY OF RELATIONS

In 2218, the *U.S.S. Ranger* transported a Federation diplomatic and anthropological team to a newly discovered world named Qo'noS. Preliminary probes had indicated that the inhabitants were named Klingons and, though occasionally violent, were exhausted after a lengthy war a century earlier (with the Romulans, as it transpired). Eager for opportunities to spread peace and perhaps to gain an ally against the Romulans, the Ranger's team made immediate contact without any more observation. This was a disaster: The Klingons massacred the diplomatic team, seized the *Ranger*, and used its technology to catapult their violent, semifeudal empire into dominance over the entire region.

Between 2223 and 2242, Klingon expansionism met desperate Federation reinforcements to what had been an empty and unthreatening border area. Finally, Starfleet checked Klingon imperialism in the Battle of Donatu V, setting the Klingon-Federation border roughly where it is now. Tensions began increasing as both sides fortified the border zone. In 2267, the two sides nearly declared an open war.

The Organians imposed an uneasy peace through the Organian Peace Treaty, effectively ending overt hostilities. The Klingons briefly entered into an

alliance with the Romulans in which the Klingons may have been the dominant partner, but it collapsed before the end of the century with the Klingons gaining only cloaking device technology and no permanent advantage. In fact, imperial overstretch coupled with the disastrous explosion of the Klingon moon Praxis in 2293 caused a Klingon-Federation detente.

Klingon Chancellor Gorkon and his daughter Azetbur pursued peace with the Federation. Azetbur's Khitomer Accords marked a new era in Federation-Klingon relations, ending hostilities and allowing for mutual aid and defense. The sacrifice of the *U.S.S. Enterprise-C* during the 2344 Romulan attack on the Klingon outpost on Narendra III cemented ties between the two powers, and a cautious alliance has developed since then.

KLINGON MILITARY: THREAT ASSESSMENT

The Klingon Defense Force operates the Empire's space fleet. The fleet employs several types of ships, many of which are equipped with cloaking devices. Klingon ships included the *Vor'cha*-class attack cruisers, the *D-7* and *K't'inga*-class battle cruisers, the *D-12* and *B'rel*-class bird-of-prey scout ships, and the *K'vort*-class bird-of-prey cruisers. The Klingon Defense Force gained the cloaking device technology, along with bird-of-prey and battle cruiser ship designs, from their Romulan alliance (roughly 2268-2289). Relations have improved enough that Starfleet and the Klingon Defense Force have officer exchange programs, in which officers of one fleet serve in a comparable position on a ship of the other fleet.

In 2365, Commander William Riker became the first Starfleet officer to serve on a Klingon ship, the *I.K.S. Pagh*. Though some Klingon officers were initially skeptical of a human's ability to command a Klingon ship, Commander Riker's Starfleet training allowed him to impress his new Klingon crew. KDF advancement and structure seem to be based on combat skill, courage, and unquestionable honor. Those displaying these attributes are the most likely to succeed in the current Klingon military force.

STRUCTURE OF RELATIONS

The Klingon homeworld, Qo'noS, houses the High Council and Emperor. The Federation has also established its embassy on Qo'noS. The establishment of the embassy provided that activities within the embassy compound are subject to Federation Law and interstellar treaty. The embassy on Qo'noS not only carries out diplomatic functions, but also serves as a contact point for scientific and cultural exchanges and an information resource for Federation citizens traveling within the Klingon Empire. Even during periods of strain on the alliance, the Klingons have never threatened the embassy, respecting its diplomatic and legal role. The Federation currently maintains cordial relations with Qo'noS, though doing so has required a great deal of skillful work by protocol officers to smooth over cultural differences.

KLINGON POLITICS

The governmental control of the Klingon Empire rests with the High Council. Klingon culture highly values family ties, resulting in a clannish societal and governmental structure. The effect of the family is so strong that honor and dishonor are passed down through several generations of family members. Through a complex system of extended family and marital ties, most Klingons belong to one house or another. High Council membership reflects this house system, with each house receiving a seat. These extended family ties also frequently determine the alliances on the High Council, resulting in powerful family voting blocs. In direct contrast to the majority of the Klingon population, which values honesty and straightforward action, the High Council seems to provide an outlet for those members of society who enjoy intrigue and cloak-and-dagger conspiracy.

The Chancellor presides over the High Council. The previous Chancellor, K'mpec, was assassinated by poison in 2367. Before his death, he appointed Starfleet Captain Jean-Luc Picard as his Arbiter of Succession to prevent his suspected assassin, Duras, from gaining control of the High Council. Duras was later killed, and Captain Picard ruled that Gowron was the only viable candidate. In the ensuing civil war, Starfleet provided assistance to Gowron's government by blockading a convoy of Romulan ships delivering supplies to the Duras family. The lack of Romulan support effectively ended the Duras family's challenge to Gowron's rule. By the end of 2368, Chancellor Gowron found it politically expedient to omit discussion of or downplay seriously the Federation's role in his selection and the subsequent civil war.

In 2369, Chancellor Gowron supported the installation of the first emperor in more than three hundred years. The Chancellor supported Kahless II, a clone of the first emperor, Kahless the Unforgettable, in hopes of avoiding a second civil war. Kahless II now serves a ceremonial role as spiritual leader of the Klingon people. The Federation believes Chancellor Gowron has strengthened his position and gained support among the houses. However, Gowron already has

proven himself to be willing to lie to and deceive both his own people and his Federation allies to serve his own political ends. It is unlikely that members of the Duras family have abandoned their hopes for reclaiming control of the Klingon Empire. As such, the Federation must remain wary of deception and eventual resumption of hostilities while still upholding the Treaty of Alliance.

KLINGON CULTURE

Culturally, several elements of Klingon culture have become well known to the Federation. Klingon opera has begun to enjoy some popularity among certain segments of the Federation population. Klingon gourmet cooking, featuring such dishes as *rokeg blood pie* and *skull stew* complemented by bloodwine, has found its way into some restaurants and replicator programs. Interest in *bat'leth* instruction and Klingonese language classes is increasing and is expected to continue to do so.

It is impossible to separate combat from Klingon culture. Most Klingon operas relate the tales of great battles, Klingon food often incorporates blood, and even the raising of a child requires combat. Klingon boys are considered men when they can hold a blade. Youths intending to be warriors, which most children do, must proclaim their intention before the age of 13. This requires the Age of Ascension ritual, in which the child walks between two lines of Klingons who prod him with painstiks. Painstiks are supposed to provide a test of endurance and promote spiritual development. The ritual also requires considerable combat expertise, as it involves a test of *bat'leth* skills. Klingons see the Age of Ascension as a second birth, the birth of the warrior, and often celebrate it in addition to or instead of a birthday.

Though Klingon culture retains many spiritual and even mystical elements, the Klingons have no religion as such. Their mythology holds that their warriors slew their gods, apparently because the gods were too much trouble. Though they do not believe in gods, they do have myths of an underworld, *Gre'thor*, which is guarded by a beast called *Fek'lhr*. They also believe that the spirit travels after death to the afterlife, *Sto-Vo-Kor*.

ORIONS

Now based in Alpha Quadrant, the Orions consider the Rigel system their original home. Tall, muscular humanoids with green skin, most Orions have long, dark hair. Forms of dress vary, but generally display their well defined bodies and elaborate tattoos. The tattoos show an Orion's family history and place in society.

Federation sociohistorians advance the following theories concerning the Orions' origins and practices: Once part of a larger empire, the Orions aggressively subjugated other races in their quest for power and religious fulfillment. Though of a high technological order, the empire fell due to its own excesses and overdependence on robot servitors and slave labor. The ruling class forgot how to maintain the advanced technology and as the robots fell into disrepair, the Orions' level of civilization fell as well. Some indications point to a disastrous interaction—perhaps an alliance with another race, who fell victim to a more advanced culture—as the true cause behind this disruption. Intriguing hints of this found within the Rigel system may account for the Orions' current extreme caution concerning their diplomatic status with other beings.

The Orions' cultural disruption and downward slide prompted them to embrace trade. As they had little of value to offer (the planets they control are resource-poor, possibly from being mined out by the earlier Orion civilization), many Orion traders turned to piracy, doing a shady business in stolen jewelry, weapons, entertainments, and other commodities. Soon they were dealing in drugs and slaves as well.

The Orions' most coveted trade item became their slave girls. Animalistic and primal, the green slave girls of Orion were regarded as the ultimate in seduction and sybaritic entertainment. More powerful captains among the traders dealt in both slaves and advanced technology stolen from dozens of sources. The traffic in slave girls has been outlawed by the Federation. Nonetheless, we suspect that this slave trade has never ceased, instead going underground and now often used to reward those who provide questionable services for the Orions (such as giving them cargo manifests, route information, and armament data on ships they wish to attack). A note of interest: Many people believe that all Orion women are slaves. This is a misperception. Those females who are not bred for the slave trade are wives, mothers, and daughters. While they stay at home (or at most engage in light shopping and social visits) and are forbidden to conduct business or perform political functions, they are not precisely slaves. Highly protected by the males, the Orion females are only now beginning to break away from their rigid, traditional roles.

Piracy and smuggling became the Orion way of life, as extended families who had once ruled metamorphosed into trade syndicates, each competing with one another, yet bound together by the desire to protect their worlds. Upon meeting Federation envoys, the Orions declared themselves independent and uninterested in joining the United Federation of Planets, the Klingon Empire, or any other group. Pretending to be isolationists, the Orions actively shunned contact with the Federation and kept to their own sector of space. Thus they were able to hide behind the pose of being both neutral and reclusive.

That pose was broken as Federation colonists continued to settle in the Rigel system and a number of incidents revealed Orion machinations and sabotage, as well as acts of piracy. In such cases (like that of the Orion operative who masqueraded as an Andorian in an attempt to disrupt the Babel Conference of 2267), those who were caught preferred death to betrayal of the syndicates. Suicides of Orions caught in extortion, assassination attempts, sabotage, piracy, and technology theft are still quite common, all in the name of protecting Orion neutrality. Nowadays, the Orions excel in disguising themselves and acting as spies, assassins, and saboteurs for the highest bidder. When Rigel V applied for Federation membership in the late 2290's, the Orion syndicates probably removed the center of their activities to other planets in the Orion sector, leaving the Rigel system as a trading post and lucrative tourism market.

Now, the Orion syndicates influence affairs on planets stretching from the Orion Sector to the borders of Ferengi space in Alpha Quadrant. On most of those planets, which have extensive Orion settlement, the government still proclaims its official neutrality and insists that such criminals act individually and without government sanctioning. This is because the corrupt syndicates rule their puppets from the shadows. In actuality, planetary ministers in "Orion space" keep their positions only as long as they please their syndicate masters. Those whom the syndicates don't own, they can bribe or intimidate. Federation monitors have noted several instances in which council members have attempted to stir honest Orions to action against the syndicates only to become the victim of an "unfortunate accident" soon thereafter. Even on technically neutral, but closely Federation-aligned, Rigel VII, the government is rumored to be a syndicate front. Starfleet needs to keep Rigel VII happy for strategic reasons, so a full-scale crackdown is impossible.

Each syndicate controls a portion of Orion space and markets. Some have become more specialized, moving from piracy to providing consummate assassins or spies or dealing exclusively in recreational drugs and poisons to those willing to pay their price. A few specialize in copied or stolen technology. While originally based around family lines, the syndicates have expanded to include peripheral members of the family as well as talented nonrelatives. Whatever their makeup or wherever they live in the belt of "Orion space," few Orions remain untouched by the syndicates' dealings. Those who engage in legitimate business are allowed to do so—as long as it doesn't conflict with any area a syndicate controls—but they never become as rich as their syndicate counterparts.

Orion syndicates are similar in many respects to the Mafia (a criminal organization prevalent on Earth during the 20th and 21st centuries). Each syndicate is led by a powerful "patriarch" who controls several lieutenants. Lieutenants and leaders of each syndicate meet together regularly to compare notes, set and control prices, and discuss problems. While the lieutenants are invited to share their views and make suggestions, the leaders make the final and absolute decisions.

Each lieutenant is responsible for a particular aspect of the syndicate's business (trade contacts, piracy, extortion, protection, drugs, etc.) and oversees those members of the syndicate involved in his area. Branching off from the lieutenants are captains who command the ships that engage in piracy. Though the captains represent the oldest form of the syndicate, they are becoming obsolete as other, less immediately dangerous methods of stealing what the syndicates want (computer theft, bribery, falsifying documents, and other such tactics) become more common. Where once a whole crew had to risk their lives for a cargo of dilithium crystals, now a single operative can supply rare weaponry to a client by accessing the manufacturer's shipping and billing department and creating a false order complete with shipping instructions!

The Federation does not maintain regular diplomatic relations with many Orion worlds because Federation officials and personnel have been targeted for extortion and kidnapping in the past. The corruption that runs rampant throughout Orion space makes any treaties or agreements with those worlds valueless. (Except, of course, on Rigel VII, which needs Starfleet and the UFP almost as much as Starfleet and the UFP need it.) It is not unheard of for one council to approve a treaty only to have a new council break it a few days later, citing misunderstanding and confusion concerning terminology as the reason. Appeals to talk to the council members who approved the treaty are met with either silence or the statement that several council members "retired" and there has been a new election. Blatant crimes against Federation officials and citizens are ignored or passed over with a shrug and the declaration that the government cannot keep track of every small pirate or thief in the system.

Nevertheless, the Federation maintains a consulate on most Orion worlds so that Federation citizens traveling there have some protection, however inadequate. Consulate personnel live in protected compounds (utilizing Federation guards, not Orion ones). Every item and person who enters or leaves the compound is thoroughly checked before they are allowed inside the compound or let out again. Visitors are rigorously screened, and consulate personnel agree to regular inspections to make certain they have not been bribed or coerced into assisting the syndicates. Occasionally, the consulate issues travel advisories for UFP citizens, usually in response to an upswing in dangerous syndicate activities (kidnappings, assassinations) or wars between rival syndicates, which often spill over into violence that kills innocents. Ruling coalitions rise and fall with great rapidity, as one syndicate gets the upper hand and forges new alliances, while another tumbles from a prime position.

The Federation must maintain some sort of diplomatic relations with these worlds because of their strategic position on the Federation's rimward flank. Starfleet Intelligence keeps an eye on the syndicates. Nevertheless, the Federation cannot recommend that any UFP citizen have business dealings with or travel to Orion space.

ROMULANS

BRIEF HISTORY OF RELATIONS

The little information known about the Romulans comes primarily from their Vulcan cousins, from Starfleet encounters with Romulan ships, and from Romulan dissidents. Historians believe Romulan ancestors left Vulcan two millennia ago when Surak popularized the logical structures on which modern Vulcan society is based. They did not want to suppress their passionate and often violent natures, deciding instead to form their own society when they failed to stop the spread of Surak's ideology. As the self-styled exiles traveled to their new home on Romulus, groups of settlers sporadically left the journey, colonizing planets along the way. The few surviving settlements have developed into their own unique societies, sharing traits with both the Vulcans and the Romulans, but truly like neither. The "twin capitals" of Romulus and Remus may actually be the results of an early civil war between Romulan factions both claiming dominion over what would become Romulan space.

The Romulans fought a century-long war with Vulcan from roughly 1270 to 1370, and in 2156 the Romulans presented Earth with its first contact with a hostile alien civilization. This contact led to the Romulan-Earth War, which ended in 2160 with the Treaty of Cheron and the establishment of the Romulan Neutral Zone. (Between those two wars, the Romulans apparently fought another long-distance war with the Klingons in the late 21st century.) The next year, partially motivated by the Romulan attacks, the Federation was formed. The Federation owes a great deal to the Romulan Star Empire, for without its aggressions the United Federation of Planets might not exist.

The Federation had little contact with the Romulans for the next hundred years. In 2266, the

Romulans emerged from their isolation to test the strength and resolve of the Federation. The Romulans proved to be a serious threat with the introduction of their cloaking device technology. Between approximately 2267 and 2287 the Romulans adopted Klingon ship designs and allied themselves with the Klingon Empire. Starfleet analysts remain relatively sure that this so-called "alliance" actually consisted of a brief period of Romulan weakness which the Klingons exploited as much as possible. In 2293 the Romulan ambassador to the Federation was involved in a plot to assassinate the Klingon Chancellor Gorkon and prevent the signing of the Khitomer Accords.

The Romulans and the Federation concluded the Treaty of Algeron as a result of the Tomed Incident of 2311. The treaty reaffirmed the Neutral Zone established by the Treaty of Cheron, and prohibited the Federation from using or developing cloaking technology. Though they apparently retained some contact with factions in the Klingon government, no contact occurred with the Federation, and the Romulans are generally believed to have entered another period of isolationism after 2311.

The next known contact with the Romulans took place in 2364, when both the Romulans and the Federation lost several bases along the Neutral Zone. Though both sides were suspicious of the other, later findings revealed that the disappearance of the bases was the result of a Borg attack. The Romulans have been active in interstellar politics ever since, planning attacks on Klingon and Federation worlds and trying to destabilize the Federation-Klingon alliance. The Romulans have attempted to prevent the ascendance of Klingon Chancellor Gowron and have planned an attack on Vulcan.

ROMULAN STAR NAVY: THREAT ASSESSMENT

Among the ships used by the Star Command are the *D'deridex*-class warbirds, the bird-of-prey smaller craft, and other capital ships that Starfleet has little detail on. Romulan ships routinely employ cloaking device technology.

Compulsory military service for all Romulans ensures that the Empire will always have an ample supply of soldiers for the fleet. Individual senators frequently command their own fleets, and the Praetor has a special Praetorian Guard, loyal only to him. The Romulan Star Command

directs the fleet as a whole. Individuals advance within the Star Command based on their service to the Empire. Unlike the intrigues of the Senate, Star Command personnel look for opportunities to expand the Empire's sphere of control in order to gain personal and political power. The Romulan Star Command also maintains an extensive network of starbases, many located along the Neutral Zone. Always elusive and secretive, the Romulans prefer to carry out their plans through subtle manipulation rather than overt action. They are generally reactionary, preferring to see their opponents' moves before planning their own.

STRUCTURE OF RELATIONS

The isolationist Romulan Empire restricts Federation diplomatic activities to very narrowly defined areas. The Ambassador is the only Federation official permitted entry to Romulus itself under normal circumstances; no UFP diplomat has ever set foot on Remus. The embassy of the Federation is located on Algeron, a planet on the very edge of the Romulan Neutral Zone. Only unarmed diplomatic transports can travel from Federation space to Algeron, and they must be escorted by Romulan war birds. While the Romulans do not maintain an embassy on Earth, the Romulans have occasionally sent special envoys to the seat of the Federation. When the Federation must contact the Romulan Empire, they do so through subspace channels or through their representative on Algeron.

ROMULAN POLITICAL STRUCTURE

The Praetor and the Romulan Senate, led by the Proconsul, rule the Romulan Star Empire. The Praetorship is believed to be partially hereditary, with the child of a Praetor being given preference, but readily replaced if shown to be ineffective. Senators are appointed based on the record of service to the Empire, though they apparently do have constituencies to represent. Senators usually prove their worth to the Empire through exemplary military service, where they gain skills, power, and fame. The Romulan Senate breeds intrigue, power plays, and assassination. It is possible that true power in the Empire constantly shifts between the Praetor, the Proconsul, and the Senate at large, with the Navy holding the balance of power.

A shadowy Romulan intelligence organization apparently also functions as the state secret police. This organization, the *Tal Shiar*, brutally suppresses internal dissent and infiltrates other agencies, both internal and external, to provide information for the Empire. The *Tal Shiar* causes widespread fear in the Romulan citizenry, among loyal groups and dissidents alike. Those who speak out against the terror of the *Tal Shiar* often find themselves or their families the subject of mysterious "disappearances" in the middle of the night.

Recently, dissidents in the Romulan Empire have become more active, trying to open an escape route for endangered citizens to defect to the Federation. They have also begun a movement to try to reunify with the Vulcans. Though initial contact with the dissidents was the result of an elaborate ruse by the Romulan government, Ambassador Spock found legitimate interest in such a movement.

ROMULAN CULTURE

Though little of Romulan culture has surfaced in the Federation, smuggling of the highly intoxicating Romulan ale is an increasing problem in the Federation. Though illegal in the Federation, the exotic blue liquor enjoys such popularity that there is always a willing market. Artistically, Romulan sculpture and architecture rank among the most dramatic in the galaxy. Romulan artists often choose military themes or landscape scenes of Romulus to depict. They benefit from the rumored spectacular scenery of Romulus. Military themes reflect the larger-than-life stature given to military heroes, and often represent preparations for a particularly glorious battle or the actual battle scenes themselves. Romulan architecture is no less grand, characterized by wide, sweeping arches and intricately worked columns, and conveys the architect's sense of the splendor of the Romulan Star Empire.

SON'A

HISTORY OF RELATIONS

The relationship between the United Federation of Planets and the people known as the Son'a is a relatively recent occurrence. Prior to 2374, the Son'a remained an enigma. The Federation knew little about them, aside from rumors from other spacefaring species. The Ferengi in particular seemed to have extensive contact with the Son'a; the two races apparently moved in the same circles, trading in precious metals, jewels and assorted commodities. The Ferengi, however, seemed decidedly uninterested in introducing the Son'a to the Federation. First contact with the Son'a occurred in 2374, when a Son'a vessel approached the *U.S.S. Tat'sahr.*

The events surrounding this change of heart revolved around an obscure planet in a region of space known as the 'Briar Patch.' An area known for its supernova remnants, false vacuum fluctuations and nebula clusters, the 'Briar Patch' made navigation nearly impossible, and precluded exploration. The Son'a discovered an inhabited M-Class planet in the midst of this inhospitable region, but because it lied within Federation territory the Son'a approached the Federation to get permission to proceed with their plans for the planet.

The Son'a presented their plight to a closed-door session of the Federation Council. After years of genetic therapy designed to extend their lifespans, the Son'a suffered from DNA breakdown which prevented them from procreating. The Son'a faced extinction. The rings around the planet in the 'Briar Patch' focused metaphasic radiation found in the region, concentrating their life-extending properties. In order to survive, the Son'a developed an orbital collector to accumulate these particles, which would result in the destruction of the planet's surface, forcing the evacuation of the planet's inhabitants. Federation scientists searched for an alternative, but to no avail. At this juncture, the Federation Council made a critical decision.

In need of allies after the catastrophic losses during the Dominion war, the Federation chose to ally themselves with the Son'a, despite the questionable rumors surrounding them (the production of mass quantities of the narcotic ketracel-white, used by the Dominion's Jem'Hadar soldiers, and the use of subspace weapons outlawed by the Second Khitomer Accord). The Son'a offered to share the regenerative properties of this radiation, doubling life-spans in the Federation, in return. The Ba'ku numbered a mere 600 inhabitants. The Federation Council authorized an operation to secretly relocate the Ba'ku to another planet, functionally stealing their world. The entire operation would operate under the ruse of a joint sociological survey.

Fortunately, Captain Picard of the *U.S.S. Enterprise-E* learned of the deception and thwarted the Son'a plan. The repercussions within the Federation Council would be swift and far-reaching. The shining example set by the crew of the *Enterprise-E* served as a reminder that the Federation's strength derived from its dedication to its principles.

With the conclusion of events surrounding the Ba'ku planet, the status of this alliance, and the reliability of the Son'a, remains unclear.

MILITARY ASSESSMENT

The Son'a maintain a handful of ships, not properly spoken of as a "fleet." The Federation knows little about their capabilities, although Starfleet Intelligence estimates these to be similar to standard Federation specifications. The few Son'a ships the Federation has encountered dwarf even a *Sovereign*-class ship, and thanks to their lucrative trade throughout the Alpha Quadrant, no doubt, the Son'a decorate their ships opulent-

ly, with latinum accents and mellawaxine flooring. History records two major Son'a conflicts within the last 100 years; the Son'a conquered and absorbed both species, the Elloran and Tarlac.

The Son'a have been known to employ subspace weapons, banned by the Second Khitomer Accord signed by the Federation, Cardassians, Klingons and Romulans. These weapons make the Son'a a dangerous threat, not only to their opponents but to the very fabric of space. These weapons literally rip subspace apart when they explode, causing an implosion of real space around the blast. Ships affected by such a blast could find themselves sucked into the spatial continuum underlying real space, if the stresses don't destroy the ship beforehand. In their conflict with the *Enterprise-E*, the Son'a exhibited decidedly straight-forward tactics, not hesitating to fire weapons without warning or provocation. Federation sociologists have subsequently theorized that this approach suggests a ruthless personality.

The Son'a employ two officer ranks, *Ahdar* (Commander) and *Subahdar* (Lieutenant Commander). According to reports from Admiral Dougherty, assigned to a Son'a ship during the Ba'ku operation, *Ahdar* seem to command unfailing loyalty among their crew; whether this suggests a unity of purpose or thorough indoctrination remains unknown. *Subahdar* appear to assume the role of a traditional Starfleet First Officer. Son'a soldiers are well trained and efficient, not unlike the Cardassians; members of the Elloran and Tarlac serve as soldiers as well. Additional ranks and duties, and the existence of those unique to the Son'a, remains unknown. Future encounters with this species will no doubt shed more light on these newly encountered aliens.

GOVERNMENT

How the Son'a govern themselves remains a mystery. They have no homeworld, instead leading a nomadic life traveling the Alpha Quadrant's spacelanes. After initial first contact with the Son'a, Federation exosociologists theorized that the original Son'a homeworld suffered a cataclysm, perhaps even a genocidal war, in which only a few specimens managed to survive. Like the Orions and the pirates of ancient Earth, the Son'a appear to recognize no authority beyond that of their *Ahdar*. They join the crew of a ship and submit to the will of their commander. The *Ahdar* commands unswerving loyalty and rules with ruthless efficiency. Overall, Son'a society is anarchic; no single governing body appears to claim authority over the Son'a people. Instead, individual Son'a ships go their own way, concerning themselves with their own well-being. Federation exosociologists believe some Son'a ships engage in piracy, while others attempt to support themselves trading in mundane commodities. Starfleet Intelligence reports suggest the Son'a occasionally supply weapons to the Nausicaans and

Breen. It remains unclear whether or not other Son'a vessels supported Ahdar Ru'afo's actions at the Ba'ku planet.

THOLIAN ASSEMBLY

THOLIAN WARS

In 2268, the Federation first officially encountered the Tholians. Myths and legends of the Tholians had been common throughout neighboring sectors, although the UFP had believed that they were simply a myth—the "Flying Dutchmen" of space. The *U.S.S. Defiant* found out differently when the Tholians trapped the starship in an interphasic field, the famous "Tholian web." The field disrupted the central nervous systems of the crew, causing mass insanity before it sublimated the *Defiant* into a pocket dimension only tangentially connected to "normal space." Investigating the disappearance of the *Defiant*, the *U.S.S. Enterprise* came "face to face" with the Tholians. Although briefly trapped in the Tholian interphase field, the *Enterprise* managed to escape before the Tholians could destroy it.

Territorial and isolationist, the Tholians would not travel far from their borders but destroyed any trespassers into a Tholian "annex." UFP policy regarding the Tholians was to avoid contact and warn vessels against venturing into Tholian space. As relations improved between the Federation and the Klingon Empire, however, more ships traveled along the borders of Tholian space. Reports of space pirates, unexplained time-space phenomena, and the disappearance of several merchant vessels prompted Starfleet to send patrols to Tholian space once again. In 2351, only the heroism of Bolian Admiral Taneko saved a Starfleet task force when he

detonated the warp core of the crippled *U.S.S. Mizar* to decimate an attacking Tholian fleet.

Starfleet constructed Starbase 277 on the Tholian border in 2352 to monitor Tholian activities and to coordinate escorts for civilian craft. Four days after Starbase 277 became fully operational in 2353, the Tholians attacked in overwhelming numbers, employing strange and deadly weapons. All personnel aboard Starbase 277 were killed except for Kyle Riker, a civilian mathematician advising Starfleet on Tholian tactical matrices. Tholian ships attacked other targets as well, devastating colonies and destroying civilian ships all along their borders. Ruthless and efficient, the Tholians left incoherent and unbelievable sensor readings and few witnesses or survivors.

The *U.S.S. Fearless* led a task force which blunted the Tholian assault and began a blockade of the border sectors, hoping to outlast the Tholians with a purely defensive strategy of attrition. Unfortunately, the Tholian appetite for war seemed unquenchable. Andorian Admiral Temrev proposed a change of strategy, suggesting an invasion in force into the heart of the Tholian Assembly. By carrying the war to the intensely territorial Tholians, Temrev hoped to increase the incentives for peace. Starfleet approved Temrev's plan, and the *U.S.S. Lor'vela* led a squadron of starships into the Tholian core sectors while the *Fearless* maintained a defensive reserve. New Tholian technologies finally stalled the *Lor'vela's* offensive, but the attack had done its work.

In 2360, Betazoid diplomats arrived in Tholian space to negotiate a truce with the Tholians. Although many veterans of the war were skeptical that peace could ever come, the Betazoids succeeded. The Tholians seemed frustrated with the war and willing to listen to peace proposals. The Tholians and the Federation signed the Tholian Accords that year, which ended open conflict between the powers and restored the border to the status quo. For years, the Tholian border remained quiet, although formal diplomatic ties remained elusive. Finally, in 2369, the Tholians stunned the Federation by proposing normalized relations between the two powers. Later that same year, both sides agreed to an exchange of ambassadors and trade.

THOLIAN NATURE

As the Tholians continue to expand their "territorial annexes," they also prefer to remain hidden. Despite our best efforts, their true appearance remains a subject of conjecture. Sensor data gathered from Federation starships confirms that the environment necessary to sustain them is vastly different from that of a Class M planet. Although contradictory sensor data exist, Tholian ships seem to contain a primarily methane atmosphere kept at a temperature of several hundred degrees. Thus, the Tholians may not even be capable of "face to face" negotiations with the Federation. Instead, they typically allow carefully chosen representatives to speak for them over long-distance communications.

The Tholians, apparently a startlingly advanced technological race, seem to place a high reliance upon scientific precision and accuracy. Even before Federation contact, legends in that region of space emphasized Tholian punctuality. This characteristic may correspond with other Tholian traits, such as their need to maintain an exact temperature as part of their exotic living conditions. After all, a deviation of a few degrees of temperature may possibly be fatal to an unprepared Tholian.

Tholian representatives seem to have a curious disregard for straightforward "human" two-dimensional thinking. Standard tactics of negotiation do not work; furthermore, the Tholians' extensive technological proficiency gives them a significant edge. Their military tactics are particularly baffling, taking advantage of multidimensional space that does not fully correspond with current theories of physics. Whether their tactics reflect the Tholian grand strategy of carefully defending "annexes" to Tholian space remains an enigma: Some Tholian annexes seem completely unnecessary to Tholian defense, while other sectors that would seem to hold great strategic value for the Tholians remain unclaimed.

Whenever dealing with representatives of this race, Federation officers should be aware that seemingly minor concerns can quickly become major threats. The situation between the UFP and the Tholian Assembly is tense, and starships must always be prepared for a possible skirmish. For this reason, and because of the unusual Tholian battle tactics, Tholian ships remain fairly common programs in Starfleet battle simulators. Extreme caution is advised. Anyone required to communicate further with the Tholians should consider the lessons we have learned from past encounters. Be precise in stating your intentions, do not vary from what you profess, respect the Tholian need for anonymity and pseudonymity, and expect the unexpected from Tholian technology.

THOLIAN ENIGMAS

From the Science Log of Ensign Vaclav Hunedoara, U.S.S. Nakashima

The *Nakashima* is preparing for its patrol along the Tholian border. Soon, I may hopefully have more data for my research. I can hardly wait. I have dreamt of such an opportunity all my life. When I was a young boy, my father would tell me stories about the ghost ship *Defiant.*. I've had nightmares of what the crew of the *Enterprise* went through when they first found it. Unfortunately, my only other choice is to relive it vicariously through the data files I have. (Note to myself: Do I have enough to program a holodeck simulation?)

To prepare myself for the next few weeks, I have been reviewing the case of the *Defiant*. Still, the more I examine what happened, the more questions spring to mind. Why was the *Defiant* trapped between dimensions? Was it an accident, or did the Tholians intend to use the ship as a trap of some kind? Why did the ship only have the appearance of a solid vessel? One theory I have is that the ship's appearance was the direct result of Tholian technology. From the events that followed, I can assume that the Tholians have a respectable command over matter and energy and over interdimensional physics; other aspects of their technology confirm this. Still, the mystery remains unsolved.

As I collate more data on encounters between our two races, the mystery grows even stranger. A few facts are clear. I know that, on the rare occasions when Tholians briefly interact with Federation ships, only one representative will communicate with the Federation at any given time. These encounters are so rigidly staged and carefully controlled that another debate has broken out among my colleagues in the xenology department: Is the image they present to outsiders the same as their actual appearance? It appears that the personal accounts of encountering Tholians "in the flesh" are scattered and contradictory. So far, I have found three different theories posed by Starfleet xenologists.

The first theory assumes that there is no deception involved. The Tholians are exactly as they first appeared, just as the ghost ship *Defiant* was an exact representation. If this is true, then I would presume Tholians to be a crystalline, possibly silicon-based, lifeform. If this is the case, however, why would they insist on maintaining an environment so hostile to Federation diplomats? The Tholian homeworld may have an exotic atmosphere, but would a silicon lifeform necessarily be so dependent on extreme temperatures? I'm afraid even my biologist colleagues still argue that point.

The second prevailing theory presumes that the Tholians we encounter may depend on some type of individual survival gear. In fact, the shape encountered by Federation officers could be a variety of "encounter suit." Yet this is puzzling, to say the least. Do they require such protection to live inside their ships, or are the conditions of their homeworld even more extreme than what we've detected on their starships? The very idea tantalizes me.

A third, more direct, theory holds that the Tholians are actually energy-based creatures. After all, Tholian engineering shows a remarkable grasp of principles involving energy management and energy shields, including the infamous "Tholian web." This would explain the contradictory accounts advanced by other races. Since the race relies on such meticulous order and logic, the practice of presenting themselves as solid geometrical forms would make sense.

I can also deduce, largely from records of intercepted communications, that the Tholians have a precise organization to their civilization. I've reread Whitehead's treatise. He presumes that their colonies designate citizens as belonging to one of three castes: the "builder" caste, the "scientist" caste, or the "ruling" caste. Current theory holds that these designations are assigned upon birth, and that these roles evolve in any given colony to further its expansion and conquest. This would also correspond to their dependence on order and precision.

Perhaps my speculation is just the overeager imagination of an ambitious ensign. I must make sure I do not betray too much enthusiasm. The rest of the crew fervently hopes that the Tholians will not take this opportunity to attack, but I would risk anything to learn more. In the meantime, I shall continue to pursue my duties ... and hopefully add more data to my files.

TREATIES

Since its formation, the Federation has been signatory to several treaties and pacts in its attempts to keep galactic peace. Some of the important treaties are described below.

TREATY OF CHERON

The Treaty of Cheron ended the Romulan wars in 2160 and established the Romulan Neutral Zone. Although the treaty was signed by the Romulan Star Empire and Earth's world government, it was upheld after the creation of the United Federation of Planets. The later Treaty of Algeron, signed by the Federation, reaffirmed the Romulan Neutral Zone.

TREATY OF ARMENS

The Federation signed the Treaty of Armens with the Sheliak Corporate in 2255. The reclusive Sheliak feel that humans are inferior lifeforms, and want little to no contact with them. The Federation accidentally violated this treaty in 2276 by establishing a colony on Tau Cygna V, a desert planet ceded to the Sheliak under the terms of the treaty. The Sheliak demanded the removal of the colony in 2366, citing the terms of the treaty.

TREATY OF CESTUS III

In 2267, the Gorn destroyed a Federation outpost on Cestus III. The Federation had been unaware that the Gorn considered Cestus III to be part of their sovereign space. The Treaty of Cestus III cleared up the misunderstanding and allowed the Federation to establish a colony on the planet.

ORGANIAN PEACE TREATY

The Organians imposed a peace treaty on the Federation and the Klingon Empire in 2267, after the Federation tried to stop the Klingons from occupying Organia. Strategically located for use as a base by either side, both felt it was important enough to go to war.

The advanced civilization of the Organians, who had evolved beyond the need for a corporeal form, declared that they would allow no hostilities. They decreed that any disputed planet would be awarded to whichever of the powers could most effectively develop and manage it, and that starship crews were entitled to use each others' facilities, such as space stations.

POLARIC TEST BAN TREATY

The treaty prohibits the use of polaric ion energy sources. Polaric ion energy can provide enough power for a planet, but its use entails a high risk of serious and uncontrolled subspace chain reactions. After the near destruction of a Romulan research colony on Chaltok IV in 2268 from such a reaction, the Romulan Star Empire, the Federation, and other galactic powers signed the Polaric Test Ban Treaty.

KHITOMER ACCORDS

Following the destruction of Praxis in 2293, Klingon Chancellor Gorkon sought peace with the Federation. The loss of energy production and environmental damage to Qo'noS were the straw that broke the back of Klingon imperial overstretch. Headed for economic ruin, the Klingon Empire made the pragmatic choice for peace.

Though Chancellor Gorkon was assassinated by forces on both sides who did not want to see hostilities ended, his daughter Azetbur was able to conclude the peace talks. The Khitomer Accords allowed the Federation and the Klingon Empire to begin to normalize relations and did away with the Klingon Neutral Zone.

TREATY OF ALGERON

The Treaty of Algeron has shaped the course of Federation relations with the Romulan Star Empire and dictated Starfleet's use of technology. Following the Tomed Incident in 2311, the Treaty of Algeron reaffirmed the Romulan Neutral Zone, which the Treaty of Cheron established in 2160, and provided that any incursion into the Neutral Zone without adequate warning to the other side would be considered an act of war. It also prohibits the Federation from employing cloaking devices on its starships or developing cloaking technology.

TREATY OF ALLIANCE

The Treaty of Alliance of 2346 not only ended the threat of war between the Federation and the Klingon Empire but established groundwork for mutual military deployments and diplomatic exchanges. Under the terms of the treaty, the Federation and the Klingons may provide mutual aid and defense, but interference in domestic governmental matters is prohibited.

THOLIAN ACCORDS

The Tholian Accords of 2360 established Federation diplomatic relations with the Tholians, a traditionally hostile civilization. The Tholian Accords established the borders of Tholian space, closed the borders to ships of both sides, and established protocols for diplomatic communications between the Federation and the Tholian Assembly.

FEDERATION-CARDASSIAN TREATY

Talks for the Federation-Cardassian Treaty began in 2367, and concluded with its signing in 2370. The treaty redrew the boundaries between Federation and Cardassian space, and created the Demilitarized Zone as a buffer. As a result of the border change, some Federation colonies came under Cardassian control, and the Federation acquired some Cardassian colonies. The treaty prohibits military activity, including outposts and fleet exercises, within the Demilitarized Zone. A treaty not popular with all parts of either society, it secures only a fragile peace.

SELDONIS IV CONVENTION

The Seldonis IV Convention outlined the treatment of prisoners of war. The Convention prohibits torture of prisoners and requires that they be provided with adequate food, shelter, medical attention, and other such basic necessities. Most major powers in the galaxy are signatories, including the Federation, the Cardassian Union, the Klingon Empire, and the Romulan Star Empire.

The Federation Merchant Marine

Not every ship traversing Federation space belongs to Starfleet. In fact, most of the craft in the Federation are personal, commercial, or scientific vessels, not the exploration and defense ships of Starfleet. Compared to, for example, Romulans or Cardassians, citizens of the Federation have virtually unrestricted freedom to travel the galaxy and see its sights.

The Federation Merchant Marine comprises by far the largest fleet of non-Starfleet vessels. An important part of the Federation economy, it is directed by the Federation government itself, not Starfleet. It performs many diverse tasks which, while often not as glamorous as the jobs assigned to a Starfleet starship, are equally vital to the prosperity and even to the continued existence of the Federation. It carries cargo from one planet to another, transports passengers, helps keep colonies supplied, and transports and sells certain types of goods to nonmember planets.

The Nature of the Organization

The Federation Merchant Marine was founded shortly after the Federation itself was created. Although the Federation Constitution did not specifically provide for a merchant marine, its provisions on economic matters did grant the Federation Council broad powers "to maintain the economic health and strength of the Federation and all of its members." One of the many things the Council did with these powers was to establish the Merchant Marine.

Historically, the broad term "merchant marine" means the commercial or mercantile fleet of a nation, whether owned directly by that nation or by its citizens. In the spacefaring age, it includes the commercial starships of a particular species, planet, or government, and it is of course this aspect of commerce with which the Federation was primarily concerned when it established the Federation Merchant Marine. Individual planetary surface merchant marines do not fall within the Federation's jurisdiction, and neither do the individual starfaring merchant marines of the Federation's members.

The Andorian Merchant Marine remains the largest and most professional of these, with a tradition extending back to the days of the Earth-Romulan War. Many Andorian Merchant Marine crewmen joined the new Federation Merchant Marine, giving it a cadre of experienced captains and engineers during the early crises of the Klingon wars and the Axanarian secession. Grandsons and granddaughters of these captains served the Federation well during the emergency mobilizations against the Borg, the immense human crises of the Cardassian border relocation, and the more conventional support roles during the Tholian War. This tradition still holds strongly enough that even human and Tellarite crewmen enlist in the Andorian Merchant Marine in hopes of being able to join the Federation Merchant Marine some day.

THE ROLE OF THE MERCHANT MARINE

The Federation has always recognized a need to transport certain goods, or goods in bulk. Transporter and replicator technologies, marvels that they are of modern society, do not remove the need to move various types of goods, or large amounts of goods, across space. First, the range of transporters is limited. Federation space is hundreds of light years across, and even the best cargo transporters only have a range of about 40,000 kilometers. Second, the amount of material which can be transported at any one time is limited, as is the size of the object to be transported; only a few very large planet-based transporters are capable of transporting extremely large objects (such as some vehicles). Third, not every person or every planet has access to transporters—although they are not rare, they are not ubiquitous either. This reasoning also applies to replicator technology, though large-scale industrial replicators are more common than large transporters (and, of course, there are some goods which some people prefer not to replicate, as discussed below).

What this all means is that there are many occasions when the Federation, or someone within the Federation, needs to transport goods, products, or people in the old-fashioned way—by loading them onto a ship and carrying them to where they need to go. Starfleet's ships could handle such tasks, but only do so in the gravest of emergencies. At any other time, that's where the Federation Merchant Marine comes in. Carrying cargo and passengers is its job. As such it forms a vital economic link between many members of the Federation, and acts as a lifeline to distant colonies and outposts which would otherwise have, at best, a very difficult time getting the supplies they need.

However, the Federation Merchant Marine should not be mistaken for a profit-driven private mercantile enterprise; it's far from that. The reason some of those worlds and far-flung colonies sometimes have difficulty obtaining goods is that merchants who work for profit do not find it profitable to visit them. Either they are too far away, or there aren't enough customers, or whatever it is they need is not profitable enough to make it worth a private merchant's time to visit them. But the Federation Merchant Marine, operated under the auspices of the Federation, is able to visit anyone or any planet and bring what is needed to survive and thrive. The Federation Merchant Marine isn't concerned with profit; instead, it focuses on providing needed goods to Federation citizens, and on keeping vital colonies supplied.

THE FEDERATION MERCHANT MARINE AND STARFLEET

As one might expect, the Merchant Marine enjoys good relations with Starfleet. In essence the two complement each other. While Starfleet does on occasion transport goods or personnel (especially those which are dangerous, or which are going to particularly dangerous areas), it is primarily engaged in missions of

exploration, scientific investigation, and defense. Its ships are not set up to carry large amounts of cargo or passengers. That's what the Merchant Marine is for; Starfleet's highly trained personnel can be put to better uses. Unless there's an emergency of some sort requiring high warp speed and a potential military response, Starfleet prefers to let the Merchant Marine transport goods and people. Even in those grave emergencies, the Merchant Marine often follows right behind Starfleet in bringing vaccines or doctors to a plague-stricken world, or phaser rifles to a Federation garrison under attack.

Conversely, the ships of the Merchant Marine, while well equipped for commerce, are not designed for combat or similar missions. They have low-strength shields and phasers, but would find themselves out of their depth fighting off anything more powerful than technologically backward pirates or brigands. Nor do Merchant Marine ships have the sophisticated sensor arrays which Starfleet ships use to chart systems and investigate stellar anomalies. When a Merchant Marine vessel has to go into a dangerous area, or its commander fears that Orions or other threats may attack the ship, Starfleet might be called on to escort the mercantile ship to its destination. (Of course, some Merchant Marine captains trust to their own skills rather than calling on Starfleet, and a surprising number of them succeed.) Thus, the two fleets have a healthy respect for each other and work well together.

In the eyes of many Federation citizens, the Merchant Marine is a sort of "junior" or lesser

Starfleet. This is unfair. It lacks a high profile and prestige, but its job is in many ways equally important. Its members do not possess the powers or prerogatives which Starfleet personnel do, but they enjoy respect throughout the Federation because of their important role in the galactic economy. Federation families are proud to have their sons and daughters join the Merchant Marine; many families have been serving in its ranks for generations.

ORGANIZATION AND STRUCTURE

The Federation Merchant Marine ultimately answers to the Federation Council. The Council's Merchant Marine Committee meets on a regular basis to assess the performance of the Merchant Marine, determine where its services are needed, and allocate its resources. (Actual direction of the Merchant Marine falls to the Department of Commerce in the Secretariat.) If there were any difficulties or problems with the service, the Committee would hold hearings to investigate them, but no such hearings have ever been necessary.

Daily command of the Federation Merchant Marine is vested in an Admiral; currently, Admiral Jenidox Parl, a Tellarite, holds the position. Sometimes the Admiral has Starfleet experience, but more often the post serves as the pinnacle of a successful mercantile career for a civilian captain. The Admiral is responsible for seeing that the Merchant Marine fleet is properly and efficiently deployed, for ensuring that all ships are sufficiently maintained and staffed, and for evaluating requests for Merchant Marine assistance and prioritizing them. To help him with these tasks he has a staff consisting of several Vice-Admirals (each of whom is responsible for the portion of the Merchant Marine fleet in a particular area of Federation space) and lesser officers, bureaucrats, and functionaries. The Admiral is headquartered on Alpha Centauri; his headquarters facilities include a large starport and extensive planetary and space-based starship repair bays.

The Merchant Marine organization more or less follows "astrographical" lines. The ships which serve a particular sector or group of sectors comprise a particular "fleet." Each such fleet is commanded by a Vice-Admiral, to whom the captains of the fleet's ships report. Usually a fleet remains in its designated territory, but on occasion it is necessary to assemble several fleets for an important task (such as responding to an emergency or supplying Starfleet ships in time of war). Independent merchants of Federation registry may be called upon to serve under the Vice-Admiral of their sector in emergencies (such as the Cardassian border evacuation), and usually report any rumors of pirates or navigational hazards to his office.

TRITANIUM SHIPS AND IRON MEN

A life in the Federation Merchant Marine isn't necessarily for everyone. It requires a certain combination of discipline, adventurousness, and willingness to work hard. While these qualities might also recommend a person for Starfleet service, these individuals may fail the rigorous Starfleet entrance tests and screenings, prefer a less-structured lifestyle, or choose to join the Merchant Marine without ever considering a career in Starfleet.

JOINING THE MERCHANT MARINE

It's a lot easier for a Federation citizen to join the Merchant Marine than to join Starfleet. (In fact, unlike Starfleet, the Merchant Marine does not require Federation citizenship.) Although there are some entrance requirements and tests, they mainly concern physical and mental fitness for the job; they do not approach the rigors or difficulties of the Starfleet Academy admission procedure.

The Merchant Marine has recruiting stations on most Federation planets, and at some starbases and outposts as well. To join, a potential recruit need only go to the local recruiting office and apply. If he passes the tests mentioned above, he's in—easy as that. Typically the new member, known as a "sailor," will ship out on his first cruise within a year.

Before that, however, he has to learn a little more about the job he's just signed up for. The Merchant Marine sends him to its own academy on Danula II for a period of about six months. During that time he learns the rudiments of stellar cartography, starship operations, and the like. He then spends another three months studying whatever he has chosen to specialize in—command, flight control, or what have you. While his skills may never approach those of a similarly positioned Starfleet officer, he usually isn't exposed to dangerous situations where such a high level of skill is necessary, either (a tradeoff many sailors are more than happy with). After completing his time at the academy, the sailor is assigned to a ship; he may return to the academy periodically for retraining, officer training, and other purposes.

A standard tour of duty in the Federation Merchant Marine is four years; all persons who attend the academy must serve one such term. After his four years are up, a sailor is free to leave to pursue another career. In practice, most sailors remain in the service for two or more terms; many make it a lifetime occupation. After serving their first tour, sailors are eligible to request transfer to a different ship or fleet. Many of them do so, since this allows them to take on new challenges, visit new areas of space, and make new friends.

WHY THE MERCHANT MARINE?

Sailors give many reasons for wanting to join the Merchant Marine. First and foremost among them is a desire to "see the galaxy." More than the members of any other Federation organization except Starfleet, the sailors of the Merchant Marine travel extensively. Even if a sailor remains in the same fleet for several tours of duty, he is still likely to visit more planets and see more of space than most Federation citizens will in an entire lifetime. Those sailors who truly long for a nomadic life transfer from fleet to fleet and ship to ship, getting to know the galaxy as well as some Starfleet officers.

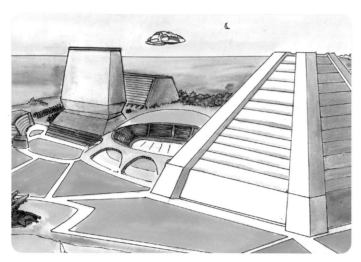

A second reason is a lack of desire to join Starfleet. Many Federation citizens want to go into space for some reason, but not as part of Starfleet. It's hard to get into Starfleet, and just as hard to make it through the Academy. When you finally get posted to a starship, you're likely to be exposed to dangers both commonplace and exotic—anything from warp-core breaches, to collisions, to starship combat, to encounters with bizarre galactic phenomena and playful omniscient energy beings. Not everyone wants that kind of pressure, danger, and "excitement." Some prefer the more sedate life of a sailor in the Merchant Marine. It's not a relaxing job—sailors work hard, and they're proud of it—but compared to serving on board a Starfleet vessel it's a mighty calm job most of the time.

It's much the same for citizens who want to join Starfleet but can't for some reason (typically because they cannot meet the entrance requirements). Starfleet's standards are tough to meet, and not every Federation citizen can get into the Academy. For those citizens who are still desperate to work in space on board a starship, even though they cannot become a part of Starfleet, the Merchant Marine is often a perfect solution. Although it's not nearly as difficult to join, the Merchant Marine still teaches its sailors many valuable spacefaring skills—and on occasion it may even serve up a dose of adventure or two. Plus, every member of the Federation acknowledges the valuable services the Merchant Marine provides, and it's considered an honor to be a member of it, even if its entrance requirements aren't as hard to meet as Starfleet's.

SERVICE IN THE NAME OF PROSPERITY

"Service in the Name of Prosperity" is the motto of the Federation Merchant Marine, and it perfectly sums up the sailors' desire to serve the Federation by increasing the prosperity and ease of life of its citizens. The Merchant Marine was formed to serve the needs of the Federation's citizens, and has always done an admirable job at its appointed task.

The assignments given to a Merchant Marine vessel may remain more or less the same for long periods of time, but typically they vary. Merchant Marine vessels and sailors rarely undertake specific "tours of duty" in the sense that Starfleet uses the term. Instead, the ship will handle a wide variety of jobs—everything from transporting cargo or passengers to towing stranded ships into stardock—which must be performed within its "territory." This variety appeals to many sailors. However, some ships, due to their nature or their sector, tend to perform the same types of missions repeatedly. It's not uncommon for a ship to spend long periods of time simply transporting goods and passengers between the planets in its sector, for example. On the bright side, this usually allows the sailors to develop a routine which lets them maximize their free time, during which they can study, pursue hobbies, and maybe even take a bit of shore leave.

Some of the more typical duties assigned to Merchant Marine ships include:

• *Transporting goods*: The most common "mission" for a Merchant Marine vessel is transporting goods which Federation citizens cannot or prefer not to replicate. While most of the needs of many Federation citizens can be met with replicated goods, not everyone has easy access to replicators (or industrial replicators big enough to make large items). Some items cannot, or should not, be replicated. One good example is artwork and craftwork, such as Mintakan tapestries. While it is possible to replicate such an item, a replicated copy would lack many of the qualities of an original, handmade, one, and certainly would have little or no value as a work of art. Therefore a lively Federation trade in such items has sprung up. Similarly, some Federation citizens claim to be able to tell the difference between the taste of replicated food and "real" food, so there is trade in homegrown grains, meat animals, and similar products. Because of their access to such foodstuffs, some sailors are accomplished cooks who eat quite well.

• *Transporting passengers*: The Merchant Marine is not a commercial transportation service. Citizens of the Federation can't simply contact the Merchant Marine via subspace radio and book passage to Risa whenever they feel like taking a trip; for that, they must use private commercial transportation companies. However, there are many occasions when the Federation must transport large numbers of people. Some examples include establishing colonies, evacuating failed colonies, evacuating planets which are suffering from an attack or natural disaster, and ferrying large numbers of diplomats to important conferences. In these cases the Merchant Marine usually does the transporting. In fact, some Merchant Marine vessels are specifically designed as personnel transports, and come equipped with amenities such as holodecks for the passengers' use.

• *Trade*: The Federation does conduct some official trade with nonmember species. Typically this involves exchanging Federation goods for goods of equal value which the other race has but the Federation cannot manufacture, especially minerals like dilithium or

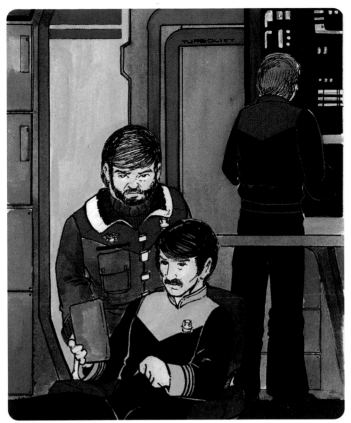

topaline. However, sometimes these trade missions are conducted solely to generate goodwill and help cement relations between the species and the Federation; whether the Federation obtains anything else of value in return is inconsequential.

• *Colony support*: The Federation has established many colonies and outposts throughout its space. Many extremely isolated colonies lie in deep space without any other inhabited planets for light years around them. With no one else to trade with, and often nothing to trade until the colony becomes firmly established, the colonists remain dependent upon the Federation to provide supplies, check up on them periodically, and bring news of the rest of the galaxy. These jobs often fall to the Merchant Marine. Because of this, more than one sailor has met the person of his dreams at some colony and left the service to settle down and become a colonist.

• *Technology transfer*: The races of the Federation frequently exchange newly developed forms of technology with each other. Acquisition of Federation technology is also a prime motivating factor behind some species' requests to join the Federation. Such exchanges of scientific knowledge and equipment usually fall within the purview of the Merchant Marine, since it is better prepared to carry large amounts of equipment than Starfleet. It can also easily accommodate diplomats or other personnel who accompany the items so that the transfer can be effectuated.

• *Tugboat detail*: Even as advanced and sophisticated as they are, Federation ships sometimes become stranded for one reason or another. It may be damage caused by an attack, equipment failure, loss of power, or some other reason, but the ship still has to be retrieved. Most Merchant Marine ships have powerful engines and tractor beams designed to help them perform such a task.

• *Repair ship*: Similarly, ships which have been extensively damaged often need a large supply of parts to make repairs—parts which cannot be replicated (either because the replicators are inoperational, or the items needed are too large for a ship's replicators). In such cases the Merchant Marine is usually called upon to ferry parts and repair personnel to the damaged ship (although in the case of ships which require classified military technology, Starfleet may instead take this duty upon itself). Some Merchant Marine craft specialize in repair work, with a large complement of engineers and equipment the next best thing to a full spacedock.

A SAILOR'S LIFE

While it is usually less dangerous than a life in Starfleet, the life of a sailor in the Merchant Marine isn't always an easy one. The work can be hard and the hours long, but the reward—helping the Federation and its citizens prosper—is well worth the sacrifice.

Compared to Starfleet vessels, Merchant Marine ships feel uncrowded. It doesn't take many persons to keep one of the relatively simple and easy-to-maintain freighters operational, or to make sure cargo is safe. Some ships, despite their rather large size, have a crew of only a dozen or so. However, those ships specifically designed to carry large numbers of passengers often have extensive crews.

Regulations in the Merchant Marine are not nearly as strict as those in Starfleet; after all, the Merchant Marine is not a quasi-military organization. Discipline tends to be more lax, and the officers and crew more easygoing, than usually seen in Starfleet. However, the Merchant Marine is required to abide by all pertinent Federation regulations, especially the Prime Directive. Common-sense safety regulations also apply, and most sailors observe them conscientiously, since they know the risks of space travel better than most people. The Merchant Marine also falls under the Federation's commercial regulations and laws; most Command officers have a thorough knowledge of such laws.

On long journeys, life aboard a Merchant Marine vessel can get a little routine. Most Merchant Marine vessels do not have holodecks or similar forms of entertainment, so the crew often contents itself with studying, gambling, athletics, art, or other hobbies or diversions.

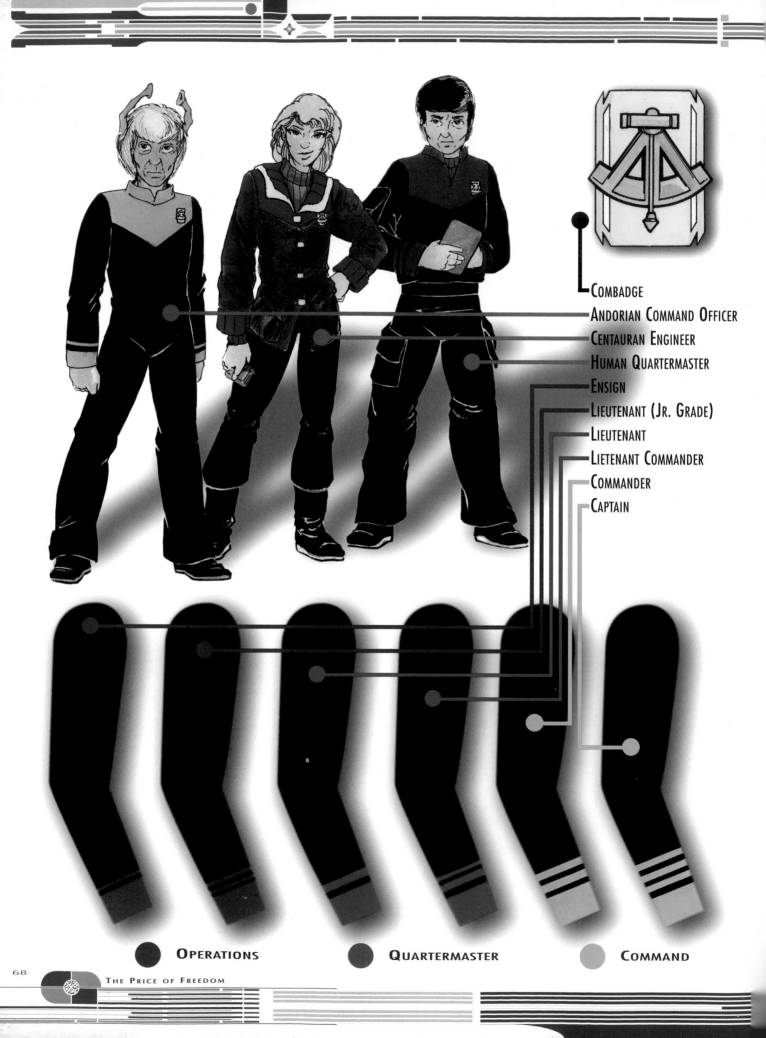

COMBADGE

ANDORIAN COMMAND OFFICER

CENTAURAN ENGINEER

HUMAN QUARTERMASTER

ENSIGN

LIEUTENANT (JR. GRADE)

LIEUTENANT

LIETENANT COMMANDER

COMMANDER

CAPTAIN

OPERATIONS   QUARTERMASTER   COMMAND

RANKS AND DEPARTMENTS

The ranks used in the Merchant Marine are virtually identical to those used in Starfleet. Each ship is commanded by a Captain who has total authority over the vessel and his crew (subject, of course, to being removed from duty for medical reasons and the like). The Captain is assisted by a First Officer. Lieutenant Commanders (or, in some cases, Lieutenants) head the various departments on board the ship, such as Security and Engineering. Enlisted personnel compose the bulk of the crew.

The departments typically found on a Merchant Marine ship include:

• *Command:* This department is more or less self-explanatory and very similar to the same department on board a Starfleet vessel. However, in addition to typical Command duties, Command officers are expected to perform whatever negotiating, bargaining, or trading is needed with regard to their cargo. Even more than Starfleet captains, Merchant Marine commanders have to run every aspect of a (sometimes very) isolated world on their ships.

• *Engineering:* First, Engineering must make sure the ship is in fit condition to fly, and must conduct all routine maintenance which is required to keep it in proper shape. Second, it must make whatever emergency repairs are necessary. Third, when necessary Engineering must assist the Quartermaster with bringing goods onto the ship, safely securing them, and then offloading them. Engineers may be called on for assistance if special uses of the tractor beam are required for a particular cargo, when a dangerous cargo is being brought on board and it is necessary to activate multiple safety measures, when tests have to be performed on the cargo, or just when the crew needs extra hands to do the lifting.

Since Merchant Marine ships usually do not have a dedicated Science Officer, Engineering personnel fill such roles whenever there is a need. This rarely happens, but Merchant Marine engineers have the closest thing to training for it nevertheless.

• *Flight Control:* The Flight Control officer is responsible for astronavigation, steering the ship, making sure the ship enters a proper orbit, and the like. He also usually operates the ship's sensors. His duties usually don't involve anything more complicated than entering an orbit or towing another ship, but occasionally more difficult situations crop up, so he's got to be ready for them.

• *Operations Manager:* The Operations Manager has several related duties. First, he is responsible for the allocation of the ship's power in time of need; it's up to him to decide which systems get power when the warp engines can't produce enough to go around. Second, he monitors the status of any groups of personnel which leave the ship to conduct negotiations, retrieve or deliver cargo, and so forth (these are usually called "Trade Teams"). Finally, if necessary he assists the Quartermaster.

• *Quartermaster:* The Quartermaster is responsible for the loading, offloading, and maintenance of cargo and passengers on the ship. He supervises most such operations, though lesser ones are usually delegated to subordinates. A Quartermaster has to be precise and meticulous, since even a seemingly tiny or trivial error regarding the cargo may cause serious repercussions. In some cases the Quartermaster also assists the Captain with negotiations regarding trades and transportation. Outside the Federation, the Quartermaster oversees any purchases the ship makes. He also works closely with Security. Often the Quartermaster serves as the ship's First Officer. On smaller ships, he often serves as Operations Manager as well.

• *Security:* The Security Officer is responsible for the safety and security of the ship and its passengers, crew, and cargo. Typically he and his subordinates are the only officers on the ship trained in the use of phasers; most sailors never learn how to use one, since they have little (if any) need for weapons. He, or a trusted junior officer, usually accompanies the Captain on any negotiation or trade mission which may pose some danger.

It's also important to note what a Merchant Marine ship doesn't have in comparison to a Starfleet vessel. There's no Tactical Officer, for example; the Tactical station will usually be taken by a Security, Flight Control, or Command officer in times of crisis. There isn't much of a medical staff, either; a doctor or two, at most, is usually enough for a Merchant Marine ship. As noted above, there's no Science Officer, since Merchant Marine missions usually have little, if anything, to do with scientific investigation. If necessary, a Starfleet Science Officer can be temporarily assigned to the ship.

TRADE TEAMS

The Merchant Marine equivalent of the Away Team is the Trade Team—a group of crewmen whose purpose is to negotiate trades, obtain and deliver goods, and so forth. The typical Trade Team consists of one or more Command officers (who do most of the talking), one Security officer (sometimes more), and someone from the Quartermaster department. If large numbers of Merchant Marine personnel are involved, an Operations Manager may also accompany the Team.

STEPPING UP

"Stepping up" is Merchant Marine slang for leaving the service to join Starfleet. (Less polite sailors call it "waxing.") While this is rare, it does happen from time to time. Many sailors are people who wanted to join Starfleet at first, but were prevented from doing so for some reason, such as inability to pass the entrance exams. However, Starfleet is neither a rigid nor an unforgiving organization, and sometimes a Federation citizen can qualify to join later on in life. Many of the skills learned in the Merchant Marine, such as piloting a ship, coordinating groups of people to reach a goal, and interacting amicably with many different species, translate well to a Starfleet career. For more details on stepping up, see p. 74.

MERCHANT MARINE VESSELS

The Merchant Marine uses a wide variety of vessels. The two things most of them have in common are (1) a great deal of room for cargo and/or passengers, and (2) engines strong enough to move all that weight, even though their top speed is not particularly high. Here is a template for a typical Merchant Marine ship:

MERCHANT MARINE STARSHIP

CLASS AND TYPE: MERCHANT MARINE CARGO/PASSENGER CARRIER
COMMISSIONING DATE: N/A
HULL CHARACTERISTICS
   SIZE: 5 (500 METERS LONG, 11 DECKS)
   RESISTANCE: 2
   STRUCTURAL POINTS: 80
OPERATIONS CHARACTERISTICS
   CREW/PASSENGERS: 50/2,000   [6 PWR/ROUND]
   COMPUTERS: 2   [2 PWR/ROUND]
   TRANSPORTERS: 2 PERSONNEL, 8 CARGO, 2 EMERGENCY   [6 PWR/ROUND]
   TRACTOR BEAMS: 1 AV, 1 FD   [2 PWR/RATING USED]
PROPULSION AND POWER CHARACTERISTICS
   WARP SYSTEM: 4.0/6.0/8.0 (8 HOURS)   [2/WARP FACTOR]
   IMPULSE SYSTEM: .25 C/.5 C   [2/5 PWR/ROUND]
   POWER: 120
SENSOR SYSTEMS
   LONG-RANGE SENSORS: +0/10 LIGHT YEARS   [6 PWR/ROUND]
   LATERAL SENSORS: +0/1 LIGHT YEAR   [4 PWR/ROUND]
   NAVIGATIONAL SENSORS: +0   [5 PWR/ROUND]
   CLOAK: NONE
   SENSORS SKILL: 3
WEAPONS SYSTEMS
   TYPE IV PHASER:
      RANGE: 10/30,000/100,000/300,000
      ARC: 90 DEGREES FORWARD, 90 DEGREES AFT
      ACCURACY: 4/5/7/10
      DAMAGE: 8
      POWER: [8]
   WEAPONS SKILL: 3
DEFENSIVE SYSTEMS
   STARFLEET DEFLECTOR SHIELD
      PROTECTION: 30/40
      POWER: [30]
DESCRIPTION AND NOTES
THIS TEMPLATE DEPICTS A TYPICAL MERCHANT MARINE CARGO AND PASSENGER CARRIER. ALTHOUGH LARGE, MOST OF ITS SIZE IS TAKEN UP WITH CARGO BAYS AND PASSENGER ACCOMMODATIONS, NOT THE ADVANCED EQUIPMENT FOUND ON STARFLEET VESSELS. ITS WARP ENGINE IS STRONG ENOUGH FOR IT TO TOW LARGER SHIPS AND TO OPERATE ITS TRACTOR BEAMS, WHICH ARE AS POWERFUL AS THOSE ON *GALAXY*-CLASS STARSHIPS.

FOR ANOTHER EXAMPLE OF A TYPICAL CARGO CRAFT, SEE THE *ANTARES*-CLASS SHIP DESCRIBED ON PAGE 222 OF THE *STAR TREK: THE NEXT GENERATION ROLE PLAYING GAME* CORE RULEBOOK.

THE FEDERATION MERCHANT MARINE IN YOUR SERIES

The Federation Merchant Marine makes an excellent addition to just about any *Star Trek: The Next Generation Role Playing Game* series. Whether you make the Merchant Marine the basis for the series, or simply use it to generate story seeds and plot threads in a typical series, it can add another level of depth and interest to your game.

MERCHANT MARINE CHARACTER GENERATION

Here are some Overlays, alternate Background History stages, and Archetypes with which to create Federation Merchant Marine characters. Since Merchant Marine personnel are less broadly skilled than the equivalent Starfleet personnel, these Overlays, Background History stages, etc. are built on fewer points than standard *Star Trek: The Next Generation RPG* ones. Narrators who wish to give Merchant Marine characters extra points to balance the series for all players, or for any other reason, are encouraged to do so.

OVERLAYS

Overlays for a Merchant Marine Commander, Engineer, Flight Control Officer, Quartermaster, and Security Officer are provided below. Players who want to play other roles (such as a Medical Officer) can adapt the Overlays in the core rulebook or, with the Narrator's assistance, create their own.

MERCHANT MARINE COMMANDER

A member of the Command branch of the Merchant Marine can be anything from a ship's captain to an administrative officer posted at a Merchant Marine starbase somewhere in the galaxy. They tend to be not only experts on commercial regulations but skilled trade negotiators and administrators.

A character who wants to be First Officer or Captain of a Federation Merchant Marine ship must purchase both the Department Head and Promotion Advantages, and must have some knowledge of other shipboard duties.

MERCHANT MARINE COMMANDER
ADMINISTRATION (MERCHANT MARINE SHIP ADMINISTRATION) 2 (3)
BARGAIN (CHOOSE SPECIALIZATION) 1 (2)
COMMAND (MERCHANT MARINE SHIP COMMAND) 2 (3)
COMPUTER (CHOOSE SPECIALIZATION) 1 (2)
DIPLOMACY (COMMERCIAL TREATIES) 1 (2)
HISTORY (FEDERATION MERCHANT MARINE) 1 (2)
LANGUAGE
      FEDERATION STANDARD 1
LAW (FEDERATION MERCHANT MARINE REGULATIONS) (FEDERATION COMMERCIAL REGULATIONS) 2 (3) AND (3)
MERCHANT (CHOOSE SPECIALIZATION) 1 (2)
PERSONAL EQUIPMENT (CHOOSE SPECIALIZATION) 1 (2)
VEHICLE OPERATIONS (SHUTTLECRAFT) 1 (2)

MERCHANT MARINE FREIGHTER

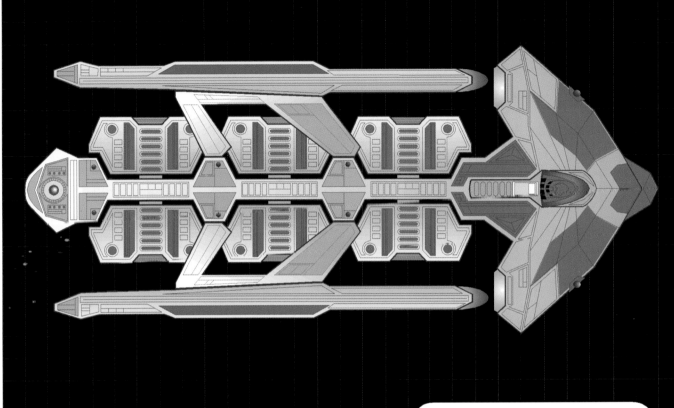

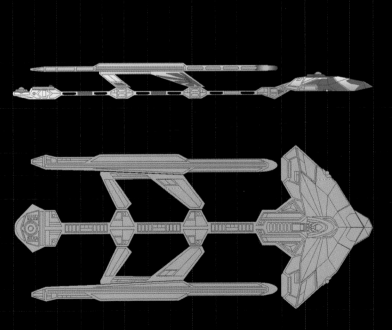

CLASS AND TYPE:
  MERCHANT MARINE
  CARGO/PASSENGER CARRIER

COMMISSIONING DATE: N/A

HULL CHARACTERISTICS
  SIZE: 5 (500 METERS LONG,
    18 DECKS)
  RESISTANCE: 2
  STRUCTURAL POINTS: 80

Merchant Marine Engineer

As described above, a Merchant Marine Engineer not only keeps his ship functioning properly, but helps evaluate and store cargoes properly and assists the Quartermaster. This makes him slightly less "focused" than a Starfleet Engineer.

ENGINEER
Computer (Modeling) 2 (3)
Engineering, Any (choose Specialization) 2 (3)
Engineering, Any Other (choose Specialization) 1 (2)
History (Federation Merchant Marine) 1 (2)
Language
    Federation Standard 1
Law (Federation Merchant Marine Regulations) 1 (2)
Personal Equipment (choose Specialization) 1 (2)
Physical Science, Any (Materials Science) 1 (2)
Science, Any Other (choose Specialization) 1 (2)
Shipboard Systems (choose Specialization) 2 (3)
Vehicle Operations (Shuttlecraft) 1 (2)

Merchant Marine Flight Control Officer

Merchant Marine Flight Control officers pilot their ships, operate sensors, and sometimes fill in at Tactical in emergencies. In some cases they assist Command officers with negotiations and trade decisions.

FLIGHT CONTROL OFFICER
Administration (Merchant Marine Ship Administration) 1 (2)
Computer (choose Specialization) 1 (2)
History (Federation Merchant Marine) 1 (2)
Language
    Federation Standard 1
Law (Federation Merchant Marine Regulations) 1 (2)
Merchant (choose Specialization) 1 (2)
Personal Equipment (choose Specialization) 1 (2)
Science, Any (choose Specialization) 1 (2)
Shipboard Systems (Flight Control) (Sensors OR Tractor Beam) 2 (3) and (3)
Space Sciences (Astrogation) 2 (3)
Vehicle Operations (Shuttlecraft) 1 (2)

Merchant Marine Quartermaster

The Quartermaster is responsible for the ship's cargo and passengers. Thus, he's one of the most important officers on the ship. He does his best to keep things running smoothly and efficiently. Many Quartermaster officers eventually transfer into Command.

QUARTERMASTER
Administration (Merchant Marine Ship Administration) (Logistics) 2 (3) and (3)
Bargain (choose Specialization) 2 (3)
Computer (choose Specialization) 1 (2)
History (Federation Merchant Marine) 1 (2)
Language
    Federation Standard 1
Law (Federation Merchant Marine Regulations) 1 (2)
Merchant (choose two Specializations) 2 (3) and (3)
Personal Equipment (choose Specialization) 1 (2)
Physical Science (Chemistry OR Physics) 1 (2)
Vehicle Operations (Shuttlecraft) 1 (2)

Merchant Marine Security

The Security officers on a Merchant Marine vessel are primarily responsible for preventing successful attacks on the ship and/or thefts of cargo. However, they also make sure that internal rules and regulations are followed.

SECURITY
Computer (choose Specialization) 1 (2)
Dodge 1
Energy Weapon (Phaser) 1 (2)
History (Federation Merchant Marine) 1 (2)
Language
    Federation Standard 1
Law (Federation Law) 2 (3)
Personal Equipment (choose Specialization) 1 (2)
Security (Security Systems) 2 (3)
Shipboard Systems (Tactical) 1 (2)
Starship Tactics (Federation Merchant Marine Tactics) (Pirate Tactics) 2 (3) and (3)
Unarmed Combat (Starfleet Martial Arts) 1 (2)
Vehicle Operations (Shuttlecraft) 1 (2)

Background History: Federation Merchant Marine Academy Training and Tours of Duty

Since Merchant Marines don't attend Starfleet Academy or have Starfleet tours of duty, they need their own Background History stages to represent their training.

As noted above, the Merchant Marine doesn't usually have dedicated tours of duty the way Starfleet does. Instead, the Tour of Duty History stage represents the activity which the character (or the character's ship) has most often been engaged in during the character's career prior to the start of the series—in essence, what he's gotten best at through practice and experience.

MERCHANT MARINE ACADEMY LIFE HISTORY

THE CHARACTER RECEIVES 6 DEVELOPMENT POINTS TO SPEND DURING ACADEMY LIFE.

ACADEMY TRAINING PACKAGES (EACH COSTS 6 DEVELOPMENT POINTS)

ENGINEERING TRAINING: ENGINEERING, ANY (CHOOSE SPECIALIZATION) 1 (2), SHIPBOARD SYSTEMS (CHOOSE SPECIALIZATION) 1 (2)

LEGAL TRAINING: DIPLOMACY (COMMERCIAL TREATIES) 1 (2), LAW (FEDERATION LAW) 1 (2)

NEGOTIATOR TRAINING: LANGUAGES (CHOOSE ANY TWO), PERSUASION (DEBATE) 1 (2), SHREWD +1

QUARTERMASTER TRAINING: ADMINISTRATION (MERCHANT MARINE SHIP ADMINISTRATION) 1 (2), CONTACT(S) (3 POINTS' WORTH)

SECURITY TRAINING: ENERGY WEAPON (PHASER) 1 (2), SYSTEMS ENGINEERING (SECURITY SYSTEMS) 1 (2)

ATTRIBUTES AND EDGES
  ANY

SKILLS
  BARGAIN
  CHARM
  COMMAND
  DIPLOMACY
  ENERGY WEAPON
  FAST TALK
  FIRST AID
  GAMING
  MERCHANT
  SCIENCE, ANY
  SECURITY
  SHIPBOARD SYSTEMS
  STARSHIP TACTICS

ADVANTAGES
  ALERTNESS (+2)
  ENGINEERING APTITUDE (+3)
  HIGH PAIN THRESHOLD (+2)
  INNOVATIVE (+1)
  LANGUAGE ABILITY (+2)
  MATHEMATICAL ABILITY (+3)
  SHREWD (+1)
  TACTICAL GENIUS (+3)

DISADVANTAGES
  ZERO-G INTOLERANCE (-2)

TOUR OF DUTY LIFE HISTORY

THE CHARACTER RECEIVES 7 DEVELOPMENT POINTS TO SPEND DURING HIS FIRST TOUR OF DUTY.

TOUR OF DUTY PACKAGES (EACH COSTS 7 DEVELOPMENT POINTS)

CARGO TRANSPORT/TRADE MISSIONS: ADMINISTRATION (MERCHANT MARINE SHIP ADMINISTRATION) 1 (2), LANGUAGE (CHOOSE ONE) 1, MERCHANT (CHOOSE SPECIALIZATION) 1 (2)

COLONY SUPPORT: ADMINISTRATION (MERCHANT MARINE SHIP ADMINISTRATION) (COLONY ADMINISTRATION) 1 (2) AND (2), PLANETSIDE SURVIVAL (CHOOSE SPECIALIZATION) 1 (2)

PASSENGER TRANSPORT: CONTACT +1, GAMING (CHOOSE SPECIALIZATION) 1 (2), SYSTEMS ENGINEERING (ENVIRONMENTAL SYSTEMS) 1 (2)

REPAIR MISSIONS: FAVOR OWED +1, PROPULSION ENGINEERING (CHOOSE SPECIALIZATION) 1 (2), SYSTEMS ENGINEERING (CHOOSE SPECIALIZATION) 1 (2)

TRADE TREATY NEGOTIATION & IMPLEMENTATION: DIPLOMACY (COMMERCIAL TREATIES) 1 (2), LANGUAGE (CHOOSE ONE APPROPRIATE TO NEGOTIATIONS) 1, PERSUASION (DEBATE) 1 (2)

ATTRIBUTES AND EDGES
  ANY

SKILLS
  COMMAND
  PSIONIC SKILLS (IF APPLICABLE)
  SECURITY
  SHIPBOARD SYSTEMS
  STARSHIP TACTICS
  STRATEGIC OPERATIONS

ADVANTAGES
  ALERTNESS (+2)
  COMMENDATION (+1 TO +3)
  INNOVATIVE (+1)
  PROMOTION (+2 TO +6)

DISADVANTAGES
  BLOODLUST (ALMOST ALWAYS TIED TO VENGEFUL) (-2)
  CHRONIC PAIN (-2)
  LOW PAIN THRESHOLD (-2)
  MEDICAL PROBLEM (-1 TO -3)
  PHYSICALLY IMPAIRED (-1 TO -2)
  POOR CHEMORECEPTION (-1)
  POOR HEARING (-1)
  POOR SIGHT (-2)
  SLOW HEALING (-2)
  WEAKNESS (-2)

ARCHETYPES

In case you need to get going quickly with your Merchant Marine character, here are two Archetypes to get you started: a Human Command officer and a Bolian Quartermaster.

HUMAN MERCHANT MARINE COMMANDER ARCHETYPE

ATTRIBUTES
  FITNESS 2
  COORDINATION 2
      REACTION +1
  INTELLECT 2
  PRESENCE 2
      WILLPOWER +1
  PSI 0

SKILLS
  ADMINISTRATION (MERCHANT MARINE SHIP ADMINISTRATION) 2 (3)
  ATHLETICS (PARRISES SQUARES) 2 (3)
  BARGAIN (MACHINED EQUIPMENT) 1 (2)
  COMMAND (MERCHANT MARINE SHIP COMMAND) 2 (3)
  COMPUTER (PROGRAMMING) 1 (2)
  CULTURE (HUMAN) 2 (3)
  DIPLOMACY (COMMERCIAL TREATIES) 1 (3)
  HISTORY (FEDERATION MERCHANT MARINE) 1 (2)
          (HUMAN) (2)
  LANGUAGES
      BOLIAN 1

Federation Standard 3
Ferengi 1
Tellarite 1
Law (Federation Commercial Regulations) 2 (3)
(Federation Merchant Marine Regulations) 2 (3)
Merchant (Self-sealing Stem Bolts) 1 (2)
Personal Equipment (Communicator) 1 (2)
Persuasion (Debate) 1 (2)
Space Science (Astrogation) 1 (2)
Vehicle Operations (Shuttlecraft) 1 (2)
World Knowledge (Earth) 1 (2)
Advantages/Disadvantages
Athletic Ability +2
Contact +1
Promotion (Lieutenant) +3
Shrewd +1
Courage: 5
Renown: 1

Initiative 1

BOLIAN QUARTERMASTER ARCHETYPE

Attributes
Fitness 2
Strength -1
Coordination 2
Dexterity +1
Reaction +1
Intellect 2
Presence 2
Psi 0

Skills
Administration (Bureaucratic Manipulation) 2 (3)
(Logistics) (3)
(Merchant Marine Ship Administration) (3)
Culture (Bolian) 2 (3)
Diplomacy (Commercial Treaties) 1 (2)
(Ferengi) (2)
History (Bolian) 1 (2)
Language
Bolian 2
Federation Standard 1
Ferengi 2
Law (Federation Merchant Marine Regulations) 1 (2)
(Ferengi Rules of Acquisition) (2)
Merchant (Dilithium Market) 2 (3)
(Ferengi Markets) (3)
Personal Equipment (PADD) 1 (2)
Persuasion (Debate) 2 (3)
Physical Science (Material Science) 1 (2)
Social Science (Economics) 1 (2)
Vehicle Operations (Shuttlecraft) 1 (2)
World Knowledge (Bolarus IX) 1 (2)
(Ferengi Space) (2)
Advantages/Disadvantages
Ally +1
Contact(s) (3 points' worth)
Multitasking +2
Courage: 3
Renown: 1

Skill 1

STEPPING UP

Once a character has established an appropriately meritorious record in the Federation Merchant Marine, he may apply for admission to Starfleet. Whether he is accepted is up to the Narrator, of course; the decision should be based on what's best for the series. However, at a minimum the character must satisfy these standards:

— A minimum skill level of 3 in the character's "primary" skill (the one he will pursue as part of Starfleet, such as Propulsion Engineering for some Engineers), plus a minimum skill level of 1 in two skills related to that skill or proposed career in Starfleet.

— A minimum Renown of 15, 10 of it in Starfleet-favored Aspects. (This indicates an "appropriately meritorious record," as mentioned above.)

— Enough saved Experience Points to buy the following skills, if the character does not already possess them: Energy Weapon (Phaser) 1 (2), History (Federation) 1 (2), Planetside Survival (any Specialization) 1 (2), and Law (Starfleet Regulations) 1 (2). These Specializations may be bought as such if the character already knows the base skill. This represents an accelerated nine-month training program at Starfleet Academy. Narrators may wish to make this course part of the series, or simply cut to graduation day and the character's first posting.

THE FEDERATION MERCHANT MARINE IN A STARFLEET SERIES

The most common use for the Federation Merchant Marine is as an element or aspect of an existing *Star Trek: The Next Generation* Role Playing Game series, one based on the adventures of a Crew of Starfleet personnel based on a particular ship. The Merchant Marine typically serves one of several roles in such a series.

First, Merchant Marine personnel can take a common supporting cast role: victims to be assisted or rescued. Somehow they get themselves into a situation where they need help (such as an escort), or they're in danger (or maybe just in some kind of trouble) and Starfleet has to get them out of it. This can range from relatively comedic situations (a Merchant Marine ship which has accidentally picked up a load of tribbles, or one run by Pakleds) to deadly danger (a Merchant Marine ship which has lost power and is about to crash into a planet, or with a crew suffering from a virulent disease). In any case, it's up to the Crew and their ship to rescue the hapless Merchant Marines.

Second, the situation can be reversed—the Starfleet ship or Crew is in trouble and the Merchant Marine has to help them out. This may not necessarily be very pleasant for the Crew, since Starfleet ships usually do the rescuing rather than the reverse, but any port in a storm, after all. A clever Narrator may even be able to have some fun building up a bit of a friendly rivalry between the Crew and the sailors on the Merchant Marine vessel.

Third, a Merchant Marine ship may serve as a source of new crewmen for the series' normal starship—maybe even some new Crew members. A player who's tired of the usual run-of-the-mill character types might enjoy creating a character who has "stepped up" from a Merchant Marine ship. Similarly, the Narrator might enjoy roleplaying a former Merchant Marine NPC as he adapts to Starfleet rules, regulations, and standards while at the same time bringing a fresh, "unorthodox" perspective to the Crew's problems.

Regardless of how the Merchant Marine is used in the series, the Narrator should remember to maintain a "human touch." *Star Trek* is, in large part, about the human condition and how people interact with other people and species, and the differences between standard Starfleet characters and

Merchant Marine characters can help cast a spotlight on this aspect of the series. Love, rivalry, friendship, or envy between the characters of the two types of ships can give rise to many interesting episodes.

EPISODE SEEDS

Here are a few suggested plots for episodes featuring the Merchant Marine in a standard *Star Trek: The Next Generation Role Playing Game* series:

• *Matters of the Heart*: While on shore leave on Risa, the captain of the Crew's starship meets and becomes attracted to a Command officer on a Merchant Marine vessel. This results in increased contact between the two ships. However, during a crisis in which the Merchant Marine vessel is endangered, the Crew may have to question whether their captain is acting rationally when he orders extremely dangerous rescue measures in the hopes of saving his significant other's ship.

• *The Ties That Bind*: A Merchant Marine cargo freighter becomes caught in the gravitational well of a cosmic string fragment. The Crew's vessel, when it responds to the emergency, becomes trapped itself (perhaps due to a panicked reaction on the part of a Merchant Marine sailor). The crews of both ships must work together to determine a way to break free from the string's effect—and then to determine why the string suddenly appeared in the middle of a well-traveled trade route. The entire situation is complicated by a relationship many years ago between a Crew member and a high-ranking officer on the Merchant Marine vessel which ended badly, causing some strain between them.

• *Shadow War*: The Crew's ship is assigned to escort a Merchant Marine vessel through dangerous territory to resupply an important outpost or colony. Along the way the Crew detects subspace burst transmissions from the Merchant Marine ship which its crew denies making. A short time later, an enemy (pirates, raiders, or a threat race) attacks the convoy in an effort to steal or destroy the freighter's cargo. The Crew manages to beat off the attack, but both ships suffer severe damage in the process. Then the Crew picks up another burst transmission. Both ships' crews must race to effect repairs and uncover the traitor whose transmissions draw the enemy to them before more attackers arrive.

• *Pirouette*: A Merchant Marine vessel carrying a large number of passengers is taken over by terrorists (or some similar threat) who take the other passengers (and most of the crew) hostage. They threaten to kill the hostages unless their demands are met. The Crew must initiate a dialogue with the terrorists while simultaneously secretly contacting the Merchant Marine sailors who evaded capture, rendezvousing with them to strike at the terrorists, and freeing the ship. Complicating the matter is the fact that one or more Crew members have relatives among the hostages.

• *Full Contact*: The Crew and some tough-talking Merchant Marine sailors compete in an athletic contest while on shore leave at Starbase 82. (The Narrator should choose a contest which at least some Crew members are skilled at, but not all.) The sailors manage to win—barely—and then proceed to brag about their "great victory" all over the Starbase. A few days later, after both ships are back in space, the Crew's ship receives a distress call from the sailors' ship, which has been badly damaged by some odd stellar phenomena and is in danger of destruction. The Crew must put aside their dislike of the sailors and help rescue their ship, teaching the sailors a valuable lesson and turning them into friends instead of rivals.

• *Selling Short*: A Merchant Marine crew and vessel go rogue, leaving Federation space to become for-profit traders in the backwaters of the galaxy (or perhaps in Gamma Quadrant via the Bajoran wormhole). The Crew must pursue the ship and bring it back. One member of the Crew, who used to be good friends with a high-ranking officer on the Merchant Marine vessel, is extremely puzzled by the sailors' behavior. This should lead to an investigation which shows that the Merchant Marine crew has been taken over by some sort of strange, and possibly hostile, alien species which wants to use the ship and crew for its own ends.

THE FEDERATION MERCHANT MARINE SERIES

Instead of working the Merchant Marine into an existing series, a Narrator in search of something new or different may actually base a whole series around a Merchant Marine vessel. The Crew in this case would take the roles of the leading officers (or most interesting personnel) aboard a Merchant Marine ship.

A CHANGE OF PACE

A Merchant Marine series is similar to a regular Starfleet series in some ways, but very different in others. The main similarity is that both involve extensive travel through space. Both types of ships traverse the space lanes, seeking the next star or other destination. The difference, of course, is the nature of the missions they undertake. While Starfleet explores, assists in emergencies, and defends the Federation, the Merchant Marine is engaged in commerce and trade. Usually its routes are relatively predetermined and its missions are dictated by the Federation. However, some Merchant Marine ships have greater leeway and act more like private merchants—they go wherever they feel they can acquire goods they need or want instead of sticking to predefined routes and cargoes. This latter type of Merchant Marine vessel is most likely to appeal to the Narrator as a series vehicle, since it gives the Crew a lot more freedom to go where it wants—and thus to encounter the latest adventure or threat which the Narrator has prepared for them.

Another important difference is the outlook of the respective Crews. Starfleet Crews, bound by the occasionally rigid rules and regulations of Starfleet, must uphold Starfleet ideals. Merchant Marine sailors, as loyal citizens of the Federation, abide by the Prime Directive and other important principles (such as rescuing ships in distress), but outside emergency duty they're not as restricted by regulations as Starfleet. They're a lot more easygoing, in a sense. This provides the Narrator with a little bit of an opportunity to explore some of the darker sides of the Federation—the renegades, rogues, nomadic merchants, and scam artists who live mainly on the outskirts of Federation space.

A Merchant Marine ship might also secretly be used by Starfleet to spy out opposition or extend "feelers" for the Federation in situations where bringing in a Starfleet vessel would only heighten tensions or cause problems.

Merchant Marine vessels also report anything odd in the course of their travels to Starfleet. Merchant Marine vessels became an important part of the Federation-wide search for Borg intruders after 2366, for example. Some Merchant Marine captains come to prefer seeking out anomalies for Starfleet to the tedium of convoy duty. Often, Merchant Marine ships that provide useful information or intelligence get better assignments from the Federation in the future—and their officers find promotion comes faster, as well.

It's also important for the Narrator to remember that the Crew of a Merchant Marine vessel is not likely to have the breadth and depth of skills which a Starship crew will have. Most of them may not know how to use a phaser, for example. This has its drawbacks, since the Narrator can't count on the Crew being able to deal with some situations, but it also has benefits. First, it gives the Crew room to grow and learn new things. Second, it allows the Narrator to put the Crew in situations where the players' ability to think through problems and roleplay becomes more important than the skills on their characters' sheets.

SERIES STRUCTURE

Superficially, the structure of a Merchant Marine series and episodes is just like that of a regular Starfleet series. The characters are the Crew of a ship. They travel through space, encountering new phenomena, threats, and events in each episode which they must cope with in an appropriate fashion. However, the Narrator should take the differences between the two types of series into account when planning a game.

Even the most freewheeling Merchant Marine vessel isn't likely to encounter as many threats as a Starfleet ship. Merchant Marine vessels are often assigned to preexisting trade routes, or to sectors which they cannot normally leave. This means the Narrator has to be prepared for adventures focusing on the two aspects of the series which don't change: the Crew; and the ship's assigned sector or route (or be prepared to change them repeatedly for good reason).

Before the game begins, the Narrator should have copies of all of the Merchant Marine Crew's character sheets so that he can begin to build episodes around their personalities and backgrounds. If the players can be persuaded to write out detailed histories for their characters, so much the better—that's even more material for the Narrator to work with. With just a little bit of effort the Narrator can build up a stock of "episode seeds" which revolve primarily around the characters and their histories and interrelationships.

Then the Narrator should spend some time preparing a description (for himself, if not the players) of the trade routes or sectors which the Crew's vessel frequents. Since this is the other constant in the campaign, use it. Put a generous scattering of inhabited planets, strange uninhabited planets (or similar phenomena, like asteroid belts), stellar events, starbases and outposts, and maybe even unexplored (or casually explored) space. This provides plenty of places for the Crew to have encounters and meet new people, and for the Narrator to spring threats upon them. Imagine, if you will, a trade route which takes the Crew by Risa every couple of months, or a sector which includes a suspicious asteroid belt where Breen raiders or Romulan spies may hide.

EPISODE SEEDS

With those two bits of planning out of the way, the Narrator should have an excellent framework around which to base a Merchant Marine campaign, as well as more than a few episode seeds. Here are a few more seeds to get you started:

• *Invaders*: The Crew's ship receives a distress call from a relatively young colony. They get there and beam down to discover that there's a medical emergency—and now they're infected, too! They have to work with the colony's small medical staff to find out what's happening and locate a cure. It turns out that the problem results from a civilization of microscopic organisms (who communicate and even think by psionic gestalt) which precolonization scans did not detect. The microorganisms regard the colonists as invaders, and have returned the favor by invading and infecting their bodies. Once the lines of communication are opened, the two races can figure out a way to live in peace.

• *Just in Time*: The Crew's vessel encounters an uncharted temporal anomaly which throws them back to 20th-century Earth. Lacking the advanced scientific facilities and training of Starfleet, the Crew will have to be very clever to figure out a way home without alerting the primitive humans to their existence or reason for being there. A more mercenary Crew might even try to get some amusing souvenirs for trade back in the future.

• *Food Fight*: A semihumorous episode in which tribbles infest the Crew's ship and eat most of the food, damaging the replicators in the process. After coping with the tribbles, the Crew must deal with the passengers, who stage a "revolt" for more food and other amenities. The Crew has to placate them without breaking into the ship's cargo stores.

• *Enemy Unseen*: A cargo taken on by the Crew proves to be not what it was represented to be. In fact, it's something much more dangerous, a substance which gives off waves of psychotropic energy which cause the Crew to experience hallucinations. The Crew has to solve the mystery and figure out how to get rid of the cargo without damaging the ship or themselves.

• *Jolly Roger*: What's a Merchant Marine series without some pirates and raiders? A clever Narrator should be able to come up with plenty of twists on this theme, such as Ferengi pirates who aren't as interested in stealing the ship's cargo as they are in forcing the Crew to buy or barter for their cargo.

Starfleet

The Federation Constitution provides for a fleet of ships, with the mandate to seek out new life forms and new civilizations. The signatories understood that by combining their resources and efforts, they could explore more of the universe. A combination deep-space exploration agency, diplomatic corps, and defense force, Starfleet is perhaps the Federation's greatest monument, a symbol of the UFP's strength and ideals. Citizens of over 150 member planets stand side by side, united in a desire to go where no one has gone before, to unlock the galaxy's secrets, to push the boundaries of sapient understanding. Starfleet trains its personnel not only to execute their exacting duties under the most adverse conditions, but also to serve as examples for the rest of the citizenry and to use that role responsibly. The allure of adventure encapsulated in Starfleet's motto ("To boldly go where no one has gone before"), combined with extremely selective entrance requirements, ensure that Starfleet welcomes only the Federation's best, boldest, and brightest into its ranks. As a result, across its two-hundred-year history, Starfleet has produced far more than its share of legends, including a number of men and women who have single-handedly shaped the destiny of the Federation.

In fact, to much of the galaxy, Starfleet is the Federation—its officers and agencies are the UFP's only real representatives across huge swaths of space, both inside and outside Federation borders. Starfleet personnel bear a heavy responsibility, protecting the fringe colonies against pirates and raiders, delivering critical medical supplies to remote outposts, intervening to prevent astronomical catastrophes, making first contact with newly discovered species, and negotiating important treaties with alien governments.

STARFLEET AND THE FEDERATION

Starfleet serves as an arm of the Federation, enacting Federation policy, whether a mandate to explore space or defend against attack. While Starfleet sees itself as primarily an organization dedicated to exploration and diplomacy, it follows a military structure. Harkening back to the grand naval traditions of many worlds, notably Earth's, Starfleet employs military ranks and organization in its operations. However, the framers of the UFP Constitution placed Starfleet under civilian control, mandating it answer to the Federation Council in full accord with traditional democratic principles.

Ultimately, the whole of Starfleet answers to the Federation President, who in turn answers to the Council. The UFP Constitution clearly appoints the President to act as Starfleet's Commander-in-Chief. This role gives the President complete authority over all of Starfleet's activities: ship deployments, exploratory missions, starbase and deep space commands, etc. The Federation Council has the responsibility to declare war, while the President has the power to deploy the fleet. In practice, the President defers to the advice of qualified Starfleet officers, notably the Joint Chiefs, and does not meddle in the fleet's daily operations. As with other Federation departments, Starfleet officers are ultimately answerable to the Federation Council. For more information on the relationship between Starfleet, the Federation President, and the Council, see chapter two, "UFP Structure & Government."

STARFLEET HEADQUARTERS

The headquarters for Starfleet stand on a lush, four-hundred-twenty-acre facility, located just outside of San Francisco on planet Earth. Housed in several buildings, Starfleet Headquarters consists of offices for each of the Joint Chiefs, various departments and agencies, Starfleet's spacious strategy and status rooms, a host of research labs, the collected archives of Starfleet Intelligence, massive subspace transmitters and computers, and the command center for Earth's Planetary Defense Forces. A large spaceport handles the numerous shuttlecraft traveling to and from Starfleet Command. Starfleet Academy can be found to the east of Starfleet Command on its own, separate campus.

In all, some eight thousand personnel are stationed at Starfleet Command, most of whom work for the Intelligence Corps, the Communications Corps, or one of the agencies under the aegis of the Joint Chiefs. Additionally, the staffs of the various Joint Chiefs are all housed at Starfleet Command along with Starfleet Medical, the Center for Advanced Instruction, and various other agencies that make up the Starfleet bureaucracy. Although Starfleet maintains a few dormitories on the campus, most of the personnel stationed at Starfleet Headquarters live in and around San Francisco.

Among San Francisco's civilian population, Starfleet Headquarters is most famous for the Fosse Menagerie, an enormous zoo maintained by Starfleet and situated on a parcel of land adjoining the Starfleet Command campus. Open to the public, the Menagerie houses the most impressive collection of alien flora and fauna in Alpha Quadrant. Joining the thousands of tourists who visit the Menagerie each day are hundreds of scientists and researchers from across the Federation who study the unique lifeforms housed in the zoo. Among the Menagerie's most impressive attractions are a pair of Bardakian pronghorn moose, one of the few remaining Corvan gilvos, a pride of Kryonian tigers, a swarm of lynars, and a pod of deadly Denevan parasites. An impressive garden landscaped in the traditions of ancient Earth and Vulcan surrounds the Menagerie, serving as another favorite destination of tourists from across the Federation. By tradition, Starfleet officers hold their marriage ceremonies in this garden, though the rigors of duty often make this tradition difficult to uphold.

STARFLEET ORGANIZATION

With nearly 8,000 square light years and thousands of sectors, maintaining communication and organization across Federation space becomes an operational ordeal. An organization as large and far-flung as Starfleet requires a complex command structure capable of keeping everyone cooperating and working efficiently. To combat this problem, Starfleet maintains bases, outposts, and offices

throughout Federation space. Each department within the Starfleet bureaucracy has its own duties and responsibilities, and ultimately reports back to one of the five Joint Chiefs of Staff. Thanks to powerful computer systems and a complex web of subspace communications arrays, Starfleet can keep track of the entire organization, from tiny *Oberth*-class ships to entire fleets. While disputes between various agencies occur from time to time, they are relatively rare thanks to Starfleet's unparalleled leadership and superb communications infrastructure.

In all, there are hundreds of agencies, offices, and programs that comprise Starfleet—so many that it's unlikely that any single individual is aware of them all. Starfleet Command manages the entire organization from a cavernous room at the heart of main building. Ringed with giant display screens and staffed by dozens of officers, this command center allows Starfleet to supervise deployments and communicate with the fleet. Massive computers keep track of all information flowing into Starfleet, which can be called up at a moment's notice. Thus, the Chief-in-Command or any other admiral can quickly assess a situation as it develops. If an admiral needs to know where the *U.S.S. Enterprise* is currently deployed, for example, he need only ask one of the watch commanders to locate it on a starmap.

The key to smooth organization and rapid communication is clear lines of authority. Starfleet groups its vessels into a number of fleets, each commanded by a fleet admiral posted at a major starbase facility. When an order needs to be relayed to a particular ship, the appropriate agency contacts the fleet admiral at a particular starbase. The admiral then transmits the order to the appropriate captain. Communication from a starship or starbase to Starfleet Command works similarly. Upon discovering a new civilization, for example, a starship captain notifies his fleet admiral, who relays the information to Starfleet Command. There, the information is disseminated to the appropriate offices—the First Contact Division, Planetary Sciences office, and Fleet Operations, for example. Of course, Starfleet Command can communicate with a starship directly, if needed, and vice versa. But for routine operations, Starfleet prefers the use of the normal chain of command.

THE JOINT CHIEFS

Like other departments within the Federation, Starfleet is far too large for any one person to oversee directly, particularly someone with as many additional responsibilities as the Federation President. For the most part, Starfleet's day-to-day operations are conducted by a five-member panel known as the Joint Chiefs of Staff. Each of the five chiefs has his own sphere of authority. The Chief of Fleet Operations oversees fleet deployments, personnel assignments, and so forth. The Chief of Research and Exploration supervises Starfleet's scientific activity, technological investigations, and engineering activities. Starfleet's interplanetary initiatives, from first contact to diplomacy, are organized under the Chief of Interplanetary Affairs. The Chief of Strategic Operations is responsible for the Federation's overall strategic defense, coordinating with Fleet Operations to ensure adequate disposition. Overseeing and coordinating all of Starfleet's operations is the Chief-in-Command of Starfleet.

The Chiefs are chosen from among Starfleet's most capable and experienced officers. Whenever a vacancy exists among the Chiefs, the Federation President chooses a qualified candidate to fill the post. The Federation Council must ratify all appointments. Typically, a Chief is chosen from among Starfleet's most qualified admirals. The Federation's Security Council often requests a briefing from the Joint Chiefs on military matters.

All Starfleet operations are decided in meetings of the Joint Chiefs. Each office brings its concerns and requirements to the meeting, for discussion. If Strategic Operations believes there is a need for additional starships, the Chief makes his request at a meeting of the Joint Chiefs. There, the other members discuss the relative merits of the request. Starfleet Medical may need a starship to transport a vaccine to a colony, while Exploration requires a ship in the same sector to explore a T Tauri star; the Joint Chiefs together prioritize such requests. Once a decision has been made, the Chief-in-Command enforces the committee's decisions.

STARFLEET AGENCIES

Starfleet is organized into a number of offices, departments, and agencies to supervise its numerous operations. Each level of the bureaucracy reports up the organizational chain to its immediate superior. Using these descriptions as illustrations, Narrators should find it easy to create new agencies when necessary to fill holes in adventures and campaigns, and easy to place these agencies appropriately within Starfleet's overall structure.

Starfleet Command and its organization could come up in a *Star Trek: The Next Generation RPG* session in several ways. First, the visiting expert story is a staple of the *TNG* series. A visiting expert arrives on the ship for some reason—to research a particular topic, to travel to a planet for negotiations, to inspect the ship and her crew, etc. Of course, because these individuals work so close to headquarters, they're a bit more "spit and polish." Commander Shelby, from "Best of Both Worlds" [TNG], makes a good example, as does Sirna Kolrami from "Peak Performance" [TNG]. These episodes generally focus on the differences between the people in the field and those back at headquarters, though this need not be the only theme. A Crew member could fall in love with someone bound for duty back on Earth, or the officer could bring a needed skill that the Crew lacks.

The second way to use Starfleet Command is to post temporarily some or all of the Crew to duty back on Earth. Perhaps some emergency requires the Crew's special talents, and now they have to learn to work within an even more structured environment. Put them in charge of Earth security for awhile, or have them work on the design of a new starship at Utopia Planitia. If they had first contact with a new species, they might be asked to work with the First Contact Division to assess the planet. This makes a nice break from the typical starship adventure, and gives them a better sense of what Starfleet operations are like.

Finally, an entire series could focus on a particular department back at Starfleet headquarters. While this doesn't make for exciting roleplaying—who wants to play a game where everyone sits around pushing papers?—some agencies make for interesting stories. A group might be assigned to the Judge Advocate General's office, the players taking on the roles of intrepid investigators. Or they might receive a posting to Starfleet's Diplomatic Corps, responsible for negotiations with an Orion syndicate, the Klingon Empire, or the Tholians. It might be a refreshing change of pace to play the officials visiting a starship, perhaps getting in the way and stepping on some toes.

OFFICE OF THE CHIEF OF FLEET OPERATIONS

Headquartered at Starfleet Command on Earth, the Chief of Fleet Operations manages the operation and deployment of all the vessels in Starfleet. This includes assigning starships to a particular sector or fleet, personnel assignments, and appointing starships to fulfill missions requested by other Starfleet offices.

The Chief of Fleet Operations serves as liaison between the vessels that comprise the fleet and Starfleet's various agencies. Should the Office of Research and Exploration require a starship to examine a newly discovered star, the request is passed on to Fleet Operations, which in turn coordinates the mission with the Chief-in-Command. For the most part, Fleet Operations maintains a tactical focus—it doesn't decide what the fleet's starships should do, it decides how to accomplish the missions devised by other agencies. The CFO is responsible for maintaining the preparedness of the fleet as a whole and managing Starfleet's resources efficiently. Among the CFO's most important duties is to keep accurate records on every starship and crewman in the fleet. The Fleet Operations Central Records Office makes sure every vessel undergoes its regularly scheduled maintenance cycle and every crewman remains current in his training.

The current Chief of Fleet Operations, Admiral Yoshi Fukazima, maintains a personal staff of forty-seven officers (including his executive staff of six) at Starfleet Command. While most of these officers handle the numerous daily reports generated by managing such a large fleet of ships, several can be found inspecting the fleet (sometimes on a surprise basis). This is the most common way starship personnel interact with the CFO's office, during one of its meticulous inspection tours. An extremely capable officer, Fukazima is also noted for his sometimes extreme dedication to the regulations. When one of his inspection teams discovered a variance in the phase inducers in the warp drive of the U.S.S. LaSalle, he followed up personally.

ADMIRAL FUKAZIMA

DESPITE HIS FAMILY'S HISTORY OF STARFLEET SERVICE, ADMIRAL FUKAZIMA ROSE THROUGH THE RANKS FROM ENSIGN, NEVER CALLING ON ANY FAVORS OR RECEIVING SPECIAL TREATMENT. HIS FATHER COMMANDED A STARSHIP FOR FIFTEEN YEARS BEFORE RECEIVING A DESK POSTING BACK AT STARFLEET COMMAND, AND HIS MOTHER SERVED AS ASSISTANT TO THE THEN CHIEF OF FLEET OPERATIONS. FUKAZIMA LEARNED THE IMPORTANCE OF STRICT ADHERENCE TO REGULATIONS DURING HIS UPBRINGING. DESPITE HIS REPUTATION, HE MAINTAINS A FRIENDLY, COMFORTABLE ATMOSPHERE IN HIS OFFICE. ONE OF HIS FAVORITE EVENTS IS THE ANNUAL ADMIRAL'S BANQUET.

OFFICE OF THE EXECUTIVE ADMIRAL AND THE FLEET ADMIRALTIES

This office oversees the various admirals posted throughout Federation space. Because of the size of its operational theater, Starfleet organizes its vessels into twenty-seven separate fleets, each consisting of between five and twenty-five starships. Each fleet has a unique numerical designation (i.e., First Fleet, Second Fleet, Third Fleet, etc.), and is commanded by a fleet admiral. Assigned to a starbase, these fleet admirals oversee the disposition of the ships under their command, and serve as a vital linchpin in Starfleet's operational chain. Orders are communicated from Starfleet Command on Earth to the fleet admiral, and from him to the appropriate starship. Similarly, changes in a starship's assignment status—

if, for example, a vessel alters its course to investigate an emerging phenomenon—are relayed up the chain of command to Earth. Each fleet admiral reports to an officer known as the Executive Admiral, who in turn reports directly to the Chief of Fleet Operations. Typically, the Executive Admiral maintains a staff of fourteen experienced officers to help him issue fleet deployment orders, including an executive staff of four.

In the early days of Starfleet, fleet admirals took command of one of the vessels in their charge, known as the "flagship" of the fleet. Harkening back to ancient Earth naval tradition, the custom refers to an admiral flying his personal flag from his ship. Although most modern fleet commanders operate out of convenient starbases, the tradition of nominating a flagship continues. Today, "flagship" is a purely honorary title traditionally bestowed upon each fleet's top-performing vessel and crew. The Enterprise, for instance, is the flagship of Admiral Necheyev's Sixteenth Fleet. During the Borg invasion of 2369, however, Admiral Necheyev "flew her flag" from the U.S.S. Gorkon, taking command of the ship personally.

Starfleet further divides its fleets into one of two categories: standing fleets and mobile fleets. Standing fleets are permanently assigned to a single sector and perform missions only within that sector, such as patrol. Most of Starfleet's standing fleets hold defensive positions along the Romulan and Cardassian borders, though Earth, Vulcan, and a few other, strategic planets also have their own standing fleets. Mobile fleets, on the other hand, are continuously redeployed across the Federation to respond to a variety of situations. In this way, Starfleet attempts to keep potential adversaries guessing as to the precise disposition of the fleet while providing maximum maneuverability.

FLEET DEPLOYMENT

ASSIGNED TO SECTOR 001, THE FIRST FLEET SERVES AS THE LAST LINE OF DEFENSE FOR EARTH. ITS SHIPS PATROL THE ROUTE BETWEEN EARTH, VULCAN, AND ANDORIA. ADMIRAL WAGNER SERVES AS ITS CURRENT FLEET ADMIRAL. SMALLER, SPECIALIZED VESSELS COMPRISE THE FIRST FLEET, SUCH AS THE SABER CLASS, STEAMRUNNER CLASS, AND AKIRA CLASS.

THE 8TH FLEET (MOBILE), UNDER THE COMMAND OF ADMIRAL ANKORA, AN ANDORIAN, EXPLORES UNCHARTED REGIONS OF ALPHA QUADRANT. ADMIRAL ANKORA COMMANDS THIS FLEET FROM STARBASE 201. THE FLAGSHIP OF THIS FLEET IS THE U.S.S. YAMATO, WITH THE REST OF THE FLEET MADE UP OF OLDER AMBASSADOR-CLASS AND NEWER NEBULA-CLASS STARSHIPS.

ELEMENTS OF THE 4TH, 5TH, AND 7TH FLEETS MASSED AT WOLF 359 FOR THE DISASTROUS BATTLE WITH THE BORG. THE 7TH FLEET, UNDER THE COMMAND OF ADMIRAL VAYOS, IS ASSIGNED TO PROTECT BETAZED, WHILE THE 4TH FLEET SERVES AS A MOBILE FLEET PATROLLING THE FEDERATION'S CORE WORLDS. THE 5TH FLEET PATROLS THE ANDORIAN SECTOR.

THE U.S.S. ENTERPRISE-D IS PART OF ADMIRAL NECHEYEV'S 16TH FLEET (MOBILE). THESE SHIPS ARE ROUTINELY SENT TO PERFORM DIPLOMATIC AND EXPLORATORY ASSIGNMENTS ALONG THE FEDERATION'S BORDERS WITH THE CARDASSIANS, KLINGONS, AND ROMULANS. ADMIRAL NECHEYEV COMMANDS HER FLEET FROM STARBASE 310.

THE 20TH FLEET PATROLS THE RIMWARD REGIONS OF FEDERATION SPACE. BECAUSE THE REGION IS RELATIVELY EMPTY, THESE SHIPS TEND TO BE OLDER — SUCH AS THE AMBASSADOR AND EXCELSIOR CLASSES — AND SEE LITTLE ACTION. SHIPS OF THE 20TH FLEET PARTICIPATED IN THE BLOCKADE OF KLINGON SPACE DURING THE KLINGON CIVIL WAR.

SHIPS OF THE 22ND FLEET, COMMANDED BY ADMIRAL J. P. HANSON, SERVE AS THE FIRST LINE OF DEFENSE AGAINST THE ROMULANS AND BORG. A STATIC FLEET, THEY PATROL ALONG THE ROMULAN NEUTRAL ZONE. THE FLEET CONSISTS OF AMBASSADOR-, NEBULA-, AND INTREPID-CLASS VESSELS.

In addition to the twenty-seven standing and mobile fleets, Starfleet maintains several specialized fleet classifications to handle particular missions. It is not uncommon for Starfleet Command to assemble ad hoc fleets (composed of vessels from various standing and mobile fleets) to complete special assignments.

•*Colonization Fleet:* This collection of thirty-four vessels contains the necessary equipment for conducting complex terraforming missions, as well as all the transports necessary to establish a colony of one hundred thousand individuals. Although most Federation colonies begin on a much smaller scale under the aegis of private citizens, the colonization fleet is deployed to assist the governments of Federation member worlds in establishing large, official, incorporated outposts.

•*Evacuation Fleets:* There are three evacuation fleets stationed at strategic points within the Federation, each consisting of between ten and eighteen vessels. The evacuation fleets are used to house millions of citizens temporarily when their planet, moon, or colony is threatened by an unavoidable natural disaster. The 26th Fleet (Mobile) is one such fleet, and consists primarily of *Excelsior*-class ships.

•*Rapid Response Fleets:* The rapid response fleet is a new and relatively controversial addition to Starfleet. Combining the flexibility of a mobile fleet with the stability of a static fleet, the ships assigned to rapid response are expected to be the first vessels to respond to a crisis in a remote locale, whether the crisis is a military situation, a natural catastrophe, or a civil defense emergency. The brainchild of Admiral Fukazima, each fleet remains stationed in a strategic sector of space, waiting to respond to an emerging crisis. Each ship—one of the Federation's new *Steamrunner*- or *Akira*-class vessels—reports directly to the Executive Admiral, and thus circumvents the usual chain of command. Fukazima launched the rapid response program in the wake of the Borg invasion, the Klingon Civil war, and the attempted Romulan invasion of Vulcan (all which took place within the span of two years). Among the various controversial powers granted to the rapid response commanders are the option to escalate to the use of force much more quickly than the average starship captain and wider latitude in the interpretation of various Starfleet regulations. One particularly vocal critic of the rapid response philosophy is the starship *Enterprise* First Officer William T. Riker, who turned down an opportunity to command one of the cruisers.

STANDING AND MOBILE FLEETS

THE CONCEPTS OF STANDING AND MOBILE FLEETS PROVIDE STAR TREK: THE NEXT GENERATION RPG NARRATORS WITH MAXIMUM FLEXIBILITY WHEN DESIGNING THEIR CAMPAIGNS. STATIONING YOUR PC'S ABOARD A VESSEL ATTACHED TO A STANDING FLEET ALLOWS YOU TO DEVELOP THE INHABITANTS AND WORLDS OF A PARTICULAR SECTOR IN GREAT DETAIL. YOU CAN RUN DETAILED, CONTINUING STORYLINES REVOLVING AROUND THE POLITICAL RELATIONSHIP BETWEEN TWO NEIGHBORING PLANETS, EXTENDED CONFRONTATIONS WITH ONE OF THE FEDERATION'S MAIN ADVERSARIES, OR A LENGTHY PURSUIT OF A BAND OF FUGITIVES ACROSS AN ENTIRE SPACE SECTOR. THE FRAGILE PEACE CAMPAIGN BOOK IS A GOOD EXAMPLE OF THE BENEFITS OF MAKING THE CREW'S SHIP PART OF A STANDING FLEET.

A MOBILE FLEET, HOWEVER, ALLOWS YOU TO SET YOUR STORIES ALL OVER THE FEDERATION AND BEYOND. AS A SHIP ASSIGNED SIMPLY TO TRAVEL THE GALAXY, YOUR CREW CAN ENCOUNTER A WIDE VARIETY OF ALIENS, ADVERSARIES, AND SITUATIONS. YOU SHOULD CHOOSE THIS OPTION IF YOU'D LIKE YOUR SERIES TO UNFOLD ALONG THE LINES OF THE STAR TREK: THE NEXT GENERATION TELEVISION SERIES.

OFFICE OF STARBASE OPERATIONS

The Office of Starbase Operations oversees the administration of Starfleet's numerous starbases, deep space stations, long-range sensor arrays, and monitor stations. This office reviews the need for Starfleet facilities in a particular area, depending on a number of factors such as Starfleet's overall needs and the feasibility of maintaining such an operation. The Office of Starbase Command reports to the Chief of Fleet Operations, and its headquarters orbit Earth on Starbase 1.

When hearing mention of Starfleet, most people (both Federation citizens and aliens) think of impressive ships traveling faster than light. They forget about the numerous orbital and planetary facilities that

allow those starships to operate far beyond their operational means, much as military bases allowed the old United States to deploy its resources around the Earth. Starbases allow the Federation to project its influence in the same way as starships.

In addition to providing support to starships, however, starbases provide a host of other benefits. Officers detailed to the Astronomical Science Services train starbase long-range sensors on various astronomical phenomena. Planetary Survey scientists supervise various expeditions and relay their reports back to Starfleet Command. Starfleet Intelligence personnel staff starbases and monitor stations to conduct long-range reconnaissance on potential threats. Starbases serve as home to various attachés belonging to the Starfleet Diplomatic Corps, who represent the Federation both to indigenous populations and throughout the sector. Frequently, the best medical care can be found at a starbase. Even the Starfleet Marines utilize starbases as forward outposts. Coordinating all of these activities is the Office of Starbase Operations.

OFFICE OF THE JUDGE ADVOCATE GENERAL

Under the jurisdiction of the Chief of Fleet Operations, the Office of Judge Advocate General enforces all administrative law within the ranks of Starfleet. The JAG carries out investigations of wrongdoing by Starfleet officers and convenes courts martial when necessary. Although the Judge Advocate General herself is headquartered at Starfleet Command, the JAG maintains offices on all major starbases. Any incident requiring the intervention of the JAG is referred to the nearest local office, though extremely important cases or those involving high-ranking officers are often pulled back to Starfleet Command for the JAG's personal attention.

In addition to upholding Starfleet's Uniform Code of Justice, the JAG investigates and prosecutes cases involving violations of Starfleet's General Orders, the Constitution of the United Federation of Planets, and the laws of Federation member worlds. The Judge Advocate General's office has jurisdiction over any member of Starfleet accused of wrongdoing, even if the violation occurred under local law. Normally, on a member planet, local authorities remand the accused officer to Starfleet's custody, and the officer is tried under the Uniform Code of Justice. On a nonaligned planet, however, this is largely a question of custody; once in an alien jail, it is within the planet's rights to try the accused. Starfleet, however, works hard to convince the planet's government to surrender the accused for court martial proceedings. This isn't always successful, and more than one officer has faced trial on an alien world, under unfamiliar (and sometimes poorly understood) laws. Often, in the case of laws broken on a nonmember world, the JAG office will invite a representative of the local government to observe, or even present evidence.

The current Judge Advocate General is Admiral Phillipa Louvois. After unsuccessfully prosecuting Captain Jean-Luc Picard following the loss of the

U.S.S. *Stargazer*, then-Captain Louvois left Starfleet. Later, she returned to head the JAG office in Sector 23, where she presided over the famous case which determined Data's status as a lifeform and not as Starfleet's property. That difficult case propelled her to a posting at Starfleet Command, and eventually to the position of Starfleet's Judge Advocate General.

> ### JAG OFFICER—COMMAND
>
> SERVING UNDER THE JUDGE ADVOCATE GENERAL, JAG OFFICERS ARE THE LAWYERS AND SLEUTHS OF THE JAG CORPS. AS AGENTS FOR THE PROSECUTION AND DEFENSE, THEY MUST CONDUCT INQUIRIES, TAKE DEPOSITIONS, INTERVIEW WITNESSES, AND GENERALLY PLAY SHERLOCK HOLMES. IT'S IMPORTANT TO REMEMBER, HOWEVER, THAT THE INVESTIGATION BY AN OFFICER WORKING FOR THE DEFENSE WILL TAKE A MUCH DIFFERENT ROUTE THAN THAT OF ONE WORKING FOR THE PROSECUTION. BOTH, HOWEVER, MUST HAVE EXTENSIVE KNOWLEDGE OF TRIAL LAW.
>
> LAW (STARFLEET REGULATIONS AND CHOOSE SECOND SPECIALIZATION) 2 (3) AND (3)
>
> COMPUTER (RESEARCH) 2 (3)
>
> HISTORY (FEDERATION) 1 (2)
>
> PERSUASION (DEBATE AND ORATORY) 2 (3) AND (3)
>
> INTIMIDATION (INTERROGATION) 2 (3)
>
> ATHLETICS (CHOOSE SPECIALIZATION) 1 (2)
>
> DODGE 1
>
> ENERGY WEAPON (PHASER) 1 (2)
>
> LANGUAGE
>   FEDERATION STANDARD 1
>
> PERSONAL EQUIPMENT (TRICORDER) 1 (2)
>
> PLANETSIDE SURVIVAL (CHOOSE SPECIALIZATION) 1 (2)
>
> SEARCH 1
>
> VEHICLE OPERATIONS (SHUTTLECRAFT) 1 (2)
>
> PROMOTION — LIEUTENANT (J.G.) +1

JAG INVESTIGATIONS

Characters from the JAG office will most often appear in a series as special guest stars, investigating some error or reviewing an incident for potential wrongdoing. If your group wants to play a campaign centered on the JAG Corps, they should be posted to the JAG office on a particular starbase, and travel around the sector as needed. This need not be limited to Command officers; Operations and Science officer may be needed to assist in the investigation. If, for example, a crewman dies inexplicably in a sensor pod ("*Court Martial*" [Star Trek]) or a nacelle's warp field coils ("*Eye of the Beholder*" [*TNG*]), and the JAG Corps looks into the matter, an Engineer would be necessary to examine the potentially faulty equipment. This could lead to charges of negligence or murder, depending on the circumstances. Overall, this type of series does not have the range of adventure as one based on a starship, though it makes a nice change of pace for a night's play.

Most JAG offices retain several highly trained investigators to inquire into wrongdoing, or possible wrongdoing. Typically, these investigators travel with their own security teams, and standard protocol calls for a starship captain (or starbase commander) to put the ship's (or base's) security forces at a visiting investigator's disposal. Their task is to gather facts and evidence and determine if a court martial is warranted. JAG investigations continue until the case is solved, or no clear determination can be made (at which point the file is left open until new evidence may be brought to light). Although all Starfleet captains can call for a JAG investigation of personnel under their command, most ranking officers prefer to conduct their own inquiries and submit their own subordinates for court martial. Normally, JAG investigators become involved in a case only when a member of Starfleet is accused of wrongdoing by someone outside of his chain of command. If no JAG officer is available to conduct an investigation, it falls to the highest ranking officer to appoint an investigator—normally the ship's Security Chief.

Starfleet personnel who show particular aptitude in law, or who attended law school on their homeworlds, are frequently tapped to serve in the JAG Corps for at least one tour of duty. This is not restricted to those with a legal bent, however. The JAG office requires officers with a nose for the truth and an unswerving devotion to the principles, rules, and regulations that govern Starfleet. Security officers, science officers, or other experts in the field could find themselves detailed to the JAG Corps for a particular investigation. The Center for Advanced Training provides classes to those who desire legal training, most notably those Command personnel aiming for promotion to Starfleet's upper echelons.

COURTS MARTIAL

Although most infractions can be handled through less severe reprimands, or short incarceration in a brig, some crimes are so severe as to warrant a court martial. A court martial is a trial under Starfleet's Uniform Code of Justice, as opposed to Federation civilian law, and is conducted by a committee of officers.

Any officer of the rank of Captain or higher can submit a subordinate officer for immediate court martial (though frivolously abusing this right is itself a court martial offense). Officers of the Judge Advocate General's office have the power to submit any member of Starfleet for court martial, as long as they first submit an approved finding to a JAG officer of the rank of Captain or higher. Once it has been called, a court martial is typically convened within seventy-two hours. As part of the formal order of court martial, the presiding representative of the JAG's office nominates both a prosecuting advocate and an advocate for the defense. Typically, both advocates are officers from the local JAG office. If no suitable JAG advocates are available, however, the JAG representative can nominate any available Starfleet officers as ad hoc advocates. The accused always has the right to refuse the nominated defense advocate and either serve as his own lawyer or appoint an eligible officer of his choice.

A panel of three judges presides over a court martial proceeding, usually officers from the JAG office. If none are available, the JAG office typically appoints an ad hoc judge—the fleet admiral for the sector. Only officers ranked Commander or higher can serve as judges, and no officer with an obvious conflict of interest, such as friendship, is allowed to serve. If possible the JAG representative who signs the order for court martial appoints a full three-judge panel.

Procedurally, a court martial is handled very much like a civilian criminal trial. Both sides make opening statements, the prosecution presents its witnesses and evidence, the defense presents its case, and both sides make closing arguments. Each side has the right to cross-examine the witnesses presented by the other side, and almost all the rules of evidence and courtroom procedure applicable to civilian trials apply

CRIME AND PUNISHMENT

A COMPLETE LIST OF ALL STARFLEET'S REGULATIONS AND THE PENALTIES FOR BREAKING THOSE REGULATIONS IS BEYOND THE SCOPE OF ANY SOURCEBOOK. FOR THE MOST PART, VIOLATIONS OF STARFLEET REGULATIONS ARE FAIRLY OBVIOUS, SUCH AS INSUBORDINATION, GROSS NEGLIGENCE, INFRACTIONS OF THE RULES, CAPITAL CRIMES LIKE MURDER, ETC. SIMILARLY, YOU CAN ASSUME THAT A CRIMINAL OFFENSE ON 20TH-CENTURY EARTH IS PROBABLY A VIOLATION OF THE UNIFORM CODE OF JUSTICE AS WELL.

THE PENALTIES IMPOSED BY COURT MARTIAL VARY WITH THE SERIOUSNESS OF THE OFFENSE, BUT RANGE ANYWHERE FROM IMMEDIATE DISCHARGE FROM STARFLEET TO PRISON TIME AT ONE OF STARFLEET'S PENAL SETTLEMENTS. THE FEDERATION CONSTITUTION FORBIDS THE USE OF CAPITAL PUNISHMENT, THOUGH STARFLEET DID NOT ABOLISH THE PRACTICE UNTIL THE MID-23RD CENTURY. (FOR A TIME, VISITING TALOS IV WARRANTED THE DEATH PENALTY.) THE MOST SERIOUS PUNISHMENT A COURT MARTIAL CAN DISH OUT IN THE 24TH CENTURY IS LIFE IMPRISONMENT.

equally to courts martial. Unlike civilian trials, however, court martial proceedings do not employ juries; guilt or innocence is determined by the panel of judges. Courts martial tend to be less formal affairs, moving along at a much faster pace than a civilian trial, and rarely take more than a week to complete.

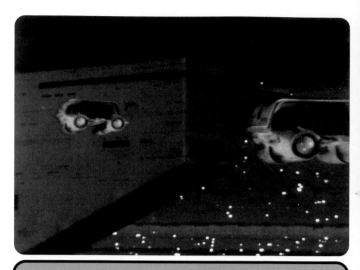

COURTS MARTIAL AND ADVENTURES

THE "COURT MARTIAL EPISODE" IS A STAPLE OF THE VARIOUS *STAR TREK* TELEVISION SERIES (SEE "*COURT MARTIAL*" [*STAR TREK*] FOR A GOOD EXAMPLE), AND AN OCCASIONAL EPISODE BASED AROUND A COURT MARTIAL MIGHT SPICE UP YOUR *STAR TREK: TNG RPG* SERIES. NATURALLY, FIRST YOU NEED A CRIME OF SOME SORT, COMMITTED BY EITHER AN NPC (LIKE THE SHIP'S CAPTAIN) OR ONE OF THE CREW. THE LATTER CAN BE DIFFICULT TO ORCHESTRATE, SINCE THE PLAYER HAS TO HAVE HIS CHARACTER DO SOMETHING ILLEGAL. THAT DOESN'T HAVE TO BE AS DIFFICULT AS IT SOUNDS; PLAYERS FREQUENTLY HAVE THEIR CHARACTERS "BEND" THE REGULATIONS, LIKE SHOOTING FIRST AND ASKING QUESTIONS LATER. SIMPLY WATCH THE PLAYERS FOR ANY VIOLATIONS, AND THEN SIC A JAG INVESTIGATOR ON THEIR CHARACTERS. SIMILARLY, POSSESSION BY AN ALIEN INTELLIGENCE WORKS WELL, AS IN THE *STAR TREK* EPISODE "*A WOLF IN THE FOLD*," BUT BE SURE TO DISCUSS THIS WITH THE PLAYER FIRST. ALWAYS REMEMBER, IF THE COURT MARTIAL DOESN'T FAVOR THE ACCUSED, HE COULD END UP IN PRISON FOR A LONG TIME. WHICH BRINGS US TO THE FINAL CONSIDERATION: BE SURE YOU HAVE AN "OUT" FOR THE COURT MARTIAL, SOME WAY THE OFFICER'S INNOCENCE CAN BE PROVED.

COURT MARTIAL STORIES GIVE YOU AN IDEAL OPPORTUNITY TO CONFRONT THE PLAYERS WITH A PUZZLE REQUIRING THEIR COOPERATION AND WITS TO SOLVE ("YES, BUT HOW ARE WE GOING TO PROVE YOU'RE INNOCENT!"). THEY'RE GREAT OPPORTUNITIES FOR PLENTY OF ENTERTAINING ROLEPLAYING, AS THE ACCUSED AND THE VARIOUS ADVOCATES GET PLENTY OF CHANCES TO MAKE DRAMATIC SPEECHES AND HEARTFELT PLEAS TO THE JUDGES. OBVIOUSLY, IF AT ALL POSSIBLE, YOU'LL WANT TO TAKE ADVANTAGE OF THE "AD HOC" PROVISION TO SEE THAT ONE OR MORE PLAYER CHARACTERS SERVE AS ADVOCATES.

COURT MARTIAL STORIES GENERALLY REQUIRE THE CREW TO MAKE LAW (STARFLEET REGULATIONS) AND PERSUASION (ORATORY) SKILL TESTS. THESE SHOULD BE OPPOSED TESTS AGAINST EACH JUDGE'S PERSUASION OR INTELLECT. AS ALWAYS IN THESE CASES, NARRATORS SHOULD RELY ON GOOD ROLEPLAYING RATHER THAN DICE ROLLS. BUT IT'S NOT ALL ARGUING AND LEGAL MANEUVERING. IN THE BEST *STAR TREK* TRADITION, THE ADVOCATE AND FRIENDS OF THE ACCUSED HAVE TO GET TO THE HEART OF THE CASE (PARTICULARLY IF THE ACCUSED IS BEING FRAMED). THIS COULD MEAN ALL SORTS OF SKILL TESTS, FROM TRICORDER ROLLS TO MIND MELDS. TRIALS, LIKE SCIENTIFIC EXPLORATION, ARE ABOUT GETTING TO THE TRUTH, AND THE COURT MARTIAL WILL ULTIMATELY BE DECIDED ON THE FACTS. IF THE CREW CAN PRESENT A CONVINCING ARGUMENT, THEY'LL SAVE THE DAY.

OFFICE OF SHIPYARD OPERATIONS

The Admiral of Shipyard Operations directs all construction of new Starfleet vessels and substantial repairs on active vessels. The Chief of Fleet Operations, to whom the Admiral of Shipyard Operations reports, issues build orders based upon the perceived needs of the fleet and the resources authorized by the Federation Council. In general, Starfleet launches several hundred new ships each year, from one of four primary construction yards— Utopia Planitia, Antares, the San Francisco Yards, or Earth Station McKinley. The Admiral of Shipyard Operations maintains his office at Utopia Planitia, on Mars, along with hundreds of engineers.

ASSEMBLY SPECIALIST—OPERATIONS

BASICALLY A CONSTRUCTION WORKER, ASSEMBLY SPECIALISTS PHYSICALLY PUT SHIPS AND STATIONS TOGETHER. WHILE MANY SMALL COMPONENTS OF SHIPS CAN BE REPLICATED, SHIPS THEMSELVES AND THINGS OF SIMILAR SIZE MUST STILL BE BUILT MANUALLY. SINCE MANY SHIPS ARE ASSEMBLED IN ORBIT AND MANY WORLDS HAVE UNDERWATER STATIONS, THESE ENGINEERS MUST BE SKILLED IN WORKING IN ZERO-G AS WELL AS UNDERWATER AND IN A VARIETY OF ENVIRONMENTS. AN ASSEMBLY SPECIALIST SPENDS HOURS A DAY HAPPILY WELDING PLATES TO OTHER PLATES AND DOING OTHER BASIC FUNCTIONS OF STRUCTURAL ENGINEERING. NOT AS INTELLECTUALLY DEMANDING AS BEING A QUANTUM COSMOLOGIST, BUT VERY FULFILLING NONETHELESS. AFTER ALL, AT THE END OF HIS DAY HE CAN SAY HE JUST PUT A SHIP TOGETHER!

ENGINEERING, ANY (CHOOSE SPECIALIZATION) 2 (3)
PERSONAL EQUIPMENT (ENVIRONMENTAL SUITS, CONSTRUCTION EQUIPMENT) 2 (3) AND (3)
SYSTEMS ENGINEERING (CHOOSE SPECIALIZATION) 2 (3)
COMPUTER (CHOOSE SPECIALIZATION) 1 (2)
VEHICLE OPERATIONS (SHUTTLECRAFT) 1 (2)
ATHLETICS (CHOOSE SPECIALIZATION) 1 (2)
DODGE 1
ENERGY WEAPON (PHASER) 1 (2)
HISTORY (FEDERATION) 1 (2)
LANGUAGE
    FEDERATION STANDARD 1
LAW (STARFLEET REGULATIONS) 1 (2)
PHYSICAL SCIENCES (PHYSICS) 2 (3)
PLANETSIDE SURVIVAL (CHOOSE SPECIALIZATION) 1 (2)
ZERO-G TRAINING +2

SHIPYARD FACILITIES

FOUR FACILITIES ARE RESPONSIBLE FOR THE PRIMARY CONSTRUCTION OF MOST OF STARFLEET'S VESSELS.

UTOPIA PLANITIA FLEET YARDS: STARFLEET'S MAIN CONSTRUCTION FACILITY IS A HUGE SHIPYARD ORBITING MARS. SINCE THE ADMIRAL OF SHIPYARD OPERATIONS AND THE ADVANCED RESEARCH AND DEVELOPMENT TEAM ARE BOTH HEADQUARTERED AT UTOPIA PLANITIA, MOST OF STARFLEET'S MOST IMPORTANT SHIPS ARE CONSTRUCTED HERE (INCLUDING THE LAST THREE STARSHIPS *ENTERPRISE*). OF ALL THE CLASSES OF STARSHIPS LAUNCHED BY THE FEDERATION OVER THE LAST TWENTY-THREE YEARS, MANY OF THE PROTOTYPES WERE CONSTRUCTED AT UTOPIA PLANITIA.

EARTH STATION MCKINLEY: MCKINLEY IS A LARGE SHIPYARD THAT ORBITS THE EARTH. MUCH SMALLER THAN UTOPIA PLANITIA, MCKINLEY MAINLY

SERVES AS A MAINTENANCE AND ORBITAL REPAIR FACILITY, THOUGH IT ALSO CONSTRUCTS A GOOD NUMBER OF SMALLER STARSHIPS AND SUPPORT VESSELS.

SAN FRANCISCO FLEET YARDS: THE OTHER OF EARTH'S SHIP CONSTRUCTION FACILITIES, STARFLEET CONTINUES TO USE THIS VENERABLE DOCK IN ADDITION TO MCKINLEY. THIS IS WHERE THE *HORIZON* CLASS, ONE OF THE FIRST STARSHIPS BUILT BY THE FEDERATION, AND *CONSTITUTION* CLASS WERE BUILT. ITS STAFF CONTINUES A LONG TRADITION OF SHIPBUILDING, INCLUDING THE MODERN *NEBULA* CLASS, AND STARFLEET COMMAND RECENTLY AUTHORIZED THE SAN FRANCISCO FLEET YARDS TO BEGIN CONSTRUCTION ON THE EXPERIMENTAL *SOVEREIGN* CLASS.

ANTARES SHIPYARDS: THE NEWEST FEDERATION SHIPYARD, ORBITING THE SECOND MOON OF ANTARES IV, IS EVEN LARGER THAT UTOPIA PLANITIA, THOUGH ITS FACILITIES ARE FAR INFERIOR. MOST OF THE SHIPS CONSTRUCTED HERE ARE OLDER CLASSES SCHEDULED TO BE DEPLOYED IN THE STANDING FLEETS STATIONED ALONG THE CARDASSIAN BORDER.

STARFLEET CORPS OF ENGINEERS

The special projects division of Starfleet, the Corps of Engineers, handles major construction projects throughout the Federation. The Advanced Starship Design Bureau supervises the design of new starship classes, such as the *Galaxy*-class and the projected *Sovereign*-class. The Galaxy Class Starship Development Project, for example, operated under the auspices of this department. Unlike the Shipyard Facilities division, the Starfleet Corps of Engineers does not build starships and starbases. It works with that department, however, during construction of a prototype ship. It also designs and constructs additional projects, such as massive irrigation works, as needed. The Starfleet Corps of Engineers is overseen by the Chief of Starfleet Engineering, who reports directly to the Chief of Fleet Operations.

One of the most desirable assignments for engineering students graduating from Starfleet Academy is the Advanced Research and Development Team that is part of the Starfleet Corps of Engineers. Advanced R&D is responsible for evolving new and improved shipboard systems for deployment across the fleet. Broken down into several technology development groups, such as the Spaceframe Technologies Group, the Warp Technologies Group, and the Tactical Ops Group, the groups are responsible for innovations such as quantum torpedoes and bioneural circuitry. While at the Academy, future officers have an oppor-

tunity to attend the Advanced Research Engineering school at the Utopia Planitia shipyards, the headquarters for the Corps of Engineers. Those engineers who show particular aptitude can also attend this school for additional training, as part of the Center for Advanced Training. Starfleet typically assigns promising Engineering personnel to the Corps of Engineers after they complete their studies, though many select postings on Starships to apply their advanced engineering skills.

THEORETICAL ENGINEER—OPERATIONS

POSTED TO THE CORPS OF ENGINEERS, THEORETICAL ENGINEERS WORK AT A STARBASE WITH OTHER DESIGNERS ON NEW SHIPBOARD SYSTEMS, FROM IMPROVED WARP DRIVES TO MORE EFFICIENT CONTROL SURFACES. BECAUSE STARSHIPS SPEND A CONSIDERABLE AMOUNT OF TIME IN DEEP SPACE, FAR FROM STARBASE REPAIR FACILITIES, HAVING A THEORETICAL ENGINEER ON BOARD CAN BE A CONSIDERABLE ASSET. WHEN CAUGHT IN THE GRIP OF AN ACETON ASSIMILATOR, A THEORETICAL PROPULSION ENGINEER COULD MAKE THE DIFFERENCE BETWEEN CONTINUING ON A VOYAGE WITH LITTLE MORE THAN A BRIEF INTERLUDE, OR TRAVELING UNDER IMPULSE FOR WEEKS.

PLAYERS SHOULD CHOOSE THE AREA IN WHICH THEIR CHARACTER SPECIALIZES. A THEORETICAL PROPULSION ENGINEER WOULD SPECIALIZE IN SKILLS RELATED TO WARP DRIVES, FOR EXAMPLE. SUITABLE ENGINEERING SPECIALIZATIONS INCLUDE WARP THEORY, TRANSPORTER THEORY, AND SUBSPACE DYNAMICS.

ENGINEERING, THEORETICAL (CHOOSE SPECIALIZATION) 2 (3)
ENGINEERING, SYSTEMS (CHOOSE SPECIALIZATION) 1 (2)
COMPUTER (SIMULATION/MODELING AND RESEARCH) 2 (3) AND (3)
SCIENCE, ANY (CHOOSE TWO SPECIALIZATIONS) 2 (3) AND (3)
PHYSICAL SCIENCES (PHYSICS AND CHOOSE SECOND SPECIALIZATION) 2 (3) AND (3)
DODGE 1
ENERGY WEAPON (PHASER) 1 (2)
HISTORY (FEDERATION) 1 (2)
LANGUAGE
     FEDERATION STANDARD 1
LAW (STARFLEET REGULATIONS) 1 (2)
PERSONAL EQUIPMENT (TRICORDER) 1 (2)
PLANETSIDE SURVIVAL (CHOOSE SPECIALIZATION) 1 (2)
VEHICLE OPERATIONS (SHUTTLECRAFT) 1 (2)

THEORETICAL ENGINEERING—OPERATIONS SKILL

THIS IS THE SCIENCE OF ENGINEERING. ALTHOUGH AN ENGINEER HAS TO KNOW THE UNDERLYING PRINCIPLES BEHIND THE EQUIPMENT HE WORKS ON, ENGINEERS WITH THIS SKILL FOCUS ON THE ABSTRACT, CONJECTURAL ASPECTS OF THEIR CHOSEN FIELD. IT REPRESENTS ACADEMIC KNOWLEDGE OF HOW A WARP DRIVE WORKS, RECENT ADVANCES IN TRANSPORTER TECHNOLOGY, OR CONJECTURAL HOLOGRAPHIC INTERFACES. AN ENGINEER WITH THIS SKILL COULD FIGURE OUT HOW TO USE WARP FIELDS IN NEW AND INTERESTING WAYS, OR DESIGN A NEW, MORE POWERFUL PHASER. IN 20TH-CENTURY TERMS, THE AVERAGE ENGINEER HOLD AN ENGINEERING B.S., WHILE A THEORETICAL ENGINEER HOLDS A PH.D. THIS SKILL IS TYPICALLY POSSESSED BY ACADEMICS, THEORETICAL ENGINEERS, AND SCIENTISTS.

SPECIALIZATIONS: CYBERNETICS SUBSPACE FIELD GEOMETRY, TRANSPORTER THEORY, WARP THEORY

OFFICE OF PERSONNEL MANAGEMENT

The Office of Personnel Management, headquartered at Starfleet Command, ensures that all Starfleet operations, vessels, starbases, and agencies receive

adequate staffing. The OPM assigns ensigns to their first tours of duty upon graduation from the Academy. Personnel requests and requests to transfer are made to this agency. This office also handles any qualified civilian advisors required. Although the Admiral of Starfleet Personnel retains complete authority over the assignment of all personnel (subject to review by the Chief of Fleet Operations, of course), the OPM rarely acts without the advice and consent of active commanders in the field. In other words, the Office of Personnel Management normally transfers only those officers and crewmen who have submitted transfer requests approved by their commanding officers.

In addition, in order to keep Starfleet running efficiently, Personnel Management makes great efforts in accommodating officers, both in honoring assignment requests and meeting a species' biological requirements. A number of factors are taken into account: Is the person qualified for the requested assignment? Where is there a need for someone with a particular set of skills? Is there an opening on the requested ship? Frequently, those requesting a particular assignment research the answers to these questions before requesting the posting.

When a planet joins the Federation, officers from OPM survey the species to determine any special requirements and evaluate its technical skills. Those species with sufficient training and skill are rapidly integrated into Starfleet, through accelerated training at Starfleet Academy. Here, they learn the skills necessary to function on a starship. Sometimes an alien species has difficulty adjusting to Federation standards and must be integrated more slowly.

OFFICE OF THE CHIEF OF RESEARCH AND EXPLORATION

The Chief of Research and Exploration supervises Starfleet's myriad scientific endeavors, from exploring new planets to conducting experiments on the effects of warp drive on the fabric of space. Based on Earth, at Starfleet Command, this office oversees all of Starfleet's scientific personnel, whether posted to a starship or starbase, and serves as a clearinghouse of scientific information. It reviews various discoveries, critiques scientific theories, and keeps abreast of current projects. All scientific endeavors undertaken by Starfleet personnel are subject to review from the Office of Research and Exploration, through the appropriate department. Mission requests are submitted to the Office of the Chief of Fleet Operations through this office, in coordination with the C-n-C. The CRE maintains the records at Memory Alpha, as well as orchestrating research efforts with the Daystrom Institute, the Vulcan Science Institute, and the Psychology Institute on Betazed.

Admiral Stenn, a Vulcan, currently serves as the Chief of Research and Exploration. After a lengthy tenure at the Vulcan Science Academy, he joined Starfleet. He served for fifteen years on board various starships, first as a science officer specializing in subspace mechanics, then working his way up to Chief Science Officer on the *U.S.S. T'Pau* (prior to its

decommission in 2364). His paper on electromagnetic waves in subspace garnered him the attention of the Federation Science Council, and he was transferred to the Office of Scientific Research. There, he supervised the development of improved subspace communications relays, eventually improving the time it took messages to travel across space. Afterward, Stenn achieved the rank of Admiral, and was assigned to head the Office of the Chief of Research and Exploration.

ADMIRAL STENN

STENN, SON OF ALIDOK, STANDS SLIGHTLY SHORTER THAN THE AVERAGE VULCAN. HE STUDIED FOR A WHILE UNDER T'VAN, A VULCAN MASTER, WHENCE COMES HIS SINGLE-MINDED DEVOTION. HIS ABILITY TO REMAIN AWAKE FOR UNUSUALLY LONG PERIODS OF TIME (EVEN FOR A VULCAN) SERVES HIM WELL IN HIS CURRENT POSITION. STENN DOES NOT STAND FOR DELAY OR EXCUSES. BY ASKING POINTED QUESTIONS, HE QUICKLY GETS TO THE HEART OF A MATTER. STENN WILL MOVE HEAVEN AND EARTH TO GET AROUND AN IMPASSE, ALLOCATING WHATEVER RESOURCES ARE REQUIRED TO FINISH A PROJECT DEEMED VITAL TO STARFLEET.

ASTRONOMICAL SCIENCE OPERATIONS

Astronomical Science Operations is responsible for monitoring known space to track and investigate astronomical phenomena, and oversees Starfleet's ongoing efforts to map the galaxy. Using long-range sensors and reports from ships in the field, its scientists maintain Starfleet's central galactic condition database, issue warnings about unsafe regions of space, and conduct research into enigmatic phenomena such as singularities, wormholes, and quasars. Whenever a starship visits a starbase, it downloads detailed recordings of objects encountered during its travels for inclusion in the database. Scientists stationed on starbases train their long-range sensors on stellar objects to record the locations and proper motions of stars, nebulae, dust clouds, and pulsars. Because of the immense size of the galaxy, they also search the sky for new phenomena. Should one of these monitor stations detect a change, or identify new stellar objects, it alerts Starfleet Command.

In the case of a particularly interesting discovery, the Astronomical Services office requests a starship to investigate. Sometimes it dispatches specialists to a starship to provide assistance. It is not uncommon for scientists from Starfleet headquarters to lead an expedition, with the starship at the scientist's disposal. Normally, the Director of Astronomical Science Operations approves such requests and then submits them directly to the Chief of Research and Exploration, who then coordinates the request with the Chief of Fleet Operations and the Chief-in-Command.

Information on the sort of phenomena that attracts the attention of Astronomical Science Operations can be found in the *Star Trek: The Next Generation* core rulebook.

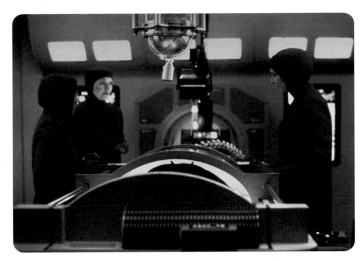

PLANETARY SCIENCE OPERATIONS

Just as Astronomical Science Operations observes space for new scientific developments, this agency conducts planetary surveys. One of the largest organizations that falls under the Chief of Research and Exploration, the Office of Planetary Science Operations monitors conditions on various worlds across the Federation. Unusual and interesting phenomena, from odd crystal formations to previously unknown ecologies, attract these scientists' attention. Scientists with expertise in related disciplines, such as exozoology and exobotany, also work with this office as needed. Frequently, it dispatches specialists to participate in these surveys. In addition, these scientists survey planets to determine the feasibility of terraforming, or their suitability for colonization (both conducted jointly with the appropriate departments). Lastly, emergency survey teams are dispatched to planets with troubles, from unusually poor soil to unpredictable tectonic activity, with an eye toward finding solutions.

This agency is headed by the Director of Planetary Science Operations, who reports to the Chief of Research and Exploration. In times of emergency, this office communicates directly with the Chief-in-Command. When a starship discovers a new planet, the initial report is sent to this agency, which then determines whether or not the planet warrants further study. Typically, when a ship receives orders to explore a planet, it comes from this office.

STARFLEET MEDICAL

With offices at Starfleet Command on Earth, Starfleet Medical looks after the health and well being of Starfleet personnel: It determines Starfleet's fitness requirements; conducts advanced medical research into diseases like irumodic syndrome and transporter psychosis; researches diseases newly encountered by starships, like the Psi 2000 virus and hyperaccelerated aging disease; and keeps Starfleet's doctors up to date on the physiologies of alien species. All this information, and more, can be found in the Starfleet Medical Database. In addition to tending Starfleet's medical needs, this office tracks and combats epidemics, dispatches personnel to assist civilian medical authorities when necessary, and conducts training programs that prepare Starfleet medical personnel for the unique situations they routinely encounter. Frequently, this agency receives requests from member planets and colonies suffering from epidemics, coordinating appeals for medical supplies with the CFO and Chief-in-Command.

SCIENCE OPERATIONS

This office manages Starfleet's scientific operations that do not fall under the jurisdiction of Astronomical Science Operations or of Planetary Science Operations. These include the physical sciences such as chemistry, computer science, and mathematics; the "soft" sciences of archeology, political science, and sociology; and life sciences. This agency is divided into a number of smaller departments, each dedicated to a particular area. Archeological expeditions, for example, report to the Office of Archeological Studies. Overall, Science Operations disseminates Starfleet's scientific discoveries throughout the Federation, particularly the Federation Science Council. With offices at Starfleet Command, the Chief of Science Operations answers to the Chief of Research and Exploration.

Science officers throughout the fleet send their reports to Science Operations for review. In this way, Starfleet remains up to date on the activities of all its scientists. It often sends promising Starfleet officers to the Daystrom Institute to conduct their experiments or to teach. Scientific outposts fall under this office's authority, as well. It works with Advanced Research and Development to improve sensor technology, coordinates its activities with the other scientific offices, and coordinates scientific expeditions through the Office of Fleet Operations.

OFFICE OF THE CHIEF OF INTERPLANETARY AFFAIRS

While the Chief of Fleet Operations sees to the deployment of the fleet, and the Chief of Research and Exploration directs Starfleet's exploratory and scientific endeavors, this office oversees Starfleet's interplanetary affairs—first contact efforts, diplomatic initiatives, and colonization programs. From Starfleet Command, the staff of the Chief of Interplanetary

Affairs coordinates its activities with other departments. When a starship makes contact with a new spacefaring species, for example, a report goes to the Diplomatic Corps, which then determines whether or not to pursue diplomatic initiatives. Should a survey uncover a new civilization, the CFO will forward the report to the First Contact Division. Any requirements are transmitted up the chain of command to the CIA, who then coordinates with the CFO. This office also keeps the C-n-C abreast of any developments in interplanetary affairs, and briefs officers as needed.

Talented individuals might receive a posting to one of the departments associated with this office. The Office of Personnel Management might transfer an officer with a particular talent at negotiation, for example, to the Starfleet Diplomatic Corps. Similarly, those officers who desire advanced training in the diplomatic arts can request admission to the Diplomatic School operated by the Center for Advanced Training and the Diplomatic Corps.

The current Chief of Interplanetary Affairs is Admiral Adena Imari. A graduate of the University of Betazed's School of Interplanetary Affairs, she received a posting to the *U.S.S. Discovery*. There, while a Lieutenant (J.G.), she played an instrumental role in a peace mission to Syliss V. After a second tour of duty on the *Discovery*, she applied for and received a seat at the Starfleet Diplomatic School. Graduating at the top of her class, the Office of Personnel Management assigned her to the Starfleet Diplomatic Corps. Admiral Imari has participated in some of the Federation's seminal negotiations—the Parliament Initiative banning subspace proximity detonators, the treaty with the Evangelion, and the opening initiative with the Tholians.

ADMIRAL IMARI

ADMIRAL IMARI IS A PLAIN-LOOKING, MIDDLE-AGED BETAZOID. A DAUGHTER OF THE HOUSE OF IMARI, HER FAMILY IS THE HEREDITARY KEEPER OF THE HOLY DIADEM OF ANU. SHE PUTS LITTLE STOCK IN HER NOBLE ANCESTRY AND PREFERS TO BE TREATED NORMALLY; SHE HATES BEING REMINDED OF HER HERITAGE, TYPICALLY BROUGHT UP BY OTHER BETAZOIDS. SHE WORKS HARD TO BRING PEACE TO THE GALAXY, WHICH SHE SEES AS A DUTY OF HER PRIVILEGED UPBRINGING. IMARI POSSESSES HIGHLY DEVELOPED TELEPATHIC ABILITIES, BUT ASSIDUOUSLY AVOIDS THE URGE TO USE THEM DURING HER NEGOTIATIONS. WHEN ON BETAZED, HOWEVER, SHE PREFERS TO COMMUNICATE TELEPATHICALLY. THOSE WHO WORK WITH ADMIRAL IMARI DESCRIBE HER AS A "DEN MOTHER." SHE MOST OFTEN FINDS HERSELF IN DISAGREEMENTS WITH THE CHIEF OF STRATEGIC DEPLOYMENT, THE TWO FREQUENTLY ADOPTING DIAMETRICALLY OPPOSED POSITIONS.

OFFICE OF COLONIAL AFFAIRS

Colonization efforts are an important strategy to handle the persistent need for habitable worlds to combat potential overpopulation. To manage the growth of colonies within Federation space, this department supervises most colony efforts within the Federation. Under the command of the Chief of Colonial Affairs, this office utilizes dozens of executive staff and inspectors. The Office of Colonial Affairs is based at Starfleet Command and reports to the Chief of Interplanetary Affairs. While the Secretariat's

Bureau of Colonization oversees a colony once established, this office is responsible for setting one up.

Starfleet plays a vital role in the establishment of colonies, even though they fall under civilian authority. This office works closely with the Federation's Bureau of Colonization. When the Bureau decides to establish a new colony, officers from this office perform a feasibility study to determine whether or not the planet is suitable for colonization. Once Starfleet has deemed a planet safe for colonization, it sends a report to civilian authorities. When the Bureau authorizes a colonization request, Colonial Affairs handles the logistics of moving manpower and material to the site, coordinating with the Office of Fleet Operations. For the first five years, the colony remains on probationary status. The Office of Colonial Affairs periodically checks up on the fledgling colony, to ensure things proceed apace, and reports to the Bureau. Inspectors look to make sure the colony can support itself in the time frame specified in the colonization plan, and may identify areas of potential improvement. Before a colony becomes fully established, Colonial Affairs schedules needed shipments of food and supplies with the Federation Merchant Marine. Should the Colonial Affairs office determine a colony unsuitable to continue, it reports to the Bureau of Colonization, which may recall the colonists. In some cases, the OCA may appoint one of its own staff to oversee a colony until it is capable of standing on its own and electing its own leadership.

Once a colony is capable of standing on its own, Colonial Affairs no longer retains jurisdiction. The colony then becomes the responsibility of the Bureau of Colonization, which maintains the Federation's relations with the colony. Yet OCA still has a role to play in an established colony. In times of emergency, the Colonial Affairs office supervises rescue operations and evacuation proceedings if needed. During the negotiations with the Cardassian Union, a representative of this agency advised the negotiating team on the disposition of Federation colonies. Afterward, it was this agency's responsibility to orchestrate and supervise the evacuation of Federation citizens according to the treaty's timetable.

Despite these far-ranging oversight responsibilities, some colonies manage to slip through the cracks.

Thirty years ago, in spite of a visit from an inspection team, Turkana IV deteriorated into civil war. It is also important to note that not all colonies are under Colonial Affairs' jurisdiction: Science outposts—such as the Darwin Genetic Research Station—remain under the purview of the Federation Science Council, for example. Rogue outposts—those established without Federation consent—also do not normally fall within Colonial Affairs' grasp, though it works to shut such operations down.

For more information on Starfleet's relationship with colonies, see chapter four, "Membership."

FIRST CONTACT DIVISION

The Director of Exosocial Relations heads up the First Contact Division, based on Vulcan. It assembles teams to survey a society covertly before establishing contact, then sends specially trained experts to handle the delicate situation of revealing the existence of other spacefaring cultures (like the Federation). The First Contact Division maintains strict protocols for its personnel, to prevent the kinds of disasters caused by John Gill, a cultural observer stationed on the planet Ekos. In violation of the Prime Directive, Gill imposed a government based on Earth's Nazi Germany, in an attempt to eliminate Ekosian anarchy ("*Patterns of Force*" [*Star Trek*]). A society must possess a stable world government and sufficient technological capability (i.e., faster than light travel) before first contact is made.

First contact can only be made once the First Contact Division has established that a civilization is ready for such contact, and that it would not unduly upset the society. After monitoring a society's broadcasts, it moves on to the next stage—surveillance on the ground. Assembling a team of qualified officers from various other departments and disciplines, this office quietly inserts them into the local society. This may take the form of a base hidden by a holographic projector, or specialists disguised as local inhabitants who live among the indigenous population. If the team determines a planet is ready for first contact, it reports to the Chief of Research and Exploration, who informs the Federation Council and the Chief-in-Command. The actual first contact mission is passed

on, through the Office of Fleet Operations, to the appropriate starship. If any experts are warranted, the First Contact Division dispatches a specialist to assist the crew.

Once first contact has been successfully established, this office notifies the Starfleet Diplomatic Corps if diplomatic ties are to be established. It also submits a report to the Office of the Chief-in-Command with its recommendation. That office, in turn, passes it along to the Federation Council.

FIRST CONTACT SPECIALIST—COMMAND

SERVING UNDER THE FIRST CONTACT DIVISION, FIRST CONTACT SPECIALISTS ARE A RARE BREED. A HYBRID OF EXPLORER AND DIPLOMAT, THEY ARE ASSIGNED TO SPECIFIC WORLDS WHERE THEY WILL COVERTLY OBSERVE THE INHABITANTS. THIS OFTEN MEANS SETTING UP HOLOGRAPHIC "DUCK BLINDS," WHICH REPRODUCE AN AREA OF THE TERRAIN, BEHIND WHICH THEY WATCH, UNSEEN, LEARNING THE DETAILS OF THE SPECIES' CULTURE AND SOCIETY. IN EXTREME CASES, THEY WILL UNDERGO COSMETIC SURGERY, ALLOWING THEM TO GO "UNDERCOVER" FOR UP TO MONTHS AT A TIME.

CULTURES IGNORANT OF THE EXISTENCE OF OTHER SPECIES IN THE GALAXY COME IN MANY FORMS. A FIRST CONTACT SPECIALIST MUST BE SKILLED NOT ONLY IN THE SOCIOLOGICAL RAMIFICATIONS OF FIRST CONTACT IN ALL ITS VARIETIES, BUT ALSO IN WHAT FEDERATION LAW ALLOWS ITS REPRESENTATIVES TO DO IN SUCH CIRCUMSTANCES, AND THE RAMIFICATIONS OF FAILURE.

CULTURE (CHOOSE TWO SPECIALIZATIONS) 2 (3) AND (3)
DIPLOMACY (FEDERATION LAW) 1 (2)
LAW (STARFLEET REGULATIONS) 1 (2)
PERSONAL EQUIPMENT (HOLOGRAPHIC PROJECTOR AND TRICORDER) 1 (2) AND (2)
SOCIAL SCIENCES (ANTHROPOLOGY AND SOCIOLOGY) 2 (3) AND (3)
ATHLETICS (CHOOSE SPECIALIZATION) 1 (2)
CHARM (INFLUENCE) 1 (2)
COMPUTER (CHOOSE SPECIALIZATION) 1 (2)
DODGE 1
ENERGY WEAPON (PHASER) 1 (2)
HISTORY (FEDERATION) 1 (2)
LANGUAGE
    CHOOSE SKILL 2
PLANETSIDE SURVIVAL (CHOOSE SPECIALIZATION) 1 (2)
VEHICLE OPERATIONS (SHUTTLECRAFT) 1 (2)

STARFLEET DIPLOMATIC CORPS

One of Starfleet's primary missions is to seek out new life and new civilizations, with an end toward fostering friendly relations and intergalactic peace. The diplomats of the Federation Diplomatic Service represents the UFP through its numerous embassies on alien worlds. The members of the Starfleet Diplomatic Corps are responsible for opening dialogs with newly contacted species. Trained in a variety of disciplines—from negotiation and history to specific alien cultures and exosociology—the Starfleet Diplomatic Corps seeks to foster peaceful relations throughout the galaxy. In times of conflict, these officers attempt to resolve differences—whether involving the UFP or through the use of the Federation's "good offices"—through arbitration. These individuals may eventually go on to fulfilling civilian careers with the Federation Diplomatic Service, or even represent the Federation on alien worlds.

The chief diplomat for Starfleet, known as the Director of Foreign Affairs, reports to the Chief of Research and Exploration. Diplomats often work with Federation ambassadors, and closely with the Federation Council. The Council, through the Foreign Relations Committee, typically authorizes any diplomatic missions, and the Diplomatic Corps keeps them apprised of developments. When a planet requests Federation intervention, the assignment usually goes to these officers. The Diplomatic Corps coordinates with the Chief of Fleet Operations and the C-n-C, as needed. Its headquarters are on Earth, at Starfleet Command.

The Diplomatic Corps frequently dispatches its personnel to serve as special consultants, although most starship crews are imminently qualified to handle negotiations when a diplomat is unavailable. Starships often play host to Starfleet diplomats on their way to delicate negotiations, or, on a happier note, to welcome a new member into the Federation. They host alien dignitaries, showing the flag when it suits the Federation, alongside an expert from Starfleet Diplomatic. Finally, especially delicate negotiations may require a specialist to handle the situation.

DIPLOMATIC CAMPAIGNS

RATHER THAN FOCUSING ON THE EXPLOITS OF A STARSHIP, TRAVELING FROM PLANET TO PLANET IN SEARCH OF THE UNKNOWN, A NARRATOR CAN RUN A SERIES BASED ON THE EFFORTS OF THE STARFLEET DIPLOMATIC CORPS. EACH OF THE PLAYERS TAKES ON THE ROLE OF SOMEONE FROM THIS OFFICE — A COMMAND OFFICER TRAINED IN NEGOTIATION, SECURITY OFFICERS TO PROVIDE PROTECTION, SCIENCE OFFICERS AND ENGINEERS SENT TO ASSIST THE LEAD DIPLOMAT. ONE WAY TO USE THIS IDEA IS TO SEND THE CREW ON A VARIETY OF DIPLOMATIC MISSIONS. ONE WEEK THEY MIGHT BE SENT TO NEGOTIATE WITH THE SHELIAK. THE NEXT THEY COULD BE SENT TO THE BIENNIAL TRADE CONFERENCE ON BETAZED, TO NEGOTIATE DILITHIUM MINING RIGHTS WITH THE TROYANS. THE DRAMATIC TENSION COULD ARISE FROM ISSUES OF VERIFICATION — DO THE CARDASSIANS ACCURATELY REPRESENT THE NUMBER OF MUTAGENIC BOMBS THEY HAVE? — TO OUTRIGHT ESPIONAGE — THE KTARIANS USE THE NEGOTIATIONS AS A COVER FOR SOMETHING ELSE, OR SOMEONE DOESN'T WANT TO SEE THE NEGOTIATIONS WITH THE ARTELINES SUCCESSFULLY CONCLUDED. WHILE IT MIGHT BE ENJOYABLE TO ROLEPLAY A NEGOTIATION WITH THE BARZANS OR ARBITRATE A DISPUTE BETWEEN THE ANTICANS AND SELAY, THE DIPLOMATIC CAMPAIGN COMES INTO ITS OWN WHEN THE FOCUS IS ON A SINGLE PLANET.

AFTER A STARSHIP MAKES INITIAL CONTACT WITH A NEW CIVILIZATION, IT BECOMES THE PURVIEW OF THE DIPLOMATS ACTUALLY TO FORGE A PEACEFUL RELATIONSHIP. SIMILARLY, IF A PLANET REQUESTS FEDERATION MEMBERSHIP, A GROUP OF DIPLOMATS MUST ASSESS THE PLANET AND NEGOTIATE THE ARRANGEMENTS. ONE OF THE PLAYERS MIGHT PLAY THE ROLE OF A DIPLOMAT FROM THE FEDERATION DIPLOMATIC SERVICE OR THE DIPLOMATIC CORPS. IN ADDITION TO THE LEAD DIPLOMAT, STARFLEET ROUTINELY SENDS CULTURAL AND MILITARY ATTACHÉS TO ADVISE ON A VARIETY OF SUBJECTS, SEVERAL SCIENTIFIC AND ENGINEERING EXPERTS TO STUDY THE PLANET'S TECHNOLOGY, AND SECURITY OFFICERS TO PROTECT THE DELEGATION. EXPERTS IN THE "SOFT" SCIENCES OF POLITICS, SOCIOLOGY, AND PSYCHOLOGY — NORMALLY GIVEN SHORT SHRIFT IN THE TYPICAL STARSHIP CAMPAIGN — CAN REALLY SHINE WHEN EVALUATING A CULTURE. OVER THE WEEKS AND MONTHS, THE CREW WILL BECOME INTIMATELY FAMILIAR WITH THE SETTING. NARRATORS WHO ENJOY "WORLD-BUILDING" — CREATING A SINGLE WORLD IN GREAT DETAIL — WILL LIKE THIS TYPE OF SERIES. TO KEEP THE SERIES ENTERTAINING, THE NARRATOR MUST PROVIDE ENOUGH INFORMATION TO MAINTAIN THE PLAYERS' INTEREST. THE LOCAL CULTURE, HISTORY, AND SOCIETY SHOULD BE EXHAUSTIVELY DETAILED. ANCIENT RUINS TO EXPLORE, UNUSUAL CULTURAL MORES, AND THE OCCASIONAL MEDDLING OUTSIDER (FERENGI ALWAYS MAKE A GOOD CHOICE HERE) CAN PROVIDE ENDLESS ADVENTURE OPPORTUNITIES.

STARFLEET DIPLOMAT—COMMAND

WHILE MANY STARFLEET OFFICERS USE DIPLOMACY AS A TOOL, THE TERM "DIPLOMAT" IS RESERVED FOR A SELECT GROUP OF PEOPLE: THOSE WHO MAINTAIN THE FEDERATION'S RELATIONSHIPS WITH ITS MEMBERS AND ALLIES, AND THOSE WHO WORK TO ESTABLISH RELATIONS WITH OUTSIDERS. SPECIFICALLY, STARFLEET'S DIPLOMATS NEGOTIATE TREATIES, SERVE AS ARBITERS DURING POLITICAL DISPUTES, AND REPRESENT THE FEDERATION ON ALIEN WORLDS; THEY ARE OFTEN ON THE FRONT LINES OF THE FEDERATION'S EXPLORATION EFFORTS. SOMEONE WHO SPECIALIZES IN CONTACTING NEW CIVILIZATIONS CERTAINLY RELIES HEAVILY ON DIPLOMACY, BUT ONLY INDIVIDUALS SUCH AS AMBASSADOR SPOCK — ONE OF THE GREATEST POLITICAL NEGOTIATORS THE FEDERATION HAS EVER KNOWN — PROPERLY WEAR THE TITLE "DIPLOMAT."

DIPLOMACY (FEDERATION LAW AND CHOOSE SECOND SPECIALIZATION) 2 (3) AND (3)

PERSUASION (NEGOTIATION) 2 (3)

SOCIAL SCIENCES (CHOOSE TWO SPECIALIZATIONS) 1 (2) AND (2)

CULTURE (CHOOSE TWO SPECIALIZATIONS) 2 (3) AND (3)

WORLD KNOWLEDGE (CHOOSE TWO SPECIALIZATIONS) 1 (2) AND (2)

COMPUTER (CHOOSE SPECIALIZATION) 1 (2)

DODGE 1

ENERGY WEAPON (PHASER) 1 (2)

HISTORY (FEDERATION AND CHOOSE SECOND SPECIALIZATION) 1 (2) AND (2)

LANGUAGE
    FEDERATION STANDARD 1

LAW (STARFLEET REGULATIONS AND CHOOSE SECOND SPECIALIZATION) 1 (2) AND (2)

VEHICLE OPERATIONS (SHUTTLECRAFT) 1 (2)

PROMOTION — LIEUTENANT +3

STARFLEET ATTACHÉ—COMMAND

USUALLY ASSIGNED TO A SPACE STATION OR AN EMBASSY ON A FOREIGN PLANET, STARFLEET ATTACHÉS DIVIDE THEIR TIME BETWEEN OBSERVING AND RESEARCHING LOCAL CUSTOMS AND EDUCATING THE NATIVE INHABITANTS IN THE CONVENTIONS OF FEDERATION CULTURE. THEY SOMETIMES ATTEND STARSHIP CAPTAINS DURING DIPLOMATIC MISSIONS, ADVISING ON LOCAL CUSTOMS. SPECIALIZING NOT ONLY IN A SPECIFIC CULTURE'S MORES AND FOLKWAYS BUT ALSO ITS ECONOMY AND TECHNOLOGY, AN ATTACHÉ MUST BE ABLE TO LEARN THESE THINGS QUICKLY AND ADAPT TO NEW SITUATIONS AND ASSIGNMENTS.

CULTURE (CHOOSE SPECIALIZATION) 2 (3)

DIPLOMACY (PLANETARY AFFAIRS [CHOOSE PLANET]) 2 (3)

LAW (STARFLEET REGULATIONS) 1 (2)

SOCIAL SCIENCES (CHOOSE TWO SPECIALIZATIONS) 2 (3) AND (3)

WORLD KNOWLEDGE (CHOOSE SPECIALIZATION) 1 (2)

COMPUTER (RESEARCH AND CHOOSE SECOND SPECIALIZATION) 1 (2) AND (2)

DODGE 1

ENERGY WEAPON (PHASER) 1 (2)

HISTORY (FEDERATION AND CHOOSE SECOND SPECIALIZATION) 1 (2) AND (2)

LANGUAGES
    CHOOSE ONE 1
    FEDERATION STANDARD 1

PLANETSIDE SURVIVAL (CHOOSE SPECIALIZATION) 1 (2)

VEHICLE OPERATIONS (SHUTTLECRAFT) 1 (2)

PROMOTION — LIEUTENANT (J.G.)

OFFICE OF THE CHIEF OF STRATEGIC OPERATIONS

Although one of the smallest departments in Starfleet, the Chief of Strategic Operations holds one of the most important posts in the whole of Starfleet— the planning of the strategic defense of Federation space. While the Chief of Fleet Operations oversees the disposition of the fleet to tackle the large volume of missions required by Starfleet, the Office of Strategic Operations draws up Starfleet's battle plans and defensive schemes. In concert with Starfleet Security, the Office of the Chief of Strategic Operations dispatches experts to the field to brief starship captains on the strategic operations and tactics of threat species, and develops training simulations against enemy vessels. While there can be no substitute for a good starship captain and a dedicated crew, the incredible speed at which battles unfold in the 24th century makes good strategic planning a more crucial element of tactical success than ever before.

The Chief of Strategic Planning oversees Starfleet's intelligence efforts, because they are so closely related to the Chief of Strategic Operations' defensive responsibilities. In fact, the current chief, Admiral Venahil, rose through the ranks of Starfleet Intelligence to receive his current assignment. The Office of Starfleet Security falls within Admiral Venahil's sphere, as well.

ADMIRAL VENAHIL

A SOFT-SPOKEN ANDORIAN, VENAHIL IS A MATHEMATICAL GENIUS AND BRILLIANT STRATEGIST. VENAHIL BELIEVES STARFLEET DOES NOT DO ENOUGH TO SAFEGUARD THE SECURITY OF THE FEDERATION. HE CITES THE RECENT BORG INVASION, THE POTENTIAL FOR DISASTER DURING THE KLINGON CIVIL WAR, AND THE ROMULAN ATTEMPT TO INVADE VULCAN AS WARNING SIGNS FOR AN EVEN GREATER CONFLICT. SIMPLY PUT, HE BELIEVES THE FEDERATION'S ENEMIES PERCEIVE IT AS WEAK AND UNFOCUSED, AND THUS RIPE FOR INVASION. ADMIRAL VENAHIL PUSHES THE C-N-C FOR MORE AGGRESSIVE FLEET DEPLOYMENTS AND A RAPID INTEGRATION OF NEW WEAPONS TECHNOLOGY. AMONG THE JOINT CHIEFS, HIS MOST VOCAL OPPONENT IS ADMIRAL IMARI.

STRATEGIC PLANNING COUNCIL

Headed by the Starfleet Security Advisor, this office reports to the Chief of Strategic Operations. "Strategic Planning Council" is actually a misnomer; it is not one council, but several. Combining the talents of Starfleet officers and specialists with qualified civilian experts, members are divided into working groups. The Council on Borg Strategy, the Tholian Defense Council, and the Committee on Cardassian Strategy are but some examples. Each council is responsible for evaluating a threat species' military capabilities, determining likely strategic operations, and developing a course of action. When the Romulans mounted the assault that would come to be known as the Tomed Incident, for example, the Federation was prepared thanks to the efforts of the Neutral Zone Defense Council. Because of its simulations Starfleet could anticipate the Romulans' movements, and thus respond with a lower loss of life.

The members of this office do more than sit back comfortably on Earth and dream up battle scenarios. Lieutenant Commander Shelby was placed in charge of Starfleet's defensive planning against the Borg after serving on the appropriate committee. Kyle Riker, after his near-fatal experience with the Tholians in 2353, joined the Tholian working group and later visited the U.S.S. Enterprise-D to brief Captain Picard and his command staff. Sirna Kolrami, a Zakdorn strategist, served on a number of vessels as a tactical consultant. Starships anticipating conflict with a known threat species, or which have new tactical information on an enemy, can expect a visit from someone at the Strategic Planning Council.

STARFLEET INTELLIGENCE

The director of Starfleet Intelligence reports directly to the Chief of Strategic Operations. Based on Earth, Starfleet Intelligence collects data concerning the military, industrial, and diplomatic activities of the Federation's neighbors. SI operates a number of long-range sensor arrays and listening posts throughout the Federation, to obtain information on subjects ranging from enemy fleet deployments to agricultural production—anything that contributes to a threat species' military capabilities. While Starfleet Intelligence handles counterintelligence activities throughout Starfleet, on starbases and starships, the Federation Intelligence Service protects nonmilitary locations and Federation personnel. The two groups sometimes work together, SI providing intelligence on possible spies within the Secretariat. Starfleet normally directs its intelligence efforts outward, along the Federation's frontier and inside "unfriendly" space.

Most of the officers in Starfleet Intelligence serve as data analysts, sifting through information and developing detailed reports for the Federation President, the Security Council, and the Joint Chiefs. Yet as good as satellite intelligence can be, it does not take the place of an agent on the ground. SI makes use of a number of agents who undertake a wide variety of dangerous assignments. Some of these agents are assigned to unfriendly regions, where they act as "spies" in the Cardassian, Romulan, and Gorn empires. Others work with the Federation Intelligence Service to uncover and capture enemy spies who have infiltrated the Federation. These individuals are highly trained, and often operate for extended periods without direct supervision.

Because the number of available special ops agents is so small, any dangerous missions in enemy territory that do not require a long-term infiltration are usually handed off to Fleet Operations and assigned to personnel aboard an appropriate starship. A starship Crew might find itself conducting long-range scans of a potential enemy during an emergent situation, or assisting in a covert rescue mission. It might play host to a Cardassian defector, or provide the first look at a new Romulan weapon. These missions provide for Federation security as much as patrolling the Neutral Zone or working to resolve a dispute peacefully.

For more information on Starfleet Intelligence and its organization and operations, see the upcoming **Starfleet Intelligence** supplement .

OFFICE OF STARFLEET SECURITY

This office reports to Admiral Venahil, the Chief of Strategic Operations, and oversees all matters of security for Starfleet, on starships, starbases, and other Federation installations. It serves two distinct functions. As an interstellar police force, it enforces Federation law throughout Alpha and Beta Quadrants, as well as Starfleet regulations on its installations. Local law enforcement, however, remains responsible for infractions of the local law. If a criminal breaks Andorian law, for example, it remains an Andorian matter. If the crime took place on a starbase, on the other hand, it would become the jurisdiction of Starfleet Security. Issues of jurisdiction are left to the Federation sector courts to decide. Generally, any violation of interstellar law becomes the responsibility of Starfleet Security. Starfleet Security works with local security forces as needed, either providing support to member planets or apprehending local criminals who flee off-world. To these ends, the Office of Starfleet Security issues wanted posters for criminals within Federation space. The Office of Starfleet Security operates penal colonies throughout Alpha Quadrant, from the Federation Penal Settlement in New Zealand to Tantalus V. This office works with the Federation Intelligence Service, which serves a similar function.

Starfleet Security handles the larger question of Federation security as its other function. Just as security officers on a starship handle both internal and external security, this office keeps apprised of potential threats to Federation security. Working with the Office of Strategic Planning, the Chief of Starfleet Security enacts its recommendations. The staff receives regular reports from Starfleet Intelligence as

to fleet movements and coordinates with Fleet Operations to respond to any potentially dangerous situation. It develops tactical protocols, such as General Order 12, which requires adequate precautions be taken when approached by a spacecraft with whom contact has not been made. In times of war or extreme emergency, the Chief of Starfleet Security provides for the planetary defense of Earth. With proper authorization from the Federation President, Starfleet Security can enforce martial law.

STARFLEET RAPID RESPONSE TEAMS

Some might say that on the 24th-century battlefield, with its powerful ships and weapons of awesome destructive power, the need for ground forces becomes irrelevant. When a starship can lay waste to a planet's surface from orbit, what need is there for trained soldiers? Starfleet no longer condones this type of action, rescinding General Order 24, the command to destroy the surface of a planet unless the captain countermands the order within a specified time period, for obvious reasons. The Borg invasion of 2367 highlighted the need for ground forces, when the prospect of retaking captured planets became very real. Since then, Starfleet developed the concept of the Rapid Response team. In the rare times when Starfleet must respond with controlled, overt force—retaking a starbase captured by Cardassian soldiers or rescuing prisoners from Breen pirates, for example—it calls upon the special services of its Rapid Response forces.

The members of Starfleet see themselves primarily as explorers and diplomats, and Starfleet prefers to resolve conflicts as quickly and peacefully as possible. There are times, however, when force becomes the only option. Starfleet's Rapid Response forces respond quickly to situations requiring specialized, armed training. They differ from more traditional security officers in that they receive extensive training in personal combat, such as guerrilla warfare, demolitions, and weapons training, at the expense of more well-rounded Starfleet training (in the sciences and diplomacy, for instance). Although the first to be deployed in a hostile situation, Starfleet's Rapid Response forces remain an option of last resort. It specializes in the traditional arts of assaulting and holding a position (known as point defense), and trains to tackle situations as divergent as storming a well defended position, hostage rescue, and antiterrorism actions.

Starfleet maintains few of these personnel, because of their lack of utility in other areas. Certain elements at Starfleet Command have proposed expanding the program, and improving the capabilities of these forces, citing Dominion aggression. Should the Dominion manage to conquer a Federation planet, the idea is to provide a large enough force capable of fighting a traditional, ground-based war. So far, cooler heads at Starfleet and on the Federation Council have prevailed. Starfleet would prefer to allocate personnel and resources to more positive endeavors, like exploration. It currently maintains some 10,500 personnel throughout the Federation, stationed at strategic locations, such as along the Cardassian border and near Gorn space. In times of peace, they occupy their time with training and conventional security activities. In order to make them more "useful," the Chief of Starfleet Security has authorized a program assigning individual members to starships, to serve in the more typical role of security officer.

The Superintendent of Starfleet's Rapid Response Teams answers directly to the Chief of Starfleet Security. Contingents are posted at Starbases 82, 221, and 500, typically using *Steamrunner-* and *Saber-* class starships for rapid deployment. Starfleet outfits these individuals with the newly developed compression phaser rifle, a type-II phaser, and a tricorder. Additional equipment is assigned as needed. The typical team consists of one Command officer, one Medical officer, and eight specially-trained security officers.

SECURITY (RAPID RESPONSE) — OPERATIONS

UNLIKE THEIR KLINGON OR CARDASSIAN COUNTERPARTS, STARFLEET GROUND FORCES ARE NEVER ASSIGNED TO CONQUER A WORLD. THEIR TIME IS DEVOTED INSTEAD TO DEFENDING THE MEMBERS OF THE FEDERATION FROM MARTIAL THREATS. THESE THREATS MAY BE INTELLIGENT AGGRESSOR SPECIES, THE UNINTELLIGENT INDIGENOUS INHABITANTS OF COLONIZED WORLDS, OR SOME ENTIRELY UNFORESEEN THREAT. AS A RESULT, THE TYPICAL MEMBER MUST HAVE A WIDE ARRAY OF WEAPONS AND VEHICLE KNOWLEDGE, AS WELL AS ENGINEERING AND COMPUTER REPAIR SKILLS.

DEMOLITIONS (CHOOSE SPECIALIZATION) 2 (3)
OR
HEAVY WEAPONS (CHOOSE SPECIALIZATION) 2 (3)
ENERGY WEAPON (PHASER AND PHASER RIFLE) 2 (3) AND (3)
PERSONAL EQUIPMENT (CHOOSE TWO SPECIALIZATIONS) 1 (2) AND (2)
PLANETSIDE SURVIVAL (CHOOSE TWO SPECIALIZATIONS) 1 (2) AND (2)
VEHICLE OPERATIONS (CHOOSE TWO SPECIALIZATIONS) 1 (2) AND (2)
ATHLETICS (CHOOSE SPECIALIZATION) 1 (2)
COMPUTER (CHOOSE SPECIALIZATION) 1 (2)
DODGE 1
ENGINEERING SYSTEMS (WEAPONS) 1 (2)
LANGUAGE
    FEDERATION STANDARD 1
LAW (STARFLEET REGULATIONS) 1 (2)
PRIMITIVE WEAPONRY (KNIFE) 1 (2)
UNARMED COMBAT (CHOOSE SPECIALIZATION) 2 (3)
ZERO-G TRAINING +2

RESPONSE TEAM COMMANDER — COMMAND

OVERSEEING HIS TEAM IN THE FIELD, A UNIT COMMANDER MUST BOTH MANAGE THE PERSONNEL UNDER HIS COMMAND AND KEEP THE UNIT'S TACTICAL GOALS IN CLEAR SIGHT. REQUIRING AN INTIMATE KNOWLEDGE OF THE CHAIN OF COMMAND, AS WELL AS HIS UNIT'S PERSONNEL RESOURCES, THE TEAM COMMANDER MUST BE BOTH DECISIVE AND INTROSPECTIVE, REQUIRING GOOD JUDGMENT AND UNPARALLELED COMMAND LEADERSHIP.

COMMAND (COMBAT LEADERSHIP) 2 (3)
PLANETARY TACTICS (SMALL UNIT) 2 (3)
ENERGY WEAPON (PHASER RIFLE) 2 (3)
STRATEGIC OPERATIONS (CHOOSE SPECIALIZATION) 2 (3)
VEHICLE OPERATIONS (SHUTTLECRAFT) 1 (2)

ATHLETICS (CHOOSE SPECIALIZATION) 1 (2)
COMPUTER (CHOOSE SPECIALIZATION) 1 (2)
DODGE 1
LANGUAGE
    FEDERATION STANDARD 1
LAW (STARFLEET REGULATIONS) 1 (2)
PERSONAL EQUIPMENT (CHOOSE SPECIALIZATION) 1 (2)
PLANETSIDE SURVIVAL (CHOOSE SPECIALIZATION) 1 (2)
ZERO-G TRAINING +2
PROMOTION — LIEUTENANT +3

FIELD SURGEON — MEDICAL

WHILE THE TYPICAL STARFLEET MEDICAL OFFICER HAS AT HIS DISPOSAL A WIDE ARRAY OF MEDICAL EQUIPMENT ALL KEPT IN PERFECT WORKING CONDITION, THE RR FIELD SURGEON MUST MAKE DO WITH WHATEVER IS HANDY. RARELY A CLINICIAN, THE FIELD MEDIC SPECIALIZES IN SURGERY: PUTTING BROKEN PEOPLE BACK TOGETHER. OFTEN FACING CONDITIONS THAT NO DOCTOR IN A HOSPITAL WOULD EVER ENCOUNTER, THE FIELD SURGEON MUST ALSO BE A SKILLED COMBATANT, FIGHTING SIDE BY SIDE WITH HIS COMPATRIOTS.

MEDICAL SCIENCES (SURGERY AND CHOOSE SECOND SPECIALIZATION) 2 (3) AND (3)
FIRST AID (COMBAT TRAUMA AND CHOOSE SECOND SPECIALIZATION) 2 (3) AND (3)
ENGINEERING, SYSTEMS (MEDICAL EQUIPMENT) 1 (2)
PERSONAL EQUIPMENT (MEDICAL TRICORDER) 2 (3)
PLANETSIDE SURVIVAL (CHOOSE TWO SPECIALIZATIONS) 1 (2) AND (2)
ATHLETICS (CHOOSE SPECIALIZATION) 1 (2)
COMPUTER (CHOOSE SPECIALIZATION) 1 (2)
DODGE 1
ENERGY WEAPONS (PHASER AND PHASER RIFLE) 2 (3) AND (3)
LANGUAGE
    FEDERATION STANDARD 1
LAW (STARFLEET REGULATIONS) 1 (2)
VEHICLE OPERATIONS (SHUTTLECRAFT) 1 (2)
ZERO-G TRAINING +2

USING RAPID RESPONSE TEAMS

As stated above, Starfleet's ground forces are used as a last resort, in situations where diplomacy has failed. Thus, a campaign centering on surface conflict is not in keeping with the general tone of *Star Trek: The Next Generation*. Only rarely needed to carry out mass assaults, Rapid Response teams see little action.

Narrators might use these ground troops during extraordinary times, such as when a Cardassian army forcibly seizes a Federation colony, when hostage negotiations break down and force is the only remaining option, or to act as a temporary security force on a planet in upheaval. They might even by deployed to cope with a natural disaster. Always remember, however, the Federation is loath to use overt force to deal with these kinds of situation unless absolutely necessary. More often than not, Rapid Response team members will make an appearance as supporting cast, as a starship transports them to some hot spot. In this case, the Narrator can play up the difference in outlook between the typical Starfleet officer and the more military ground troops. Instead of being the focus of an entire series, one of the PC's might take on the role of a former officer, assigned to serve on a starship.

• *Prison Riot:* The prisoners at the Federation Penal Colony on Korba IV riot, taking the guards hostage. They demand freedom and a starship in return for the guards. The Federation cannot afford to allow these dangerous prisoners to roam the galaxy freely, and negotiations fail to produce a solution. For an added twist, the prisoners might be Orion syndicate members or captured Romulan spies who receive outside assistance. To recapture the penal colony, Starfleet sends out these highly trained security officers. They must circumvent the prison's security systems, now under the control of the prisoners, and free the hostages. In order to preserve life, Starfleet has not authorized the use of deadly force; to complete their mission, they may only stun the antagonists. To complicate things further, something or someone of great importance may also be involved, such as a famous former captain, competing factions of prisoners, or a captured destructive superweapon.

OFFICE OF THE CHIEF-IN-COMMAND

The Chief-in-Command supervises the whole of Starfleet, coordinating the activities of its many departments, and serves as Chairman of the Joint Chiefs. Should the Office of Research and Exploration elect to send a starship to investigate a wormhole, for example, the Chief-in-Command coordinates with Fleet Operations to see that the order is communicated to the appropriate vessel. Should the Office of Strategic Operations identify a need for additional starships, the Chief-in-Command coordinates the request with Fleet Operations and the Starfleet Corps of Engineers. The C-in-C's office makes sure all departments are up to date on the disposition of the fleet.

The C-n-C also functions as a special advisor to the Federation President and serves in the President's cabinet. In many respects, the ·C-n-C is the liaison between the President and the rest of Starfleet. Although the President occasionally attends the regular meetings of the Joint Chiefs, the Chief-in-Command is often the only Starfleet officer with whom the President regularly interacts. Therefore the C-n-C's most important duty is to keep the President informed of Starfleet's activities and to make him aware of any special situations requiring an executive decision. Although only the Chief-in-Command regularly meets with the President, it would be an extreme breach of protocol for the President to refuse any other member of the Joint Chiefs who requests a meeting.

The standard term of office for the Chief-in-Command is ten years. In the unlikely (and in fact unprecedented) event the C-n-C abuses his powers and responsibilities, several safeguards quickly curb such behavior. At any time, the Joint Chiefs can meet and elect to remove the current Chief from his post; this vote of no confidence is passed on to the President and Council for review. In practice, the Joint Chief's recommendations have been followed. The Federation President can request the resignation of any C-n-C deemed unfit for duty. Finally, the Federation Council can call for an investigation into the C-n-C's actions, and vote to remove him from office.

The current Chief-in-Command at Starfleet is William Castillo. An older man in his late sixties, Castillo rose through the ranks to Captain in record time. After a stint commanding a starship, Castillo received a posting to the Office of Strategic Planning. He's been at Starfleet Command ever since. Eventually, he moved up to the Office of Strategic Operations, and a seat on the Joint Chiefs. During his tenure, he witnessed the invasion of the Borg, which caught him and his staff by surprise. With the retirement of Admiral Kapella, he received the appointment to his current position. Since then, he's focused on strengthening Starfleet, authorizing new ship construction to replace the forty-nine ships lost at Wolf 359; the construction of the new *Defiant-*, *Steamrunner-*, and *Akira*--classes; and improving Earth's planetary defenses.

ADMIRAL CASTILLO, CHIEF-IN-COMMAND

ADMIRAL CASTILLO, AT 41 YEARS OLD, IS THE YOUNGEST MAN TO HOLD THE OFFICE OF CHIEF-IN-COMMAND IN STARFLEET'S TWO-HUNDRED-YEAR HISTORY. HE WORKS CLOSELY WITH HIS STAFF TO KEEP ABREAST, AS WELL AS ANYONE CAN, OF STARFLEET'S OVERALL ACTIVITY. SURROUNDED BY HIS EXECUTIVE STAFF, CASTILLO CAN QUICKLY LAY HIS HANDS ON THE LOCATION OF A STARSHIP AND ITS CURRENT MISSION. CASTILLO LEAVES MUCH OF HIS OFFICE'S DAILY OPERATIONS — THE COORDINATION OF STARFLEET'S MANY ACTIVITIES AND THE RECORDING OF MILLIONS OF REPORTS — TO HIS STAFF, AND ONLY GETS INVOLVED WHEN A DECISION NEEDS BE MADE. HE ENJOYS A CLOSE RELATIONSHIP WITH THE JOINT CHIEFS AND PRESIDENT JARESH-INYO. INWARDLY, HE WORRIES THAT STARFLEET, BECAUSE OF ITS RECENT CONFLICT WITH THE BORG, MAY LOSE ITS DEDICATION TO EXPLORATION, INSTEAD FOCUSING SOLELY ON MATTERS OF DEFENSE.

STARFLEET ACADEMY

Before a person can join Starfleet, he must first attend Starfleet Academy. The Academy has primary responsibility for upholding Starfleet's demanding entrance requirements and preparing recruits for the myriad of unexpected situations they are likely to encounter in service. From simple ensigns all the way up to the most decorated admiral, all Starfleet personnel are united by, and can proudly point to, their experiences at the Academy.

The Academy is located in San Francisco's historic Presidio district on Earth, just a few miles from Starfleet Command. With an impressive campus and its well manicured gardens, the Academy fosters an environment conducive to study. Cadets live on campus, in one of twenty dormitories. Cadets receive room assignments based on a policy of diversity. Befitting the institution's motto—*Ex Astris, Scientia* ("*From the stars, knowledge*")—the Academy houses some of the quadrant's finest research laboratories and libraries, making it an important center of study and learning. In addition to the main campus on Earth, the Academy runs a number of auxiliary facilities, like the Academy Flight Range near Saturn.

BOOTHBY

A MAN WITH A MYSTERIOUS PAST, BOOTHBY HAS BEEN THE GROUNDSKEEPER AT STARFLEET ACADEMY FOR ALMOST FIFTY YEARS. DESPITE THE FACT THAT HIS DUTIES DON'T INVOLVE HIM IN THE FORMAL INSTRUCTION OFFERED AT THE ACADEMY, BOOTHBY HAS FORMED CLOSE RELATIONSHIPS WITH SEVERAL CADETS ACROSS HIS FIVE DECADES OF SERVICE. IN FACT, THOSE CANDIDATES WHOM BOOTHBY BEFRIENDS ALMOST ALL GO ON TO STAND AMONG STARFLEET'S BEST AND BRIGHTEST, DEMONSTRATING THAT HE HAS AN UNCANNY CAPACITY TO IDENTIFY GREATNESS.

IN REALITY, THERE ARE MANY BOOTHBYS AT THE ACADEMY. ANYONE WHO TAKES THE TIME TO ACT AS A MENTOR, CONFIDANT, OR CONSCIENCE IS A "BOOTHBY." WHILE NOT ON THE EDUCATIONAL STAFF, THESE PEOPLE PROVIDE CADETS WITH AN UNQUANTIFIABLE SOMETHING, BE IT AS SOUNDING BOARD OR FRIEND. USE THE INFORMATION HERE TO COME UP WITH SIMILAR CHARACTERS; PLAYERS MIGHT REFER TO SOMETHING THEIR "BOOTHBY" TAUGHT THEM, OR MEET UP WITH HIM LATER ON IN LIFE. NARRATORS MIGHT HAVE A CHARACTER'S MENTOR SHOW UP TO CHECK UP ON HIS OLD CHARGE, OR PLACE HIM IN DANGER FOR THE CHARACTER TO RESCUE. IF PLAYING AN ACADEMY CAMPAIGN, SUCH CHARACTERS TAKE ON A CENTRAL SUPPORTING ROLE.

ATTRIBUTES
FITNESS: 2
COORDINATION: 2
INTELLECT: 3
  PERCEPTION +1
PRESENCE: 4
  EMPATHY +1
PSI: 0

SKILLS
ARTISTIC EXPRESSION (GARDENING) 1 (5)
CULTURE (HUMAN) 3 (4)
GAMING (THREE-DIMENSIONAL CHESS) 2 (3)
HISTORY (HUMAN) 2 (3)
LANGUAGE
  FEDERATION STANDARD 2
LIFE SCIENCES (BOTANY) 2 (3)
PERSUASION (STORYTELLING) 3 (4)
VEHICLE OPERATIONS (GROUND VEHICLES) 1 (2)
WORLD KNOWLEDGE (EARTH) 2 (3)
COURAGE: 2
RENOWN: 4
AGGRESSION: 0 DISCIPLINE: 0 INITIATIVE: 1 OPENNESS: 3 SKILL: 0
RESISTANCE: 2
WOUND LEVELS: 2/2/2/2/2/2/0

ADMISSION

Starfleet Academy has high standards for entrance. Beginning with the application process, the candidate must demonstrate not only extraordinary academic accomplishment, but also exhibit a fine character. Here, recommendation letters—from planetary leaders, Federation officials, or Starfleet officers—help. If the applicant meets certain basic standards, he receives an invitation to a nearby starbase for physical and written examinations. These tests are often not what the applicant expects. Rather than simply testing a person's knowledge, problem-solving, and reasoning ability, they also test character, teamwork, and emotional stability. A common test, for example, consists of a malfunctioning testing computer. The purpose of this is simple—do the other test-takers attempt to help their hapless comrade, or simply, and selfishly, ignore him?

Those prospects who pass the written and physical exams receive an invitation for yet another visit to a nearby starbase for another round of testing. During this final screening process, groups of qualified candidates are thrown together and asked to cooperate on a wide variety of physical and mental challenges as a team. This last test is exceptionally grueling; often, only a single candidate from a team of eight or ten is chosen for admission. In part, much of what makes this final test so challenging is the fact that Academy personnel often tailor their challenges to hammer away at the potential physical, mental, and emotional weaknesses detected in the candidates during previous exams.

THE ACADEMY PROGRAM

Those candidates who pass these tests receive admission to Starfleet Academy. Cadets participate in a six-week preparatory program to hone their specialized faculties (such as spatial orientation and deductive reasoning) before beginning classes. Generally, each cadet spends four terms at the Academy before graduation, each term lasting approximately one solar year. In the first year, cadets learn the basics necessary for life in Starfleet, such as transporter theory and warp dynamics. The second

year consists of basic training in Starfleet protocol and operations; by the end of the second year, a cadet must choose a particular field of study. During the third year, cadets receive advanced training in their chosen fields. Fourth-year studies include classes designed to prepare the cadet for a life in Starfleet—practical training in simulators and the like. Academy students are also required to participate in extracurricular activities such as sports teams or special interest clubs. At the end of each term, Academy instructors rank the students against each other, based upon performance. Graduating from the Academy with a high rank is quite an honor, and such students are usually placed on the fast track for top assignments and quick promotions. Beyond class rank, cadets have an opportunity to obtain various special honors that might greatly influence their post-Academy careers. These include membership in the Academy's prestigious precision flight team and selection to the ultraselective *Red Squad* composed of the Academy's top students.

Newer programs like *Red Squad* and *Nova Squadron*, in which a select body of cadets receives special training and privileges, have recently sparked controversy. The brainchild of the former Academy Commandant, Admiral Tokk, these programs are meant to produce elite officers. Many within Starfleet, however, including Admiral Fukazima, disagree with this new policy. Their argument: All Academy cadets should be treated equally, receiving equal training. Critics complain that these programs foster elitism. Only time will tell the effects on Starfleet's cohesion and esprit de corps.

Upon graduation from the Academy, all midshipmen must embark on, and pass, one final challenge—the cadet cruise. This final test takes the form of a year-long probationary period during which the former cadet is expected to perform the duties of an actual Starfleet officer out in the field. Here, the midshipman learns the practical ins and outs of working in Starfleet, by serving alongside full-fledged officers on active duty. Upon completion of this tour, the midshipman receives the rank of ensign and a posting somewhere in Starfleet.

THE ACADEMY CAMPAIGN

The *Star Trek: The Next Generation* RPG assumes players want to portray accomplished officers, long out of Starfleet Academy and well on their way to a life of adventure. In the *Narrator's Toolkit*, we suggested playing a "lower decks" campaign, where the players portray very junior officers working far away from the usual center of activity. Narrators can take this a bit further, setting their series at the Academy.

This opens up an entirely new vista for roleplaying in Starfleet. The players take on the roles of young, hopeful Academy cadets, newly arrived from across the Federation. They don't have a ship to unite them, only a desire to join Starfleet. They have no specialized skills. Thrust together, they have to get along, learn to overcome whatever handicaps they may have, and succeed.

Perhaps one episode focuses on a character's choice between two difficult options—saving a fellow classmate in danger or allowing the mission to fail. Another might follow the cadets on a few days' leave.

The Academy isn't only about study; cadets must be prepared for any eventuality, from being thrust into a bridge simulator for the infamous Kobiyashi Maru test to a ten-mile hike on the Moon. Many episodes will focus on personal development, both emotional and academic. A character might drop out, the others faced with the very real possibility of failure. But the range of stories the Narrator can tell are not limited to classroom experience. Anything can happen at the Academy, from a mysterious accident in the training simulator to an experiment gone horribly wrong. The most rewarding aspect of an Academy campaign is that the experience points the characters earn will directly reflect their own education—from the early days with few skills to the cadet cruise.

To begin an Academy campaign, have each of the players choose a Template, but forego selecting an Overlay. Then go on to the Early Childhood background stage, but stop there. Give each character between 5 and 8 points to reflect additional skills he's picked up along the way; because roleplaying the early years at the Academy can be tedious ("Okay, in this session, your characters attend Dr. Whately's Transporter Theory class."), spend some of these points on one or two skill levels in Starfleet-oriented skills, and begin the series during the second year at the Academy. Experience points should be spent on the skills listed on the Overlay for the position the character will eventually assume. From time to time, test the characters by having them make Skill Tests. If they fail, they might possibly wash out of the Academy (after all, all tests have consequences for failure, but only after consistent failure).

ADMIRAL BRAND, STARFLEET ACADEMY COMMANDANT

AFTER A LONG AND ILLUSTRIOUS CAREER IN STARFLEET, ADMIRAL BRAND WAS REWARDED WITH THE HONOR OF SERVING AS THE COMMANDANT OF STARFLEET ACADEMY. THROUGHOUT HER CAREER, SHE EXHIBITED AN ABILITY WITH INNOVATION, COMBINED WITH A FINE SENSE OF RESPONSIBILITY AND MORALITY. SHE SERVED ON A VARIETY OF STARSHIPS, FROM THE *U.S.S. VICO* TO COMMANDING THE *U.S.S. HORATIO*. SHE BECAME FAMOUS FOR DISCOVERING THE HET, A SMALL EMPIRE ON THE FRINGES OF CARDASSIAN SPACE.

BRAND TAKES HER POSITION SERIOUSLY, WORRYING NOT ONLY ABOUT HER CADETS' TECHNICAL SKILLS, BUT ALSO THEIR MORAL COMPASSES. SHE FRETS THAT LATELY THE ACADEMY HAS FOCUSED TOO MUCH ON PRODUCING HIGHLY CAPABLE OFFICERS AT THE EXPENSE OF THEIR CHARACTER. SHE EXHIBITS A MATRONLY DEMEANOR SOME FIND DISARMING. THOSE WHO HAVE FACED HER ANGER DISCOVER SHE HAS AN IRON CORE BENEATH HER GRANDMOTHERLY EXTERIOR. CADETS CALLED INTO HER OFFICE FOR DISCIPLINARY ACTION LEAVE FEELING AS THOUGH THEY'VE LET BRAND DOWN PERSONALLY, AND MANY WORK HARD NOT TO DISAPPOINT HER AGAIN. ON A PERSONAL NOTE, ADMIRAL BRAND ENJOYS A WARM RELATIONSHIP WITH THE ACADEMY INSTRUCTORS. SHE HOSTS A TEACHER-STUDENT BANQUET ONCE A YEAR.

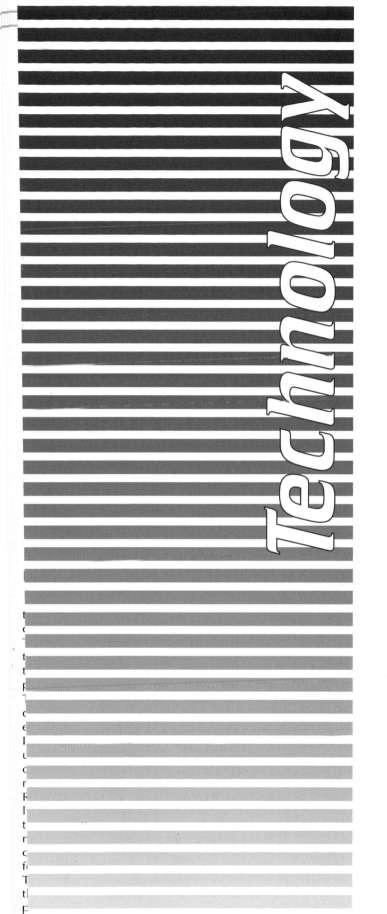

Technology

Because it is supported by the resources and expertise of the entire Federation, Starfleet possesses the highest technology in the Federation. This same level of technology and these same devices can be found, adapted to civilian uses, on most of the highly advanced world of the Federation. Tricorders, personal communicators, and similar equipment can be found in widespread private use on Earth, Alpha Centauri IV, Vulcan, Andoria, and many other worlds. However, on the less advanced worlds, and especially new colonies or Federation allies like Bajor, the level of available technology may be notably less. Most less advanced members of the Federation have access to technology similar to mainstream Federation technology, but behind it by as much as a century in some cases. In general, communicator, sensor, and weapon ranges are somewhat reduced, and equipment is somewhat bulkier and missing some of the more advanced functions.

The widespread use of replicator technology has had a profound impact on the entire Federation, including the availability of these various technologies. All of the devices listed here and in the main rulebook may be replicated. The only cost associated with producing them is the energy necessary to operate the replicators, so all of these devices are quite inexpensive in those areas which use some form of currency and lie near Federation space. Only handicrafts, luxuries which suffer when replicated, large items like antimatter plants, complex and large technologies like starships, and illegal items which must be smuggled or stolen are significantly expensive.

Most member worlds in the Federation prefer to design their own devices, but the vast majority of non-restricted Federation devices are available at low cost to all citizens who want or need them. On a number of worlds, including Vulcan, the local economy, if it can be termed that, rests upon perceived need. Most devices remain freely available to anyone trained in their effective use.

Regardless of the method of acquisition, most Federation citizens will be at least vaguely familiar with the equipment listed in this chapter, and many will own several of the devices described here. The only exceptions are restricted devices such as weapons and specialized technologies like medical equipment which require special licenses and training to use.

On most thickly settled Federation worlds local laws limit personal weapons to knives, stun rods, and modified Type I phasers capable only of using settings 1-3, or in some cases settings 1-2. Only police, local military and security forces, and Starfleet personnel are allowed to own or carry more powerful weapons. On some worlds, only the police and military can carry any weapons at all. Of course, on some colonies (or on worlds like Andoria with strong surviving military traditions), ownership of any weapon short of heavy artillery is allowed, or even mandatory. Similarly, on most worlds in the Federation, specialized medical equipment and other devices that can be easily used in a dangerously incorrect fashion may only be possessed and operated by personnel well trained in their use. On some worlds like Vulcan, everyone who completes such training is freely provided with such devices.

13	Heavy Disrupt D	80+18D6	70	Explode 100 cubic meters of rock into rubble
14	Heavy Disrupt E	100+12D6	80	Explode 160 cubic meters of rock into rubble
15	Heavy Disrupt F	120+12D6	90	Explode 400 cubic meters of rock into rubble
16	Heavy Disrupt G	160+12D6	100	Explode 600 cubic meters of rock into rubble
17	Heavy Disrupt H	[240]	120	Vaporize 50 cubic meters of solid duranium
18	Heavy Disrupt I	[300]	150	Vaporize 100 cubic meters of solid duranium, explode up to 1,200 cubic meters of rock into rubble

TRANSPORT INHIBITOR

There are times when transport is undesired, particularly in hostile situations, when a transporter could be used to extract personnel against their will. Similar to the pattern enhancer, the transport inhibitor creates an energy field which prevents a transporter from establishing a pattern lock. The transport inhibitor creates a field of tetryonic energy which causes a transporter's annular confinement beam to dissipate. Without the confinement beam, the transporter is unable to acquire a target lock on the matter to be transported.

To use a pattern inhibitor, it must first be placed at the target location. When activated, these devices produce a transporter secure area 10 meters in diameter around the inhibitor. Multiple inhibitors can be used to increase the area protected, and can be arranged to establish a perimeter. By placing these devices around the perimeter of the Ba'ku village, for example, Captain Picard and his crew created overlapping fields to protect the entire site. The strength of the tetryonic field can be adjusted from a minimum of one meter up to the maximum.

Size: An upright cylinder 1.5 m tall and 8 cm in diameter, with a tripod base
Mass: 6 kg each
Duration: 1,000 hours

GENETICS AND BIOTECHNOLOGY IN THE FEDERATION

The Federation attitude toward genetic manipulation and biotechnology mirrors the distaste for cybernetics. Although genetic research for improved crops, extinct species restoration, and disease fighting is routine, genetic alteration of humans or other races outside the elimination of congenital diseases, birth defects, etc. is almost unknown. On Earth, at least, this rejection of "inhuman" technological and genetic change dates from the disastrous Eugenics Wars, when scientists deliberately altered humans to create "supermen."

However, most of the other races in the Federation turned out to have equally strong philosophical objections to seriously modifying their physical natures. Although even the Vulcans would be hard pressed to find any logical reason for this unease, the fact is that it exists throughout the Federation and genetic alteration of sentient beings for any reason short of medical emergency (even by consent) is frowned on.

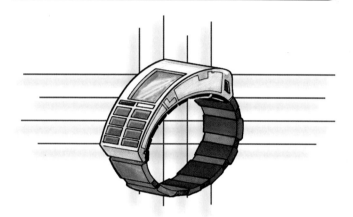

WRIST COMMUNICATOR

While some variant of the Starfleet combadge is used by most official UFP organizations, other options are popular with civilians. On most advanced worlds like Earth or Andoria, the vast majority of residents wear some form of communicator to allow them to remain in constant contact with the worldwide information network. The wrist communicator is one of the more common models of civilian communicators in use throughout the Federation.

Based on a style of communicator used briefly by Starfleet in the 2070's and discarded because it was not durable enough for field use, the wrist communicator has all of the features of a Starfleet combadge, as well as possessing a miniature camera and a small viewscreen. The ability to transmit visual as well as audio information has made these devices quite popular. For many people, the wrist communicator is used as a more convenient and portable substitute for a PADD. This device can act as a sophisticated terminal to the global computer network as well as a communication device. In addition, a wrist communicator can record up to 100 hours of audio and visual input on its optical microchip memory. Wrist communicators have the same range limitations as Starfleet combadges, and, like combadges, most models include miniature universal translators.

Size: A 1 cm thick, 5 cm wide wrist band
Mass: 0.1 kg
Duration: 1,000 hours

starships

When an average citizen of the Federation thinks about the vast interstellar community of which he is a small part, his thoughts invariably turn to Starfleet and its vessels. The ships of Starfleet have become synonymous with the ideals upon which the UFP stands, and the brave men and women who serve on them command respect in every corner of the galaxy.

Images of *Deneva*-class transports running the Draconis IX blockade, of *Niagara*-class cruisers in orbit above Arcalion during the Reunification, of *Steamrunner*-class frigates standing bravely against the Borg—these images have come to embody the wide-ranging spirit of Starfleet, a tangible expression of Federation ideals for all the galaxy to see.

A ship's crew may be the heart of Starfleet, but the bone and sinew of the organization remain the vessels that allow these dedicated souls to fulfill their missions. While historians often speak of the 23rd century as a golden age of starship development, the engineers and scientists of Starfleet's Advanced Technologies Division have made great strides throughout the 24th century as well. Stronger spaceframes, more efficient shields, higher sustainable velocities—each of these innovations has played a role in making Starfleet the most potent exploratory and defensive force in the galaxy.

The latter half of the 24th century remains an exciting time to wear the Starfleet uniform. With new contacts come new threats, and the Federation coexists with powerful spacefaring neighbors on nearly every border. It is a time of unequaled vigilance throughout the UFP, and as a result more new ship classes have been introduced in the latter half of this century than at any time before.

Spaceframes have become lighter and stronger, and vessel designs more streamlined and efficient. More than ever before, ships are designed for increasingly narrow mission profiles, while still retaining the versatility that has become a hallmark of Starfleet. New classes and subclasses take shape on R&D drawing boards and PADD's every day, while existing classes enjoy longer and longer service lifetimes.

In many ways, the current situation within the UFP reminds a casual observer of the Old West on Earth—the more a nation expands, the more frontiers it has to defend. The primary instrument of this defense, in the core worlds as well as on the frontiers, remains the Federation Starfleet.

VESSEL CLASSIFICATIONS

Starfleet Command classifies all vessels in service according to their primary (and, in some cases, secondary) mission profiles. Although in the past these profiles have revolved largely around exploratory and scientific missions, the heightened threat environment of the late 24th century has seen an increasing number of military profiles introduced as well.

While nearly all Starfleet vessels are capable of a diverse array of missions and mission profiles, most ships do have a specific use for which they were designed. Narrators can use these designations when choosing ships or designing encounters for episodes.

A science vessel will rarely appear on the main battle line during a major engagement, just as an escort won't normally be assigned to a routine planetary tectonic survey. Of course, in times of emergency all bets may be off.

The following ship classifications build on the basic divisions introduced in the *Star Trek: The Next Generation* core rulebook. These classifications will be further expanded in the upcoming *Engage!* starship miniatures game. The accompanying Classification Table provides the standard abbreviations used by Starfleet Command for each of the vessel types. Feel free to use these in your own games, either to add spice to fleet or command decisions, or simply as a useful shorthand when detailing starships for individual episodes or series.

CLASSIFICATION TABLE

EXPLORERS
EXPLORER	EX

CRUISERS
CRUISER	CA
EXPLORATORY CRUISER	CEX
FAST CRUISER	CF
HEAVY CRUISER	CH
LIGHT CRUISER	CL

FRIGATES
FRIGATE	FR
FAST FRIGATE	FF
HEAVY FRIGATE	FH
LIGHT FRIGATE	FL

ESCORTS
ESCORT (PERIMETER DEFENSE)	ES
LIGHT ESCORT (CORVETTE)	EL
HEAVY ESCORT	EH

SCOUTS
SCOUT	SS
HEAVY SCOUT	SH

SPECIALIZED
COURIER	SC
FIGHTER	XF
MEDICAL	MD
SURVEYOR	SV
DEEP SPACE SURVEYOR	SVH
RESEARCH/LABORATORY	SRS/SRL

SUPPORT/AUXILIARY
CARGO CARRIER	TC
TANKER	TA
TENDER	TN
TRANSPORT	TT
ARMORED TRANSPORT	TTA
TUG	TG

EXPLORERS

A mainstay of Starfleet since its inception, the *Explorer* classes of vessels have become metaphors for UFP ideals throughout the galaxy. These ships represent the pinnacle of versatile and efficient starship design; most explorers fulfill numerous mission profiles and are capable of extended, multiyear missions far beyond the borders of Federation space.

Although design philosophies and priorities have changed significantly in the latter part of the 24th century, explorers still form the historical core of the fleet. These vessels remain the flagships of both the Federation and its Starfleet, carrying the UFP into uncharted reaches of the galaxy on their voyages of exploration and discovery.

Vessel profiles in this class have evolved significantly during the 24th century. Working from many of the foundations established by the *Constitution*- and *Endeavor*- classes in the 23rd century, most of the current explorer classes retain design elements inspired by the heavy and exploratory cruisers of yesteryear. Although these elements have stood the test of time from a design perspective, they also continue to imbue the modern vessels with a valuable sense of nostalgia.

All explorers are large ships; as an overall vessel type, they represent the largest ship classes built by Starfleet. All of the various explorer classes thus far have employed the now familiar saucer-hull-nacelles design, and most possess saucer-separation capability. In addition, all explorers normally have two additional things in common: They are well armed considering their diverse mission profiles, and their internal designs cater to the long-term needs and desires of their crews. Starfleet understands the demands placed on officers forced to spend years in space, and these considerations play a prominent role in most new vessel designs. After all, a happy crew is a productive crew.

Several new explorer classes have entered service in the 24th century. While the *Galaxy*-class is perhaps the most famous, its sister classes have all served with distinction. The *Ambassador*-class paved the way for the design documents that would eventually launch the Galaxy Class Development Project. Although smaller and designed for more limited mission pro-

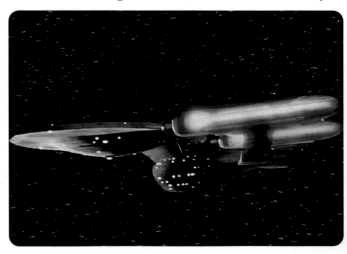

files, *Ambassador*-class vessels possess an enviable track record as a class. Aside from vessels destroyed in combat or lost during the course of duty, none of these ships have been decommissioned. All continue to serve, most in diplomatic or near-interstellar exploratory capacities.

Commissioned a scant five years after the maiden voyage of its *Galaxy*-class siblings, the *Ascendant* class of explorers entered service in the rimward sectors of the UFP in 2361. Equipped for extreme deep-space exploration missions, *Ascendant*-class vessels were designed with maximum comfort in mind and quickly became something of a favorite among officers whose families also lived aboard ship. Starfleet plans an ambitious production schedule for the class through the end of the decade, with three vessels per year being commissioned at the venerable Deneb Orbital Docks at Deneb IV.

Finally, rumors abound about a new *Explorer* class scheduled for commissioning sometime during the next few months. While much of the information surrounding the new class remains highly classified, conventional wisdom in the fleet suggests that the new ships will advance starship technology to an extent not witnessed since the Galaxy Class Development Project. Commonly known throughout Starfleet as the "Theta Project," speculation abounds regarding the name of the new class. If the whispers coming out of Advanced Technologies are to be believed, the prototype vessel has already been christened the *U.S.S. Sovereign.*

A SELECTION OF EXPLORER CLASSES CURRENTLY IN SERVICE

CLASS	TYPE
AMBASSADOR	EX
ASCENDANT	EX
GALAXY	EX
SOVEREIGN	EXH

CRUISERS

For well over a century, the numerous cruiser classes have been the workhorses of Starfleet. While explorers continue to serve as flagships for most sector fleets, cruisers form the backbone of these units. Smaller and lighter than their high-profile cousins, most cruiser designs stress utility and function. These midsized to large vessels serve in every sector of the UFP, in capacities ranging from deep-space patrols to sectorwide interdiction duties.

The updated design parameters of the 24th century have favored the cruiser. New spaceframe technology, more specific weapons and sensor platforms, and new warp field advancements have allowed Starfleet designers to expand and enhance the role of the cruiser within the fleet. As mission profiles continue to diversify and more new classes are commissioned, Starfleet has found it necessary to fine-tune its cruiser classification methods. These subclasses serve to define a class' primary mission objectives, and they provide the casual observer with a better idea of the class' role within the fleet.

Direct descendants of the larger explorer classes, exploratory cruisers such as the *Constellation* and *Nebula* classes continue to chart new worlds and contact new species on the frontiers of Federation space. Because of their size and their more limited scientific capabilities (relative to the larger explorer classes), most exploratory cruisers perform their missions of discovery within the bounds of the Federation. The UFP covers a vast amount of space, and the exploration of many sectors has only just begun. As a result, most cruisers of this type do not venture beyond the frontiers of the UFP, and most mission profiles are of shorter duration than those performed by their explorer counterparts.

Cruisers fill many other roles in the fleet, as well. Midsized vessels of the *Miranda* and *Renaissance* classes continue to ply the spacelanes, performing missions as diverse as long-term research surveys and preliminary first contact cultural studies. These "classic" cruisers generally fall into one of three categories—those outfitted with large scientific/sensor packages, those upgraded for military and interdiction duties, and those outfitted with enhanced drive systems for long-range sector patrol missions and diplomatic contacts. The *Miranda* class falls into the first category, while *Renaissance* vessels fall into the second. In the latter half of the 24th century, most

New cruiser designs enter development constantly, and the importance of these crucial ship classes is recognized at the highest levels of Starfleet Command. Economical and utilitarian, most light cruiser profiles incorporate current technology with a minimum of ground-breaking innovation. As a result, ships in these classes can be constructed quickly and cheaply, with most of the larger shipyards able to produce in excess of six vessels per year. Starfleet plans to introduce several new cruiser classes before the end of the century; the first classes commissioned will include the new *Odin*-class light cruisers, the *Legacy*-class heavy cruisers, and the proposed *Nova*-class strike cruisers.

A SELECTION OF CRUISER CLASSES CURRENTLY IN SERVICE

CLASS	TYPE
MIRANDA	CA
RENAISSANCE	CA
NORWAY	CA
CONSTELLATION	CEX
EXCELSIOR	CEX
NEBULA	CEX
HERMES (APOLLO REFITS)	CF
ISTANBUL	CF
NIAGARA	CF
OSAKA	CF
AKIRA	CH
WAMBUNDU	CH
APOLLO	CL
CHEYENNE	CL
SABER	CL
LEGACY (PROPOSED)	CH
ODIN (PROPOSED)	CL
NOVA (PROPOSED)	CS

long-range patrol and interdiction missions are gradually being transferred to the newer fast cruiser and fast frigate classes.

The heavy cruiser has been a staple of the fleet since the early 23rd century, and heavy cruisers still serve as flagships for many sector deployment commands. In active threat situations, these ships are often seen commanding reserve forces or anchoring the primary fleet battle lines. Starfleet has several heavy cruiser classes in ongoing production, although specifications have evolved in the wake of the recent Borg incursions. The new *Akira*-class vessels represent the pinnacle of current design thinking, while the older *Wambundu*-class remains a solid performer even as it approaches the end of its production life. There are currently no fewer than five new heavy cruiser classes on Starfleet R&D drawing boards.

Originally designed for sensitive long-range diplomatic and courier missions, fast cruisers are relative newcomers to Starfleet (the first *Niagara*-class vessels were commissioned in 2349). Capable of extended journeys at high speeds, these ships have considerable defensive punch. Although the *Niagara*-class continues to serve a primarily diplomatic function, its larger *Istanbul*- and *Osaka*-class cousins are often assigned to long-range patrol, interdiction, and forward observer duties throughout the UFP. Along with the new fast frigate classes, these ships have redefined rapid deployment and response times within the fleet, and have thus assumed important roles in late 24th-century fleet operations.

Boasting some of the most impressive service records of any vessel classification, the various light cruiser classes often form the primary support and reconnaissance arms in many outlying sector commands. These ships are veritable jacks-of-all-trades for the fleet, and they can be found serving throughout the UFP in almost every capacity imaginable. From the legendary *Apollo*-class patrol craft to the venerable *Cheyenne*-class reconnaissance/sensor vessels, the utility offered by these ships remains unmatched. Because of this, updates and refits are common for all classes, and most light cruisers enjoy extended service lifetimes (see the *Apollo*-class description later in this chapter).

FRIGATES

Until recently, most frigate classes were the misunderstood stepchildren of Starfleet. While their utility was well known throughout the fleet, the stable threat environment of the early 24th century had relegated many of these vessels to simple police and patrol duties. However, as tensions gradually began to increase along the UFP frontiers, the usefulness of these smaller, well armed ships became quickly apparent once more. Today, there are more frigates and frigate classes in active Starfleet service than any other type of vessel.

Although certain heavier frigate classes are actually larger than some cruisers, most frigates are medium-sized vessels designed for military, escort, patrol, and rapid response missions. These vessels normally incorporate the latest technological developments and the most sophisticated weapons platforms available. For these reasons, frigate classes are often chosen to lead many detachments of Starfleet's rapid deployment forces. Affectionately referred to as "space tanks" by their crews, frigates tend to be the most overtly "military" vessels commissioned by Starfleet.

Descended from the warships of old, the heavy frigates of Starfleet can be found on the main battle lines of every major UFP conflict. Although most frigates are technically considered support vessels for the larger cruisers, the firepower and defensive capabilities of many newer classes are impressive by themselves.

Foremost among these recent additions to the fleet are the sleek *Steamrunner*-class vessels. Based on specifications developed under the auspices of the Perimeter Defense Directive, the *Steamrunner*-class has already distinguished itself as a formidable offensive craft, and frigates of this class have become common sights in regions where tensions run high. Building on the success enjoyed by the *Steamrunner*-class, an even more heavily armed ship is scheduled to begin active production in early 2371. Christened the *U.S.S. El Dorado*, the prototype of the new *El Dorado*-class of heavy frigates has become the current topic of the moment among the Starfleet rank and file.

With the growing emphasis on military vessels, a new appreciation has developed for the functional elegance of many of the older frigate designs. Vessels of the *New Orleans*-and *Mediterranean*-classes still serve with distinction alongside their more youthful descendants. The wider range of mission profiles built into these ships has made them ideally suited for more diverse and wide-ranging roles, such as convoy and close orbital support, reserve line support in battle, and hostile escort and evacuation duties.

In fact, the success of these older vessels has encouraged designers to appreciate the value of narrower development parameters. For example, the new *Shi'Kahr*-class frigates were designed for sensitive scientific and research duties in hostile or threat environments, while the scheduled *Mediterranean*-class refit project will upgrade these older ships based on their use as orbital and near-system support ships (the *Aegean*-class is the tentative designation for the refitted vessels).

In addition to the new fast cruiser classes, several classes of fast frigate have entered service in recent years. Collectively, these vessels have played a large role in redefining conventional strategic thinking among the top brass at Starfleet Command. Where regular border patrols were once a necessity, modern perimeter and rapid deployment forces enjoy much greater mobility and freedom. Instead of stringing numerous patrol ships over a segment of the frontier, integrated operational bases now serve as staging areas for rapid response sorties and perimeter actions. Frigate groups are dispatched to trouble zones and "hot spots," while escorts assume many of the more conventional patrol duties. The nature of frontier and border operations has changed forever.

The chief instruments of this change have been the various new "fast" ship types. While fast cruisers often anchor such response forces, fast frigates provide much of their muscle. Although frigates are normally attached to larger cruiser mission groups during times of crisis, they often operate independently during more peaceful interludes (i.e., most of the time). In fact, in outlying or "sleepy" sectors it is not uncommon to see frigates leading the response and patrol teams themselves. Starfleet has initiated aggressive production schedules for both the *Ariel*-and *Chimera*-classes of fast frigate, and both ships appear with

clockwork regularity at outposts all along the various borders of the UFP.

Another common sight along the frontier, the newer light frigate classes have also established themselves as important aspects of Starfleet's ongoing perimeter defense strategy. Designed for more static patrols in dense sectors with low to medium levels of activity, light frigates are the heavily armed equivalents of the CL's—small, maneuverable, economical to produce, and able to defend themselves admirably in a pinch. In recent years, some design overlap has occurred between these classes and certain escort classes; however, this is less an innovation issue and more a result of increasingly similar mission profiles as new, more advanced escort classes enter service.

Springfield-light frigates remain in heavy use along the spinward frontiers of the UFP, primarily because of the dense nature of most of the border sectors there. Still bearing a slight resemblance to their warship forebears, the *Springfield*-class ceases active production in 2375. The newer *Newport*-(*Santa Fe*-class refit) and *Ukora*-classes currently enjoy active production schedules, with over twenty of each vessel due for commissioning over the next three years.

A SELECTION OF FRIGATE CLASSES CURRENTLY IN SERVICE	
Class	**Type**
Mediterranean	FR
New Orleans	FR
Shi'Kahr	FR
Chimera	FF
Ariel	FF
El Dorado	FH
Steamrunner	FH
Newport	FL
Santa Fe	FL
Springfield	FL
Ukora	FL
Aegean (upcoming Mediterr. refit)	FR
Pyrenees (proposed)	FR
Oberon (proposed)	FH

ESCORTS

Dedicated escort classes were not produced on a large scale until the early 24th century. Used primarily for convoy and transport escort duties, the reduced threat environment of the late 23rd and early 24th centuries did not require heavily armed support vessels, and thus the early escort classes were often viewed as ships looking for a role to fill. The advent of the Cardassian wars during the mid-24th century changed their duties considerably.

As threats began to escalate on several frontiers, escorts started to fill roles previously reserved for frigates. Starfleet Command recognized the utility of the small, well armed escorts for a wide variety of missions, including perimeter and frontier defense, close orbital and planetary support for ground forces, fleet support during major engagements, and troop transport. While escorts remain the primary choice for convoy and sensitive transport missions, their expanded mission profiles have led to the introduction of no less than eight new ship classes in the latter half of the century.

Heavy escorts form the nucleus of Starfleet's perimeter defense and patrol forces in many sectors. Designed as a heavily armed alternative to the larger frigate classes, these vessels (commonly referred to as perimeter defense vessels, or PDV's) have distinguished themselves in numerous frontier and police actions, freeing their larger frigate counterparts for more specific "hot spot" response and interdiction duties. Two heavy escort classes—*Pinnacle*-and *Frontier*-are currently in production, with several more (including the new *Defiant*-class) scheduled for commissioning over the next few years. The *Defiant*-vessels promise to offer a departure from traditional small ship designs, incorporating defensive elements that would almost classify the vessel as a small warship.

Despite the success of the heavy escort classes, Starfleet still commissions escort vessels designed according to the more "classic" model. Used for lower-risk patrol missions and battle line support during times of crisis, these vessels are normally deployed several to a sector in regions of light activity or where threats are minimal. In addition to mundane patrol missions, escorts are often assigned to guard troop convoys and military transports. They are always a familiar sight along supply routes during major Federation engagements or during extensive fleet movements. The *Capella*-and *Pollux*-classes have become fleet standbys, while the proposed *Bolarus*-vessels would add additional firepower to this well established ship type.

More specialized than most of the escort classes, light escorts (also known as corvettes) generally perform specialized transport and support duties. While they are often called in to "back up" perimeter defense forces in times of crisis, their primary roles consist of acting as troop and personnel transports in

tense regions of space. Most ships in this class are also equipped to provide close orbital and atmospheric support for ground troops during planetary engagements, as well as performing actual troop drops and landings in enemy hot zones where conventional transports would be placed under extreme risk. Several light escort classes are currently in production, with the *Merced*-and *Nomad*-classes serving as the most prominent examples of the type. A new class, developed in conjunction with the Starfleet Marine Corps, will enter service in the mid-2370's.

A SELECTION OF ESCORT CLASSES CURRENTLY IN SERVICE

CLASS	TYPE
CAPELLA	ES
POLLUX	ES
MERCED	EL
NOMAD	EL
PINNACLE	EH
FRONTIER	EH
BOLARUS (PROPOSED)	ES
DEFIANT (PROPOSED)	EH

SCOUTS

Scout vessels have changed perhaps more than any other ship type over the past century. Originally designed to perform a diverse array of missions, including long-range observation, contact, survey, and courier duties, many of these additional mission profiles have since been subsumed by other, more specialized vessels.

The Federation's needs with regard to deep space exploration and reconnaissance have also changed drastically over the past century. Where the UFP once encompassed only a handful of sectors near its present core, expansion eventually brought the Federation to its current considerable size. Vessels can no longer travel from the core worlds to the frontier in a matter of days. Journeys have become longer, and the require-

ments for long-range Scout vessels have changed as well.

These changes have led the rank and file of the fleet to begin calling the new ships "flying nacelles," a reference to the large propulsion systems these small ships are often forced to carry. *Rigel*-class heavy scouts regularly travel beyond the boundaries of the UFP; their mission profiles normally consist of basic stellar charting, surveillance, and system reconnaissance. The information gained is then used to plan longer, more extensive missions to these unexplored regions. Such follow-up missions are normally carried out by the larger explorer and cruiser classes. In times of crisis, heavy scouts are often employed as patrol and surveillance vessels along the front of a conflict.

Starfleet continues to commission more conventional, shorter-range scout vessels as well. *Hokule'a*- and *Vigilant*-class scouts ply the empty spaces of many outback sectors, and can often be found in uncharted regions along the UFP frontier. While these vessels are not capable of the extended missions performed by their heavier brethren, their value as surveillance, communication, reconnaissance, and courier vessels is appreciated throughout Starfleet.

As more explorer type vessels are called to trouble spots and frontier sector commands, the long-term utility of the heavy scout classes has become more important to the powers-that-be in Starfleet Command. As a result, the Long Range Survey Directive was implemented in late 2369. Under this directive, additional resources will be allocated to new scout vessel design and development, as well as to the development of new specialized courier and surveyor ships. The first vessels produced under this initiative—the *Orion* class of heavy scouts—will enter service in the mid-2370's.

A SELECTION OF SCOUT CLASSES CURRENTLY IN SERVICE

CLASS	TYPE
HOKULE'A	SS
VIGILANT	SS
RIGEL	SH
ORION (PROPOSED)	SH

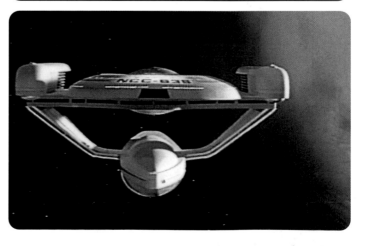

SPECIALIZED, AUXILIARY, AND SUPPORT VESSELS

Any organization the size of the Federation Starfleet requires tremendous support to function effectively. For every ship of the line in Starfleet, there are probably three additional support vessels operating in the background. Such specialized and auxiliary ships perform a staggering array of so-called "low profile" missions—everything from planetary surveys to fleet hospital duty to the delivery of sensitive communiqués. It is this vast secondary fleet that in many ways keeps Starfleet "afloat" and operating at peak efficiency.

An impressive number of classes and ship types compose the various specialized and support vessels of Starfleet, and only a small portion of the whole will be covered here. It is important to remember that many of these ship classes are also used by departments or divisions within the UFP government proper; since such vessels are technically civilian ships, their government or civilian variants normally carry different class designations and numbering schemes than their Starfleet counterparts. While your average Federation citizen might not know that a Starfleet *Deneva*-class transport is essentially the same vessel as a civilian *Ceres*-class ship, the distinction remains an important one.

More specialized versions of the standard scout vessel types, survey and courier vessels are attached to nearly every sector fleet. Survey ships are generally sent in after the scouts and explorers to perform extensive surveys and analyses of new worlds or regions of space. As such, these ships are equipped with state-of-the-art sensor and scientific packages, often to the exclusion of defensive systems that would be considered standard on most ships of their size. When traveling to trouble spots or sensitive areas, most survey vessels will be accompanied by an escort of some sort. The *Sagan*-, *Korolev*-, and *Copernicus*-classes are the most common dedicated surveyor classes currently in service; while the larger *Korolev*- and *Sagan*-class deep space surveyors perform deep space, long-term missions, the smaller *Copernicus*-class vessels are usually dispatched for simpler, near-system or core world missions.

Sacrificing many of the amenities found on other vessels of their size, effective courier design hinges on a single requirement—speed. Boasting limited comforts and even more limited offensive and defensive capabilities, courier classes were the origin of the "flying nacelle" nickname that has since stuck to the scout classes. Although not many of these vessels are produced each year, they can be found in every corner of the Federation. Their primary mission profile includes the delivery of sensitive (or secret) documents and information, as well as the transport of extremely valuable or rare goods and supplies. *Loki*-class couriers represent the bulk of courier vessels in service, but many of their more critical duties will probably be subsumed by the new *Mercury*-class when it enters active production in 2373.

Representing the apex of specialized spaceframe and interior vessel design, the various classes of research, laboratory, and medical ships represent critical and invaluable mainstays of every group in the fleet. Although a large number of different configurations exist for each of these ship types, many are refit or rebuilt for very specific missions or mission profiles—the requirements of a botanical research vessel are worlds away from those of a warp field test ship. As a result, an officer never knows what he might find when assigned to such a specialized vessel.

Medical and hospital ships in particular are dispatched according to perceived need; while most sector groups have several small medical frigates attached to them, large hospital cruisers are reserved for threat-heavy regions or main battle line support during times of war. Numerous classes of specialized research and medical vessels are used by Starfleet—these include *Olympic*- and *Geneva*-class medical ships, *Fermi*- and *Oppenheimer*-class research vessels, *Nobel*-class laboratory ships, and the large *Graceful*-class hospital cruisers.

According to their crews, the "real" workhorses of Starfleet are not the explorers, cruisers, and other ships of the line, but rather the support ships that function in the background. These vessels—the various classes of transport, cargo carrier, tanker, tug, and tender—provide the ongoing support and assistance necessary to keep the rest of the fleet operational.

Transports, cargo carriers, and tankers are attached to every Starfleet installation, both planetary and space-based, no matter what its size. Transport missions generally involve the movement of personnel or troops from place to place, although in times of crisis they may be commandeered to move fleet supplies or materiel. Armored transports are specifically designed to move troops, weapons, and supplies to the front lines of a conflict or through hostile territory (although since these vessels are not heavily armed, escorts are often substituted when transporting personnel or equipment through an actual war zone or in the heat of a pitched battle). Transport classes include the older *Sydney* personnel transports, the newer *Deneva*-

class light transports, and the Iowa-class armored transports.

Cargo carriers are large vessels, well protected but carrying little or no armament. Their primary role is the transport of goods and supplies of all kinds, from nonreplicable foodstuffs and medicines to hazardous materials and military hardware. Although officially designated "cargo carriers," most Starfleet personnel simply refer to them collectively as "transports" (thus not distinguishing them from proper transports). Classes include the light *Fiji* ships, the heavier *Rakota* class (used for perishable or biological substances), and the new *Midway* vessels (used for hazardous or weapons-grade material). Tankers are essentially cargo carriers with reinforced spaceframes and shielding; they transport the raw dilithium and deuterium required for warp core function, and are attached as reserve or support ships to most sector groups.

Tenders and tugs normally operate within a static theater of operations, rendering assistance to disabled ships when necessary. Vessels of each type are often assigned to specific starbases, deep space stations, or shipyards, and only travel with larger fleet groups in times of full-scale battle or war. Neither ship type carries significant armor, shielding, or weapons systems. Tenders perform space-based or orbital repairs, and serve as support and resupply vessels during large-scale conflicts. The larger examples of the class resemble small-scale, floating dry docks. Tender classes currently in service include the smaller *Ural* -class and the larger *Andes*-class fleet tenders. *Sierra*-class impulse tenders are a common sight around most starbases and deep space stations.

Tugs are responsible for moving vessels into and out of space and ground-based dry docks, as well as towing disabled vessels to repair facilities. They employ heavy tractor beams to accomplish these duties, and several tug classes are in fact warp-capable. In times of crisis, these ships are sometimes dispatched to the front lines as aid vessels for ships that become crippled during battle. Tug classes currently in service include the *Hogan* and *Piper* classes. Impulse versions of several warp-capable tender and tug classes are produced as well.

A FINAL NOTE ON SUPPORT AND AUXILIARY VESSEL CLASSIFICATIONS

Although not officially incorporated into most support ship class names, most Starfleet personnel have adopted traditional colloquial descriptions for many of these ships. For example, while *Olympic*-class medical ships are simply classified as medical vessels for administration purposes, they are commonly known as "medical cruisers." In this case, the "cruiser" designation serves more as a reference to the ship's overall size than it does as a description of its capabilities. Whenever possible, we have chosen to employ these traditional Starfleet colloquialisms.

A SELECTION OF SPECIALIZED, AUXILIARY, AND SUPPORT CLASSES CURRENTLY IN SERVICE

CLASS		TYPE
COURIERS		
	LOKI	SC
	MERCURY (PROPOSED)	SC
MEDICAL		
	GENEVA	MD
	GRACEFUL	MD
	OLYMPIC	MD
SURVEYORS		
	COPERNICUS	SV
	KOROLEV	SV
	SAGAN	SV
RESEARCH/LABORATORY		
	FERMI	SRS
	OPPENHEIMER	SRS
	NOBLE	SRL
CARGO CARRIERS		
	FIJI	TC
	MIDWAY	TC
	RAKOTA	TC
TANKERS		
	LAURO	TA
	WEI-FA	TA
TENDERS		
	ANDES	TN
	SIERRA (IMPULSE)	TN-I
	URAL	TN
TRANSPORTS		
	DENEVA	TT
	SYDNEY	TT
	IOWA	TTA
	UTAH	TTA
TUGS		
	HOGAN	TG
	PIPER	TG

STARSHIP TEMPLATES

The following starship templates detail thirteen new vessels for use in your *Star Trek: The Next Generation* episodes. These ships represent a general cross-section of mission profiles and design philosophies, and their commissioning and service dates include every period of the 24th century.

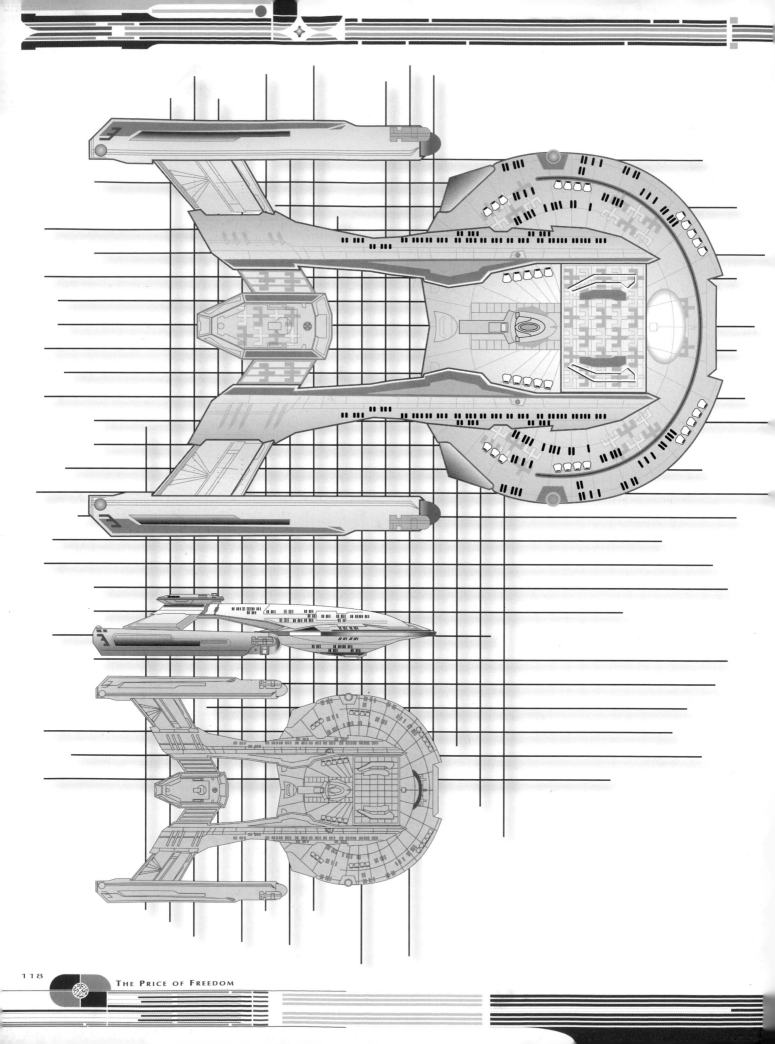

AKIRA–CLASS STARSHIP

CLASS AND TYPE: *AKIRA*–CLASS HEAVY CRUISER
COMMISSIONING DATE: 2368
HULL CHARACTERISTICS
> **SIZE:** 7 (465 METERS LONG, 26 DECKS)
> **RESISTANCE:** 5
> **STRUCTURAL POINTS:** 140

OPERATIONS CHARACTERISTICS
> **CREW/PASSENGERS/EVAC:** 500/1750/4500
> [6 PWR/ROUND]
> **COMPUTERS:** 5
> [5 PWR/ROUND]
> **TRANSPORTERS:** 4 PERSONNEL, 4 CARGO, 4 EMERGENCY
> [6 PWR/ROUND]
> **TRACTOR BEAMS:** 1 AD, 1 FD, 1 FV
> [2/RATING USED]

PROPULSION AND POWER CHARACTERISTICS
> **WARP SYSTEM:** 6.0/9.4/9.8 (12 HOURS)
> [2/WARP FACTOR]
> **IMPULSE SYSTEM:** .75c/.95c
> [7/9 PWR/ROUND]
> **POWER:** 190

SENSOR SYSTEMS
> **LONG-RANGE SENSORS:** +2/17 LIGHT-YEARS
> [6 PWR/ROUND]
> **LATERAL SENSORS:** +2/1 LIGHT-YEAR
> [4 PWR/ROUND]
> **NAVIGATIONAL SENSORS:** +2
> [5 PWR/ROUND]
> **SENSORS SKILL:** 5

WEAPONS SYSTEMS
> *TYPE X PHASER*
> **RANGE:** 10/30,000/100,000/300,000
> **ARC:** ALL (720 DEGREES)
> **ACCURACY:** 4/5/7/10
> **DAMAGE:** 20
> **POWER:** [20]

TYPE II PHOTON TORPEDOES
> **NUMBER:** 275
> **LAUNCHERS:** 1 AD, 1 FV
> **SPREAD:** 10
> **ARC:** FORWARD OR AFT, BUT ARE SELF-GUIDED
> **RANGE:** 15/300,000/1,000,000/3,500,000
> **ACCURACY:** 4/5/7/10
> **DAMAGE:** 20
> **POWER:** [5]
> **WEAPONS SKILL:** 5

DEFENSIVE SYSTEMS
> *STARFLEET DEFLECTOR SHIELD*
> **PROTECTION:** 60/80
> **POWER:** [60]

DESCRIPTION AND NOTES

FLEET DATA: Starfleet's new *Akira*–class vessels represent the epitome of fast, maneuverable threat-response design. First launched in 2368, the *Akira*–class ships were the first vessels authorized by the Perimeter Defense Directive to enter active service. (Additional ships designed under this classified directive—including the *Norway*, *Steamrunner*, and *Saber*-classes—would enter active duty over the next several years.) Although smaller and lighter than many of the larger *Explorer*–type vessels, these ships boast one of the heaviest armaments ever seen on a Starfleet ship of this size.

Of the twelve new ship classes placed in accelerated development by the PDD, the *Akira*–class Heavy Cruisers remain one of the most versatile. Although primarily designed for active defense duties and long-range perimeter actions, *Akira*–class vessels have proven themselves time and time again on a wide variety of Starfleet missions. In the modern age of Borg incursions, such versatility has become a necessity.

NOTEWORTHY VESSELS/ SERVICE RECORDS/ ENCOUNTERS: *U.S.S. Akira*, prototype; *U.S.S. Black Elk*, lost during routine patrol along Cardassian border; *U.S.S. Nez Perce*, participated in Romulan blockade (2368); *U.S.S. Susquehanna*, engaged the Tholians during the Draconis IX Perimeter Action (2371); *U.S.S. Thunderchild*, participated in defense of Sector 001 during the Borg incursion of 2373. Also in service: *U.S.S. Geronimo*, *U.S.S. Mateo*.

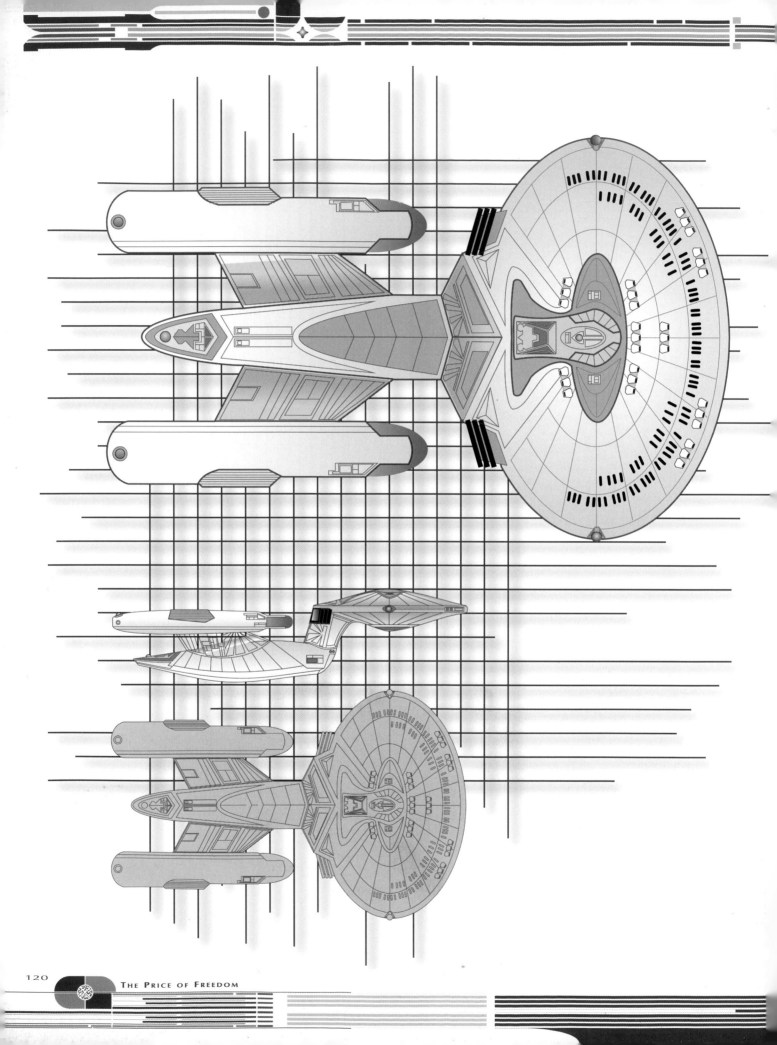

APOLLO–CLASS STARSHIP

CLASS AND TYPE: *Apollo*–class Light Cruiser
COMMISSIONING DATE: 2325
HULL CHARACTERISTICS
    SIZE: 5 (315 METERS LONG, 16 DECKS)
    RESISTANCE: 3
    STRUCTURAL POINTS: 100

OPERATIONS CHARACTERISTICS
    CREW/PASSENGERS/EVAC: 100/700/2500
        [6 PWR/ROUND]
    COMPUTERS: 4
        [4 PWR/ROUND]
    TRANSPORTERS: 4 PERSONNEL, 3 CARGO, 3 EMERGENCY
        [5 PWR/ROUND]
    TRACTOR BEAMS: 1 AD, 1 FV
        [2/RATING USED]

PROPULSION AND POWER CHARACTERISTICS
    WARP SYSTEM: 6.0/9.2/9.6 (12 HOURS)
        [2/WARP FACTOR]
    IMPULSE SYSTEM: .75c/.95c
        [7/9 PWR/ROUND]
    POWER: 160

SENSOR SYSTEMS
    LONG-RANGE SENSORS: +1/15 LIGHT-YEARS
        [6 PWR/ROUND]
    LATERAL SENSORS: +1/1 LIGHT-YEAR
        [4 PWR/ROUND]
    NAVIGATIONAL SENSORS: +2
        [5 PWR/ROUND]
    SENSORS SKILL: 4

WEAPONS SYSTEMS
    TYPE VIII PHASER
        RANGE: 10/30,000/100,000/300,000
        ARC: ALL (720 DEGREES)
        ACCURACY: 5/6/8/11
        DAMAGE: 16
        POWER: [16]

    TYPE II PHOTON TORPEDOES
        NUMBER: 150
        LAUNCHERS: 1 AD, 1 FV
        SPREAD: 4

        ARC: FORWARD OR AFT, BUT ARE SELF-GUIDED
        RANGE: 15/300,000/1,000,000/3,500,000
        ACCURACY: 4/5/7/10
        DAMAGE: 20
        POWER: [5]
        WEAPONS SKILL: 4

DEFENSIVE SYSTEMS
    STARFLEET DEFLECTOR SHIELD
        PROTECTION: 50/70
        POWER: [50]

DESCRIPTION AND NOTES

FLEET DATA: A Starfleet workhorse for nearly fifty years, the *Apollo* class of light cruisers has had one of the most distinguished service careers in the fleet. First launched in 2325, *Apollo*–class cruisers were originally intended to replace the older *Philadelphia*–class vessels of the 23rd century, which reached the end of their production lives in 2312. The *Apollo* vessels were small, quick, and capable of extended mission profiles, thus making them ideal for sector patrol and interdiction duties. In fact, they are still used in this capacity today, and as a class comprise the most common patrol craft encountered in Federation space.

The *Apollo* class remains one of the most reliable spaceframe designs ever to come out of Starfleet's Advanced Technologies division, and many of its concepts can be seen reflected in the newer *Galaxy*–class vessels. As a result of the current threat climate in the UFP—and because of their exemplary maintenance record as a class—many *Apollo*-class vessels are currently being refit into the updated *Hermes*-class of fast cruiser. The *Apollo* class itself ceased production in 2358, when the last vessel was delivered to Starbase 674 from the Utopia Planitia fleet yards.

NOTEWORTHY VESSELS/ SERVICE RECORDS/ ENCOUNTERS: *U.S.S. Apollo*, prototype; *U.S.S. Agamemnon*, a member of Task Force Three during the expected Borg invasion of 2369; *U.S.S. Ajax*, used as test vessel for experimental warp drive upgrade in 2364; *U.S.S. Clement*, assigned to core world patrol duties in late 2360's; *U.S.S. Gage*, lost in the Battle of Wolf 359; *U.S.S. T'Pau*, decommissioned in 2364, later stolen and used to transport Romulan troops during an attempted invasion of Vulcan in 2368. Also in service: *U.S.S. Chronos, U.S.S. McHenry.*

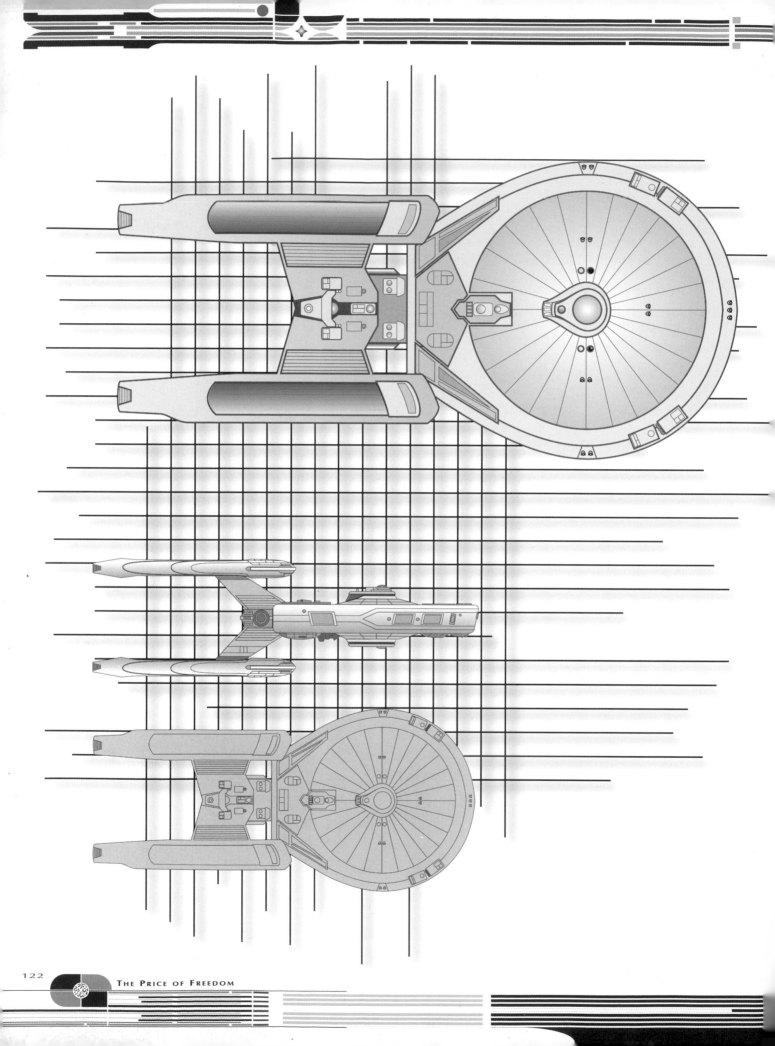

THE PRICE OF FREEDOM

CONSTELLATION–CLASS STARSHIP

CLASS AND TYPE: *CONSTELLATION*–CLASS EXPLORATORY CRUISER

COMMISSIONING DATE: 2304

HULL CHARACTERISTICS

SIZE: 5 (302 METERS LONG, 17 DECKS)

RESISTANCE: 3

STRUCTURAL POINTS: 100

OPERATIONS CHARACTERISTICS

CREW/PASSENGERS/EVAC: 350/1500/3500

[6 PWR/ROUND]

COMPUTERS: 4

[4 PWR/ROUND]

TRANSPORTERS: 4 PERSONNEL, 4 CARGO, 4 EMERGENCY

[6 PWR/ROUND]

TRACTOR BEAMS: 1 AD, 1 FV

[2/RATING USED]

PROPULSION AND POWER CHARACTERISTICS

WARP SYSTEM: 5.3/9.0/9.2 (8 HOURS)

[2/WARP FACTOR]

IMPULSE SYSTEM: .75C/.9C

[7/9 PWR/ROUND]

POWER: 150

SENSOR SYSTEMS

LONG-RANGE SENSORS: +2/15 LIGHT-YEARS

[6 PWR/ROUND]

LATERAL SENSORS: +1/1 LIGHT-YEAR

[4 PWR/ROUND]

NAVIGATIONAL SENSORS: +1

[5 PWR/ROUND]

SENSORS SKILL: 4

WEAPONS SYSTEMS

TYPE VIII PHASER

RANGE: 10/30,000/100,000/300,000

ARC: ALL (720 DEGREES)

ACCURACY: 5/6/8/11

DAMAGE: 16

POWER: [16]

TYPE II PHOTON TORPEDOES

NUMBER: 160

LAUNCHERS: 1 AD, 1 FV,

SPREAD: 5

ARC: FORWARD OR AFT, BUT ARE SELF-GUIDED

RANGE: 15/300,000/1,000,000/3,500,000

ACCURACY: 4/5/7/10

DAMAGE: 20

POWER: [5]

WEAPONS SKILL: 4

DEFENSIVE SYSTEMS

STARFLEET DEFLECTOR SHIELD

PROTECTION: 48/70

POWER: [48]

DESCRIPTION AND NOTES

FLEET DATA: Direct descendants of the legendary *Constitution*–class ships, *Constellation*–class vessels built and improved on many of their predecessors' most important innovations. Utilizing expanded navigational and lateral sensor templates, as well as a four-nacelle warp drive configuration, the *Constellation* class assumed a leading role in both deep space exploration and long-range perimeter defense during the early 24th century.

Although some of these duties were subsumed by the new *Ambassador*–class vessels when they were launched in 2322, the *Constellation* class remained in many ways the more versatile design. Perhaps the best testament to the class' utility is the fact that many remain in active service today, despite the fact that the class' production life ended nearly twenty years ago.

NOTEWORTHY VESSELS/ SERVICE RECORDS/ ENCOUNTERS: *U.S.S. Constellation*, prototype; *U.S.S. Gettysburg*, former command of Admiral Mark Jameson; *U.S.S. Hathaway*, participated in battle simulation with *Enterprise-D*; *U.S.S. Magellan*, commanded by Captain Conklin; *U.S.S. Stargazer*, former command of Captain Jean–Luc Picard, destroyed in the Battle of Maxia (2355); *U.S.S. Victory*, commanded by Captain Zimbata, posting of Geordi LaForge prior to his service aboard *Enterprise–D*. Also in service: *U.S.S. Antietam, U.S.S. Fading Sun, U.S.S. Vespucci*.

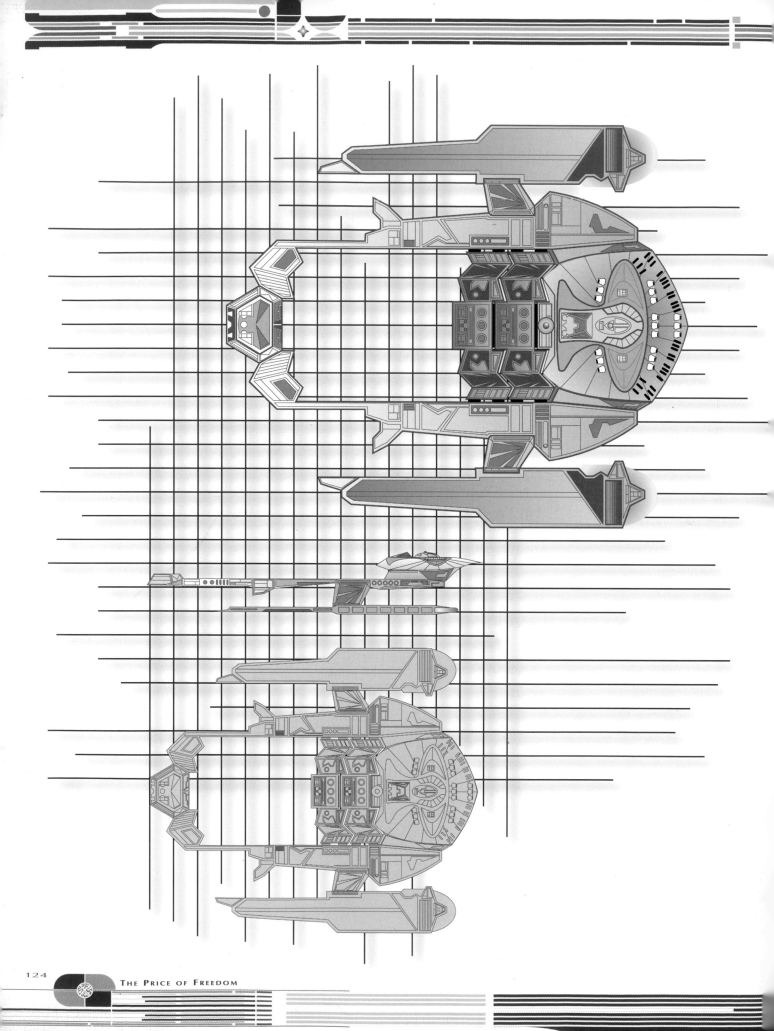

DENEVA–CLASS STARSHIP

CLASS AND TYPE: *DENEVA*–CLASS LIGHT TRANSPORT
COMMISSIONING DATE: 2318
HULL CHARACTERISTICS
    SIZE: 4 (210 METERS LONG, 11 DECKS)
    RESISTANCE: 2
    STRUCTURAL POINTS: 80

OPERATIONS CHARACTERISTICS
    CREW/PASSENGERS/EVAC: 90/1100/2000
      [6 PWR/ROUND]
    COMPUTERS: 3
      [3 PWR/ROUND]
    TRANSPORTERS: 3 PERSONNEL, 8 CARGO, 3 EMERGENCY
      [7 PWR/ROUND]
    TRACTOR BEAMS: 1 AD, 1 FV
      [2/RATING USED]

PROPULSION AND POWER CHARACTERISTICS
    WARP SYSTEM: 5.0/9.0/9.2 (6 HOURS)
      [2/WARP FACTOR]
    IMPULSE SYSTEM: .5c/.75c
      [5/7 PWR/ROUND]
    POWER: 110

SENSOR SYSTEMS
    LONG-RANGE SENSORS: +1/12 LIGHT-YEARS
      [6 PWR/ROUND]
    LATERAL SENSORS: +1/1 LIGHT-YEAR
      [4 PWR/ROUND]
    NAVIGATIONAL SENSORS: +1
      [5 PWR/ROUND]
    SENSORS SKILL: 4

WEAPONS SYSTEMS
    TYPE VI PHASER
      RANGE: 10/30,000/100,000/300,000
      ARC: ALL (720 DEGREES)
      ACCURACY: 5/6/8/11
      DAMAGE: 12
      POWER: [12]
      WEAPONS SKILL: 3

DEFENSIVE SYSTEMS
    STARFLEET DEFLECTOR SHIELD
      PROTECTION: 30/48
      POWER: [30]

DESCRIPTION AND NOTES

FLEET DATA: *Deneva*–class transports are a familiar sight on worlds and at starbases throughout Federation space. One of the most common types of Starfleet transport vessel, the class has been in service since the early 24th century. These ships are used by Starfleet sector commands to transport everything from deuterium to photon warheads.

Its unique modularity accounts for much of the popularity of this versatile design. The main compartments can be configured to accept any of several prefabricated designs, including passenger quarters, standard cargo bays, hydroponic transport modules, security modules, and biological/medical transfer modules. Most starbases have several of each type of module on hand.

NOTEWORTHY VESSELS/ SERVICE RECORDS/ ENCOUNTERS: *U.S.S. Deneva*, prototype; *U.S.S. Arcos*, lost over Turkana IV; *U.S.S. LaSalle*, discovered series of radiation anomalies in the Gamma Arigulon system (2367). Also in service: *U.S.S. Eridani*, *U.S.S. Indi*.

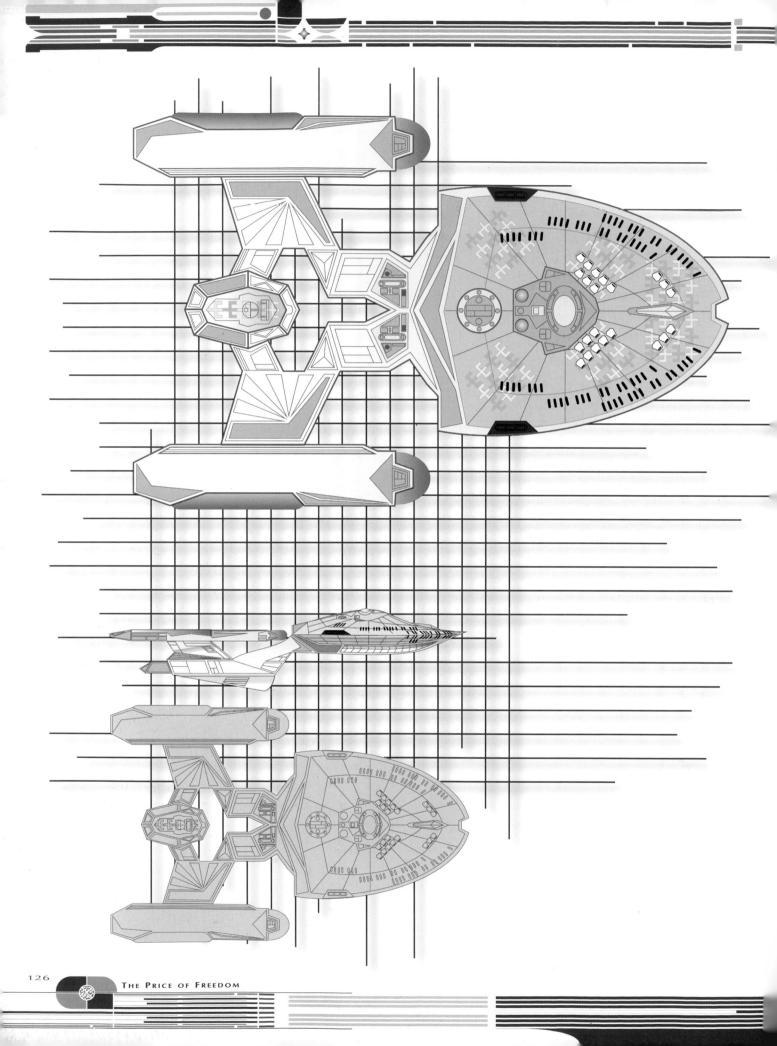

MERCED–CLASS STARSHIP

CLASS AND TYPE: *MERCED*–CLASS LIGHT ESCORT (CORVETTE)

COMMISSIONING DATE: 2312

HULL CHARACTERISTICS

    SIZE: 4 (187 METERS LONG, 9 DECKS)

    RESISTANCE: 3

    STRUCTURAL POINTS: 80

OPERATIONS CHARACTERISTICS

    CREW/PASSENGERS/EVAC: 50/150/400

        [5 PWR/ROUND]

    COMPUTERS: 3

        [3 PWR/ROUND]

    TRANSPORTERS: 2 PERSONNEL, 2 CARGO, 2 EMERGENCY

        [3 PWR/ROUND]

    TRACTOR BEAMS: 1 AD, 1 FV

        [2/RATING USED]

PROPULSION AND POWER CHARACTERISTICS

    WARP SYSTEM: 5.0/9.0/9.2 (12 HOURS)

        [2/WARP FACTOR]

    IMPULSE SYSTEM: .7C/.9C

        [7/9 PWR/ROUND]

    POWER: 125

SENSOR SYSTEMS

    LONG-RANGE SENSORS: +1/15 LIGHT-YEARS

        [6 PWR/ROUND]

    LATERAL SENSORS: +1/1 LIGHT-YEAR

        [4 PWR/ROUND]

    NAVIGATIONAL SENSORS: +1

        [5 PWR/ROUND]

    SENSORS SKILL: 4

WEAPONS SYSTEMS

    TYPE VII PHASER

        RANGE: 10/30,000/100,000/300,000

        ARC: ALL (720 DEGREES)

        ACCURACY: 5/6/8/11

        DAMAGE: 14

        POWER: [14]

    TYPE II PHOTON TORPEDOES

        NUMBER: 75

        LAUNCHERS: 1 AD, 1 FV,

        SPREAD: 4

        ARC: FORWARD OR AFT, BUT ARE SELF-GUIDED

        RANGE: 15/300,000/1,000,000/3,500,000

        ACCURACY: 4/5/7/10

        DAMAGE: 20

        POWER: [5]

        WEAPONS SKILL: 4

DEFENSIVE SYSTEMS

    STARFLEET DEFLECTOR SHIELD

        PROTECTION: 48/70

        POWER: [48]

DESCRIPTION AND NOTES

FLEET DATA: First launched in early 2312, shortly after the Tomed Incident, the *Merced* class of light escorts was part of an aborted development program initiated to combat the growing Romulan threat. Originally intended to serve as support vessels for the proposed Freedom class of strike cruisers, the *Merced* program was discontinued—along with the never–launched *Freedom* project— when the Romulans entered their self-imposed isolation and Starfleet assumed a decidedly less hawkish attitude toward the Star Empire. As a result, the *Merced* class has the curious distinction of having the shortest production lifespan of any vessel in Starfleet history (only sixteen ships were produced over a period of four years).

Despite their limited production life, *Merced* vessels represent prime examples of early 24th-century functional design. Well armed, sleek, and uncompromising, these ships have an unusually short range for Starfleet craft (they were originally designed for fleet escort, troop transport and interdiction duties—most *Merced* mission profiles last less than a year). Because of this, most are attached to starbases and deep space stations as support and defense ships. Others still serve in frontier regions as escorts for newer cruisers and frigates.

NOTEWORTHY VESSELS/ SERVICE RECORDS/ ENCOUNTERS: *U.S.S. Merced*, prototype; *U.S.S. Trieste*, stationed near Starbase 74, former assignment of Cmdr. Data. Also in service: *U.S.S. Calypso, U.S.S. Pumori*.

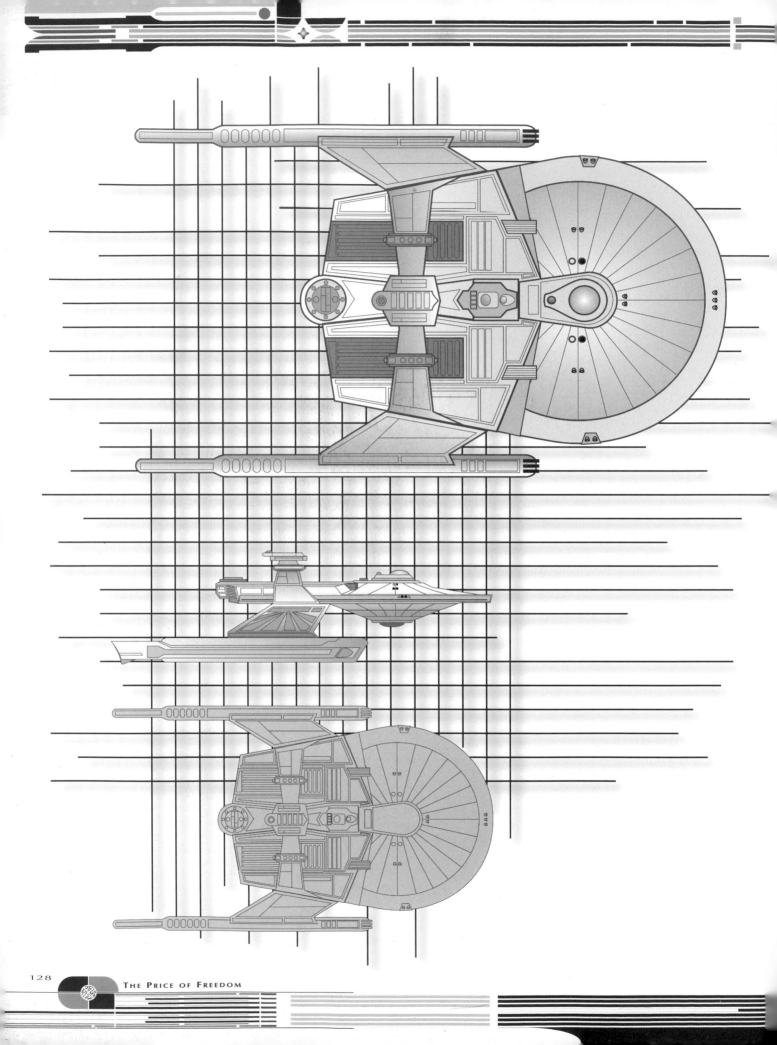

THE PRICE OF FREEDOM

MIRANDA–CLASS STARSHIP

CLASS AND TYPE: *Miranda*–class Cruiser
COMMISSIONING DATE: 2274
HULL CHARACTERISTICS
    SIZE: 5 (278 METERS LONG, 15 DECKS)
    RESISTANCE: 3
    STRUCTURAL POINTS: 100

OPERATIONS CHARACTERISTICS
    CREW/PASSENGERS/EVAC: 220/250/500
      [5 PWR/ROUND]
    COMPUTERS: 5
      [5 PWR/ROUND]
    TRANSPORTERS: 4 PERSONNEL, 3 CARGO, 3 EMERGENCY
      [5 PWR/ROUND]
    TRACTOR BEAMS: 1 AD, 1 FV
      [2/RATING USED]

PROPULSION AND POWER CHARACTERISTICS
    WARP SYSTEM: 5.0/8.8/9.2 (12 HOURS)
      [2/WARP FACTOR]
    IMPULSE SYSTEM: .6c/.8c
      [6/8 PWR/ROUND]
    POWER: 130

SENSOR SYSTEMS
    LONG-RANGE SENSORS: +1/15 LIGHT-YEARS
      [6 PWR/ROUND]
    LATERAL SENSORS: +1/1 LIGHT-YEAR
      [4 PWR/ROUND]
    NAVIGATIONAL SENSORS: +2
      [5 PWR/ROUND]
    SENSORS SKILL: 4

WEAPONS SYSTEMS
    TYPE VII PHASER
    RANGE: 10/30,000/100,000/300,000
    ARC: ALL (720 DEGREES)
    ACCURACY: 5/6/8/11
    DAMAGE: 14
    POWER: [14]
    TYPE SX-3 PULSE PHASER CANNON
    RANGE: 10/35,000/110,000/325,000
    ARC: FORWARD OR AFT
    ACCURACY: 5/6/8/11
    DAMAGE: 15
    POWER: [15]
    TYPE II PHOTON TORPEDOES
    NUMBER: 150
    LAUNCHERS: 1 AD, 1 FV,
    SPREAD: 5
    ARC: FORWARD OR AFT, BUT ARE SELF-GUIDED
    RANGE: 15/300,000/1,000,000/3,500,000
    ACCURACY: 4/5/7/10
    DAMAGE: 20
    POWER: [5]
    WEAPONS SKILL: 4

DEFENSIVE SYSTEMS
    STARFLEET DEFLECTOR SHIELD
    PROTECTION: 48/70
    POWER: [48]

DESCRIPTION AND NOTES

FLEET DATA: A Starfleet fixture of long-range scientific, supply, and exploratory missions for nearly a century, *Miranda*–class vessels have probably logged more parsecs than any other single vessel class. During the late 23rd century, Starfleet Command began to place an increasing emphasis on deep space exploration and surveying. *Miranda*–class vessels were the first ships launched after the inception of the Exploratory Vessel Initiative, and represent the most notable result of Starfleet's renewed focus on exploration and discovery.

Merging a host of diverse capabilities, versatility quickly became a hallmark of the class. Although *Miranda*–class ships primarily undertake scientific and exploratory missions, certain systems modules are swappable. These *Miranda* variants enjoyed great popularity in the early 24th century, and their expanded tactical and defensive systems are more than a match for most foes. Ships of this class have participated in every major battle of the 24th century, often serving on the secondary or reserve battle lines.

Older *Miranda*–class ships are currently decommissioned and sent to surplus depots, scrapped for parts, or used as training vessels. Although the active production life of these ships ceased over a decade ago, many *Miranda*–class vessels continue to serve with distinction throughout Federation space and beyond.

NOTEWORTHY VESSELS/ SERVICE RECORDS/ ENCOUNTERS: *U.S.S. Miranda*, prototype; *U.S.S. Brattain*, trapped in a Tyken's rift (2367); *U.S.S. Lantree*, destroyed in classified incident (2365); *U.S.S. Reliant*, support vessel for classified Genesis Project, later hijacked by Khan Noonian Singh; *U.S.S. Saratoga*, lost in the Battle of Wolf 359; *U.S.S. Tian An Men*, participated in Romulan blockade (2368); *U.S.S. Vigilant*, lost during long-range survey mission in Perseus Arm. Also in service: *U.S.S. Andover*, *U.S.S. Brisbane*, *U.S.S. Mondial*.

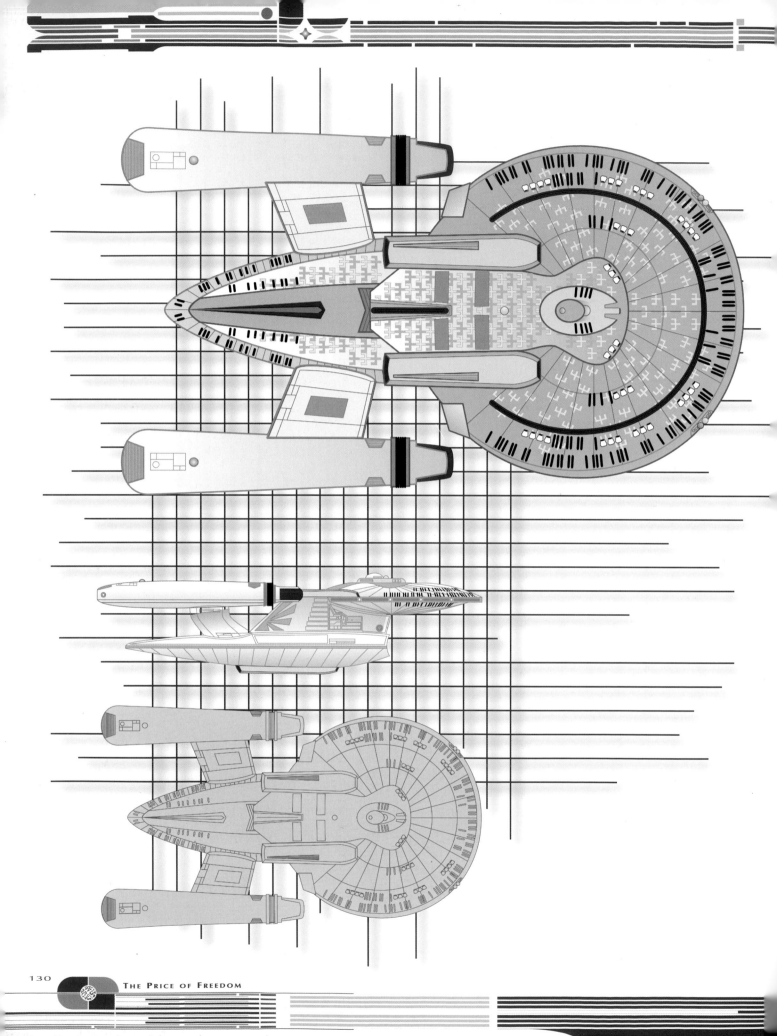

THE PRICE OF FREEDOM

NEW ORLEANS–CLASS STARSHIP

CLASS AND TYPE: *NEW ORLEANS*–CLASS FRIGATE
COMMISSIONING DATE: 2332
HULL CHARACTERISTICS
  SIZE: 7 (425 METERS LONG, 18 DECKS)
  RESISTANCE: 4
  STRUCTURAL POINTS: 140

OPERATIONS CHARACTERISTICS
  CREW/PASSENGERS/EVAC: 550/1600/4200
    [6 PWR/ROUND]
  COMPUTERS: 4
    [4 PWR/ROUND]
  TRANSPORTERS: 4 PERSONNEL, 4 CARGO, 4 EMERGENCY
    [6 PWR/ROUND]
  TRACTOR BEAMS: 1 AD, 1 FD, 1 FV
    [2/RATING USED]

PROPULSION AND POWER CHARACTERISTICS
  WARP SYSTEM: 5.0/9.0/9.3 (12 HOURS)
    [2/WARP FACTOR]
  IMPULSE SYSTEM: .75C/.9C
    [7/9 PWR/ROUND]
  POWER: 170

SENSOR SYSTEMS
  LONG-RANGE SENSORS: +2/15 LIGHT-YEARS
    [6 PWR/ROUND]
  LATERAL SENSORS: +2/1 LIGHT-YEAR
    [4 PWR/ROUND]
  NAVIGATIONAL SENSORS: +1
    [5 PWR/ROUND]
  SENSORS SKILL: 4

WEAPONS SYSTEMS
  TYPE IX PHASER
    RANGE: 10/30,000/100,000/300,000
    ARC: ALL (720 DEGREES)
    ACCURACY: 4/5/7/10
    DAMAGE: 18
    POWER: [18]

  TYPE II PHOTON TORPEDOES
    NUMBER: 200

LAUNCHERS: 1 AD, 1 FV,
  SPREAD: 8
  ARC: FORWARD OR AFT, BUT ARE SELF-GUIDED
  RANGE: 15/300,000/1,000,000/3,500,000
  ACCURACY: 4/5/7/10
  DAMAGE: 20
  POWER: [5]
  WEAPONS SKILL: 5

DEFENSIVE SYSTEMS
  STARFLEET DEFLECTOR SHIELD
    PROTECTION: 55/75
    POWER: [55]

DESCRIPTION AND NOTES

FLEET DATA: These ships are commonly found leading reserve forces and secondary battle lines during large-scale conflicts. *New Orleans*–class vessels represent an unusual departure for Starfleet—a vessel developed primarily for military use. Designed during the early period of tension with the Cardassian Union, these ships often form the core of sector defense groups. Most are assigned to regular patrol duty along the various frontiers of the UFP, and as such are often among the first vessels to respond to new threats or crises.

New Orleans–class ships descend from the old school of starship design, with individual elements and systems reminiscent of their *Daedalus*–class ancestors. Theirs is a philosophy of function above form, with the amenities found in larger explorer-type ships often absent. Instead, tactical and defensive systems receive additional space within the hull; enemies are often unprepared for the considerable offensive and defensive capabilities of these deceptively maneuverable frigates.

NOTEWORTHY VESSELS/ SERVICE RECORDS/ ENCOUNTERS: *U.S.S. New Orleans*, prototype; *U.S.S. Kyushu*, destroyed during the Battle of Wolf 359; *U.S.S. Renegade*, commanded by Captain Tryla Scott, rendezvoused with *Enterprise–D* during attempted alien takeover of Starfleet Command; *U.S.S. Rutledge*, served in Cardassian war, early posting of Miles O'Brien; *U.S.S. Santa Fe*, assigned to interdiction duty in Deneb Sector; *U.S.S. Thomas Paine*, commanded by Captain Rixx. Also in service: *U.S.S. Herbert*, *U.S.S. Jefferson*, *U.S.S. Savannah*.

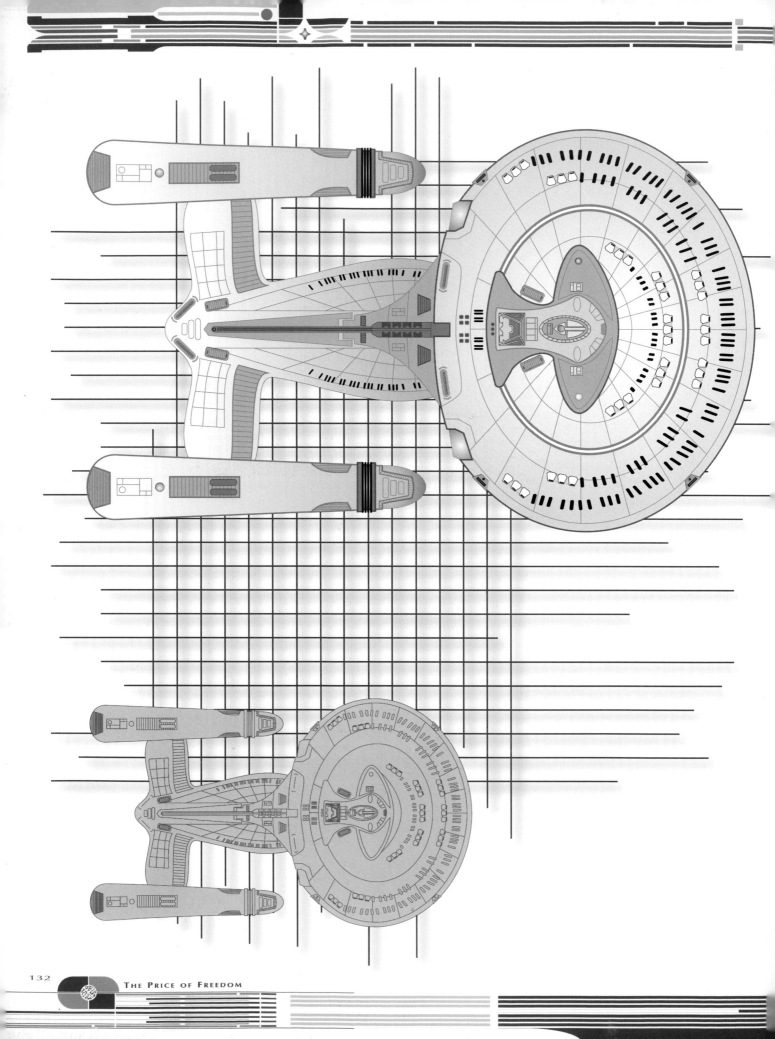

THE PRICE OF FREEDOM

NIAGRA–CLASS STARSHIP

CLASS AND TYPE: *NIAGARA*–CLASS FAST CRUISER
COMMISSIONING DATE: 2349
HULL CHARACTERISTICS
   SIZE: 5 (330 METERS LONG, 16 DECKS)
   RESISTANCE: 4
   STRUCTURAL POINTS: 100

OPERATIONS CHARACTERISTICS
   CREW/PASSENGERS/EVAC: 400/1650/3500
      [6 PWR/ROUND]
   COMPUTERS: 4
      [4 PWR/ROUND]
   TRANSPORTERS: 4 PERSONNEL, 2 CARGO, 4 EMERGENCY
      [5 PWR/ROUND]
   TRACTOR BEAMS: 1 AD, 1 FV
      [2/RATING USED]

PROPULSION AND POWER CHARACTERISTICS
   WARP SYSTEM: 6.0/9.0/9.6 (16 HOURS)
      [2/WARP FACTOR]
   IMPULSE SYSTEM: .75c/.95c
      [7/9 PWR/ROUND]
   POWER: 160

SENSOR SYSTEMS
   LONG-RANGE SENSORS: +2/17 LIGHT-YEARS
      [6 PWR/ROUND]
   LATERAL SENSORS: +2/1 LIGHT-YEAR
      [4 PWR/ROUND]
   NAVIGATIONAL SENSORS: +2
      [5 PWR/ROUND]
   SENSORS SKILL: 5

WEAPONS SYSTEMS
   TYPE IX PHASER
      RANGE: 10/30,000/100,000/300,000
      ARC: ALL (720 DEGREES)
      ACCURACY: 4/5/7/10
      DAMAGE: 18
      POWER: [18]

   TYPE II PHOTON TORPEDOES
      NUMBER: 160
      LAUNCHERS: 1 AD, 1 FV,
      SPREAD: 8
      ARC: FORWARD OR AFT, BUT ARE SELF-GUIDED
      RANGE: 15/300,000/1,000,000/3,500,000
      ACCURACY: 4/5/7/10
      DAMAGE: 20
      POWER: [5]
      WEAPONS SKILL: 4

DEFENSIVE SYSTEMS
   STARFLEET DEFLECTOR SHIELD
      PROTECTION: 50/70
      POWER: [50]

DESCRIPTION AND NOTES

FLEET DATA: Based on specifications created for the Galaxy Class Development Project, the *Niagara* class of Starfleet vessels is essentially a much smaller version of its larger, *Galaxy*–class cousins. Intended for shorter-range missions within Federation space, these ships are commonly assigned to diplomatic and cultural relations duties. They are also a common sight in orbit above political and trade conferences, since their lush accommodations make them the preferred method of travel for diplomats throughout the UFP.

The *Niagara* class represents the vanguard of a new wave of starship design and mission-specific planning. While the 23rd century saw a partial return to broad mission profiles and diversified vessel capabilities, such broad-based designs did not truly come into their own until the mid-24th century. One of the first vessels designed according to these narrower, mission-oriented profiles but capable of a wide variety of duties, the *Niagara* class would pave the way for initiatives such as the Perimeter Defense Directive in subsequent decades.

NOTEWORTHY VESSELS/ SERVICE RECORDS/ ENCOUNTERS: *U.S.S. Niagara*, prototype; *U.S.S. Princeton*, lost during the Battle of Wolf 359; *U.S.S. Raleigh*, served as location of negotiations during Rigelian Trade Accords of 2359; *U.S.S. Thims*, served as primary diplomatic transport during Cardassian peace talks; *U.S.S. Wellington*, former posting of Ro Laaren; *U.S.S. Wells*, currently assigned to diplomatic duties in Sector 001. Also in service: *U.S.S. Fairfax*, *U.S.S. Joshua Tree*, *U.S.S. T'Pavis*.

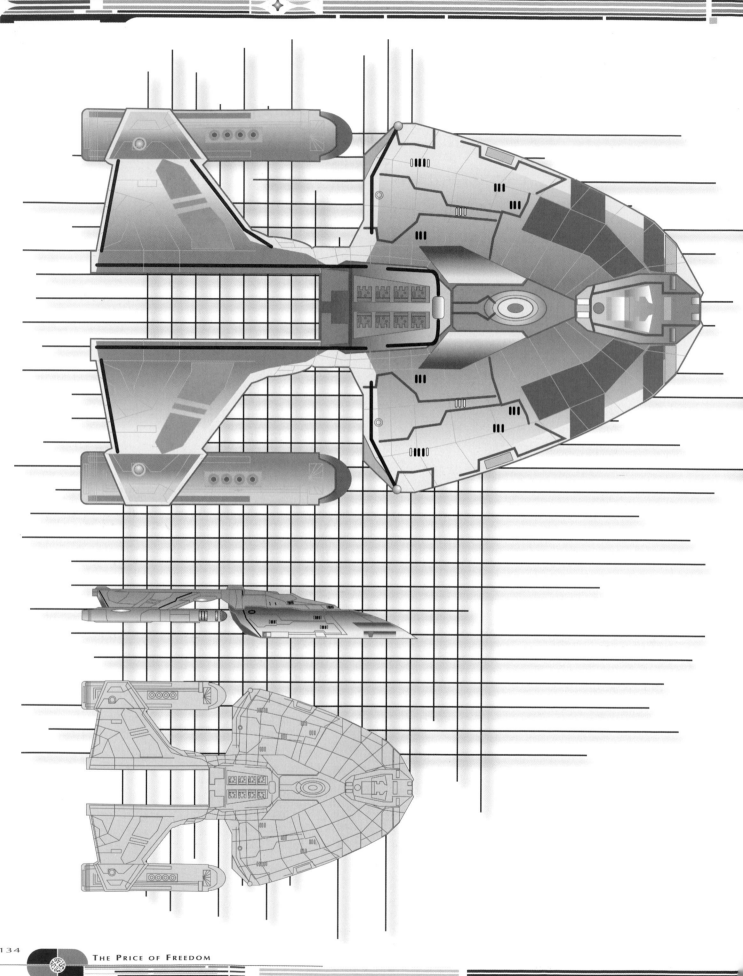

NORWAY–CLASS STARSHIP

CLASS AND TYPE: *Norway*–class Cruiser
COMMISSIONING DATE: 2369
HULL CHARACTERISTICS
  SIZE: 6 (365 meters long, 14 decks)
  RESISTANCE: 4
  STRUCTURAL POINTS: 120

OPERATIONS CHARACTERISTICS
  CREW/PASSENGERS/EVAC: 190/200/500
    [5 PWR/ROUND]
  COMPUTERS: 4
    [4 PWR/ROUND]
  TRANSPORTERS: 4 personnel, 4 cargo, 4 emergency
    [6 PWR/ROUND]
  TRACTOR BEAMS: 1 AD, 1 FD, 1 FV
    [2/RATING USED]

PROPULSION AND POWER CHARACTERISTICS
  WARP SYSTEM: 6.0/9.2/9.7 (12 HOURS)
    [2/WARP FACTOR]
  IMPULSE SYSTEM: .75c/.95c
    [7/9 PWR/ROUND]
  POWER: 175

SENSOR SYSTEMS
  LONG-RANGE SENSORS: +2/17 LIGHT-YEARS
    [6 PWR/ROUND]
  LATERAL SENSORS: +2/1 LIGHT-YEAR
    [4 PWR/ROUND]
  NAVIGATIONAL SENSORS: +2
    [5 PWR/ROUND]
  SENSORS SKILL: 4

WEAPONS SYSTEMS
  TYPE X PHASER
    RANGE: 10/30,000/100,000/300,000
    ARC: ALL (720 DEGREES)
    ACCURACY: 4/5/7/10
    DAMAGE: 20
    POWER: [20]

TYPE II PHOTON TORPEDOES
  NUMBER: 225
  LAUNCHERS: 1 AD, 1 FV,
  SPREAD: 10
  ARC: FORWARD OR AFT, BUT ARE SELF-GUIDED
  RANGE: 15/300,000/1,000,000/3,500,000
  ACCURACY: 4/5/7/10
  DAMAGE: 20
  POWER: [5]
  WEAPONS SKILL: 5

DEFENSIVE SYSTEMS
  STARFLEET DEFLECTOR SHIELD
    PROTECTION: 60/80
    POWER: [60]

DESCRIPTION AND NOTES

FLEET DATA: The third vessel class authorized by Starfleet's Perimeter Defense Directive, the *Norway* class of updated cruisers has proven itself time and again in its short history. Although only eighteen of these ships have been commissioned thus far, they have seen escort and threat response duty throughout Federation space, and are often employed as advance scout and reconnaissance vessels in hostile or unstable sectors.

Utilizing advanced ablative spaceframe technology developed for the larger *Akira*-class and refined during the *Steamrunner* Project, *Norway*–class ships are the fastest military vessels ever to serve in Starfleet. Their design and light mass give them unparalleled maneuvering capabilities, and allow them to maintain high cruise velocities for extended periods of time. Maneuverable and versatile, the *Norway* class has quickly assumed an important role in Starfleet's ongoing threat-response and long-range reconnaissance programs.

NOTEWORTHY VESSELS/ SERVICE RECORDS/ ENCOUNTERS: *U.S.S. Norway*, prototype; *U.S.S. Budapest*, defended Earth against Borg in 2373; *U.S.S. Denmark*, currently assigned to deep frontier patrol; *U.S.S. Prague*, assigned to perimeter action duties in Sol Sector. Also in service: *U.S.S. Arian*, *U.S.S. Luxembourg*, *U.S.S. Triumph*.

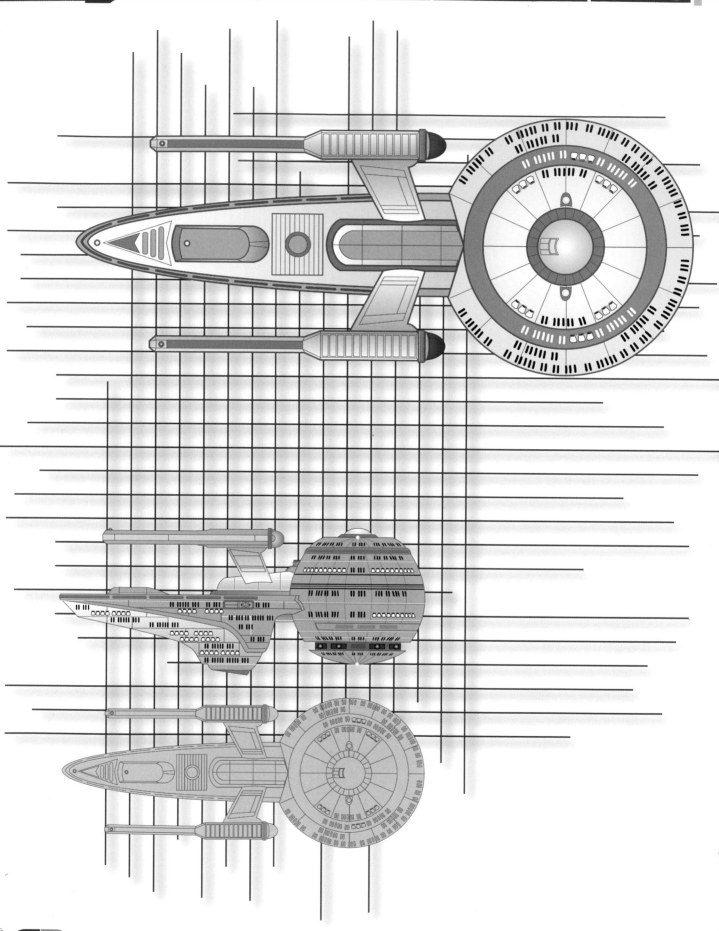

THE PRICE OF FREEDOM

OLYMPIC–CLASS STARSHIP

CLASS AND TYPE: *Olympic*–class Medical Cruiser
COMMISSIONING DATE: 2361
HULL CHARACTERISTICS
  SIZE: 5 (310 METERS LONG, 27 DECKS)
  RESISTANCE: 3
  STRUCTURAL POINTS: 100

OPERATIONS CHARACTERISTICS
  CREW/PASSENGERS/EVAC: 750/2600/8000
    [7 PWR/ROUND]
  COMPUTERS: 5
    [5 PWR/ROUND]
  TRANSPORTERS: 6 PERSONNEL, 2 CARGO, 6 EMERGENCY
    [7 PWR/ROUND]
  TRACTOR BEAMS: 1 AD, 1 FV
    [2/RATING USED]

PROPULSION AND POWER CHARACTERISTICS
  WARP SYSTEM: 6.0/9.0/9.2 (6 HOURS)
    [2/WARP FACTOR]
  IMPULSE SYSTEM: .7C/.9C
    [7/9 PWR/ROUND]
  POWER: 140

SENSOR SYSTEMS
  LONG-RANGE SENSORS: +1/15 LIGHT-YEARS
    [6 PWR/ROUND]
  LATERAL SENSORS: +1/1 LIGHT-YEAR
    [4 PWR/ROUND]
  NAVIGATIONAL SENSORS: +1
    [5 PWR/ROUND]
  SENSORS SKILL: 5

WEAPONS SYSTEMS
  TYPE VI PHASER
    RANGE: 10/30,000/100,000/300,000
    ARC: ALL (720 DEGREES)
    ACCURACY: 5/6/8/11
    DAMAGE: 12
    POWER: [12]
    WEAPONS SKILL: 3

DEFENSIVE SYSTEMS
  STARFLEET DEFLECTOR SHIELD
    PROTECTION: 48/70
    POWER: [48]

DESCRIPTION AND NOTES

FLEET DATA: A familiar sight throughout the Federation core worlds, *Olympic*-class medical cruisers form the core of Starfleet's mobile emergency platform. Essentially floating hospitals, these vessels perform a multitude of rescue, medical, evacuation, aid, and emergency missions. Seen as saviors on many outlying worlds, *Olympic*-class cruisers can often mean the difference between life and death during periods of natural disaster or emergency.

While their patient and treatment capacity exceeds all other Starfleet medical ship classes except the huge *Graceful*-class hospital vessels, the *Olympic* class is perhaps best known for the large number of variants in active production. Mission-specific subclasses based on the basic *Olympic* design abound; such redesigns includes medical research vessels, evacuation/triage vessels for threat regions, dedicated surgical ships for large-scale conflicts or fleet movements, and aid ships for all-around humanitarian and relief missions. The class has served with distinction for nearly twenty years, and Starfleet Command shows no sign of curtailing its production any time soon.

NOTEWORTHY VESSELS/ SERVICE RECORDS/ ENCOUNTERS: *U.S.S. Olympic*, prototype; *U.S.S. Biko*, assigned to emergency patrol duties in Beta Quadrant; *U.S.S. Hope*, assigned to emergency support duty in sector 001; *U.S.S. Noble*, searched for *U.S.S. Hera* in 2370; *U.S.S. Pasteur*, commanded by Captain Beverly Picard in anti-time future created by Q; *U.S.S. Peace*, currently assigned to perimeter transfers of humanitarian aid. Also in service: *U.S.S. Hippocrates*, *U.S.S. Mayo*, *U.S.S. Moore*, *U.S.S. Tranquility*.

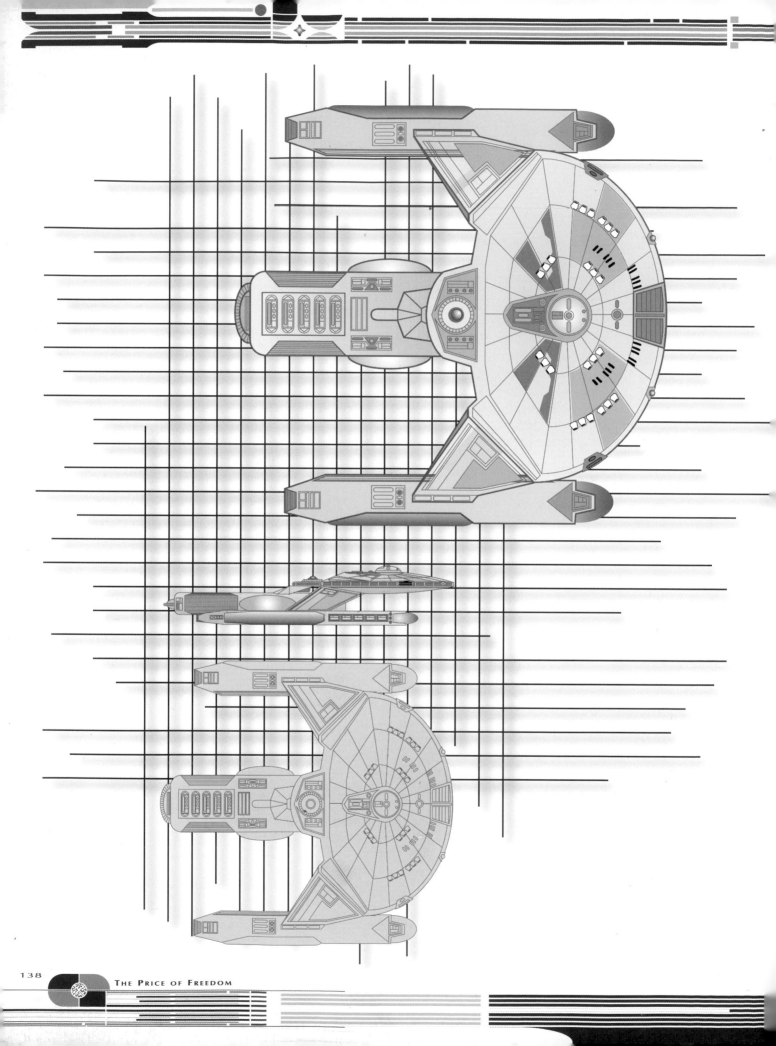

RIGEL–CLASS STARSHIP

CLASS AND TYPE: *RIGEL*–CLASS HEAVY SCOUT
COMMISSIONING DATE: 2327
HULL CHARACTERISTICS
   SIZE: 4 (215 METERS LONG, 6 DECKS)
   RESISTANCE: 3
   STRUCTURAL POINTS: 80

OPERATIONS CHARACTERISTICS
   CREW/PASSENGERS/EVAC: 70/125/400
      [4 PWR/ROUND]
   COMPUTERS: 3
      [3 PWR/ROUND]
   TRANSPORTERS: 2 PERSONNEL, 2 CARGO, 2 EMERGENCY
      [3 PWR/ROUND]
   TRACTOR BEAMS: 1 AD, 1 FV
      [2/RATING USED]

PROPULSION AND POWER CHARACTERISTICS
   WARP SYSTEM: 5.0/9.0/9.2 (12 HOURS)
      [2/WARP FACTOR]
   IMPULSE SYSTEM: .7c/.9c
      [7/9 PWR/ROUND]
   POWER: 125

SENSOR SYSTEMS
   LONG-RANGE SENSORS: +2/17 LIGHT-YEARS
      [6 PWR/ROUND]
   LATERAL SENSORS: +2/1 LIGHT-YEAR
      [4 PWR/ROUND]
   NAVIGATIONAL SENSORS: +2
      [5 PWR/ROUND]
   SENSORS SKILL: 4

WEAPONS SYSTEMS
   TYPE VII PHASER
      RANGE: 10/30,000/100,000/300,000
      ARC: ALL (720 DEGREES)
      ACCURACY: 5/6/8/11
      DAMAGE: 14
      POWER: [14]

   TYPE II PHOTON TORPEDOES
      NUMBER: 75
      LAUNCHERS: 1 AD, 1 FV,
      SPREAD: 4
      ARC: FORWARD OR AFT, BUT ARE SELF-GUIDED
      RANGE: 15/300,000/1,000,000/3,500,000
      ACCURACY: 4/5/7/10
      DAMAGE: 20
      POWER: [5]
      WEAPONS SKILL: 4

DEFENSIVE SYSTEMS
   STARFLEET DEFLECTOR SHIELD
      PROTECTION: 48/70
      POWER: [48]

DESCRIPTION AND NOTES

FLEET DATA: First commissioned during the early part of the 24th century, *Rigel*-class vessels were originally designed to specifications outlined in the Coreward Exploratory Directive of 2321. This directive was largely responsible for the mid-century expansion of the UFP along its coreward border between Alpha and Beta Quadrants, and *Rigel*-class scouts were often at the forefront of the contacts and discoveries made along the way.

Because of their long-range capability and self-sufficiency, *Rigel*-class heavy scouts have become a staple of the Merchant Marine refit program. While the Merchant Marine builds its own mission-specific vessels and transports, the refit program mandates the refit (and in some cases redesign) of older Starfleet models that may otherwise be relegated to the orbital salvage yards. The versatility of these ships as deep space transports, as well as their proven exploratory capabilities, have allowed them to assume primary roles in the growing Merchant Marine fleet.

NOTEWORTHY VESSELS/ SERVICE RECORDS/ ENCOUNTERS: *U.S.S. Rigel*, prototype; *U.S.S. Akagi*, part of the blockade armada in 2368; *U.S.S. Arcturus*, discovered Coreward Rift during long-range reconnaissance mission in 2355; *U.S.S. Barnard*, assigned to scout/response duties in Bajor Sector; *U.S.S. Sirius*, assigned to deep space observation duties along coreward frontier; *U.S.S. Tolstoy*, lost in Battle of Wolf 359. Also in service: *U.S.S. Deneb, U.S.S. Polaris, U.S.S. Vega.*

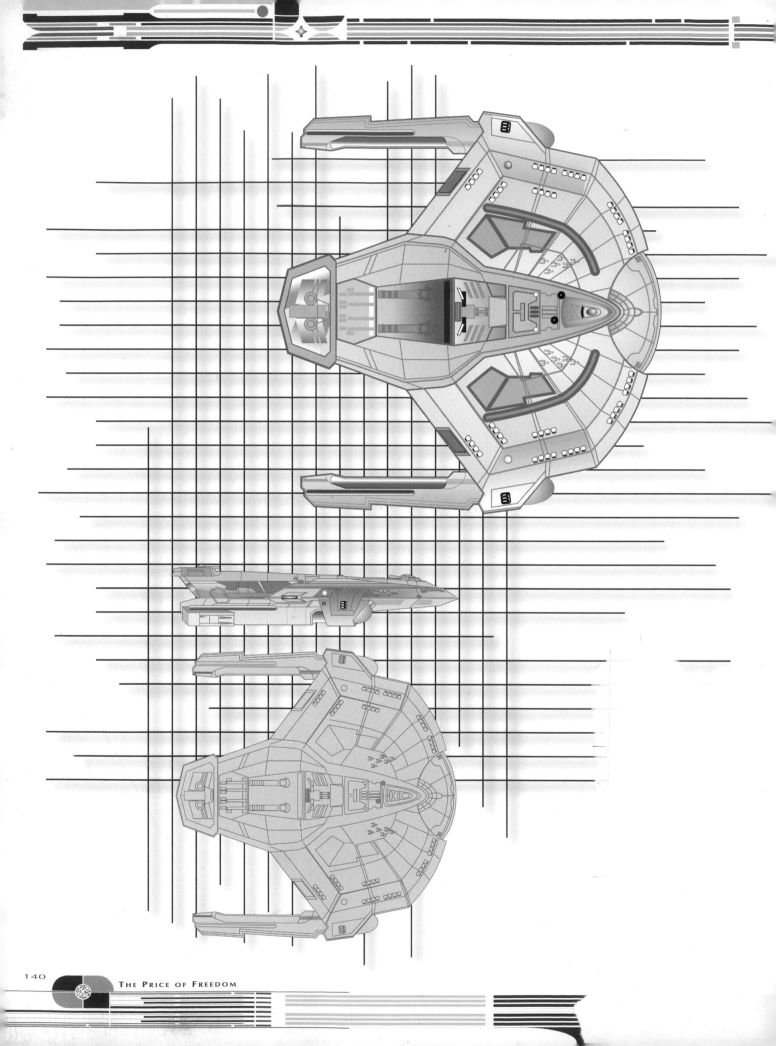

SABER–CLASS STARSHIP

CLASS AND TYPE: *Saber*–CLASS LIGHT CRUISER
(PERIMETER DEFENSE VESSEL)
COMMISSIONING DATE: 2370
HULL CHARACTERISTICS
 SIZE: 4 (160 METERS LONG, 6 DECKS)
 RESISTANCE: 4
 STRUCTURAL POINTS: 80

OPERATIONS CHARACTERISTICS
 CREW/PASSENGERS/EVAC: 40/80/200
 [4 PWR/ROUND]
 COMPUTERS: 3
 [3 PWR/ROUND]
 TRANSPORTERS: 2 PERSONNEL, 2 CARGO, 2 EMERGENCY
 [3 PWR/ROUND]
 TRACTOR BEAMS: 1 AD, 1 FV
 [2/RATING USED]

PROPULSION AND POWER CHARACTERISTICS
 WARP SYSTEM: 5.0/9.2/9.7 (12 HOURS)
 [2/WARP FACTOR]
 IMPULSE SYSTEM: .75c/.92c
 [7/9 PWR/ROUND]
 POWER: 130

SENSOR SYSTEMS
 LONG-RANGE SENSORS: +1/15 LIGHT-YEARS
 [6 PWR/ROUND]
 LATERAL SENSORS: +1/1 LIGHT-YEAR
 [4 PWR/ROUND]
 NAVIGATIONAL SENSORS: +1
 [5 PWR/ROUND]
 SENSORS SKILL: 4

WEAPONS SYSTEMS
 TYPE X PHASER
 RANGE: 10/30,000/100,000/300,000
 ARC: ALL (720 DEGREES)
 ACCURACY: 4/5/7/10
 DAMAGE: 20
 POWER: [20]

TYPE II PHOTON TORPEDOES
 NUMBER: 100
 LAUNCHERS: 1 AD, 1 FV,
 SPREAD: 4
 ARC: FORWARD OR AFT, BUT ARE SELF-GUIDED
 RANGE: 15/300,000/1,000,000/3,500,000
 ACCURACY: 4/5/7/10
 DAMAGE: 20
 POWER: [5]
 WEAPONS SKILL: 5

DEFENSIVE SYSTEMS
 STARFLEET DEFLECTOR SHIELD
 PROTECTION: 60/80
 POWER: [60]

DESCRIPTION AND NOTES

FLEET DATA: The fourth vessel to enter active service as a result of the Perimeter Defense Directive, the *Saber* class of Light Cruisers has already seen extensive action on several frontiers. Using materials technology and spaceframe elements borrowed from the ASDB Defiant Development Project, the first *Saber*-class vessels were commissioned in late 2370 as fast perimeter-defense ships.

Initially assigned to hostile frontier regions, these agile vessels quickly proved that they could hold their own against much larger opponents. The internal nacelle configuration, suggested by Cardassian embedded-warp technology and explored by Starfleet R&D during the Defiant Project, makes the ship a compact target and saves additional weight and space that would otherwise be required for nacelle field conduits and containment structures. Of course, this design also makes these vessels more vulnerable to core breaches when full armor penetration occurs.

Small and designed for easy mass production, no less than five major yard facilities currently produce *Saber*-class vessels. As a result, there are already more *Saber*-class ships in active service than any of the other new classes that have come out of the Perimeter Defense Directive.

NOTEWORTHY VESSELS/ SERVICE RECORDS/ ENCOUNTERS:: *U.S.S. Saber*, prototype; *U.S.S. Denmark*, currently assigned to deep frontier patrol; *U.S.S. Shepard*, assigned to perimeter action duties in Sol Sector; *U.S.S. Yeager*, defended Earth against Borg in 2373. Also in service: *U.S.S. Arian, U.S.S. Luxembourg, U.S.S. Triumph.*

Part of the fun of roleplaying is interacting with your favorite fictional characters. In your games, you might run into Commander Riker on Risa, attend a diplomatic function with Captain Picard, or rescue the crew of the *Enterprise-D* from an unusual astronomical phenomenon. You might even set your series on the *Enterprise-D*, with your characters serving alongside the likes of Commander Riker, Lieutenant Commander La Forge and Reginald Barclay.

CAPTAIN JEAN-LUC PICARD

Captain of the *U.S.S. Enterprise-D*. Born in Labarre, France in 2305 Picard entered Starfleet Academy at age 18. Rather reckless in his younger days, shortly after his graduation in 2327 Picard suffered severe injuries in a fight with three Nausicaans, and required a cardiac replacement. His first command came when the captain of the *U.S.S. Stargazer* was killed in action and Picard took command of the ship. In 2363, Picard assumed command of the *U.S.S. Enterprise-D*. While captain of the *Enterprise-D*, he came under scrutiny for numerous actions including several violations of the Prime Directive, though he also saved the Federation on numerous occasions (including repelling several attacks by the Borg Collective). Picard's hobbies include archeology and music.

ATTRIBUTES
FITNESS: 4
    VITALITY -1
COORDINATION: 3
INTELLECT: 4
    PERCEPTION +1
    LOGIC +1
PRESENCE: 5
    WILLPOWER +1
PSI: 0

SKILLS
ADMINISTRATION (LOGISTICS) 4 (5)
    (STARSHIP) (6)
ANIMAL HANDLING (HORSE) 1 (4)
ARTISTIC EXPRESSION (RESSIKAN FLUTE) 1 (5)
ATHLETICS (FENCING) 3 (4)
    (RUNNING) (4)

COMMAND (STARSHIP) 5 (6)
COMPUTER (RESEARCH) 3 (4)
CULTURE (BORG) 4 (5)
    (HUMAN) (6)
    (KLINGON) (5)
DODGE 4
DISGUISE (ROMULAN) 3 (4)
ENERGY WEAPON (PHASER) 2 (5)
ESPIONAGE (INTELLIGENCE TECHNIQUES) 1 (3)
GAMING (POKER) 2 (3)
HISTORY (HUMAN) 4 (5)
    (FEDERATION) (5)
LANGUAGE
    FEDERATION STANDARD 4
    FRENCH 3
    KLINGON 2
LAW (FEDERATION) 4 (5)
    (KLINGON) (4)
    (STARFLEET REGULATIONS) (6)
PERSONAL EQUIPMENT (TRICORDER) 3 (4)
    (ENVIRONMENT SUIT) (5)
PLANETARY SCIENCES (GEOLOGY) 1 (3)
PLANETARY TACTICS (SMALL-UNIT) 3 (4)
PLANETSIDE SURVIVAL (DESERT) 2 (3)
SOCIAL SCIENCES (ANTHROPOLOGY) 1 (4)
    (ARCHEOLOGY) (5)
SEARCH 3
STEALTH 3
SHIPBOARD SYSTEMS (FLIGHT CONTROL) 4 (5)
    (COMMAND) (6)
SPACE SCIENCE (ASTROGATION) 3 (4)
    (ASTRONOMY) (6)
    (STELLAR CARTOGRAPHY) (5)
STARSHIP TACTICS (STARFLEET) 5 (6)
    (BORG) (6)
STRATEGIC OPERATIONS (FEDERATION) 4 (6)
    (KLINGON) (5)
    (ROMULAN) (5)
SYSTEMS ENGINEERING (COMMAND) 4 (5)
VEHICLE OPERATION (SHUTTLECRAFT) 1 (4)
WORLD KNOWLEDGE (EARTH) 4 (6)

ADVANTAGES/DISADVANTAGES

BOLD +1
DEPARTMENT HEAD (EXECUTIVE OFFICER)
MEDICAL REMEDY (2 PTS) (ARTIFICIAL HEART)
PHYSICAL IMPAIRMENT (2 PTS.) (HEART)
PROMOTION (CAPTAIN)
VENGEFUL (BORG)

COURAGE: 4
RENOWN: 71   *AGGRESSION:* -12   *DISCIPLINE:* 16
INITIATIVE: 14   *OPENNESS:* 14   *SKILL:* 15
WOUND LEVELS: 3/3/3/3/3/3/0

COMMANDER WILLIAM T. RIKER

Executive Officer of the *U.S.S. Enterprise-D*. Born in Alaska, he graduated eighth in his class at Starfleet Academy. He was first assigned to the *U.S.S. Pegasus*, where he helped his captain escape a mutiny attempt resulting in the death of the crew and the destruction of the ship. In 2361, during the evacuation of Nervala IV, a freak transporter accident created a duplicate of Riker, who was marooned on the planet for eight years. Riker joined the crew of the *Enterprise-D* in 2364, as second in command. He became the first Starfleet officer to serve on board a Klingon vessel when, in 2365, he served as First Officer under the Officer Exchange Program. Happy with his position on the Enterprise, Riker refused several promotions to captain of his own ship. He enjoys cooking and playing jazz trombone.

ATTRIBUTES

FITNESS: 4
    VITALITY +1
COORDINATION: 4
    REACTION +1
INTELLECT: 4
PRESENCE: 4
    WILLPOWER +2
PSI: 0

SKILLS

ADMINISTRATION (LOGISTICS) 3 (4)
    (STARSHIP) (5)
ARTISTIC EXPRESSION (COOKING) 1 (4)
    (TROMBONE) (5)
ATHLETICS (LIFTING) 3 (4)
    (ANBO-JYUTSU) (5)
COMMAND (COMBAT LEADERSHIP) 4 (5)
    (STARSHIP) (5)
COMPUTER (RESEARCH) 3 (4)
CULTURE (HUMAN) 2 (4)
DIPLOMACY (INTERGALACTIC AFFAIRS) 3 (4)
DODGE 4
ENERGY WEAPON (PHASER) 2 (5)
GAMING (POKER) 3 (5)
HISTORY (HUMAN) 2 (4)
    (FEDERATION) (4)
LANGUAGE

FEDERATION STANDARD 4
LAW (KLINGON MILITARY REGULATIONS) 3 (4)
    (STARFLEET REGULATIONS) (4)
PERSONAL EQUIPMENT (TRICORDER) 3 (4)
PLANETSIDE SURVIVAL (MOUNTAIN) 1 (4)
SHIPBOARD SYSTEMS (FLIGHT CONTROL) 3 (4)
    (COMMAND) (5)
SPACE SCIENCE (ASTRONOMY) 4 (5)
STARSHIP TACTICS (PLANETARY SUPPORT) 3 (4)
    (STARFLEET) (5)
    (THOLIAN) (4)
SYSTEMS ENGINEERING (COMMAND) 3 (4)
VEHICLE OPERATION (SHUTTLECRAFT) 3 (4)
WORLD KNOWLEDGE (EARTH) 4 (5)

ADVANTAGES/DISADVANTAGES
BOLD +1
COMMENDATION (X5)
DEPARTMENT HEAD (FLIGHT CONTROL)
INNOVATIVE
PROMOTION (COMMANDER)

COURAGE: 4

RENOWN: 60   *AGGRESSION: -10*   *DISCIPLINE: 13*
INITIATIVE: 14   *OPENNESS: 12*   *SKILL: 11*
WOUND LEVELS: 5/5/5/5/5/5/0

COMMANDER DEANNA TROI

Ship's Counselor about the *U.S.S. Enterprise-D.* Born on Betazed, to ambassador Lwaxana Troi and Ian Andrew Troi, she is only half Betazed and an empath (rather than a full telepath). After studying psychology at the University of Betazed, she joined Starfleet. While a psychology student, she became romantically involved with William T. Riker, but the relationship ended when Riker's career plans interfered. In addition to her duties as ship's counselor, Troi frequently uses her powerful empathic abilities to assist in numerous missions, such as when the *Enterprise* makes contact with newly discovered lifeforms or other ships. Deeply caring and compassionate, she takes her job as ship's counselor very seriously. She enjoys vigorous exercise and fine chocolate.

ATTRIBUTES
FITNESS: 3
COORDINATION: 3
INTELLECT: 3
    PERCEPTION +2
PRESENCE: 3
    EMPATHY +1
PSI: 4
    FOCUS +1
    RANGE +2

SKILLS
ADMINISTRATION (STARSHIP PERSONNEL) 2 (5)
ATHLETICS (CLIMBING) 2 (3)
CHARM (INFLUENCE) 3 (5)
COMMAND (STARSHIP) 1 (2)
COMPUTER 1 (4)
CULTURE (BETAZOID) 4 (5)
DIPLOMACY (BETAZED) 3 (4)
    (FEDERATION FRONTIER) (4)
DODGE 3
ENERGY WEAPON (PHASER) 1 (3)
FIRST AID 3
GAMING (POKER) 2 (4)
HISTORY (BETAZOID) 3 (6)
    (FEDERATION) (4)
LANGUAGE
    BETAZOID 3
    FEDERATION STANDARD 3
LAW (STARFLEET REGULATIONS) 1 (4)
MEDICAL SCIENCE (PSYCHOLOGY) 2 (6)
PERSONAL EQUIPMENT (TRICORDER) 1 (3)
PERSUASION (COUNSELING) 4 (6)
PLANETSIDE SURVIVAL (FOREST) 1 (2)
PROJECTIVE TELEPATHY 2
RECEPTIVE EMPATHY 5
STARSHIP SYSTEMS (FLIGHT CONTROL) 1 (3)
    (SENSORS) (3)
UNARMED COMBAT (MOK'BARA) 1 (4)
VEHICLE OPERATION (SHUTTLECRAFT) 1 (4)
WORLD KNOWLEDGE (BETAZED) 1 (5)

ADVANTAGES/DISADVANTAGES
MIXED SPECIES HERITAGE
PROMOTION (COMMANDER)
DEPARTMENT HEAD (COUNSELOR)
PACIFISM (HIPPOCRATIC OATH)

COURAGE: 3

RENOWN: 43   *AGGRESSION: -10*   *DISCIPLINE: 5*
INITIATIVE: 8   *OPENNESS: 13*   *SKILL: 7*
WOUND LEVELS: 2/2/2/2/2/2/0

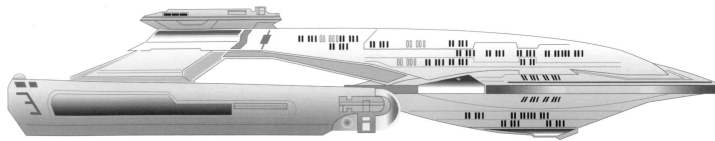

AKIRA-CLASS STARSHIP   **465** METERS

NEW ORLEANS-CLASS STARSHIP   **425** METERS

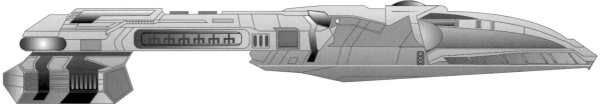

STEAMRUNNER-CLASS STARSHIP   **375** METERS

NORWAY-CLASS STARSHIP   **365** METERS

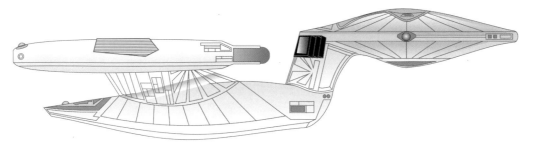

APOLLO-CLASS STARSHIP   **315** METERS

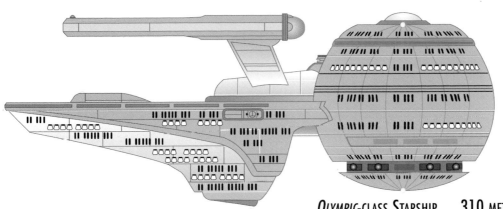

OLYMPIC-CLASS STARSHIP   **310** METERS

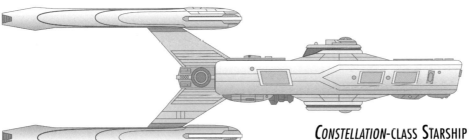

CONSTELLATION-CLASS STARSHIP   **302** METERS

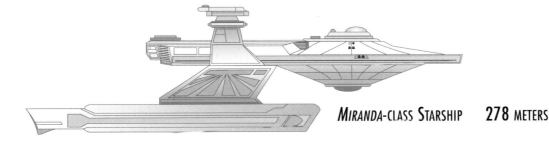

MIRANDA-CLASS STARSHIP   **278** METERS

RIGEL-CLASS STARSHIP   **215** METERS

DENEVA-CLASS STARSHIP   **210** METERS

MERCED-CLASS STARSHIP   **187** METERS

SABER-CLASS STARSHIP   **160** METERS

SHIP SIZE REFERENCE CHART

STAR TREK®

DEEP SPACE NINE™

ROLEPLAYING GAME

COMING JUNE 1999

STAR TREK®

ROLEPLAYING GAME

COMING AUGUST 1999

Order Form

Look forward to all these great upcoming Star Trek® RPG products in 1999 and beyond! You'll be able to find them at finer game, comic and book stores everywhere, but if by some twist of fate you're not able to find them at your favorite retailer and they are unable to special order these products, you can always be assured of getting them directly from Last Unicorn Games!

Item #	Title	Price	Availabil
#25000	ST: TNG Core Game Book	$35	Now
#25001	Narrator's Toolkit (screen)	$15	Now
#25600	UFP Away Team Miniature Boxed Set	$19.99	Now
#25100	The Price of Freedom: The United Federation of Planets (HC)	$25	Mar '99
#25300	Neutral Zone Campaign Vol. 1	$15	Mar '99
#35000	Star Trek: Deep Space Nine Core Game Book	$35	June '99
#25103	The Way of Kolinahr: The Vulcans	$15	Mar '99
#25101	Starfleet Intelligence: The First Line	$15	Mar '99
#55000	Star Trek: Voyager Core Game Book	$35	Feb '00
#65000	ENGAGE! Starship Mission Simulator: Battle of Wolf 359	$35	Sep '99
#25102	Planets of the UFP	$20	Apr '99
#25301	Planetary Adventures	$15	Apr '99
#45000	Star Trek: The Original Series Core Game Book	$35	Aug '99
#25500	Romulan Star Empire Boxed Set	$35	May '99

Allow 4-6 weeks for shipping. All orders must be paid in US funds. Visa/Mastercard Accepted

Shipping and Handling Charges apply as follows:
Ground (Continental US only) 1 item $3, each additional item $2
Priority Mail (Continental US only) 1 item $4, each additional item $2
Canadian Shipping 1 item $5, each additional item $3
Overseas Shipping (surface) $10 per order
Overseas Shipping (air) $20 per order

Name
Address
City
State/Province
Zip/Postal Code
Country
Daytime Phone
Email Address

I've enclosed a
O Check
O Money Order
O Credit Card
    Card #
    Exp Date
    Name on Card

Mail to:
LUG
Department M
9520 Jefferson Blvd.
Suite C
Culver City, California
90232

MERCHANDISE :
TAX :

TOTAL :